T0063341

Champagne for Tea

Ann Bailey

Order this book online at www.trafford.com
or email orders@trafford.com

Most Trafford titles are also available at major online book retailers.

Printed in the United States of America.

ISBN: 978-1-4907-3703-4 (sc)
ISBN: 978-1-4907-3702-7 (e)

Trafford rev. 08/27/2014

 www.trafford.com
North America & international
toll-free: 1 888 232 4444 (USA & Canada)
fax: 812 355 4082

PART ONE

An Innocent Cup of Tea

EMILY AND JACK

S he GRIMACED AS SHE WATCHED Jack and Rob standing together by the garden doors. Jack gave Rob one of his friendly smiles and Rob placed his hand on Jack's shoulder.

She pressed her lips together in annoyance for as much as she loved Jack she did not always like him and this afternoon was one of those times. As for Rob, well, she had never got the hang of him and Jack defended him like an overprotective father, or a too loyal friend. She was unsure which one it was, only she knew Rob drove a wedge between them.

'Just go away,' she muttered, sighing with relief as she fell back into a deep leather chair, kicked off her shoes, and got down to the serious business of her life in general and Will in particular.

It was not so much his looks, though she had to admit he was not entirely unattractive, but rather his brilliant smile and, seemingly, unlimited humour. She had met him some weeks before while walking Daisy across the heath. A donated park bench between crossing paths had become their meeting place, their rendezvous, a word she associated with shady clandestine meetings.

She had not told Jack about Will though she was unsure why not. Perhaps he was her secret, a very small secret. She decided she could cope with any twinge of guilt.

'William Windsor,' he had said, introducing himself, enthusiastically. 'Call me Will.'

'Emily Nielson. Call me Emy. Windsor that sounds very prestigious.'

'Yeah, but what's in a name.'

'Do you have a dog?' she asked, looking over the heath.

'No, but I do have a pair of trainers', he laughed. 'I like to get a breath of fresh air before I start the day.'

'And what is the start?'

'Nothing. I'm in between, if you know what I mean.'

'Between can be interesting.'

'Between two fires, that could be interesting.'

'Between the devil and the deep blue sea.'

'Same thing. All dangerous,' he had chuckled, softly, as though remembering some past incident. 'Well, I must be off,' he said, standing up. 'I'm sure we'll meet again.'

'I'm sure we will.'

She had watched him walk back down a path leading to several old houses, acutely aware that the timing of their almost daily meetings was perhaps too coincidental.

She returned to the present and Rob's wife, Helen, who was neatly slicing the cooked ham with almost surgical precision. Helen looked up as though aware she was being watched and gave a friendly grin as she walked over to her.

'I haven't cooked a ham for years,' she said, sitting down and carefully smoothing a large paper napkin over her thin knees. She stared across the lawn at the beds of flowers. 'Gardens are hard work,' she observed, as she neatly bayoneted pieces of potato salad onto a fork.

'That's for sure,' she agreed, attaching the remark to their husbands as they strolled towards the greenhouse.

She sat up in bed that night listening to Jack under the shower and later to the whine of his electric shaver which he pulled across his face several times, followed by the vibration of his electric tooth brush, running water and a great deal of spitting in the wash basin. She knew his routine well and somehow it endeared him to her, at least when she allowed herself the luxury of such an emotion.

Eventually, he got into bed, smelling strongly of aftershave lotion, and settled down next to her. She lay against him but he did not react to her subtle interest, instead he turned his full attention to a magazine which gave advice on how to invest wisely, the Federal Bank and the European Union. She drew away and opened a book from the library pretending not to notice she came second to the world economy and wondered what it would take to divert his attention, or whether it was even worth the effort.

'Saw Rosie the other day', she informed him.

He grunted as a reply.

'She showed me around her house. It's enormous. She's terribly untidy.'

Jack turned a page of his magazine too absorbed to be bothered with Rosie's untidy house.

She laid the book on her lap and considered her visit.

'The best thing about an old place is that it's held together by decades of dirt. I think it would most probably collapse if I were to clean it.' Rosie laughed. 'My family has lived here for over a hundred years and I'm only going to leave between six planks.'

She warmed to this interesting, ruddy faced, woman whose long cotton frock hung loosely over her slim body and with her hair tied up as though she had just got out of bed. All in all, she liked her rather dishevelled appearance for it made her recall the time when she had also dressed as Rosie with rows of 'hippie' beads and, sometimes, even a bandana. She wondered why it was necessary to follow a new fashion just when the last one had become so comfortable. It was like having to change colour to please the emotions of the fashion designers, rather like an obedient chameleon. She thought Rosie had got it right by wearing what she liked best and she wondered why she didn't do that.

She looked around the antique kitchen and

smiled at the piles of books and magazines stacked on the floor and the cluttered tops of the cupboards. She could relate to Rosie's untidy hoarding, valuing the valueless, for she had her own weakness.

'Do we have to be posh or can I use mugs?'

'Mugs.'

'I work from home, mostly here in the kitchen,' Rosie informed her, seeing how she gazed at the piles of books.

'I've heard you paint.'

'I do a bit of illustrating, I should clear this up,' she said, looking around. 'But not yet,' she laughed.

'It must be nice to be artistic.'

'Okay as a hobby but it doesn't bring home the bacon.'

'My first husband was an Account Manager for a Public Relations company.'

Rosie caught her eye and chuckled. 'They are a special breed. Are you in a hurry?' she quickly added.

'No, not at all.'

'Well, then, I'll show you my crumbling house.'

Rosie had led her through darkly furnished rooms where threadbare carpets covered creaking floors and old velvet or brocade curtains hung forlornly over unwashed windows; all culminating in an odour which she associated with stuffy, unaired, cupboards where the contents had seldom seen the light of day.

'I don't know how you live here all alone,' she commented, more to herself than to Rosie, as she climbed the stairs, glancing up at poorly painted portraits of the long dead. She shivered as she felt the past still lingered in the present.

'Well, I'm not always alone,' Rosie replied softly, obviously not expecting to be heard.

She grinned at the thought of this socially benevolent woman having a secret lover.

'This is my bedroom,' Rosie stated, closing the door a little too quickly. 'There's a lovely view from the tower,' she informed her, as she climbed the last turn of a narrow staircase.

'Oh, it's beautiful. I didn't realise you could see so far,' she answered, feeling apprehensive since Rosie could, most likely, see the bench at the 'Crossing' where she met Will.

'I can see everything with my trusty binoculars,' she smiled, pointing to a pair on the windowsill. 'You haven't been here long, have you?' she added.

'Just over a year.'

'Well, then, you have a lot to learn about the history of this area, particularly the 'Crossing'. People were very spiritual long ago, they lived at one with nature. Not like nowadays.'

'I can think of someone I know rather well.'

'Lights have been seen there at night,' Rosie whispered, as though she was unsure whether she should divulge such a piece of information.

'Really, what sort of lights?'

'I suppose they're 'Will o' the Wisp' lights, what else can they be?' Rosie chuckled, as she started back down the stairs of the tower.

'Have you seen any?'

'Maybe,' Rosie answered, vaguely. 'Let's have another coffee.'

'And?' Jack was asking.

'And what?'

'Rosie. Still healing?'

'She doesn't heal. She just happens to have a small chapel attached to her house. She keeps the door unlocked several hours a day so that troubled people can go there to meditate. Although, I must say there is something special about Rosie. And the Chapel,' she added, unsure why the place made her feel uneasy.

'They must be pretty troubled,' he smirked. 'And are there any miraculous interventions?'

'Not that I know. But I could use a couple,' she mumbled.

'And while I'm at it,' he continued. 'I don't like that statue thing staring at me every night.'

He nodded his head towards the chest of drawers.

She looked across to a statue of the Madonna which had been given to Jack by an enthusiastic Chinese trader, who had taken it for granted his colleague revered his Belief as he did his. Jack had seemed embarrassed by the gift and she had miraculously intervened just in time to save her from the garbage collector. Now she stood in all her glory between the family photographs which she guessed irritated Jack.

'You mean my Madonna. Why should she bother you?'

'She doesn't.'

'Perhaps she makes you feel guilty about something,' she insinuated.

'For God's sake.'

He sighed and closed his eyes. He knew he was being unreasonable but the statue brought back memories of his youthful conflicts with the local priest. He could clearly remember his visit in the summer of his last school year.

'I kissed her, Father, and then I squeezed her breast.'

He could hear a gasp from the other side of the Confessional; the squeaking floorboards as the now aged man stood up and told him to leave the church unless he was prepared to change his ways.

He had given a sigh of relief as he was offered his freedom and walked quickly over the threshold, past the enormous doors which guarded God's domain, leaving behind the smell of incense which mingled with the musk from the hassocks and the dark corners where footsteps echoed. The part of the church he had feared as a child. He had glanced back and noticed how the sun streamed through a coloured glass window onto the Cross and Christ and, for a split second, he had hesitated but the promise of Charlene waiting in the park was stronger than the call of God.

He smiled as he thought of her, how she had fallen in love with him and how he had fallen in love with what love brought. Charlene was his first and no one forgets their first.

He returned his thoughts to the present. 'What are you reading?' he asked, dismissing the latest EU meeting in Brussels and hoping to make good his puerile opposition to the 'holy one'.

'Local history. Rosie has a tower above her bedroom, you can see the 'Crossing' from there. It was once a pagan offering place until the first monk built his church there.'

He laughed dryly. 'That was not very Christian, pinching someone else's land.'

'Well, I guess he must have done some P.R. work first,' she agreed, trying not to smile because that might indicate forgiveness. 'Rosie said she has seen lights there at night.'

'Rosie looks too deep in her glass.'

'Like you,' she whispered.

Jack picked up his magazine to indicate he had heard her remark.

'Are you interested or not?'

'Not really. I'm reading about the 'now' and not the 'then'. Okay, what must I listen to?'

'Nothing,' she replied, sharply, having already decided not to tell him anything except the most banal happenings in her life. 'You're a Philistine, Jack.'

'That's what you think of all men,' he answered, shortly, as he turned the light out.

'Not all.'

He laid on his back and allowed pictures and thoughts of his bachelor days to drift through his mind. He had known he was handsome and, along with his shyness and quietness, found he could disarm others, particularly women. Once in a while, he wondered whether he should feel uncomfortable about some aspects of his past, whether his non-commitment had caused others pain. He mentally shrugged his shoulders and decided he had only used what had been given to him and, anyway, it was all too long ago to worry about.

Emy, he considered, was typical of her gender; unable to control her female 'need to know' instinct; the need to extract vital information required to control relationships; unable to accept the moment for what it was; always searching for rhyme and reason and possibly a happy ending. He had remained the silent type, perhaps it was his strength or even his weakness. In the end, he considered all relationships to be power struggles only some were gentle others deadly.

'Are you awake?' he whispered, as he nestled his head on her shoulder.

She did not answer, irritated he had ignored her earlier intentions by choosing for the economy and laughing at Rosie.

He lay motionless for a moment waiting for her to give a sign but she gave none so he gently held her hand, as though regretful of his earlier scorn.

She stirred, she loved his hands, his touch. She tried to remember who had written a touch could never be forgotten. She would never forget Jack's. She turned towards him.

'Sophie's dropping by Sunday afternoon', she whispered, as she kissed his hand and he her breast.

*

Sophie had her doubts whether her planned visit would achieve its purpose. She dreaded her mother's bombardment of 'pro's and con's' and 'why's and why not's' and the inevitable pursuing tension. She felt it was unfair that she should have to break the news, that was not the original agreement.

She had already decided that if the opportunity did not present itself then she would see her visit as a normal social call, have a good dinner, crash down in the guest room and let her news go its passionate course for a few more weeks.

She could see Jack weeding the flower beds as she drove up the drive, she lightly sounded the horn and he straightened his back and waved. She did not particularly like him, which was probably reciprocated, so they had kept as far apart as possible until she gone to college, met Peter and carelessly conceived Tom a few years later.

They had married which seemed to have stunned her mother who reckoned her eldest daughter was too modern for such correctness, or did she say sincerity. Their marriage had broken amicably, both of them had signed documents admitting their incompatibility and kissed each other goodbye. Well, it was hardly a farewell kiss since Tom was hanging on her skirt waiting for his promised reward, which was to stay the weekend with his now bachelor father. Neither of them had blamed the other, which she considered rather clever, not like her mother who never really forgave her father for their failed marriage, though she swore that was not so and would willingly be good friends with Guy and his second wife, Angie, if they wished.

The fact was they did not wish and neither did she and the idea of her mother making polite conversation with her father and Angie made her shudder, for anything either party might say would sound disingenuous and serve no purpose other than to score off each other.

She pulled her headscarf off as she stepped carefully out of her sports car and paused to clip straggling curls back to where they belonged in her long auburn hair. Then, picking up a rather large overnight bag, she walked towards her mother who was already waiting by the open front door.

'Saw Jack in the garden', Sophie remarked, pouring herself a glass of wine after settling down in the kitchen.

'Surprise me. Where else would he be.'

'How is he?'

'Good question,' she replied, dryly.

'And?'

'And nothing. He's so difficult nowadays.'

'Probably a delayed menopause.'

'Probably.'

'Men also have hot flushes, only they're not where you can see them.'

'Sophie,' she said, drawing her name out to show she was becoming embarrassed. 'Call Jack, tell him dinner's ready.'

'How's that jogger you meet on the heath?' Sophie asked, after she had shouted for Jack.

'Oh, I hardly ever see him,' she lied, regretting telling her daughter that once in a while she met up with a rather nice man.

'Don't do anything I wouldn't do.'

'As if,' she murmured, wondering what she would do if the opportunity presented itself.

Jack came through the back door, washed his hands, gave her a light kiss and picked up a bottle of red wine.

'Bumped into George this afternoon,' he informed her, as he pulled the cork out of the bottle. 'They're coming for a drink Saturday night. Is that okay?'

*

She had reluctantly made plates of the usual appetisers as she pictured herself dragging behind Jack, George and Pat at the local garden centre while they debated which shrubs or flowers they should plant to improve their immaculate herbaceous borders. Now, she physically flinched at the thought of an evening between the greenhouse and the compost heap. She convinced herself that George and Pat were nice kind people, good citizens who obeyed the laws of the land, while she admired those who stood up to the 'establishment'.

The conversation was exactly as she had predicted. The three of them enthused over new products which promised to get rid of the moss in the grass and the Aphides on the roses. Eventually, she slipped into the kitchen wishing she was at Rosie's or stumbling with Will along small paths between the heather or even watching television. She thought anything was better than listening to the three of them and that there must be something else to talk about other than the local flora.

'Jack tells me you are going on holiday,' she mentioned, casually, on her return to the lounge.

'Oh yes, we are. We're going down to the coast for a week, aren't we?' replied Pat, licking her thumb and index finger after devouring a date filled with cream cheese. She glared over at George for his support. He immediately sat up straight as though being reprimanded.

'Yes,' he agreed, obediently. 'We've booked a holiday bungalow outside a small village. There are good seaworthy boats to hire in the harbour. I thought I might potter around the coast for a few hours every day. I used to sail a great deal. In fact, I had my own boat up until a few years ago.'

'That's not such a good idea, you know I don't like you sailing alone,' complained Pat, with a worried tone to her voice and sitting with her chubby legs so far apart she could see the leg of her sensible pink knickers.

'I'll come with you,' offered Jack, without any hesitation, oblivious to the sight of the old fashioned drawers. 'You know, I have been thinking for ages about buying a small sailboat.'

'I've heard that for years,' she sighed, wishing to God she had never brought up the subject.

'I used to do a lot of sailing,' continued Jack, ignoring her. 'Every weekend. Great times.' He stood up and poured himself a whisky. 'What will it be?'

'I'll join you,' grinned George.

'Whisky is a good clean drink,' stated Jack, dropping ice cubes into their glasses.

'Happy days,' toasted George, as he raised his glass enthusiastically.

'Cheers,' replied Jack, his face flushed from a

large quantity of alcohol which he had already thrown back before his horticultural friends arrived.

She glanced over to Pat who sat smiling, happy her adventurous husband would have support at sea.

'I don't want to sound a spoilsport,' she interrupted. 'But it is a hell of a long time since you sailed at sea, Jack. I mean warm tropical waters are not exactly comparable to the Atlantic Ocean. Or do I see that wrongly?'

'You see it wrongly,' Jack replied, sharply.

'It's all the same, a boat is a boat, wherever you sail,' agreed George, who didn't want these brilliant new plans dampened by some redundant wife.

'That's right,' supported Jack, avoiding her warning glances.

'Shall I 'phone the holiday people first thing tomorrow? I was under the impression there were more houses in the area to rent. We are going out of season so you might be lucky,' offered Pat, aware she was on to a good thing.

They were still discussing sailing when she finally offered the salmon mousse.

'Oh, my dear, you really shouldn't have gone to so much trouble.'

'You're so right,' she thought.

Later, she tried to persuade Jack that going on holiday with people he did not really want to be with, or rather she did not want to be with, was not such a good idea.

He ignored her advice. 'I meant what I said. I want to sail again. Feel the wind in my face.'

She felt a lump in her throat for she understood how he felt and wished she didn't. She wanted to say that they were all in some kind of a gilded cage like birds who knew no better but were vaguely aware that there must be something more, somewhere else. She thought the 'more' became more unreachable as more years passed.

'Well,' she said, clearing her throat. 'There's a sailing club ten miles away.'

'That's nothing.'

'At least you sail with Rob around his lake.'

'That boat is little more than a dingy with a pole stuck in the middle and the lake's not what you would call spectacular.'

'So, how come the two of you go off for hours at a time.'

'Fishing,' he replied, obviously irritated. 'I want to sail at sea like I use to do. What's wrong in that?'

'Nothing is wrong in that. I'm only saying that perhaps the sea is a bit dangerous if you're alone.'

'What do you think I did before I met you?'

'You tell me.' She paused. 'You know what, Jack,' she said, almost tearfully, 'Buy yourself a bloody tug boat and chug off into the setting sun. I really couldn't care less what you do.'

'There you go again, always the dramatist, always over the top.'

'Send in the clown,' she murmured.

*

She could see Will in the distance, next morning, and she quickened her step in case he should leave before she arrived.

'It's a beautiful day,' she stated, unnecessarily, as she walked towards him slightly out of breath.

'It is,' he agreed.

She sat next to him and they chatted for a while about the potholes in the lane, which the Council ignored, and the misuse of the taxpayers' money. Eventually, she changed the line of conversation.

'We had a couple over for drinks. He and his wife are going away for a week. He's going to hire a yacht and Jack wants us to go with them. I don't know why but I have a bad feeling about it. Perhaps I'm wrong,' she added.

'Yep, you probably are,' he answered, aware something was bothering her.

'Maybe I shouldn't say anymore. Who knows how long we have before it's all over.'

'It's difficult to stop someone if they really want to do something. We are as butterflies, here for the moment, every day's important,' he grinned at his own cliché.

'I know but sometimes I feel as though I pick up other people's cigarette ends and get kicked in the butt as I bend over.'

He laughed. 'Are you sure you don't drop a cigarette end yourself?'

'Yes, I'm sure because I don't smoke. But I do eat crisps.'

He laughed again. 'Next time I see an empty bag lying around I'll know you've just passed by.

Don't worry,' he added. 'You'll enjoy yourselves. Often the things you dread the most turn out okay.'

'So they say.'

He kissed her hand. 'See you tomorrow,' he promised.

The sun blinded her as she watched him walk back along the path towards the houses.

She closed her eyes and absorbed the warmth of the sun and listened to the sound of crows squabbling in a nearby oak tree. A yellow butterfly flew around her as she stood up to leave.

'Poor, beautiful, thing, maybe this is your last day, maybe you will die tomorrow,' she whispered, aware her sadness was edged with fear.

A COTTAGE BY THE SEA

S he HAD TO ADMIT THE PINK painted cottage was cute with its white doors and window frames and the surrounding white picket fence. High cliffs rose slowly above a desolate golden beach which was only accessible by a goat-like path some way off. It was like a picture post card and she felt she probably would never want to return home. Jack was right to have pushed her on this holiday, she relaxed, everything was beautiful and a damned sight better than that eerie lake he and Rob were so mad about.

They met up with George and Pat in the evening. Pat, the perfectionist, had brought comfort items from home.

'Well done,' she muttered, insincerely.

George stepped forward in a pair of immaculate white trousers and dark blue polo shirt while Jack stood awkwardly in his favourite denim hipsters and a striped shirt.

'We'll drive down to the harbour, tomorrow morning,' George informed Jack. 'I've already reserved a boat. I'll show you how nicely she moves about,' he added, obviously establishing his position as captain of the two man crew.

She glanced over at Jack who listened politely to George's instructions and seafaring experiences. He tried to throw in a few of his own yarns but he had no chance.

'We have to go Jack, if you want to get up early,' she said, in a meaningful way.

Jack immediately stood up. 'Well, then, until tomorrow morning. Hope the weather holds.'

He sounded unsure and she thought he was already having reservations and wanted to say 'told you so,' but she kept quiet guessing he was already feeling miserable enough.

*

'George was in the Navy,' Jack informed her at the end of the week.

'Surprise me. Commander of the Fleet, no doubt. Aren't you getting fed up with being pushed around?'

'Only one more day before we go home.'

He sounded sad and she felt depressed, thinking about it there was little he could do at home except for the gardening which had become something of an escape hatch. She had tried to suggest various hobbies but he had dismissed them out of hand since all he wanted was to buy a yacht. She had listened to his pathetic repetitive plans for years, she even thought his sailing into the red sunset might be a relief. That living alone, without an obviously frustrated partner, might counterbalance any marital loss.

'We could look for a little place somewhere on the coast,' she suggested, abandoning her critical thoughts. 'Just a couple of rooms, so to speak. Can't we look around just for fun.'

'Thought you didn't like the sea.'

'Rubbish, I love the sea, I'm only frightened of deep water because I can't swim.'

'I'm not planning on another move.'

'Come on, Jack. Don't be so negative.'

'What is it you want?'

'What do I want? Well for starters, I would like you to be a bit more positive, take more interest in things, particularly me.'

'I am. I'm taking an interest in sailing.'

'Then do something about it.'

'I'm going to.'

'Good. But if you don't then don't blame me.'

'Why should I?'

'Yes, why should you. We all need some space. You're not the only one. I feel just as you do. That's what you want, isn't it?', she added, bitterly.

She waited for an answer but he remained silent.

'For God's sake, just do it,' she shouted. 'Then we can both be happy.' She pulled her jacket off a peg, 'I'm going to sit on the cliff top for a few minutes.'

She walked slowly in the half dark and sat a reasonable distance from the edge for she had a childish fear of it crumbling to the beach below and she with it. Not like Jack who boasted about his sense of balance. She closed her eyes and listened to the waves rolling in on the beach and hissing as they pulled back out, mesmerised by the repetitive sound while she thought about Jack and his sailing expeditions and his refusal to wear a life jacket. She thought his stubbornness was a hazard of their marriage, maybe all marriages suffered so.

She stared at the stars while she considered the beauty around her and Pat, a woman who chatted endlessly about her marvellous daughter who was going out with a successful man and would, without doubt, marry him in due course. While she, the Chairwoman of some Institute, was totally indispensible to those who depended on her good judgement She wondered whether she would like to change places with such a woman and live a simple life. She was sure not!

*

Jack laid next to Emy in bed that night aware that his longing to be unbound by compromise and obligation was paramount. He flinched as he remembered the strictness of his childhood, useless rigid rules which could not be broken simply because they had been made. His precious Sunday afternoons spent at his grandmother's house which reeked of teak oil rubbed hard into the brown furniture; the pot of tea brewing under the tea cosy and the inevitable embroidery which had been worked with meticulous love and care by her mother, his great grandmother, framed and hung on the wall for admiration.

He had tried to ignore the simple chatter of his mother, aunts and grandmother while his grandfather sat in the most comfortable chair, smoking endless cigarettes or cigars, exchanging news and views with his father and uncles How hard dining room chairs had been reserved for him and his peers and, when their boredom became too obvious, tired drawing books and crayons were brought out of the sideboard drawer to keep them from fidgeting and swinging their dangling legs too hard.

He had resented these orderly people, whose lives were straight without any noticeable untidy fraying ends, simply because they were banded together in narrowness. Stifling people sitting in their suffocating lounge. All these things were printed indelibly in his memory. He shuddered at the thought of being strangled by routine; to end his days regretting his inability to break free. To do what he wanted, when he wanted, without pleasing anyone but himself. He recognised the price could be high but once he had cut the umbilical family cord he could consider his next move. It was possible he might even return to routine and order sooner than he expected.

He glanced sideways at Emy lying on her back staring up at the ceiling. He loved her but not the way she did him and although he appreciated her intensity and loyalty that was exactly what he did not need at this moment in his life. He thought she was not the kind of woman who enjoyed walking around supermarkets, selecting unusual products, thumbing through cookery books or standing hours behind a stove. In fact, he sometimes wondered what her interests were apart from her obsession with spirits, which she assured him were always around. He tried to tolerate her New World theories but just once in a while he would tell her to forget the past and get on with the present. Dead is dead. But she would never agree to that at any cost.

He reached for her hand. 'I have to talk to you, Emy,' he whispered, almost inaudibly.

They had lain distant from each other as though an invisible barrier had been hammered between them. He had explained how he felt and she had listened and said little, probably because her scathing remarks would only strengthen his argument. She had hoped her silence would make him feel unsure of her feminine reaction, resistance, resilience, in time of danger.

It was only when she had driven down to the village for groceries, the next morning, did her anger overwhelm her. She had thumped the steering wheel with her fists and screamed, 'I hate you, I hate you', as tears trickled down her cheeks. 'I'll decide when your search for freedom is over; I'll decide if, or when, you come home.'

*

Jack was sitting on a ledge under the cliff top when she returned. He did not react to her presence as he continued to read a newspaper.

'I'm going to make some coffee,' she murmured.

'I'll be with you in a couple of minutes,' he replied, as though everything between them was normal.

George and Pat startled her as she entered the cottage.

'We just thought we would pop in, seeing how it's our last day,' announced Pat, standing in the doorway to the hall. 'I've hardly seen George all week. I thought we might explore the surroundings. Perhaps you and Jack would like to come with us.'

'Why not,' she said, not bothering to hide her obvious indifference. 'Would you like a cup coffee?' she asked, hoping they would just go away.

'That would be lovely,' gushed Pat, unable to notice the negative tone in her voice.

She sauntered into the tiny kitchen and looked at the apple tart and baguettes she had bought earlier at a patisserie. They were still warm and she had planned to have them with the Farmer's Brie for lunch. She noticed how her hands were shaking as she filled the kettle.

The enthusiastic couple were on the patio when she returned. 'Shall we sit here?' she suggested, as she stared across at the cliff top. 'Jack will be here in a minute.'

'Where is he?'

'You can't see him, he's on a ledge. He goes there every day. To stare out to sea,' she added.

'We've had a splendid week,' George informed her.

'So I've heard.'

'We must do this again,' suggested Pat, eagerly.

'I am sure Jack would like that, brought back a lot of memories. Excuse me, I think the kettle's boiling, I won't be a minute.'

They were talking about the price of property when she returned with the coffee and she joined in the conversation glancing every now and again at the cliffs.

'Biscuit?' she offered, after they had helped themselves to milk and sugar.

Pat was just on the point of taking the one nearest to her when suddenly she stood up knocking the table and slopping the coffee.

'Be careful, Jack, watch out,' she shouted, looking over towards the cliff top. She turned to George and Pat, 'did you see that gull swooping over the ledge, over Jack?'

'No, what gull, where?' asked George. 'Can you see a gull, Pat?'

They both searched the sky for gulls as she ran out of the garden shouting and waving her arms.

'Come on, we'd better see what's wrong,' Pat suggested, sounding worried as they began to walk after her, panting heavily as they quickened their pace. Suddenly, George stopped, caught his wife's arm, and gasped in horror as Emy stood by the cliff's edge and gave a heart wrenching wail. His face became flushed as he stumbled up to her and grasped her arm to pull her away but she loosened his grip and ran towards a small path. He stood for a moment before he dared himself to look over the edge. A body was sprawled out on the beach below and a seagull was standing next to it.

He turned to see Emy scrambling down a rough track to the beach.

'Come back,' he yelled. But she ignored him and he could not half-slide down the path as she did. He remained helplessly on the cliff top, wiping his forehead with a handkerchief and moaning, over and over again, 'Oh, God no. Please, God no'.

She slipped off the last rock and onto the hard golden sand which felt cold even though its colour promised warmth. She could see Jack lying further down the beach and she wondered if there were angels hovering in the endless blue sky above waiting to embrace his soul. She glanced upwards and saw George carefully leaning over the edge and shouting to her. It was then she noticed the cliff was stepped with rough, uneven, ledges like the one Jack had sat on.

A seagull was standing as motionless as a sentry next to Jack, as though guarding his lifeless body, and held its ground as she walked towards it, defying her presence until she knelt beside him. Only then did it wing clumsily off the beach.

She breathed deeply as she brushed the sand off Jack's bruised face and kissed his bleeding head.

'I'm so sorry, I'm so sorry' she whispered.

It was only when she touched his hand did

she notice a white feather. At first, she did not want to take it from him but she knew others would soon arrive and she dreaded their invasion, defiling her last moments alone with him. She pulled the feather carefully from his now limp hand and sat back on her heels running it through her fingers, aware of a suffocating pressure, a numbness which made her feel profoundly disconnected to where she was, who she was. She bent over as though to ward off faintness but she knew that was not the cause of the chilling sensation.

When she looked up, a gull was perched on the mast of a small yacht which bobbed up and down in the waves not far from the shore. It spread its wings, as though proud of itself, and then carefully tucked them back into its body. A man with short blond hair stood up from the bottom of the boat and inhaled deeply on a cigarette then, flicking it into the sea, he dived into its depths, surfaced and wiped his hand down his face and under his nose as he floated on his back.

'Come on in,' he called.

'Jack, I'm coming, wait for me,' she shouted back, wading into the lukewarm sea, jumping through the incoming waves, the humid air pressing against her body. Then, she began to swim with long swift strokes until she came alongside him. He roughly grabbed her wrist and held her as he kissed her through the salty water which covered them softly gently, dark as velvet night.

AS A SPECK OF DUST

Now FIVE DAYS LATER, she considered Jack had survived rather well considering how far he had fallen. However, she winced at the thought of the inevitable fetching and carrying associated with male patients and certainly Jack. She felt sorry for him but she did not entirely forgive the inconvenience he was causing. In any case, it was his own fault.

'Stupid idiot,' she murmured, as the front door bell rang.

Helen was standing in the porch when she opened the door. She stepped back surprised.

'Hey, come in. Come on in,' she greeted her enthusiastically because she was feeling lonely and depressed.

'I can't stay for long. I was in the area and have been meaning to pop in. How are you?'

'Fine, Jack's doing well. He'll probably be home in a few days. He was knocked out for some hours and, luckily, he only broke an arm, a leg, a few ribs and dislocated his shoulder. Not to mention the bruising. His back's okay and his brains are just as they were before,' she grinned, suggestively.

'In other words, nothing very special.'

'I think that sums it up. Come on, you must have time for a quick coffee.'

'How did it happen?' asked Helen, sitting down at the kitchen table.

'Had a fight with a seagull. The gull won.'

'Actually, I've come about the cottage,' Helen said, dismissing the information as old news.

Not back to that ghastly place, she thought, as she visualised the lonely, depressing, worker's hovel built on the side of one of several gravel pits which had, over countless decades, become tranquil lakes mirroring the clouds and willow trees and only disturbed by aquatic life.

Sometimes, she and Helen would sit on a low mooring and pull the green waterweed through their toes while Jack and Rob drunk a couple of beers before casting off in a small unstable sailboat, or rather a rowing boat with a sail.

It was a dangerous lake for it sloped quickly and was meters deep within a short distance from the bank. It was said to be haunted by swimmers who had been pulled to its depths by the tangling, swirling, weed.

Helen said she had heard the voice of a woman crying, 'Oh, God, Oh, my God', but Rob had shrugged his shoulders and said it was only the wind whistling in the willows and reeds. But she believed Helen. She pushed her thoughts away.

'What about the cottage?' she answered.

'I want to ask you what you think about our weekends.'

'The truth? You mean apart from the mosquitoes, insects and black spiders in the bathroom.'

'Yes,' replied Helen. 'The truth.'

'Well, I'm a bit bored with Jack and Rob's never-ending walk down memory lane.' She felt embarrassed. 'I shouldn't have said that.'

Helen smiled. 'No, glad you did. I feel just the same. I thought there's no need for you to go. Let Jack go alone,' she added, moving the salt and pepper pots around.

'I'll think about it,' she replied, thoughtfully.

'Perhaps, that's the only thing they have left.'

'What?'

'Walking down memory lane,' Helen replied, quickly. 'You know, life can be a bit dry, bread on bread, so to speak. Perhaps it's their way of reliving a colourful life.'

'Well, yes,' she frowned. 'I guess a thick spread of butter and jam might help. But where do you find it.' She softened her words as she thought of Will.

'Don't worry too much, there won't be any weekends for some time to come.'

'No, probably not.'

'Actually,' Helen informed her. 'Rob's going to have the place done up. He's getting a local builder to put in a new kitchen and build the bathroom onto the house.'

'Really, that is good news,' she replied, trying to sound enthusiastic.

'Listen, I've got a dentist's appointment and

I'll be late if I stay any longer. By the way, I found Jack's lighter on the bedside table. At the cottage,' she added, pulling a lighter from out of her handbag.

'Thanks, he lost it. He'll be pleased to have it back,' she replied, rubbing it, affectionately, through her fingers. 'I gave it to him years ago.'

She slowly closed the front door after Helen had driven away. She felt puzzled as she placed the lighter in an ashtray. Something felt wrong.

Later, she sat back in Jack's favourite chair and considered how Helen, the maker of patchwork quilts, sat complacently as she manoeuvred her needle and thread between colourful cotton squares while Jack and Rob, suspended in the past, sat drinking heavily as the evenings waned into late night; regurgitating stories of life as it was years ago. A place in the far east where skyscrapers broke the skyline and massive jets belched out thousands of hot and sticky tourists into the luxurious, air conditioned, halls of the airport.

She frowned as she remembered Rob boasting how he and Jack had shared their bachelor years together and that their past constituted the corner stone of their friendship, which was unlikely to be broken by any outsider. Probably meaning her. Jack had only smiled foolishly and had probably not even registered Rob's remark. Sometimes, she wondered if they had cut their hands and mixed their blood to seal their bond, like two school boys around a camp fire. She had given up and gone to bed.

Now, it seemed Helen was offering her a way out and although she felt relieved a wave of suspicion ran through her. She alone at home while they had their cosy weekends together. 'Catch twenty-two', she thought.

'Yea, Helen,' she murmured. 'You must think I'm stupid if you think I don't see through you. Me sitting at home while you get it together with Jack. Like hell,' she muttered. 'Your obvious glances and sweet smiles have not gone unnoticed, only I've never seen Jack show any interest in you. Ever thought about that? I really don't understand why you stay with Rob when he obviously irritates you. Why didn't you find someone else? After all, you're attractive enough in a sort of cool, arrogant, way. But, then again, if the right man doesn't cross your path why should you want to disturb your affluent lifestyle.'

She was uncomfortably aware that Jack was Helen's right man and she seriously thought it time to spoil these archaic memories and sentimental weekends. After all, Jack knew how she felt and also understood she used the visits as a leverage to gain concessions from him. A sort of quid pro quo arrangement which suited her, at least, up until now.

She sighed as she remembered how she had thought Jack was the 'be all and end all' of her life. How he had carried a light, the light at the end of the tunnel. Years later, she had seriously questioned her assumption.

'I don't think anyone is able to carry a torch for another, at least not for long,' she informed Daisy who lay at her feet.

She sat for a long time until the sun shone on a crystal candlestick forming coloured spectrums on the walls and ceiling, like miniature rainbows, and particles of dust floated and drifted through the light as though they were unable or unsure of where to settle.

'As a speck of dust one day you'll fall and I'll be there waiting, no rush at all.' She gave a hollow laugh. 'What do you think of that, Jack? Seeing how you did fall.'

Daisy jumped onto her lap seeking attention.

'You're the only one who loves me, unconditionally,' she whispered, stroking her black curly hair. The loyal poodle looked up sadly as though feeling her unhappiness.

'Come on, sweet girl,' she said, suddenly standing up. 'Let's go and see Rosie'

*

The narrow road to Rosie's house was lined with towering oak trees which, as beautiful as they were, gave her a feeling of anxiety although the sides of the road were pretty when the primroses pushed through the creeping undergrowth in the spring and, later in the year, blackberries and hazel nuts could be found in the hedgerows. She suppressed her feelings as her car crunched to a standstill on the gravel drive and relaxed when Rosie opened the door and lightly kissed her on the cheek.

'You can feel it's autumn,' she said, shivering as she followed Rosie into the kitchen.

'How are you?' asked Rosie, putting the kettle on the stove.

'Okay, thanks.'

'Jack was terribly lucky,' Rosie remarked, sitting down opposite her.

'Yes, he was. Some wire netting broke his fall.'

'I guess it wasn't his time,' replied Rosie, thoughtfully.

'It seems he rolled, or rather bounced, from one ledge to another.'

'It's a miracle he survived.'

'Actually, I want to ask you something.'

'Fire away.'

'Do you think you can cross time, go back in time?'

'I doubt it, though they're always making films about it. Why do you ask?'

'Because you are the only one I know who is a bit spiritual, so to speak. I know I must have dreamt it but it was so real. I can't get it out of my head. You won't tell anyone I told you,' she asked, aware that sharing a secret was no longer a secret.

'Never.'

'Well, we had one day of our holiday left. Jack said he would sit on the ledge beneath the cliff top and read the newspaper and I said I would go shopping and pick up something for lunch. Jack was still on the ledge when I returned. I sat next to him for a while and then I went back to the cottage and Jack said he would follow.

George and Pat, our holiday friends, were standing in the hall when I got back so I offered them coffee. We were outside on the patio when, suddenly, I saw a seagull flying over where Jack was sitting, it seemed to be diving at him. I ran to the cliff edge and when I looked down Jack was lying at the bottom of the cliff.'

She paused. 'I ran along a path until I could climb down to the beach. An enormous gull was standing next to Jack, a really big one. It flew away when I knelt down and when I looked up it was perched on the mast of a sailing boat.

Well, a man stood up, he must have been sitting in the bottom of the boat. It was Jack.'

'But Jack was on the beach,' Rosie interrupted, sounding puzzled.

'Yes, I know but somehow he wasn't. I know it doesn't make sense but he was also in the boat. Then he dived into the sea and wiped his hand down his face when he surfaced. Jack always did that, I could recognise him anywhere.'

'And you swam to him,' stated Rosie who had already heard something through the local grapevine.

'Yes, but the water was warm, the air really humid and I could swim. I can't swim, Rosie. Never have done.'

'But someone had to save you.'

'Yes, but that was after I reached Jack.'

'But Jack wasn't in the boat, he was on the beach!'

'I know, I can't explain it.'

'What time do you think you were in?' Rosie asked, now sounding concerned.

"I was about twenty one when I arrived in Hong Kong. Jack had already been living out there for years but I had never met him.'

'I think the only way of handling this is to think of it as a reaction to a traumatic event. It probably seemed real at the time but you know it wasn't. You should write it down and then forget about it and, if you take my advice, keep it to yourself before you get a name for being strange,' suggested Rosie, kindly.

She laughed with embarrassment. 'Yes, I'll do that. I know you're right but it seemed so terribly real at the time.' She paused as she stared into the fire. 'Jack didn't approve of our meetings in your chapel, he thought it immoral to give hope to people who are terminally ill.'

'Well, he's not the only one who thinks like that. He has a point, I guess,' Rosie replied.

She looked across at Rosie somewhat puzzled.

'I would have thought you would see it differently.'

'Everyone has their own take on life. We have ours, Jack has his.'

'You are so realistic. You should get married.'

'Does being realistic equate to being married,' she laughed. 'I'll have to think about that one.'

For a moment, she imagined Rosie living in a garret with some struggling Writer or Artist. She and Guy had started out rather poor and her becoming pregnant had not been in his planning, which understandable. In fact, she thought most men were not that keen to start a family. Added costs, second to the new arrival and less sex.

'Did I ever tell you about my first marriage?' she asked, still thinking of Guy.

Rosie shook her head and waited for her to continue but, instead, she only stared across the room remembering her first weeks in Hong Kong.

She was lying on a sunbed staring up at the creamy, waxy, flowers of a Magnolia tree when she noticed a small black spider had spun its web between the branches, waiting for its dinner to arrive. She smiled, as she relished the idea of binding up Guy as the spider would a fly, watch him struggle in her carefully spun web and then hang him out to dry. Unfortunately, he was very much alive and wasn't about to be caught in any web she might spin.

She closed her eyes and mulled over her frustrations, the pros and cons of living in the tropics with a man who did not love her, or she him, or returning home to suffer the monotony of the London suburbs. She decided to bide her time, nothing ever stayed the same. Something would happen to change the status quo. It always did.

She had been on the point of deciding it was time to cool off in the swimming pool when she became aware of someone standing next to her. She looked up to see Guy peering down at her.

'Get dressed,' he said, grinning smugly. 'I'll show you the house I've rented. See, I told you someone in my office would know somebody who had something.'

It was late afternoon when they eventually drove round a circular gravel drive and pulled up in front of an empty house some distance out of town.

'They're coming tomorrow to give it a coat of paint,' he informed her.

She leaned back against the car as she tried to absorb the state of the house. Dark stains had crept up the once white walls and the paint work had flaked on the window sills. She decided she didn't like the house and never would for it felt wrong.

She shuddered. 'Someone's walking over my grave,' she muttered, as she followed him up the steps.

Guy ignored her remark. 'I get the keys at the end of the week. Nice property,' he stated, assuming she would agree.

'Where's the front door?' she asked, peering through the bars of a black iron gate.

'You're standing in front of it, this is it. And that's the lounge behind,' he added, now irritated by her lack of enthusiasm.

She squinted as she tried to distinguish the outlay of a room dominated by a large bay window. She stepped back and tried to convince herself that her sinking feeling was due to the high grass behind her, which was once a lawn, and the padlocked gates which felt threatening.

'I don't like it.'

'That's you all over, always pre-judging. You haven't even seen inside yet.'

'I don't have to see inside, I can see outside and I'm not pre-judging. I'm listening to my inner voice.'

'Then tell your inner voice to shut up. I've signed the contract and paid a deposit,' Guy shouted, angrily.

'You could have asked me.'

'I could have but I didn't. I've told you, they're coming to paint it. You can stay another week in the hotel and if you don't like it, Emily, then piss off.'

*

She had rested her head next to the open car window as they drove home and felt the soft, warm, wind cool her damp face and ruffle her now short hair. She had closed her eyes and admitted, as she so often did, that she had not actually been in love with Guy but rather overpowered by his self-assurance, self-importance. She had long concluded that he needed a permanent sounding-board; someone who would listen to him without criticism; without an opinion; a mindless audience of one who was unable to escape his lengthy sermons.

Sadly, by the time she had understood his reason for marrying, a simple self-interest, the invitations had been sent, the 'Order of Service' printed, restaurant, cars and a three tier wedding cake were all lined up for the 'big' day. She had been too young to throw a spanner in such a well-oiled machine and that had cost her dearly.

She sighed as she remembered how she had fantasized the night before her marriage, how she had imagined legging it down the aisle, her bouquet of spring flowers crushed under Guy's shiny black shoes, her white wedding dress tearing in the sparse brown *heather while her whispery veil floated away in the cold March wind. Instead she had walked demurely down the aisle and dutifully answered all the vows which completed the contract.*

Sophie had been born just over a year later and she had seen little chance of anything changing until, one day, Guy had come home announcing he had found a job overseas.

She had packed their few possessions leaving her sentimental girlie rubbish until last so she could quietly re-read Guy's letters, the ones he had written before they had married, the ones declaring his unrequited love. She had smiled as she saw them for what they were, something between literary exercises and college essays, and her role was to be the admiring reader. Now she wished she had marked them with a nine out of ten or an A+ for they really were rather good, only their explicit content fell short of sincerity.

She had glanced sideways at Guy as he parked the car outside their hotel. His jaw was set firmly, his lips pressed into a tight thin line and she tried not to think of him kissing her that night. She had thought again of the spider in the Magnolia tree waiting for food, only she was waiting for the food of love. She yearned to be loved, passionately loved, by someone who could accept her just as she was.

*　　　*　　　*

'So, Mrs. Gaywood, have you settled in?' asked Mrs. Chung, an elderly Chinese lady who lived opposite her creepy house. The one which Guy had found when they had first arrived.

'As far as possible,' she replied, as she discreetly looked around a room full of dark Chinese furniture, vases and wood carvings, silk cushions and pictures which together gave an atmosphere of wealth and perhaps even of calm.

They spoke of everyday matters, what Guy did, her child, how long they had been in the country, nothing special.

'Was my house empty for long?' she asked, casually.

'You are the first tenants since Mr. Lee left,' Mrs. Chung replied as she dabbed her thin, cracked, lips with a lace handkerchief. 'The price of property is going up quickly so the 'Lee' family want to keep it for a while. Renting is profitable, we Chinese are very good business people. It has been an unhappy house,' she added, her voice now sounding pained.

'Why is that?'

'Not only did Mr. Lee disappear but his wife did as well.'

She gasped. 'Disappear! What happened to them?'

The old lady pursed her lips and stared across the room as though trying to remember the details of her story. 'Well,' she continued slowly, her voice trembling as though from old age or perhaps even emotion, 'Mr. Lee was older than his beautiful wife. He suddenly became very ill.' She paused. 'He knew he would die very slowly and he loved his wife so much he decided he did not want her to see him suffer.'

'How sad. What did he do?'

'Jimmy Lee was very rich. He kept a splendid boat out at the Yacht Club.' She stopped to sip her tea. 'He told his wife, Jade, he would sail away and leave his life in the hands of fate and she was to tell no one that he was gone. I heard he left a letter in which he wrote, she was never to forget that he who pushes back the waves of the sea will himself create new waves and that she must let destiny take its course.'

'That is so beautiful,' she sighed.

Mrs. Chung closed her narrow eyes and nodded her head in agreement. 'She tried hard to change his mind. Then, early one morning he kissed her goodbye and left. Neither he nor his boat were ever seen again.'

'How terrible, what did she do?'

'Oh, she was so sorry that she had been unable to stop him and, a few days later, she also disappeared. She left a letter to say that she had gone to search for him and if she could not find him here in this life then she would find his spirit.' She rested for a while, closing her eyes again. Then she suddenly added, 'she left her bird behind.'

'Her bird?'

The old lady paused and dabbed her eyes. 'One evening, Jade found a wounded seagull on the beach. I heard it had no grey or black feathers, no coloured beak. Just pure white. She took it home and looked after it herself. It became very tame and Mr. Lee called his boat 'The Gull' to please her.'

'That is so romantic. What happened to Jade?'

Mrs. Chung sipped her tea, closed her eyes and said no more.

The wind bells had gently moved in a soft breeze as she left Mrs. Chung's veranda and strolled down the small road which ran between the rough grass and tropical plants. High trees hid green lizards with meter long tails and yellow birds darted in and out of the branches. She stopped for a moment to listen to the crickets which chirped all day, and especially at night, and felt overwhelmed by the colour and humid heat. It was as though she could breathe it in and feel it cover her.

She had been young and incredibly naive when Mrs. Chung had invited her for that innocent cup of tea and the romantic story was destined to linger forever in her memory, how could it not. Who would not like to believe in perfect love, a rarity which until then had not crossed her path.

Eventually, she had left Guy and gone home to live with her parents. She had cried for the loss of the bright mornings, the warm moist evenings, the swirling fans, the chit chats which hid behind the pictures and cupboards, the street vendors selling spicy food, the little shops hanging out their wares. There was so much she would miss.

Rosie poured the tea noisily into the mugs to break the silence.

'You were saying something about your first husband,' she enquired, obviously curious.

'Oh, sorry, it's not important. Thanks for listening to me, Rosie. You're a good friend.'

'Come any time. You'll see, Jack will fully recover,' she added, gently.

'But will we?' she sighed, as she drove home.

HAPPY NEW YEAR

S he HAD UNWILLINGLY PULLED herself through the Christmas preparations behaving as though she found the massive shopping and present searching good fun while, in reality, she considered the festive season a penance for the sins of the year. She failed to understand how anyone could be deceived by her seasonal enthusiasm.

Jack had persuaded her to invite Rob and Helen over for New Year's Eve and Rob had raised his glass to all the weekends they would have at the cottage the following summer.

'The renovation is almost finished. The bathroom is built onto the house and we're doing up the kitchen,' he proudly announced.

He turned to Jack. 'Helen thinks it's about time we sold the place, she says it depresses her. I mean how could she even suggest it. Couldn't think of letting it go.' He laid his hand on Jack's shoulder as he so often did. 'You know how women are, don't you Jack?' he added.

'Tell us how we are, Jack,' she asked, her tone veiling a threat.

'Women like changes.'

'So long as they can keep their creature comforts,' Rob added, laughing at his own wit.

'And husbands are a pain in the butt,' she snapped, as she followed Helen into the kitchen.

'Or a necessary evil', Helen added, bitterly, as she lit a cigarette, inhaling deeply as she handed the packet to Emy. 'I told him, do the place up or I'm out. Listen,' she said, changing the subject. 'I've been thinking. Why don't we go down to the cottage together in a few weeks time, when the builder is finished.'

'Well, it's an idea,' she said softly. 'You know, we could also go somewhere else, somewhere warm. Get a bit of a suntan.'

Helen did not reply.

'Anyway, I might have to be around for a few more weeks to get Jack on his feet. He's going to need help for a while,' she continued, struggling to find a good reason to refuse her invitation.

'Are you sure about that?'

'What's that supposed to mean?' she asked, coughing from the inhaled smoke.

'Nothing, just a silly remark,' Helen answered, abruptly, as she returned to the lounge where Rob had changed the subject of the renovated cottage and his wife's dissatisfaction.

'My mother still lives with us,' he complained. 'I want to sell up but I don't know if I can legally make her move if she doesn't want to.'

'She won't move,' Helen interrupted. 'She's a

stubborn old bitch and anyway old people live too long nowadays.'

'It might be you, one day,' Emy retorted, still puzzled why Helen should suggest they go down to the cottage, which they both hated, while rejecting her suggestion of a more colourful, warmer, holiday location.

'I wonder if our kids will talk the same way about us in the future,' reflected Jack, sounding unsure.

'Of course they won't,' she interrupted, sharply, trying to hide her own uncertainty.

*   *   *

Beatrice Bennett firmly clenched her jaw as though to sustain her determination in resolving the unthinkable predicament which she now faced. She thought of her husband, Charles, who had died years ago. Rob and Helen had flown back from Hong Kong for his funeral and stayed on for several weeks to help with the paperwork, after which Rob had cornered her.

'I've been thinking,' he had said. 'You don't want to live in this house all alone. What if Helen and me were to buy it from you? We could build a small extension. I'm being replaced next year so we'll be back in the U.K. for good and then we can keep you company.'

'Well I don't know,' she had answered, her voice lowered with dread and uncertainty.

'If we were to buy a bit under the price then we would save a hell of a lot of death duties and could resell it later for a nice profit.´

'When I die, you mean.'

Rob turned away obviously embarrassed.

'Yes, but that won't be for ages. It's just an idea which would help us and, as I have just said, avoid at least some death duties.'

'What's the reason? How much under the price?' she added, suspiciously.

'There is no reason, except that anything can happen,' he replied, carefully avoiding the second question.

She had known it was unwise to sell her house but they had promised to build an extension and she could live in what they called a 'granny flat', a contradiction in terms since they were childless. They would take care of her for the rest of her life and she would never be lonely or lack any creature comforts. She would have money in the bank and no responsibilities. What more could she ask for? She thought the answer to that was more money in the bank than they were prepared to pay for her house. So, here she was staring out of the window at what used to be her garden. She thought of Charles and how he had taught his favourite subject, Latin, at an expensive private school five miles away.

'Belle,' Charles would say, for he had always called her that. 'Don't despair, Nil desperandum. Everything is solvable, you only have to find the right key.'

'You were right about that,' she mumbled. 'The key to my house was the right key. They can't make me move if I don't want to. I won't sign any papers.'

The door to her small lounge suddenly opened. Helen stood in its entrance.

'I've just made a cup of tea. I thought you might like to have one with me,' she said, smiling sweetly. 'And I've made a Victoria sponge cake, especially for you. I'll put the heating up. It's cold in here,' she added, turning the knob of the thermostat higher.

'That's very kind of you, dear. I'll be with you in a moment.'

'Take your time,' Helen replied, smiling again as she returned to the main house.

Belle glanced at a photograph of she and Charles at Rob's wedding. Helen had seemed so in love with their handsome Rob but it seemed to her, when she saw them two years later, their marriage had turned cold and there was no sign of an offspring. She had tried to drop a hint or two but no information was forthcoming from either of them. Charles, of course, did not notice anything, he never did, and only spoke highly of Helen which irritated her. After all, she was the lucky one to have married her son, not the other way around. Men were so blind when it came to women.

'You must understand,' Helen said, kindly, as she handed her a cup of tea. 'We are getting older. We need to live in something smaller, more compact. We will find you something you like, you will always have the last word. You don't have to take anything you don't like.'

'It's my house, you promised me I could stay here until my last breath. You promised me that.'

'I know we did, dear, but circumstances change. The price of houses around here is astronomical. We can buy something far cheaper further out in the country, put some money away and not have to worry about anything, anymore. This old house is a money pit we can't afford.'

'Then you shouldn't have bought it.' There was a tense silence. 'I don't understand, Rob has always had a more than good salary and you have no children. You should have a really healthy bank account. You shouldn't need to sell this house.'

Helen sighed. 'We would like to travel, feel free, and not have to worry about upkeep, burglars, etcetera, or whether you are alright or not.'

'You don't have to worry about me. I'm perfectly capable of taking care of myself.'

'Maybe, now, but think of the future,' Helen replied, sounding frustrated.

'No, Helen. No. You had years of freedom when you lived out east. How many times have I actually seen you and Rob over the years?'

'Of course, you're right. I know it sounds selfish but we want to live easily. We thought that perhaps we might find a really nice flat. Just lock it up and take holidays, knowing you are tucked up safely.'

'The garden is so beautiful, even this time of year,' remarked Belle, as though the conversation had not taken place.

'Please, Belle, be reasonable.'

'I have to go to the Library, I need a couple of new books,' mused Belle.

*

'It's no good, Rob,' Helen said that evening. 'She's not going to budge. You can forget about selling up.'

'Ridiculous old woman,' he grunted, pouring himself another drink. 'Just forget about it, she can't live forever.'

'She can live until she's a hundred.'

'Hardly likely.'

'Knowing her she'll live even longer just to spite us. You know we've been discussing this for more than a year.'

'Well, let's forget about it until the spring,' he said, glancing through the newspaper. 'They say it will freeze for some time yet. Why don't we go down to the cottage and do a bit of skating, the lake must be frozen over. I'll find my old skates.'

'Are you serious, do you really want to fall on your backside a hundred times?'

'They're in the loft, I'm going to fish them out,' he replied, ignoring her question.

'What about your mother?'

'What about her?'

'We could take her with us,' suggested Helen, staring at the frozen fish pond and wishing Belle would trip into it and drown in a couple of inches of water.

'You must be joking,' he replied, looking up at her puzzled.

'No, I'm not. It must be awful, always being left behind. We should try another tack, sweeten her up, be nicer to her, promise her she can come with us no matter where we go. We should take her down to the lake and let her stare out of the window at Winter Wonderland. She will appreciate that. She's never been with us before in the winter,' she smiled.

'That's very magnanimous of you,' he said, swallowing a mouthful of brandy, after he had first rolled it around in his mouth. 'You don't have to take her to please me.'

'I do it for her,' she replied, as she pictured the hard banks of the lake and the sheets of thin ice broken by the reeds in the shallows. She would take Belle for a walk then hurry home on some pretext while Belle conveniently slipped into the icy water. At least, that is how it had to look. Difficult, she thought. But everything was possible, all that was necessary was the opportunity and the right timing; Rob skating too far away to see his miserable mother nose dive into the slushy muddy shallows.

She had ignored Rob's expensive life style which included ridiculous bar bills, designer clothes, Italian shoes and large sums of money which he regularly took from their bank account. Now she wanted out and she wanted enough money to start a new life. If Belle would not let them sell the house then she would have to arrange it and the cottage was as good a place as any.

She could not allow Belle to win this, not for endless years, and she did not think she needed to feel any remorse.

*

The weather forecasters had got it right. It snowed hard on Friday night and the 'big freeze', as they called it, was to continue. The trip to the cottage was not without danger but they had arrived just before dark. Belle had sat, silently, in the back of the car between the extra blankets and duvets, her thermal underclothes under her skirt and jumper and, most importantly, her bottle of sherry. Helen, on the other hand, was worked up, talkative and lively. Once in a while, Rob glanced at her wondering why she should be so elated. After all, his mother was sitting in the back of the car and that was enough to depress anyone, let alone Helen who would normally sit with her head lowered so that her hair fell over her depressed face, rather like a funeral veil.

'Shall I let her sleep in?' queried Helen, as she spooned powered coffee into a mug next morning.

'I'm already up,' called Belle from the open staircase.

'Coffee or tea?'

'First tea, then coffee,' answered Belle, making her way towards the all-burner stove.

She glanced over to a pile of wood. 'You've been busy.'

Rob looked up. 'Brought it in to dry last time we were down here. It won't burn well if I don't do that.'

'So thoughtful, just like your father.'

'I've never thought of Rob being like Charles, interesting,' grinned Helen.

Rob zipped up his padded jacket, 'I'm going out. See you later,' he announced, slamming the door a little too hard behind him.

'Slept badly, I should think,' laughed Helen. 'It's his fault for sleeping on the sofa.'

'Why should he do that?'

'Ask him, how should I know why he wants to sleep alone. Do you want a cooked breakfast or just toast?'

Helen dropped the bread in the toaster and thought of Charles. Long school holidays and long boring home leaves had thrown them together. It was as though Belle had handed her husband to her on a plate.

She smiled at the thought of his rather untidy, scholarly, appearance and his deceiving 'lost look' which had so endeared him to her and, she thought, others.

So long ago, she thought, but it seemed like yesterday. Stupid Belle, stupid Rob, always hanging on each others' words; supporting each others' every move; going off together for hours leaving she and Charles to amuse themselves until the obvious happened. She grinned as she remembered their first time together.

'We're alone again,' Charles had grinned.

'What shall we do?', she asked, responding to the suggestive glint in his eyes, as she fell back onto the sofa with her legs slightly apart and her arm raised on a cushion.

He sat next to her and she fingered the buttons on his shirt. He kissed her hand, then bent over her. She welcomed his kisses, hot desperate kisses known to those who received too little passion, who needed to be loved and to return love.

'Oh, Helen,' he whispered. 'Sine amor, nihil est vita.'

'What's that?', she asked, softly.

'Without love, life is pointless. I teach the little morons Latin,' he added. 'Life is nothing without love,' *he groaned.*

She loosened her blouse, he smiled. She knew what he was thinking.

'Klein maar fijn,' she whispered.

He stopped. 'What does that mean?'

'I had a Dutch boyfriend, long before I knew Rob,' she lied. 'It means, small but fine.'

He smiled at her gently. 'I'm not greedy, they're enough for me. Amor est caecus.'

'And?'

'Love is blind,' he murmured.

'I hope your sight doesn't improve.'

'Klein maar fijn. I will remember that.'

And he did, whenever they met he whispered those words as he greeted her.

Years later, she laid red roses on his grave.

The card read, 'Sine amor, nihil vita'.

*

'He is still the sweet schoolboy I remember,' twittered Belle, sipping her first glass of sherry before dinner.

'If you say so,' agreed Helen, angry that she had suggested bringing Belle with them and constantly having to listen to her silly stories, which she had heard hundreds of times before. 'You know, I think we should go home tomorrow. It's too damn cold here,' she added, having given up the idea of getting Belle out of the cottage and along the slippery banks of the lake.

'I was hoping you would say that. It's nearly dark, where is he?' Belle asked, pulling the curtains to the end of the track. 'He shouldn't stay out so long, he should be back by now,' she murmured, recalling the numerous times she had said that when he was a child.

Rob was special, anyone could see that, so it had not bothered her when her husband had been too pre-occupied with his school and the English teacher who seemed to need his expertise. She had turned a blind eye to whatever it was she should have seen. So long as he did not interfere with her life, mainly Rob and her gardening, then any waywardness did not really matter. It had suited her to join in with the free-thinking extroverts of that time. She opened the back door and the icy air swept in cancelling the warmth in the house.

'It's a full moon, it's so light. I think they are having a party over there.'

'There are flashing lights,' muttered Helen, sounding puzzled.

'What is going on?'

'I'll go and have a look, perhaps he's having a drink with those new people further up. They've recently moved in.'

'That's very selfish of him to make us worry,' Belle whispered, 'I can't believe he would do that.'

Helen pulled on her fur lined boots and ski jacket. 'You had better hope he has. I won't be long.'

She stamped her way along a known track now hidden by snow and ice and pulled her scarf across her mouth to lessen the cold air. The area had brightened up a little since two other cottages had been renovated; one fairly nearby, the other out of sight at the far end of a second lake. She began to feel anxious as she neared the first cottage which had been bought by a young couple. He was said to be 'something in the City' and his wife 'something in interior decorating', which she found difficult to believe having seen her talentless ideas.

Apprehension overwhelmed her as she realised the lights were from an ambulance and police car parked a little way from the yuppie's cottage because the track was too narrow to drive down.

A young police officer walked towards her.

'Are you missing anyone, Madam? There's been an accident.'

She had known instantly that it was Rob who was lying under the ice and gave a Statement, after which she told them how his mother was over in the other cottage and she really must get back to her to break the dreadful news.

Belle was sitting near the wood stove when she eventually got home, rocking to and fro while sobbing as though in time with her movements. She hardly needed to be told the details for she seemed to know she had lost her only child, her only son, her reason for living. Then, suddenly, she stood up and ran wailing into the bright night sliding, stumbling, crawling, on the icy track while screaming. 'Oh, Rob. Oh, my Rob'.

Helen stood motionless, her mouth totally dry, her body numb to the cold, as she realised that she had heard the same scream years before. The scream Rob had said was the wind whistling through the rushes and reeds. The 'Oh my God' was 'Oh my Rob'.

She gasped, as she fell back into a chair and for the first time in years allowed herself to relax. She did not think for one moment about Belle for she was totally engulfed in the fact that one of her problems had been solved, even if tragically. She was free at last and now she could concentrate on what she really wanted, what she had wanted for so long. The 'so near and yet so far' was suddenly 'an arm's length away'.

*   *   *

Helen seemed composed when she told she and Jack how a group of young skaters had seen Rob sink slowly through the cracked ice; how they had carefully made their way to the side of the lake to find branches for him to hold onto and how they had failed.

Jack held Helen close to him, rubbing her back as tears formed in his eyes and gently rolled down his cheeks. Suddenly she drew away from him.

'Did you see Rob's mother on the way here? She wasn't in her room when I looked in on her this morning. I suppose she's by the lake,' she added, thoughtfully.

'I hope not,' she replied, immediately stepping outside into the crisp glistening snow.

A now faint moon and a few bright stars were still shining in the cold morning sky. Normally, she would have stood gazing up at the beauty of the universe and consider the force of creation but, now, she walked quickly to the edge of the lake where the reeds broke through the thin ice. She glanced around the banks and called Belle several times but there was no answer, no movement between the leafless trees. Only an unrecognisable form laid heaped in the reeds.

She suppressed the urge to call to God, God who was called upon in time of need. Instead she called for Jack.

Later, Helen walked out onto the mooring and stared across the lake which had deceived Rob and drowned so many others. 'Two out of three. Two birds with one stone. Just one to go. How is that possible,' she whispered. Now, she had to work out how she could have heard the desperate cries of a woman years before the event had taken place. In fact, she wondered if Time really existed.

*   *   *

She and Jack stood either side of Helen at the funeral. Rob and Belle's coffins laid next to each other with sheaths of white lilies placed on them, obviously by Helen who seemed amazingly composed. In fact, she assured them there was nothing they could do to help, she would immediately begin to clear out Rob and Belle's personal possessions. That way she would not have time to think about it all.

Only, maybe, Jack could help take Rob and Bell's clothes to the charity shop and ride a few times up and down to the 'tip'. She did not think Belle had anything worth keeping and Rob's collections of stamps and cigarette cards, which his father had left him, could be sold to a dealer. She would give Jack a call when she was ready.

'Actually,' Helen mentioned, casually, 'I feel free. Marriage is a kind of a cage and someone's just opened the door.'

Jack had said very little and crept, as always, into his protective shell. She really could not fathom him out and she was too angry with him to be bothered. She knew it was just a matter of time, improved weather, before he took a backward leap into his youth. Had she said anything at all it would have been to tell him to grow up but she did not want to use any more energy on him.

*   *   *

Months later, she stood at the back door while Jack revved his motorbike alongside the garage.

'Well, what do you think?' he asked, smiling broadly. 'I had one when I was eighteen. Can't wait to get her on the road.'

'Marvellous,' she answered, trying to look enthusiastic. 'Fantastic. Only I don't understand why you've bought a motorbike when you've always wanted a yacht.'

'It's cheaper to run. I did tell you how I feel.'

'Yes, I believe you said something about it.'

'I just want to be free, feel the wind in my face. Go where I want, doesn't have to be far, I won't be gone for long, just a few days here or there. Though I would like to ride around Scotland for a bit.

He had rattled off his point of view, his position, as he had done the night before he fell down the cliff. There was a glint in his eyes, a happiness she had not seen for such a long time and she really couldn't deflate him. Only she wondered where the dream of the yacht had gone, was it possible that a dream fulfilled was a dream poorer? That perhaps he was scared of being disappointed and a motorbike would avoid that emotion.

She had almost given him her blessing, almost but not quite. It's better than a yacht, she thought, and decided the bike was the lesser of two evils.

PAST LOVE

It WAS AT THE BEGINNING of May when Daisy pulled her attention to the postman at the gate. She did not rush to the post box for she could not image anything good happening in her life. But now, as she walked to the end of the front garden, she felt overwhelmed by the sureness that there would be something special. She quickly shuffled through the letters and stopped at the one with the flowery handwriting. For a moment, she thought it was from Guy though she could not imagine what he might want other than to complain about something in his life. However, the address on the back did not tally with his.

She walked back to the kitchen and carefully slit the envelope open. It was from Monty, a man she had known years ago, someone she once had a short affair with, five nights to be precise, during her disastrous breakup with Guy.

'What does he want?' she muttered, suddenly

feeling rather worried that the past was about to raise its ugly head.

He had written to express his concern over Jack's accident, which he had read about in a local newspaper some time ago, and wondered if they would like to meet up with him. He lived down by the coast and could book a small hotel at his expense, of course.

She had telephoned him to say it was already over six months ago since Jack's accident and that he had just gone away to stay with some friends. To her surprise Monty insisted she should visit him anyway, with or without Jack.

She had happily accepted his invitation for she did not consider herself to be totally married anymore.

Monty said he would book two nights in a local hotel, she thought time enough to see how the cookie crumbles.

*   *   *

Now, as she laid back in a hot bubbly bath, she wondered what she was hoping for, here in a rustic hotel on a sea front in Devon, with Monty's letter still in her handbag. She had, over the last week, successfully suppressed any remnants of guilt, dismissed any obligations she might normally have felt, and convinced herself she deserved a life of her own. After all, Jack had left home in the hope of finding his lost youth, now she felt free to do the same.

'So, Monty,' she murmured, as she let the hot tap run until only her head was above water, 'I wonder what your Agenda is?'

She closed her eyes and concentrated on the dramatic days before she left Hong Kong.

She had been, more or less, penniless when she left Guy who seemed surprised at her negative reaction to his latest affair. He had firmly informed her that she could come home, or not, her choice. Anyway, he had no intention of supporting her which, he thought, would curtail her options. She had chosen for the 'not' and the ensuing consequence which was a cheap hotel, due to be demolished, some way from the city centre. A hotel with a sleazy bar, inebriate men, and dark corners in an unkempt garden which smelt of urine, especially after it had rained.

A wide wooden staircase in the reception area led to two floors of bedrooms and communal bathrooms. She had been lucky and managed to book the only room on the first floor with an 'en suite' and which, amazingly, boasted a telephone.

The days had passed slowly with intermittent fights between she and Guy, either on the telephone or in his office, which were embarrassing since they were over money, or rather her lack of money.

She had been in a light sleep when she heard a soft knock. She jumped up and slightly opened the door. A young man who worked at the reception desk stood holding an envelope in his hand.

'For you, Madam,' he whispered, aware Sophie was sleeping.

'Thank you,' she whispered back.

She tore the envelope open, unable to recognise the handwriting. Two hundred dollars were wrapped in a small note.

'Overheard you in the office this morning, perhaps this may help you for a while, Monty.'

She stared at the note recalling Guy's office colleague. A prematurely grey haired man, around Guy's age, who Guy disliked intensely. The sympathy of an outsider was gratifying but she felt wary of someone who worked alongside her husband.

She picked up a scruffy telephone book and to her relief found that an M. Montague was listed.

'Montague,' he answered, in his refined voice, after she had dialled his number.

'It's Emily, I can't take this money, I really can't.'

The conversation went up and down for a while until he suggested they should meet.

'I'll be downstairs in the Bar in fifteen minutes,' he stated, as though it was a 'fait accompli'.

The air conditioned Bar smelt heavily of beer and ugly fluorescent lights ran around the walls causing the skin to appear unattractive, blotchy.

'Let's sit in the corner,' she suggested, in order to avoid their fatal glow.

'What will it be?'

'Just a tonic water, please.'

She gazed around at the red walls decorated with Chinese good luck symbols hanging high above statues of goddesses, ornamental lions, dragons and other mythical creatures and, as if to round it off, a contemplating, gold coloured, Buddha sat alongside a many armed Indian goddess.

Monty returned with the drinks; a whisky and a gin and tonic.

'No, not alcohol, I'm a bad drinker and Sophie is upstairs and I really can't stay long.'

'Just one,' he insisted, as she tried to refuse it. 'Nice to see you again,' he added. 'You look thinner.'

'I've lost pounds and no wonder.'

'I heard you talking in the office this morning, I couldn't help but hear.'

'Yes, I shouted as usual. I want to go home. No, actually, I don't want to go home, I have to go home. It seems everyone knows Guy has a new love in his narcissistic life. It seems I'm the last to hear. Why is it the wife is the last to know?'

'Well, I guess no one wants to tell her,' he said, looking away as though uncomfortable with the conversation.

She opened her handbag and took out the envelope. 'Please take this back, I really can't take it.'

Monty pushed it aside and insisted she kept it, she didn't have to pay him back. He just wanted to help a little.

He had ordered another gin and tonic and the room was no longer in the right place, sort of to the right. She was a bad drinker, she really should not drink at all. He rested his hand on hers and told her *what a lousy husband Guy was and how she was better off without him.*

'That's for sure,' she agreed, trying not to sound too enthusiastic at the thought of losing him.

Suddenly Monty stood up and grabbed her wrist. 'Let's get out of here,' he slurred, pulling her towards the exit.

The damp night air hit her face as she entered the hotel reception area.

'I have to lie down. Told you I can't drink.'

I'll get you to your room,' he offered, kindly.

She said nothing as she climbed the well trodden stairs to her room, handed Monty the key and waited for him to open the bedroom door. She felt herself tottering to the bed and falling onto the hard mattress. She had glanced over to Sophie, whose small bed had been placed in an alcove, and hoped she would not wake up for some hours, preferably in the morning.

She was aware of a movement next to her and gasped as she realised Monty was lying alongside her. He pulled her to him and she resisted for a while until their bodies slipped against each other's, until they reached the glorious state of ecstasy. Their different deodorants mingled as did his aftershave and her perfume. 'Why not?' she thought. 'Why not?'

Eventually, he rolled over onto his side and she noticed how his grey hair fell into small curls at the back of his neck and how grey his eyes were.

'I do love you,' he whispered.

'No, you don't but it's okay. Just see it for what it is.'

He had not answered and she had taken his silence as agreement.

Surely, she thought, the fast track was no longer for men only, what with the Pill.

*   *   *

She had met Jack a couple of years after her divorce. A girl friend had asked her to a party at the tennis club and she had happily accepted since she was no longer in the popular clique.

'Hey, Jack,' someone had called from the Bar. 'You must know Emily, she was also in Hong Kong.'

In fact, she had never met Jack. He had told her how his company had dragged him kicking and screaming back to the U.K., though he had to admit he still went back on business trips. She had told him about Guy, her divorce, and how she was coping as a single mother.

He had been honest and told her that he did not want to have children of his own but was happy to be a second father to Sophie. She had been so in love that it did not seem to matter whether he wanted a child or not, for being with him was parallel to being in heaven and she could settle for that. Though she did wonder how such a good looking guy was still free. She thought perhaps he had avoided being tied down with a wife and family.

'Why not, why not,' she muttered as she quickly reached for a pink towel. 'You looked me up, Monty. Now we'll see if the old flame still burns.'

She sprayed her body with a light perfume and applied her makeup more carefully than she normally did. Her hairdresser had already put blond streaks through her rather uninteresting coloured hair and she had treated herself to a facial and manicure. Everything she had done, she told herself, was for her benefit not for Monty's. She dressed, grabbed her handbag, and made her way down to the dining room where he was waiting.

Small red capped wall lights in the restaurant gave a soft glow on red wall paper patterned with gold fleurs-de-lis. She remembered the dreadful neon lights in the hotel bar so many years ago and shuddered at the thought of sitting under their ghastly light at her age.

Monty stood up as the waiter pulled out her chair. She paused for a second, surprised how little he had changed over the years.

'Emy,' he said, heartily, 'lovely to see you, so glad you could come.'

'You too, Monty,' she replied, feeling stunned and unsure whether she was in control of the situation. A déjà vu feeling ran through her mixed with some degree of apprehension.

The waiter remained by the table. 'Would you like to order drinks, Sir?'

'Yes,' answered Monty. 'A whisky and a tonic water.'

'Make it wine.'

'Pushing the boat out tonight? Well, then, I'll

join you.'

'So tell me about yourself,' he continued, after he had ordered.

'Well, I finally got divorced, married Jack and had a daughter, Jillie. Jack was forced to take an early retirement so we moved to Dorset. Then, last September, we went on holiday with neighbours. Jack sailed. He was enjoying himself until he fell down a cliff.'

'I read about it, it wasn't far from here.'

'Small world. Now tell me about you.'

'Well, I returned to the U.K. and since I was an only child I felt obliged to stay around. Eventually, my parents went into a Care Home, then I bought a house down here.' He paused. 'I remarried,' he added, suddenly.

'Oh, that's lovely,' she answered a little too quickly, wondering who was his first wife; what happened to her; why his second wife was not with him and why was she there without Jack.

'I lost her, Jade,' he added, softly. 'She drowned in a sailing accident.'

'Oh, I am so sorry, that's really dreadful. Was Jade your second wife?'

'Yes,' he replied, shortly, as though avoiding any further details.

'That's really bad luck,' she commiserated.

'Well, I'm hoping to change things,' he smiled, slightly. 'Anyway,' he continued, 'I still do some freelance work. Just a little, that's about it.'

They spent a long time over dinner which gave her time to find out more about his life which seemed to exist mostly of sailing and walking along the desolate beaches. All in all, he gave her the impression he and Jade had lived quietly and, in fact, he still did.

They were last to leave the restaurant when Monty walked her to the staircase.

'I won't ask you to help me to my room.'

'I'm sure you won't,' he grinned.

*

'So, this is where I live,' Monty informed her, proudly, as he drove up in front of a late Georgian house with equally distributed sash windows and a dark blue front door set firmly between them. 'Not frightened of entering the lion's den,' he teased.

'I thought lion's were afraid of mice.'

'Aren't you thinking of elephants. Had to put a lot of money into it,' he added, seriously, as he opened the front door.

'You must have done,' she agreed, glancing around.

'Had to replace all the windows and repair the roof. Apart from the central heating and the kitchen and bathrooms. Cost me an arm and a leg.'

He opened the door to the lounge and stepped back so she could admire it. 'What do you think?'

'Splendid,' she replied, gazing around the perfectly furnished room which was exactly in keeping with the period.

She tried to enthuse but she felt the room looked cold as though it was unloved.

Perhaps Monty read her thoughts for he quickly added, 'I don't use this room very often. Come on, I'll show you a room you might prefer,' he said, walking further down the hall and throwing open a door to a large conservatory full of tropical plants and rattan chairs and tables.

'Aah, this is more like it,' she drawled, not only appreciating the room but the garden beyond. 'Yes, I like it very much.'

'Come outside, the plants are coming to life. It's a lovely time of year,' he said, opening the glass panelled doors.

She strolled around the well-kept garden with various palm trees growing between the shrubs and flowers.

'Beautiful', she commented, more to herself than to Monty.

'I've got a small yacht which needs putting in the water. I'll arrange it today, if I can,' Monty was saying. 'Would you mind coming with me?'

'Fine,' she murmured, as she picked up a white feather and ran it through her fingers just as she had done with the gull's feather in Jack's hand.

'I'll keep this as a memento, if you don't mind.'

He laughed. 'I can't think why you should want that. There's plenty of feathers around these parts. Take your pick.'

There was no one in the boat yard when they arrived and Monty began to show her different types of boats and she wished she could enjoy sailing. It must be lovely, she thought, to have the wind in your face and not fear the sea and its depths, just like Jack always said.

He pointed towards a small yacht. 'This is it.'

She stood, fixated, as she read the name in gold lettering, 'The Gull'.

'You must miss your wife terribly,' she sympathised, trying to hide her surprise.

'I was in bed with a bad 'flu. It wouldn't have happened if I hadn't been ill. She didn't say anything about sailing, I thought she went down to the beach house, she said she would be back in a couple of hours. A storm was forecast. I have never understood why she did it.' He turned away as he spoke, 'They found the boat next day, she was found later.'

'I'm so sorry.'

He walked towards the car. 'I'll come back on the weekend,' he said, sounding depressed.

'Have you sailed for long?', she asked, genuinely interested and wanting to smooth over his obvious unhappiness.

He gave a hollow laugh. 'You had better ask me when I didn't sail. I've sailed all my life. My parents always had a boat, I think I was almost born on one.'

'And where was that?'

'Here, in England. My father got a job with the Hong Kong police force after the war. It's difficult to settle down back home once you've lived out east. I speak for myself, of course.'

She remembered how Jack had told her about the brown of his home when he was young and how he had yearned to go to the tropics. He said he hadn't cared where it was so long as it was somewhere in the sun.

'Monty,' she asked, as he drove away. 'Were you a member of the Hong Kong Yacht Club?'

'Yes, of course.'

'Did you know a Jimmy Lee?' she asked, her heart beating too hard as she asked the innocent question, omitting to add he had also owned a yacht called 'The Gull'.

'Very well,' he replied, curiously.

'I lived in a house owned by a Jimmy Lee. Is that the same man?'

'Yes, it is. In fact, it was because of me you came to live there.'

She gasped. 'How because of you?'

'Well, the company was looking for a house for you and Guy, that was prior to your arrival. I happened to know Jimmy Lee's house was empty.'

She laughed, 'Oh, so you were the someone who would know somebody who had something.'

'What do you mean?'

'Just something Guy said when he was house hunting.'

'Jade also lived there for a little while.'

'Really?'

'It was a long time ago. It's not important,' he said, brushing the remark away as though he regretted saying anything.

She stared out at the rugged countryside as they drove back to the village. She had never forgotten Mrs. Chung's story and she was still able to recall it with some degree of accuracy.

'I once met an old Chinese lady who lived opposite me. She told me Jimmy was married to Jade. Was that so?'

'No,' he replied, sullenly.

'This lady also told me Jade found an injured seagull which she looked after and Jimmy called his yacht 'The Gull' to please her. She also said Jimmy Lee disappeared because he was ill and did not want his wife to see him die. Then Jade went to find him and she also disappeared.'

'Rubbish, pure gossip.'

She was aware he was irritated by her story.

'Would you like to see my beach house?' he asked.

'Yes, I would love to,' she laughed. 'I thought you were going to ask me if I would like to see your etchings.'

'I'm not the artistic type but I do have a wine cellar,' he chuckled, sounding better humoured.

'Well, there you go.'

They both remained silent as they drove through the village and some miles up the coast until they came to a row of cottages, a Pub and an old red telephone box, all of which formed a deserted looking hamlet. A debris track, on the opposite side of the road, ran down the side of a small white house overlooking the sea.

'No one uses it now, so I have to open it up once in a while to air it out.'

The fresh sea air hit her face as she stood gazing across the sand dunes and the golden beach which stretched endlessly into the distance.

She relaxed. 'It's beautiful here,' she enthused, as he opened the door to the kitchen which led to a room with a large window and a glass door leading out onto a patio.

'Jade called this her sunroom,' he informed her, as she climbed a narrow staircase in the lounge which led to two small bedrooms and a minuscule bathroom.

'She came here more than I did.'

'Why was that?'

'No particular reason. I often sailed alone and she would stay here and walk down the beach to the headland or read books.'

He sounded sad and lonely when he spoke of Jade and she was overcome by sympathy, even pity. Still, she could not quite understand why they had needed a beach house when they already lived so near to the sea, unless it was to give each other some space.

She wished she had somewhere to go to when things were not easy, when the colour of life faded into grey.

'Listen,' he said later, over tea in a café on the sea front. 'I didn't want to tell you about Jade and Jimmy. It's true Jimmy went away to get treatment for tuberculosis. They broke up. No big deal.'

'That's okay. The old lady's story was way over the top. I was very young at the time and it sounded so romantic. I realised that it could not all be true.'

He touched her hand, 'I'm sorry I sounded so abrupt. It's a part of the past I don't want to dig up. If you see what I mean.'

'Of course, I understand. We all have bits of our lives we would rather forget about.'

He grinned broadly. 'I guess I'm one of those bits.'

'Actually, you're not.'

He stared across the tea room as though thinking of the past or even that he wanted to add something, but he remained silent. Eventually, in frustration, she picked up her shoulder bag as a sign to go home for she felt there was something she should know, something he was not telling her. But what?

They strolled down the little street to her hotel. Colourful beach balls, rubber rings and fishing nets were already hanging outside the shops waiting for the first onslaught of holiday makers. She thought fondly of her grandson, Tom, and bought him a fishing rod.

The aroma from a fish and chip shop filled the late afternoon air.

'That's what I would like for dinner tonight, fish and chips.'

Monty smiled. 'Are you sure?'

'Yes, very sure,' she said in a definite tone of voice for sitting in his kitchen was less formal and, perhaps, it would give her a chance to question him about Jade.

'Okay,' he agreed. 'I'll take pick you up at around seven.'

*　　*　　*

'You're very quiet, tonight,' he remarked, sitting down next to her in the formal lounge after dinner.

'No, I'm not,' she lied.

'Anything bothering you?'

'No, not really. I'm just turning things over. You must have known so many people in Hong Kong. I only had a couple of girl friends, I didn't know too many people.'

'Well, it's a long time ago. Forget about the past. Let's have a drink,' he suggested, as he walked over to a cupboard and opened a bottle of red wine.

'Here's to our renewed friendship, may it be long and happy,' he smiled kindly, as he handed her a glass.

'I really shouldn't,' she murmured.

'You shouldn't but you will,' he laughed as he sat down next to her, resting his arm along the back of the chair. She blushed as he let it slowly slide down onto her shoulder.

They sat in silence watching the flames flickering in a realistic gas fire and, perhaps because of the wine, she was overcome by desire. Asking about Jade suddenly seemed unimportant.

'It's getting late, I really should be going,' she sighed, suddenly feeling embarrassed as she recalled their affair.

Monty got up and looked out of the window.

'Have you seen the weather? It's pouring down, you can hardly see in front of you. Better stay the night,' he suggested, returning to the sofa with the bottle of wine.

*

He had obviously drunk too much when he led her to a bedroom some hours later. It seemed as though history was repeating itself as she lay next to him, pulling a duvet around her for warmth which, at the same time, formed a barrier between them as he curled around her body. His arm fell casually over her arm and she wanted to turn on her back so that he could kiss her, touch her. But, instead, she laid motionless waiting for the moment he would succumb to his most basic need.

Suddenly, he moved, she tensed expecting him to pull her towards him but instead he sat up.

'I'm sorry,' he muttered. 'I'll sleep somewhere else.'

'That's alright,' she whispered. 'I understand.'

She wanted to tell him he didn't have to leave, but she let it pass.

She woke up somewhere in the early morning and slipped downstairs to the kitchen to make some tea, she startled as she heard someone behind her. Monty was standing in the doorway.

She noticed for the first time how he had aged for his polo neck sweaters and suede jacket had made him look youthful. Now she noticed how his hair had thinned and the lines on his face were deeper than she had wanted to admit. She wondered if there was an unspoken compromise between them, a silent agreement to gloss over each others' physical inadequacies.

'Can I help you?' he asked in a worried voice.

'I woke up and thought I would make some

tea. Would you like a cup?'

'I'll make it,' he offered, wearily, filling an electric kettle.

She was looking for the tea when she noticed a photograph on a shelf, slightly hidden behind a pair of antique weighing scales.

'Is this Jade?' she asked.

'Yes, it was taken just after she arrived.'

She studied the photograph carefully. 'She was very beautiful,' she murmured, softly, as she placed the photograph back on the shelf. 'Sorry I woke you up,' she added, politely.

'No problem.'

'I couldn't stop thinking.'

'What is there to think about?'

'I can't get over you knowing Jimmy and Jade,' she said truthfully. 'It seems so strange to talk about people from the past, people who I didn't even know. Actually, it's nice you found each other.'

She noticed how Monty did not answer or react to her simple statement but only placed two mugs of tea on the table. She felt he was again being secretive which she found annoying, to the point of being impolite, so she tilted her chair back and repeated Mrs. Chung's romantic tale.

'Now you can understand why I am so interested,' she said brightly. 'By the way, what happened to Jimmy Lee?'

'I don't know,' he replied, abruptly, as he stood up and opened the back door. 'It's stopped raining,' he informed her, hinting he had heard enough of the silly story and her unending curiosity.

'That's good. I think I'll get off, Monty, make an early start,' she replied, pre-empting any suggestion he might make for her to leave.

'Can I make you some breakfast?' he offered, half-heartedly.

'No, thanks, I'd better get back. I don't particularly want the hotel staff to know I wasn't in my room last night.'

He rested his hands on her shoulders. 'You will come back, I would like us to stay friends, please forget about last night.'

'Yes, of course, we'll always be friends.'

It was only when she went back upstairs to freshen up did she realise that she had not slept in Monty's own bedroom but in a guest room, neatly laid out, empty cupboards and with absolutely nothing in it which could be called personal. She also realised that even if Monty was more than a little drunk he was still capable of choosing which room he would sleep in. She thought about it for a moment and decided that his bedroom, Jade's bedroom, was perhaps a sanctuary. Maybe her dressing table was as she had left it; her clothes still in her cupboards; her photographs by his bed. She could imagine he would not want to have some, perhaps meaningless, affair in her bed and amongst her possessions.

*

He took her arm as he dropped her off at the entrance to the hotel. 'Thank you for coming. There are some things I should have explained to you.'

'Oh, that's alright, Monty. I can imagine it's difficult talking about someone you've lost recently. It really isn't my business.'

He gave a faint smile. 'Well, have a good trip back. I'll be seeing you again soon, I expect. Give me a ring so I'll know you've arrived home safely.'

She was relieved to see the front door of the hotel open and there was no one at the reception desk. She hurried, unnoticed, to her bedroom and threw herself onto the bed. She stared at the pink and white lampshade as she tried to work out what happened in the past.

It was not until she was driving home did she realise that neither she nor Monty had discussed Jack, which was just as strange as Monty not suggesting they should wait for him to return so they could visit him together. After all, they knew each other in Hong Kong. She frowned as she wondered what had been the purpose of her visit. It was certainly not to renew their old affair. She also wondered how he knew her address.

She felt there must be more to it all and was even more than happy nothing had happened between them.

SOPHIE's SECRET

The TELEPHONE RANG the following Sunday, it was Sophie. 'I'm on my way back from a business meeting. It took longer than expected. I had to stay over. Thought I would come tonight, being Sunday, and go straight to the office tomorrow. Anyway, I've run out of groceries and I know I don't have any coffee. And I want to see you, talk to you,' she added.

She hung up wondering what her daughter had to talk about as she studied the minimal contents of her refrigerator and freezer.

Sophie looked dishevelled and tired when she opened the front door.

'How come you had to work over the weekend,' she asked, aware that it was not the first time she had dropped in on a Sunday evening after a business trip further down country, which in itself was highly unlikely.

'I told you, the original meeting was on

Thursday but we didn't finish until Friday evening and then I stayed over to rest out and here I am.'

'If it wasn't all work why didn't you come last night,' she asked, feeling she had only heard part of the story.

'Yea, Mum, what is it you want to hear?'

'Nothing, I don't want to hear anything. Where's Tom?' she snapped, now on the wrong footing with her somewhat hostile daughter.

'With his father, of course. I'm going to take a bath, if you don't mind.'

'I've got new bath salts, help yourself.'

A friendly acknowledgment came from the bathroom.

'Are you alright?' she called to Sophie, after she had finished cooking. 'You're so long in there,' she grumbled, thinking of the gas and electric bills as she went upstairs.

'Yes, I'm fine. Could you put a wash on for me, saves me doing it tomorrow night?'

'Of course,' she answered, as she opened Sophie's untidily packed holdall and quickly decided to wash everything, since it was impossible to tell what she had worn.

She emptied the bag onto the bed and ran her hand along the inside of a compartment, pulling out various bit and pieces together with a photograph.

She sagged down onto the bed, overcome by humiliation, as Sophie came through the door wrapped in a large bath towel.

'So, you've found it,' Sophie sighed, sounding relieved.

'Sorry, I don't get it. Did you intend me to find it?'

'I hoped you might, I would anyway have told you. That's one of the reasons I dropped in. Monty was supposed to tell you about us but he didn't. He said it was too difficult.'

'He's old enough to be your father,' she shouted, overpowered by anger and hurt.

'I know but it doesn't matter, I love him.'

'Don't be mad, you don't know what you're talking about.'

'I know what I'm doing, I'm not a child. You think you know everything better than me.'

'Yes, I do, you're right, I do. How long have you known him?'

'About eighteen months. Sometimes, he does some freelance work for my company. He did an article on polluted beaches and I became a sort of liaison and one thing led to another.'

'So why didn't you tell me earlier?' she choked.

'How could I. I knew you would be against it. Go mad.'

'And you knew I went down there. He knew Jack was away. You told him Jack had left, that's why he asked me down. That's really underhand, you set me up. That's disgusting.'

'Probably, yes, but you make people do things they wouldn't otherwise do.'

'He's having a fling, you're a young woman, he's using you,' she screamed, uncontrollably.

There was a silence, the kind which can occur during a heavy fight, perhaps because each side is absorbing the enemy's last remark, perhaps because each side is gathering ammunition for the next onslaught, perhaps because neither side wants to shout anymore unkind things at each other.

'I could be happy with him,' sobbed Sophie quietly, as though pleading for her mother's blessing.

'Tell me, did he know who you were when you first met him?' she asked, feeling almost sorry for her daughter.

'I guess he must have done. Monty only told me after Jack's accident that he knew you and Guy in Hong Kong. Guy got me my job with JJ through Monty. Though I didn't know that until recently. It's a very small circle, everyone knows each other.'

'So he's in contact with your father.'

'Indirectly.'

'And what did he say about him?'

'Nothing.'

'How convenient.'

'Don't get uptight. It's nice you know each other. Have something in common.'

'Yes, darling, we have a great deal in common', she paused. 'Do you know what I think?'

'No,' replied Sophie, angrily. 'But I'm sure you're about to tell me.'

'I think you're making a mega mistake, a gigantic mistake. You don't know him. He has too much past, too much baggage. He's been married twice before and he's old enough to be your father.'

'So what, you've also been married twice. Why the hell do you so dislike him?'

'I don't dislike him.'

'So, what's your problem?'

'Everything, just everything. He's too old for you. Look for someone your own age and think of Tom. He needs someone he can relate to,' she shouted, trying hard to think of something which might support her case.

'He has a father he can relate to,' snapped Sophie, coldly.

'Then Monty can be another grandfather.'

There was a difficult pause.

'I'm going home,' Sophie cried, throwing her clothes back into her case. 'Monty should have told you, not me. He said he would.'

'So why didn't he?'

'He thought you had enough problems and he didn't want to give you any more so he decided to leave it for a while. I knew you wouldn't understand, stupid of me to think you would.'

'He's a coward and so are you,' she sneered.

'That's your opinion.'

She paused, realising her approach was not going to work. 'I do understand, I really do. But whether I understand or not won't help you.'

'Didn't Monty mention me at all?' Sophie whined, sounding sad and worried.

'No, he didn't, but I did see a photograph of his second wife,' she added, trying to make a point.

'Well, I don't suppose you've been in his bedroom.'

'Come on, we have to eat,' she said, quickly

changing the subject as it dawned on her that was the reason Monty used his guest room, his own room being full of Sophie's photographs and possessions. 'Don't let's talk about it anymore and if Monty is what makes you happy then I will have to live with it.'

Sophie looked at her suspiciously. 'Do you mean that?'

'Yes, I mean it,' she answered, glancing over to the Madonna as she walked passed her bedroom.

She thought, fleetingly, of telling Sophie about her short passionate affair with Monty and the ghastly night she had recently spent in his house, but decided that was out of the question.

Later, she realised why her meeting with Monty had been tense, sometimes even difficult. He had something to tell her and he could not bring himself to do so.

'You bastard,' she murmured. 'How could you screw my daughter, how could you do that. How dare you. I'll never forgive you, never.'

*

She had telephoned Monty but he had not co-operated as she had hoped. He said he was terribly busy helping the local newspaper with important articles which had to be ready before the end of next week. He would be happy to meet her but only with Sophie present. They were in love and he hoped she would accept him.

She hung up and fell back into Jack's chair.

'Not good enough, Monty,' she choked, in anger. She sat with her head in her hands, 'I have to think, I have to think,' she muttered. 'I can't let this happen.'

She quickly decided to visit Monty again and have it out with him though, deep in her heart, she felt she was going to lose this one. She shuddered at the thought of this suave man enticing her daughter to his house, let alone his bed. The idea repulsed her, he with his hands on her child.

'Sorry, Monty,' she whispered. 'I'll do anything to break you up and if that means telling Sophie about us, then so be it.'

She closed her eyes and churned over, yet again, what Jack had said to her on the last night at the cottage. He had held her hand as though everything was normal. She hated him for that.

Then he went on to tell her how he needed to be free, feel the wind in his face, he wouldn't do anything wrong, nothing untoward. Just to follow the call of the wild, so to speak, before it was too late.

She had turned on her side and asked him, caustically, if had considered a safari tour. There were enough to choose from, she could pick up a few folders from the local travel agency. He had not replied and she had said no more.

She wished now she had fought him, beaten him on his chest with her fists, but she had lost the momentum and he had turned on his side probably more than a little surprised at her easy acceptance, probably waiting for the attack which never came.

It would have been better for him, for her, had she not acted out of character; had she not stayed in control of her emotions; had she been more predictable; more true to form; more assertive; then, perhaps, the following day might have been different.

MONTY's STORY

Monty WASN'T HOME when she arrived at his house, neither could she see 'The Gull' moored in the harbour between all the other sailboats. A wind slightly whipped the protected water as she walked towards an old man sitting on the seawall. His face was deeply lined and he wore the look of someone who had weathered the storms trolling for fish.

'Do you happen to know where 'The Gull' is?' she asked, as casually as she could.

He turned his head towards the entrance of the harbour.

'She's 'bout to come in now,' he answered, with a thick Devonshire accent.

She returned to her car and watched Monty tie up his boat and take down the sails. He chattered to some other men for a while then, picking up his sports bag, walked quickly to his parked car.

She drove off for she wanted to be at his house when he arrived home.

'What are you doing here?' Monty asked, not concealing his irritation.

'Just thought I would drop in.'

'Well, it's nice to see you but it's quite a long way just to drop in. Come in,' he invited, grudgingly, as he opened the front door.

'We have to talk,' she snapped, following him into the house. 'What the hell are you playing at?'

He turned around. 'There's nothing to talk about. I'm sorry but I have to go out, I'm already running late. Help yourself to a coffee. I'm going to take a quick shower.'

'I'll wait here,' she called, as he ran upstairs.

'Please, go home,' he shouted from the landing. 'Please just accept it as it is.'

'No way,' she shouted back as she sat down in the hall next to an antique desk. An old British passport lay on the top and she assumed it belonged to Monty. She looked inside, it had belonged to Jade.

She had studied the information and was about to return it to the desk when she saw, between the last two pages, three tightly folded sheets of thin airmail paper. She slowly walked to the kitchen and sat down at the table, aware that her behaviour was not defendable but the need to know outweighed any learnt politeness.

All three letters were from Jade to Monty. One, dated over thirty years ago to an address in Hong Kong, thanked him for his support. Two others, written seventeen years later, thanked him again for his help and details of her visit to Devon.

She startled as she heard Monty coming down the stairs and realised he would catch her with the letters. He was standing in the doorway when she stood up.

'What are you doing?' he asked, fiercely.

'Nothing. I was admiring your beautiful desk and I saw this passport. I thought it was yours.'

Monty lurched towards the table pulling everything towards him as though protecting his most precious possessions.

'You have no right nosing around. Mind your own business. Get out.'

'I will when your business no longer affects my family,' she shouted.

'Nothing has happened which would affect your family. Sophie and I have nothing to hide from each other and you have nothing to do with it. And that is putting it politely. What the hell is your problem?'

'Are you so stupid that you can't work that out? I'm going to make sure Sophie knows what happened between us,' she shouted, hysterically.

'My God, that was years ago.'

'Old sins cast long shadows, Monty.'

'There wasn't any sin. Why must you always rake everything up? Over is over. Leave it alone. Leave Sophie and me alone.'

'I can't.'

His breathing became heavy and asthmatic as he sat down, despondent. She had found his Achilles' heel.

'If I tell you everything will that shut you up?' he asked, resignedly.

'Depends on what you tell,' she answered, coldly. 'I have Sophie's interest at stake here.'

He sighed. 'I've told you, Jade was not married to Jimmy, he was already married. He was much older than she was. He bought a house for her, that's the house you rented.

Eventually, Jade wanted Jimmy to divorce and marry her. But he said he couldn't leave his wife and children. Then they began to have fights. Jimmy became ill at around the same time. He had tuberculosis and went to Switzerland for a complete cure. He was rich enough to do that. Jade went to live with relatives after Jimmy left.

I kept in touch for a while then she moved away. I didn't hear from her for almost eighteen years.'

'How did she find you?'

'My office had an old address and the people who lived there forwarded her letter on to me.'

'So, why did she stay here, why didn't she go back home?'

He paused for a while as though trying to control his feelings and she noticed how grey and drawn he looked as though he had instantly aged.

'Because we were both lonely. She had a son, Michael. I offered to send him to college. I thought it was a good idea.'

'She had a son!'

'Later, he got a job in London,' he continued. 'It worked out well. Sometimes he stayed at the beach house with Jade or his friends.'

'I wondered why you had the beach house.'

'Well, now you know,' he replied, angrily.

'He was Jimmy's child,' she stated.

'Of course.'

'Did Jimmy acknowledge his son?'

'We never discussed it.'

'Really!' she replied, her voice intonating disbelief.

He breathed deeply. 'As I've already told you, she took 'The Gull' out in bad weather. I'll never understand why she did that.'

He lowered his head as he spoke, his face now ashen and she looked away wishing she had left the whole thing alone.

'Can you get me a glass of water?', he asked, quietly.

'Please stop, you don't have to go on.'

'I want to get all this over with. I don't want you on my neck for the rest of my life.'

'Whatever,' she replied, trying to sound indifferent, as she handed him the glass.

'I was previously married, in Hong Kong, to Fleur. She and Jade were best friends.' His voice broke with emotion. 'Fleur became pregnant and had a miscarriage followed by some kind of depression. Jade left after breaking up with Jimmy Lee but Fleur could not seem to accept she had gone. She waited every day outside her house for her to come home.'

'Wasn't anybody living there?'

'No, it was empty. I don't know the details. Perhaps Jimmy didn't want to sell it. How should I know. Anyway, I couldn't get through to her that Jimmy was having treatment in Switzerland and Jade wasn't coming back. Then, one day she didn't come home, they found her dead on Jade's porch. She died of an overdose of antidepressants but it couldn't be proved whether it was an accident or suicide. I like to think of it as being an accident. You and Guy arrived a little later. Well, now you know. Satisfied?' he shouted, bitterly.

'In other words, both your wives died under strange circumstances. One by an overdose, the other in a sailing accident. And Sophie? Is she going to be the third?' she shouted, hysterically.

'What the hell are you insinuating?'

'I don't know, perhaps you can tell me.'

'Shut up. I don't want to listen to your rubbish. I wasn't there when Jade had her accident. Neither when Fleur died,' he heaved as he spoke, his body trembling with anger and emotion.

He hesitated for a moment as though he was about to say something but instead he bent over as though in pain.

'My pills, get my pills,' he gasped, staggering towards some cupboards.

'Oh, God, where are they?' she pleaded, frantically opening doors and drawers.

He tried to say something but instead he only made a strange heaving sound as he grasped his shirt and slumped down onto his knees, his face now grey and moist.

'Oh, Monty, hang on. I'll get help.'

He raised his hand but she drew away from him, sobbing as she ran to the telephone in the hall to call an ambulance, her hand shaking as she dialled.

'Please don't die. Oh, please, don't die,' she

repeated, over and over again, as she returned to Monty who was now on his side, his right arm clenched across his chest.

She bent down next to him but she had little or no idea of how to resuscitate him and was frightened of making the situation even worse than it already was.

'Air, he needs air,' she sobbed, as she rushed to the back door and staggered into the garden. She knelt on the well cut lawn, bowing her head low to stop herself from fainting. She became aware of the coolness from the shadows of the trees and the sound of trickling water from a small fountain in a fish pond. She looked up at the sun and remembered how Jack had once called it a plate of gold.

'Oh, Jack, where are you, I need you,' she pleaded.

After a while, she stood up and waited to see if anyone had heard her but no one called out or came so, slowly, she pulled herself together and convinced herself that Monty's heart attack could have happened any time. She breathed in deeply and then with some kind of false self assurance walked back to the kitchen.

Monty did not move as she quickly folded the letters back to how they were, placed them in the passport and returned it to the desk, frightened in case the ambulance came before she left the house.

She bent down next to him and whispered his name but he did not react.

'I'm so sorry this happened, it's all my fault. I just couldn't accept it.' She ran the back of her hand down his face. 'Monty, I have to go. I can't wait for the ambulance, I would have to give a statement and Sophie might find out and ask why I was here and guess we had a fight. She would never forgive me, you do understand, don't you. I'll leave the front door open.'

She stood up and looked down at him. 'Strange,' she said, thoughtfully. 'I've only ever remembered our passion. Now my emotions, my passion, may have killed you.'

She waited at the end of the road until the ambulance rushed past then, feeling that she could do no more, drove back to the harbour and sat listening to the lines of 'The Gull' clinking softly in the wind. She imagined Jade working the sails, fighting for her life against the storm until nature finally won the battle. Then, she thought of Fleur waiting on the porch of Jade's house, the house she had lived in; the house which had felt 'wrong'; the house in which she had seen a young girl standing by the iron gates for just an instance. She had dismissed her appearance at the time but now she realised she had seen Fleur's spirit. A sad pain ran through her and tears welled in her eyes as she thought of the unnecessary death of such a young woman and later that of Jade.

'Oh, Monty,' she whispered. 'You must have suffered when Jade died. Suddenly all alone and then Sophie comes along. I can really understand it all, I really can.'

She closed her eyes and listened to the waves lapping against the boats.

'I feel like the Angel of Death,' she murmured, as she remembered Jack's fall. He had survived but she didn't yet know about Monty. If he lived then she hoped he would not tell Sophie she was with him when he collapsed. She thought, coldly, that it might even be better for her if Monty died. She dismissed her thoughts before they became a wish.

'Monty,' she whispered. You really played the field. Married to Fleur and Jade and affairs with Sophie and me. You really had your share of love.'

The sun had become a flaming red ball when she eventually walked back to the car. Seagulls swooped and glided on the evening wind, their shapes silhouetted against the crimson sky.

JADE's SON

Sophie HAD CRIED FAR LESS than she had anticipated. She breathed a sigh of relief when the funeral was over and she could saunter around the cemetery while Sophie talked to Monty's friends and distant family. She liked walking around these places, reading the names on the gravestones and working out how old they were when they had died. She broke her heart over the young but dismissed the deaths of those who she considered had lived long enough; had a 'fair innings'.

Sophie was almost finished and she was on the point of returning to the car when a name on a gravestone, propped up behind Monty's grave, caught her eye. She stepped back surprised as she read the gold lettering. 'Here lies Jade Montague Lee who died tragically at sea'.

'Of course,' she murmured. 'Monty would be buried with Jade,' she had just not considered it.

'Coming?' Sophie called. 'I'm going to skip the coffee and sandwiches.'

'Why?'

'I don't fancy acting the widowed lover.'

'I can understand that.'

'I've been talking to a couple of Monty's friends. It seems he had a heart condition but not a serious one. His death was totally unexpected by his doctor.' She paused. 'He didn't tell me about it.'

'You know, darling, he probably didn't want to accept it, put his head in the sand. Men do that, it's one of their many weaknesses.'

'Anyway, thanks for coming.'

'I'm glad I could help.'

'Don't laugh, Monty once said I reminded him of you, when you were young.'

'I'm not laughing,' she replied.

Sophie 'phoned a few weeks later.

'I have something terribly nice to tell you. You know Jade had a son, Mike.'

'I think Monty might have mentioned him,' she lied.

'Well, you know Monty bought that beach house for Jade.'

'Yes.'

'Well, I've got to know Mike quite well and he has invited us to go down there for a day. He inherited everything when Monty died. We can stay somewhere overnight if we have to, he doesn't have enough beds for us all.'

'What a lovely idea,' she replied, warmly.

'He saw you at the funeral. I asked if perhaps Jillie could come along as well so he could meet us all. Apart from Jack who is anyway not around.'

'That's nice of him. Ask Jillie when she can make it, I'm always free.'

'Okay, I'll fix it.'

'How are you?' she asked, automatically.

'Not too bad. Have piles of work which keeps my mind off things, what about you?'

'Life is pretty boring, I suppose I should do something about it, only what?'

'Yes,' Sophie replied, thoughtfully. 'You are a bit between a rock and a hard place.'

She hung up feeling stunned. She was actually going to meet Jade's son. Unbelievable, she thought, feeling suddenly happy for the first time in what seemed ages.

*

Mike was already at the house when they arrived. She sized him up as he walked towards them. He was perhaps in his mid thirties, dressed in a pair of light blue denims, a leather flying jacket which accentuated his slight build and, like his contemporaries, white trainers. His straight dark hair fell into small curls on the nape of his neck, his skin was slightly tanned and he had unusually blue eyes.

He was handsome but this was not entirely the reason why she felt drawn to him, there was something about him but she could not place what it was.

'The view is magnificent. Actually, it's the location that makes this place attractive,' Mike enthused. 'I spoke to Monty the day after your visit. He told me how he had brought you down here.'

'Yes, that's right. He said he came to air it out once in a while.'

'It's becoming a bit of a problem,' he agreed. 'Sooner or later, I will have to decide what to do with it, when all the legal stuff is finished. But that's a long way off.'

She felt herself warming to this sensitive young man and wondered if he took after his mother.

'Come in,' he said, leading the way.

The damp salty smell in the house was still the same along with the sand which had collected against the sides of the room.

'You mustn't judge it as you see it now,' he said, protectively, as though he was defending a friend.

'No, I can see how nice it must have been.'

She turned around to Jillie who had remained silent. 'What do you think, darling? Nice isn't it?'

'Perfect. Why don't we take a walk on the beach?' she replied, impatiently.

'Tell you what,' she offered, 'I'll stay here and make something to eat. Leave Daisy with me,' she added. 'She's getting too old for long walks.'

'See,' said Sophie. 'I told you my mother is homely.'

Emy gave her a side glance and Sophie grinned like a naughty child.

'That's not meant as a compliment, Mike.'

'It's okay, Mrs. Nielson, I know her a bit already.'

She stood outside for a while watching them running along the shore and recognising the horse play for Mike had grabbed Sophie's coat. She struggled as though she wanted him to loosen his grip but, of course, she didn't want that at all. She remembered how Jack had done that, grabbing her wrist while she pretended to free herself.

Everything had been so good between them until he was forced to retire. She brushed her painful memories aside and was about to go back into the house when a large gull landed and paced the patio wall, as though waiting to be fed.

She thought of Jade as she threw a piece of bread to the waiting bird. It caught it in midair and, for some inexplicable reason, she called after it. 'Fly with the gull, Jade. Fly with the gull'.

A gust of wind slammed the door shut. She turned quickly as though someone stood behind her but only a gull swooped between she and the sunroom.

There was no one on the beach when she looked again and a familiar feeling of insecurity ran through her.

She was sweeping the floors when she heard them laughing as they struggled up the last sand dune.

'Mum, you can't guess what Mike's just told me,' called Sophie, as she staggered breathlessly onto the patio.

She waited for the bombshell.

'Monty has left me some money. Some of it's for Tom's education if he needs it. That is if we weren't living together or married. And we weren't,' she added, sadly.

'That was terribly kind of him,' she said, feeling guilty.

'I told you how nice he was,' snapped Sophie, staring darkly at her mother.

'My mother always said no one could have been a better friend to her than Monty and he was the best stepfather I could ever have had. She said Monty stood by her when she left my father and, after they married, he bought this little house so I had somewhere to bring my friends in the summer.'

'You're lucky,' Jillie murmured.

'Not really.'

'Come on, let's have a coffee,' she suggested, trying to liven the atmosphere and suppressing any deep emotion.

'It's so nice being here again.' Mike said, sounding sincere. 'As I said, I don't really know what to do with it. I don't want to sell it and I don't want to rent it to people with small children because of the current. The sea is dangerous around here.'

'I'd rent it, if I had a chance,' she replied, impulsively.

Mike laughed. 'That can always be arranged. In fact, that would suit me down to the ground, having it looked after by someone I know.' He stopped. 'No, I have a better idea. You just use it this summer and we'll see what happens next year.'

She felt stunned. 'I hardly know what to say. That's wonderful but I would like to do something in return. Tell you what, I'll buy some new furniture and small things to make it cosy.'

'Great. I know an odd job man, John Marlow, I'll ask him to paint it through and tidy up the kitchen and bathroom. On my account,' he added. 'Deal?'

'Deal,' she agreed.

AN OLD PHOTOGRAPH

She WALKED QUIETLY AROUND the now pristine little house waiting for the girls and Tom to arrive. The floorboards had been sandpapered and whitened and she had hung pictures of beach scenes dabbed with blue and red which, together with the new white furniture, gave it a real holiday look. In some way, she felt proud of her small achievement.

The gulls were winging across the surf and dark clouds billowed on the horizon when she looked down to the beach. A feeling of isolation ran through her and she wondered if she really wanted the same as Jack. Alone might just be that, lonely.

They tumbled out of Sophie's sports car an hour later.

'How was the traffic?' she asked, as she pulled a holdall from under Tom's feet.

'Not too bad, only we're a bit squashed,' Sophie complained.

'Yes, I can see. your jacket is terribly creased.'

'It's linen. It doesn't matter if it's creased. It's lovely here,' she added.

She smiled as Jillie stretched her back and pulled her leg muscles. She thought she looked more like Jack every year for her blond hair curled and waved just as his did, though she hadn't inherited his blue eyes.

'Oh, what is this cosy,' she cooed, almost tearfully. 'We haven't done anything like this for ages. Come on, let's have a cup of coffee then we'll walk down the beach.'

'Hope you don't mind,' interrupted Sophie, 'but Mike's going to drop by. He's slowly taking things from Monty's house to his flat and, since he was down here, he thought he would look at what the builder has done. Actually, I think he would like to see what you've done.'

'Oh, that's nice,' she answered, thinking of how she might be able to extract more information from him.

*

'Tell me about yourself, Mike,' she asked, when they had all eventually sat down for lunch. 'I hear you live in London.'

'Yes, I got a job after I finished my study and before that I lived down here for a year. And before that my mother and I lived in Hong Kong. That's where we came from. My mother suggested we 'do' Europe after I'd finished High School but in the end we only 'did' the U.K.'

She offered him a cheese and tomato roll. 'Do you miss Hong Kong?'

'Yes, a bit. Not so much anymore. Actually, it was Monty who suggested I should study here, so I took a gap year. He was terribly generous and paid for everything. Did you know my mother?' he asked, hopefully.

'No, I'm afraid not.'

Jillie attracted Mike's attention. 'I'm also studying.'

'Really, what's your subject?'

'History.'

'That's nice,' he muttered, dismissively.

Jillie turned defensive. 'We are now because of what we were then, we can't progress without a knowledge of what's preceded, world history. What did you study?' she asked, aggressively.

'Information Technology, nothing special. In fact, very boring. You're right about history, I mean it's far more interesting,' he replied, obviously trying to make good his verbal hiccup.

'So,' she interrupted, changing the subject. 'Are you a Michael or a Mike?'

'Actually, my name is James Michael John Lee. Michael was Monty's name. My mother said it pained her too much to call me Jimmy, after my father. So she called me by my second name.'

'I never knew Monty's first name,' she admitted, thoughtfully.

'Michael Montague. You didn't know?'

'No, I didn't. I only knew him as Monty. I never thought to ask him his Christian name.'

'And what is really strange is that my parents

had the same surname though they were in no way related. My mother used to say, 'whatever which way, you're a 'Lee'. 'Lee' is a very common Chinese name. I was a love child,' he added, proudly.

She managed to form a small smile. 'Well, that's the best kind of child to be,' she said, kindly. 'I can't think of anything better.'

'My mother died a few years ago. She took the yacht out in bad weather and drowned. They didn't find her for a couple of days,' he looked down as he spoke. 'Actually,' he continued, talking softly, 'when they did the autopsy they found her cancer had returned. She thought she was cured.' He paused again. 'If she did know, she didn't tell Monty or me. He was terribly upset. Of course, she might not have known she was still ill.'

'That must have been very difficult for you both,' she sympathised.

'Would you like another sausage roll?' Jillie asked, trying to attract his attention.

'No, thank you. I really should be leaving,' he replied, politely. 'I'm slowly taking a few personal things back with me from the house. I have to wait for all the legal business to be finalised before I can really clear it out and sell it. What else can I do?'

'You don't have to go,' Jillie suggested, temptingly.

'No, stay for an early supper. Perhaps you can fill me in on a few things. For example, where is everyone? No one lives here, I find it most odd,' she added, sounding concerned.

'The Pub closed and then a new housing estate was built five miles inland and everyone left.

Can't blame them. And, yes, I would love to stay for supper.'

'I never knew that,' she muttered. 'I'm not sure I want to be alone here at night.'

'Sorry, Mrs. Nielson, I should have told you.'

'That's okay, it's not important. Do you sail?' she asked, trying to turn the conversation back to Jade.

'Seldom, I hate deep water, I like to know what's lurking beneath me, not to mention the currents, especially around here.'

'I can really relate to that,' she agreed, unequivocally.

'Let's go for a walk before it rains,' Jillie suggested, obviously wanting to escape.

'I must be boring you, I talk too much,' he muttered, shyly.

'No, you don't,' she replied, fervently. 'It's nice to know someone who is honest and straightforward.'

He smiled happily. 'Are you coming with us, Mrs. Nielson?' he asked, putting on his jacket.

'No, I'll stay here, think about supper and chill out,' she laughed at her modern expression.

'Can I help?' he asked, politely.

'No, Mum enjoys doing it alone,' Jillie butted in quickly, giving her mother a warning glance not to contradict her inaccurate statement and spoil the planned getaway.

'No, of course not. You go and have a nice walk,' she replied, enthusiastically. 'I must line this up,' she muttered, as they slammed the patio door.

She turned over all that had happened as she

began to make a salad and it occurred to her that Fleur, Jade and Monty had all died. She considered life to be fragile, full of coincidences and sometimes unnatural events. She tried hard to convince others that there was another dimension though she accepted it was a difficult product to sell and her theories usually fell on death ears.

Black is black, white is white and there are no rainbow colours in between, just shades of grey.

She often said that to herself when trying to deny the supernatural.

Their faces were fresh and their feet bare when they returned from their walk.

'You've been gone a long time.'

'Mike took us to the headland, it's beautiful up there. I'm ravenous,' Jillie added.

'Good,' she replied, placing steaks in hot fat.

'You know,' Mike said, pensively. 'I think my mother knew your husband.'

'How is that possible?' she replied, trying to sound nonchalant.

'I can remember looking at old photographs when I was a little boy and how my mother said that Nielson meant the son of Niels. I can remember laughing and saying I was Leeson, the son of Lee. Perhaps you and your husband are on one of the photographs.'

'Jack is my second husband. I didn't know him in Hong Kong. Dig in, you've a long way to drive.'

She patted his back affectionately as she passed behind him with a dish of peas. He drew his shoulders up as he turned and smiled. It was that which reminded her of someone but she could not place who it was though she knew one thing, for sure, Mike was not pure Chinese.

'Any chance of seeing those photo's?' she asked, as he got ready to go back to London.

'As a matter of fact they're in my car. They're one of the things I picked up this morning. I don't suppose I will be staying at Monty's house again. I feel wrong there though I'm sure Monty would have told me to use it.'

She waited, her heart beating fast, as Mike sorted out photographs taken after he and Jade had arrived in Devon. Some of them were of Jade and Monty together and she wondered how Sophie felt. Then he picked out a packet which was carefully closed so that it should not become muddled with the more recent ones. He opened it and, after sorting through them, handed her one.

'See, Mrs. Nielson, this is my mother,' he said, proudly, pointing to a photo of a young woman in a swimsuit with her hair tied back and sun glasses perched on the top of her head. 'This was taken when she first met my father. She was beautiful, wasn't she?'

'Yes, she was very beautiful,' she replied, not revealing she had already seen Jade's photo in Monty's kitchen.

'And that's my father behind her.'

She focused on a man who was probably in his early forties. He had a broad, friendly, grin and she thought him rather dashing. She could imagine a young impressionable girl falling in love with him.

Mike shuffled through photographs of he and his mother, others of him playing on a beach or in a swimming pool with his friends. Typical photo's of a little boy growing up.

'What do you think of this, Mrs. Nielson?'

She narrowed her eyes as she focused on a photograph of a group of people sitting on the porch steps of a house. A large iron gate was behind them and a bay window to the right. Rows of Chinese crackers hung from the gutters of the bungalow, small red packets which were made to explode and emit ferocious bangs as they jumped and spluttered in all directions, frightening everyone except for the most hardened onlookers.

'There's my mother, that photo was taken before I was born,' he added.

'And your father?', she asked, carefully.

'He wasn't around, he was away at the time.'

'Yes, of course.'

'My mother lived in that house.'

'And that's where I lived.' She fell silent as various emotions passed through her, not least the loss of her youthful years. 'My first husband and I rented it for a short time,' she continued, almost choking on her words.

'That was after my mother left.'

'Yes, I guess it was. And now I'm staying in her house again. I can't believe it.'

'It's all meant to be.'

'You sound like my mother, Mike. You'll be talking next about karma's and all that stuff,' complained Sophie, who felt a hidden danger somewhere around the corner.

'My God,' Emy gasped, focusing once again on the photograph. 'That looks like Rob and Helen.'

'I met them once,' Mike said. 'We were on our way back from London and Monty took us down to their cottage by a lake.'

'Really, that's amazing. Actually,' she added, sadly, 'Rob Bennett, died there last winter.'

'He went skating and fell through the ice,' Jillie informed him.

'Rob's mother died as well, the same evening,' added Sophie, broadening the story. 'Poor woman died of heart failure.'

'Well, that's really odd. My mother said the lake was dangerous. I guess she was right.'

'Yes, I guess she was.'

'You can keep the photo,' offered Mike. 'It means more to you than it does to me.'

'I'll get it copied and give it to you back.'

'Okay, that would be nice. Listen,' he said, picking up the box. 'I must get off. It's been fantastic meeting you. I will be away for some time because I've found my father in Hong Kong and I'm going to look him up. It took me quite a time to find him.' He laughed. 'There's an awful lot of Lee's in the world.'

'Does he know you are coming?' she asked, suddenly feeling protective.

'No, not yet.'

'Oh, be careful, not everyone likes surprises from the past. On the other hand,' she added, worried in case she might have hurt him, 'it might be just what he is waiting for.'

He did not answer her and she felt instantly miserable that she had made the remark.

'Mum, it's not your business,' Sophie, blurted out, angrily.

'Oh, I don't mind, Sophie,' Mike replied. 'Tell you what, Mrs. Nielson, if you'd like to give me your e-mail address, I'll write to you,' he offered, taking out a notebook and pen.

'Well, if you have time,' she replied.

He looked at her kindly. 'You know, I don't have a family. I have friends, of course, but at the moment life is a bit empty. I would love to keep in touch with you.'

'Oh, that would be lovely,' she gushed.

'I'm going to buy a sports car,' he boasted, as he stepped into his old car. 'That is after I get back from Hong Kong,' he added, as he revved the car engine. 'We'll keep in touch,' he shouted, as he roared away.

ROSIE's BIRTHDAY

Rosie WAS ON HER ANSWERING machine when she got home asking her for tea next day since it was her birthday. The next message was from Helen asking her how she was and whether she would like to stay a few days at the cottage with her.

'Not unless I have to,' she muttered, as she began to study Mike's photograph under a magnifying glass.

She could clearly see several Europeans standing amongst Jade's friends or family. Mike had pointed out his mother, Rob and Helen and she thought she could recognise Jack and possibly Monty but none of the others. If Jack had been home he could have helped, now she would have to ask Helen, something she was not happy about.

She did not go to bed until late that night, instead she pulled out boxes of old photographs and spent hours checking them. Photographs of Jack as a child, a teenager, a bachelor and finally after they had married, but she was unable to find anything or anyone connecting him to either Jade or Jimmy Lee.

The Madonna caught her eye when she eventually went to bed.

'I have to talk to you about it, even though you know everything already. Telling you won't change anything, but I still need to explain what happened. Even if it's only for myself,' she added, quietly, as she lit a small candle at her feet.

'Jack can't remember too much about his accident. He doesn't remember falling but he does remember a gull flying overhead. Its standing next to him on the beach was amazingly coincidental and he even had a feather in his hand. He must have somehow grabbed at the gull.

But that's not all. I suppose I am responsible for Monty's death. I'm really sorry, I really am. As I tried to tell Monty, it had nothing to do with the age difference between he and Sophie, it was about our affair. Sophie was sleeping in the same room at the time. Then, years later, he's in bed with her. I mean, he must have remembered what had happened between us when he first met Sophie. He should have backed off.

And then, he had the audacity to sit next to me on the sofa, put his arm around my shoulder, kiss my forehead and go upstairs with me to bed. I know he was drunk and, even if nothing happened, Monty should have known he could never talk that straight with me. He shouldn't have thought he could. I felt like something out of the Bargain Basement, functional but out of date.

And I guess I needed Will to make me feel better. After all, Jack had gone off to find himself and Monty was screwing my daughter, let alone what Guy did all those years ago.

Nothing happened between us, Will and me, but I wanted to be loved. That's not a sin is it? To want to be loved.'

*

'Happy birthday to you,' she sang, as Rosie opened the front door looking flushed, as usual, with her hair falling in strands around her face.

'Come in, come in. I tried to 'phone you but you were still away.'

'Got back yesterday,' she said, giving her a small kiss as she handed her a large box of chocolates.

'Mmm, lovely,' enthused Rosie, moving her lips as though she could already taste them. 'Actually, my birthday was yesterday and everyone's come and gone, so we are alone.'

'That suits me fine.'

'And we're not going to sit in the kitchen. I've got my fine china out, if I don't use it a couple of times a year then I can just as well take it all to a car boot sale.'

'Couldn't agree more.'

'So,' continued Rosie, after she had settled down with a pot of tea and two slices of yesterday's sponge cake. 'What's new?'

'The girls came with me to the beach house which reminds me, would you like to come for a couple of days?'

'I'd love to. I don't get away very much, can't afford it with this white elephant around my neck,' Rosie replied, looking around the room.

'It's a pity you can't bring yourself to sell it and free some money. It must be worth a lot now.'

'Well, things will change. I've got something to tell you.'

The lounge door opened as though on cue. She looked up to see Will standing in the doorway.

'Am I intruding? he asked, sounding nervous.

'Ah, here you are. I believe you know each other.' Rosie smiled broadly. 'Will is family of mine. Not real family,' she added, quickly.

'Yes,' agreed Will, 'Rosie's mother, Stella, was my step mother. She married my father after my parents divorced. We were both very young and, actually, grew up together as brother and sister. Rosie's father died when she was young.'

'My best friend,' Rosie added, looking lovingly at Will who looked down at his shoes as though to avoid Rosie's admiration. 'Will used the house as his pied à terre when he worked abroad.'

'When I worked in the middle east,' he explained. 'The funding stopped so I took the opportunity to retire,' he added, miserably.

'Will was an Archaeologist and also studied Theology,' Rosie informed her proudly.

Emy felt her face redden. 'You must have found me an idiot when I discussed my theories.'

'Not at all, I really enjoyed our exchange of ideas. Every new view should be considered.'

'We are still debating,' laughed Rosie.

'I think to the grave,' muttered Will, now concentrating on the trees in the garden.

'Well, let's hope that's fifty years away,' she swallowed, trying to stop her voice from breaking up.

'Heaven forbid,' laughed Rosie again, her cheeks now even more flushed. 'We're going to get married,' she blurted out like a child who can't wait to tell a secret.

'Oh, that's lovely, Rosie. Congratulations Will. I can't think of any two people who are more suited to each other,' she spoke, a little too fervently. 'May I ask you something?' she added.

'Fire away,' answered Will, now appearing nervous.

'What took you so long getting together?'

'I was married for some years but my wife ran away with a Diplomat,' he grinned, shyly.

'Oh, I'm sorry,' she said, trying again to sound sincere.

'Well, the Diplomat was called Lucille,' he roared with laughter. 'She could offer my wife something I couldn't.'

'I wasn't a bit surprised, I could see it but he wouldn't listen,' giggled Rosie.

'Find me a man who does,' she replied, coldly, catching Will's glance.

'And I was engaged to a teacher for a while, when I was very young,' Rosie informed her, proudly. But he was Belgian and taught French. Eventually, he wanted to return to his own country. Everyone made me feel unsure and in the end I backed off. It just didn't work out, he being Belgian and all that. It was, of course, a long time ago and people were more narrow minded about Europeans in those days.'

Emy laughed, disparagingly. 'Actually, it's not changed that much, Britain still doesn't see itself as a part of the main continent.'

'Some people might say it's a piece of the States which broke off and floated thousands of miles to the east,' scoffed Will.

'Don't talk politics,' interrupted Rosie. 'He's quite an anarchist at heart.'

'Is that so, Will, do you like breaking the rules?' she asked, her voice hinting another meaning. 'If so, let me know next time you demonstrate, I've always wanted to carry a banner.'

'The moment I find a good cause I'll rope you in,' he answered, his eyes reflecting his thoughts.

'Do that,' she replied, laughing as she stood up. 'I have to be going,' she added, feeling she had to get out of the house as quickly as possible. She turned to Rosie. 'Give me a ring when you have time.'

Rosie walked with her to the front door.

'Nothing has to change,' she said, kindly. 'Will and I are like a pair of old slippers. He enjoys his chats with you.'

'There really was no content to our conversations. You know it was mostly about the weather, religion and politics. Jack will be back soon and he always keeps me busy.'

She gave Rosie a warm kiss. 'You deserve each other, be happy.'

*

She pieced it all together as she drove home. Rosie's remark about not always being alone and Will once said something about not being free. She could have guessed they lived together but it had not suited her to find out. She had chosen for denial which was contrary to her character for turning over the leaves on someone else's muddy path was something she enjoyed doing.

Her only option was to set her feelings aside, convince herself that her crush on Will had been irrelevant, even juvenile.

Now, she had to go down to the cottage to see Helen about Mike's photograph. Then she had to deal with Jack.

A PAST AFFAIR

Helen PURSED HER LIPS as she studied Mike's photograph. 'Wherever did you get this?' she asked. 'This goes back a long way. You know, I can remember Jade's party.'

'My daughter knows her son, Mike.'

'Really, what a small world. I had only been married a couple of years. I was so young and naive. It was enough to make you cry. See that's me, there's Rob, there's Jack. And there's Monty with his stupid little wife, Fleur.'

'Why was she stupid?'

'Took too many anti-depressants and died. All very embarrassing for super 'laidback' Monty'

'Poor girl, she looks so young.'

'She was about twenty one, not much older. What a waste of life. After all, Monty was pretty dishy. All the girls were after him. Can't think what he saw in her except her looks. And there's Jade,' she continued. 'He married her years later. What an idiot.'

'Why was that?'

'Well, she flutters by, out of the blue, and gets him to marry her, all in the space of a couple of months. Clever that.'

'Perhaps he was lonely, she couldn't have been a stranger. I mean, they must have known each other if he was at her New Year's party.'

Helen ignored her reasoning. 'Monty brought her down here one afternoon.'

'You met Jade here? What was she like?' she asked, pretending not to know about the visit.

'Very quiet, until her son borrowed a swimsuit and then got tied up in the weed. They dragged the poor boy out of the water and she began screaming and crying about the lake being dangerous. Monty took her home and we never saw them again. I think she was a bit mad here or there.'

'When did all this happen?'

'Ages ago, long before Rob and Jack met up again.'

'That was a strange thing to say about the lake. She must have felt it took lives. Actually, she was not far wrong, heaven knows how many people have drowned here over the years, not forgetting Rob and Belle who died between the reeds.'

Helen ignored her again. 'I fell in love with Rob,' she continued, returning the conversation to herself. 'But it was not really returned, not really. I realised, after I married, how Rob put Jack on a pedestal. It didn't matter how hard I tried I could not compete with him. He was always around, always more important than me. I gave up in the end and got on with my own life.'

'And that was?'

'A few love affairs, nothing serious.'

'Did Rob know?' she asked, not surprised at her confession.

'Well, if he did, he never said. I don't think he would have cared that much. Made life easy.'

'I heard Jade had an affair with a Jimmy Lee' she stated, more interested in him than Helen's youthful love life.

'Who told you that?'

'Can't remember, it was a long time ago.'

'Yes. They had an affair,' replied Helen, looking puzzled.

'What happened to him?'

'He went away for some treatment or another. That's why he wasn't on the photograph.'

'And Jade?'

'Well, she was having this affair with Jimmy up until he left. Then, almost immediately, she had another affair. I tried to find out who was the father of her son. No answer there.'

'Who did Jade have another affair with?'

'You ask too many questions.'

'It's so long ago, why shouldn't I?'

'What's it to you?' Helen replied, bitterly.

Emy frowned. 'Oh, God, not Rob,' she blurted out.

'You must be joking, someone far nearer to home.'

'Nearer to home?'

'Oh, well, I guess it doesn't matter anymore. Jack's left you and Rob's dead. Jack, of course.'

She felt the air leave her lungs and a

weakness which seemed to pass through her body.

'How do you know that?' she asked, coldly.

'Everyone knew. It was a public secret.'

'I don't want to hear it,' she said, standing up to go home.

'Oh, for goodness sake sit down. Did you really think you were his first?'

'Of course not, but I can hardly believe this.'

'Because you don't want to believe it. It's true. Jimmy Lee's family gave her a month to get out of the house. She held this party and, well, that's what happened. Jack stayed on after everyone else had left. He told Rob about it. End of story. Except her son is certainly not one hundred percent Chinese.' She smiled, obviously aware of the implication of her casual remark.

'Well, for your information, Jack hasn't left me. We have an agreement, he wants some space and so do I. He's probably coming home next week. I'll ask him about it.'

'Yes, he told me.'

'Told you what?'

'Just that he was planning to go home.'

'What are you, his confidant? Tell me, am I missing something? Is there something I should know? Is he living with you?' She paused, 'I'm going home, I hope I never see you again.'

'Please yourself. Sorry, if I've burst your bubble. That's life, sweetie.'

*

She kept back her tears as she drove home. A pain of betrayal and hurt ran through her but most of all the shock and realisation of what it would mean to Mike. Mike who thought he was about to find his father and the rejection he might have to face. She must warn him before he left.

'My God,' she murmured. 'He could be Jillie's half-brother. He could be my stepson and Sophie's whatever.'

She tried to 'phone Mike when she got home but he had already left the country.

THE DREAM

She WAS JUST OUT OF THE SHOWER when Daisy began barking and wagging her tail at the same time. The dark shadow of a man showed as a smear on the misty glass in the front door, it was the familiar form of Jack. She braced herself as he turned the key in the lock, undecided whether to greet him as the prodigal husband or throw him out for all the pain he had caused her.

He opened the door slightly as though to test the temperature of his welcome.

'Hi,' he said, awkwardly.

'So, the Lone Ranger has returned.'

He did not answer as he studied the coconut doormat.

'Well, are you coming in or not,' she snapped, as though she was talking to Daisy who often stood undecided on the back doorstep. 'Still in your black leathers,' she gibed, purposely turning her back on him as she walked towards the kitchen.

'You sound angry.'

'Should I be? It's okay, I've quite enjoyed my freedom. So, how did you fare in the uncharted waters of the big wide world?' she continued, coldly.

'Not so big anymore. I did keep in touch. You've always known where I was.'

'And what was I suppose to do with that information, file it or throw it away.'

'I haven't done anything wrong,' he replied, defensively.

'You think! You're so tied up with yourself and what you want. You're an ungrateful pig, Jack.'

'You know why I left.'

'Oh yes, of course, if I remember rightly you needed to feel the wind in your face. Running away just like before.'

'Before?'

'Yes, before. Helen has told me about your sexual encounter in Hong Kong. All those years ago.'

'I don't know what you're talking about.'

'Jade. I'm talking about Jade.'

'I can't remember.'

'Shut up, Jack. Helen told me about Jade's New Year's party and how you stayed behind. Can you remember now?'

'Helen should keep her mouth shut.'

'Why?'

'Because it was so long ago and it has nothing to do with anyone else. It makes no difference.'

'Makes no difference. How can you say that? Her son is walking around looking for his father who, by the way, he thinks he has found. He's going to get a terrible shock if he finds out it isn't him. How do you think he is going to feel?'

'It was a one night stand. How would I know if she was pregnant of not, let alone if the child was mine. She was a pick-up, one of Jimmy Lee's many. I suppose Helen also told you she came here and married Monty someone or another.'

'You have known this all the time and you didn't tell me.'

'Tell you what, that I had a fling. Why should I tell you? What the hell was there to tell?'

'I've always felt the three of you had a secret. The cosy threesome. It's always been so, I feel as though I was some kind of an outsider. You and Helen make me sick, including Rob whose dead.'

'It wasn't like that, it wasn't a secret. Just something I didn't want to talk about. For heaven's sake, it was so long ago. Anyway, why should you care? It has nothing to do with you. You weren't even around.'

The silence felt almost tangible. She wanted to tell him to get out of her life but she could not because she did not want him out of her life, nor lose everything around her, nor admit their marriage had failed. She felt hemmed in by her conflicting emotions and it was true, anything either of them had done before they met was irrelevant to their relationship. It occurred to her that none of this would have happened if she had not had a cup of tea with Mrs. Chung, so long ago. She would not have known about Jade and Jimmy and Monty's step son, Mike, would have been irrelevant, of no particular importance. The old woman had talked about not pushing back the waves, she was planning a Tsunami.

'That's absolutely true,' she replied. 'It's none of my business. Silly to think it was.' She breathed deeply to control her emotions. 'By the way, Helen tells me you're seeing each other. You didn't tell me that.'

He did not answer.

'Oh, come on, Jack. Helen blabbed everything out. She told me how much you meant to Rob and it seems to her as well. She told me how she was in competition with you for Rob's admiration. Or should I say affection.'

'Don't talk rubbish. What you're suggesting is ridiculous.'

'So, then, tell the truth.'

'Okay, yes. I've dropped in on Helen a couple of times.'

'Now, let me see. Sometime ago she gave me your lighter. When you were in hospital. She said she found it at the cottage, on a bedside table of all places. Well, I can remember you had it the last time we were there. Do you know why I can remember that?'

'Don't know what you are on about.'

'I know because I can remember you had the car window open when you were driving home and the ash blew onto your shirt and burnt a hole in it. And that was the last time we went down there, together. What do you think of that?'

'I still have no idea what you're talking about.'

'Jack, do you know what Guy used to say to me. 'Piss off'. And that for him was refined.'

'Do you want me to leave?'

'Do what you want, I couldn't care less,' she lied.

'What is it you want me to say?'

'Try the truth.'

'Yes, Helen, likes me. We have nothing together. Just talking and remembering old times.'

'Oh, I see. Now you reminisce with Helen instead of Rob. The two of you go down memory lane together. What is that cosy.'

There was the usual silence.

'If you're hungry, then get yourself something to eat,' she offered, magnanimously, as though nothing had happened.

'Thanks.'

'I'm going to bed. Make yourself at home, seeing how it's half yours anyway.'

He clutched her wrist. 'I'll make it up to you.'

'You can't. Perhaps you should think of how to solve the problems you've already made,' she replied, dejectedly. 'By the way,' she added, casually, 'did you know Jade died in a sailing accident, some years ago.'

Jack lay next to her in bed that night and, since she did not refuse his presence, she reckoned he would see it as a conciliatory gesture. She turned on her side to clarify her position, seeing how it was no small thing. It would take her ages to get over this, if she ever did.

'I've not asked about you,' he murmured.

'No, you haven't. For your information,' she chirped, as though she had recovered from the situation, 'I've tried really hard to have a couple of affairs and I have a beach house lent to me by the son of a woman who, according to an old Chinese lady, disappeared into thin air decades ago.

And some man from my murky past dropped dead just a couple of days after we met. You know, just the normal run of events.'

'Really,' he answered, in a tone of disbelief.

'Yes, really. Listen,' she said, after what seemed to her a long pause. 'I do not intend losing my way of life, my life style. I do not intend living a hand to mouth existence on some measly alimentation allotted to me by some bias man in a divorce court. So, we will live alongside each other, share the same house and you can come and go as you please.'

Jack nodded his head on his pillow and true to form said nothing.

'Good,' she confirmed.

'I know you won't believe me but I did miss you, I really did,' he whispered, gently.

'Oh, you surprise me.'

'Try to believe me.'

'I would love to believe you, Jack. But so much has happened it's almost impossible to turn it all around. I was even lucky those people were with me when you fell down the bloody cliff. Otherwise, I might even have been accused of pushing you before they arrived. In hindsight, that was not such a bad idea,' she laughed bitterly. 'I thought you were dead,' she added.

'I know, I'm sorry.'

'You should be.'

'What dead or sorry.'

'Both.'

They laid again in silence as though it was necessary to punctuate it with short sharp sentences.

'I've remembered my dream,' Jack suddenly informed her.

'What dream?'

'Well, I returned to the beach where I had my accident and, suddenly, it came back to me.'

'What came back to you?'

'I'm trying to tell you. Before I woke up in hospital I dreamt I was sleeping in the bottom of a boat when a seagull perched on the mast flapped its wings and woke me up. I stood up and thought I was somewhere else, perhaps out east, because it was so warm and humid and I felt young, like I did then. I dived into the sea and you began swimming towards me even though you can't swim. Everything felt wrong. Actually,' he added, 'I am wondering if you have dreams when you're knocked out.'

'I don't know, shouldn't think so.'

'But recently, I remembered I had a feather in my hand before I dived into the sea. That was it, strange dream.'

'My God, Jack,' she whispered. 'I didn't cross time. I shared your dream.'

'What are you talking about?'

'I shared your dream,' she repeated.

'I don't understand.'

'Neither do I.'

He nestled his head in her neck like a child seeking forgiveness and comfort from its mother.

Sympathy stirred within her as she kissed his forehead.

'To share a dream is to share a soul. I guess it's a small step to share love when the time is right. But not yet, Jack. Not yet.'

*

She met Will next day and told him how Jack had come home and hoped everything would be alright. Then she told him about a young man who was looking for his father overseas while, in fact, he could be within a couple of hours drive from where he lived.

After a tense silence, she told him about Helen who had been chasing Jack for years but there was nothing between them, so Jack said. She rambled on while he considered his forthcoming marriage to Rosie. He wanted to get away from the past, live it up a bit before it was too late and that was not going to happen while they were both weighed down by the millstone around their necks, the catastrophe she called home. He would confront Rosie and hope he could persuade her to sell the house.

He turned his attention back to Emy and suggested what the whole world would suggest, which was not to make any rash decisions. Later, he added, 'you could, of course, ask Helen. She might tell the truth, not probable but possible.

She thought about it later. Yes, she needed one last meeting with Helen the bitch. She needed to know the truth about her and Jack. To have a scene, perhaps an hysterical one, when hopefully the traitor would shout the miserable truth in a moment of feminine madness and anger.

Jack was not in the garden when she got home though the wheelbarrow, spade, fork and cutters were already on the path.

'I'm home,' she called from the hall.

Jack came out of the lounge. 'Have a nice walk?' he asked, sounding worried.

'See you've started the garden. Good you're back, saves a lot of money. I was about to look for a cheap gardener, as if they exist. Want a coffee,' she added.

He followed her into the kitchen as he always had done.

'So, what are your plans?' she asked, as she filled the kettle and plugged it in.

'Don't have any. Been looking through the mail. I have to go to the Bank tomorrow.'

'Yes, I've spent a bit of money, I told you somebody has lent me a little house on the beach. It's not a holiday home and I have a chance of renting it on a permanent basis next year. You would love it, it's so wild down there. I've made it really nice, bought some flat pack and a couple of chairs and some bits and bobs to make it cosy. Anyway, you've also spent a lot,' she added, defensively.

'Yes, I have,' he admitted.

'Perhaps we can have a weekend down there,' she suggested, returning to the beach house.

'Why not? Well, I'll get back to the weeds. You know,' he added, obviously very worried, 'I never told Rob that Jade was pregnant because of me, simply because I didn't know and even if I did know, the chances would have been minimal.'

'It's so bloody easy for men to have their fun and run away.'

'I wish you wouldn't make everything so black and white. Women also have to take some of the responsibility. Anyway, I would like to know how you met him, her son.'

'The 'him' has a name, it's Mike and what do you mean the chances would have been minimal. If he's not Jimmy's son then you can bet he is yours,' she said, angrily, unable to hide the bitterness in her tone.

'Well, it seems she went a bit crazy after Jimmy Lee left her. She slept with half the Yacht Club.'

'Really!' she replied, in a tone of disbelief. She opened her bag. 'Wait, I want to show you something.' She handed him Mike's old photograph. 'Can you recognise anyone?'

Jack walked across to the window to get more light. 'Yes, this was her New Year's party. It was a sort of last fling before she left. Before the Lee family chucked her out.'

'The night you stayed with her.'

'Can't remember.'

'You never stop lying. It doesn't matter.' she snapped, trying to sound indifferent. 'I just want to know if you can recognise any of those people.'

'That's me standing just behind Rob and Helen. That's Jade, that's Monty and his wife,' he replied coldly.

'Fleur,' she informed him.

'Yes, Fleur. I see you've done your homework.'

'Only what's necessary. I want to know who the others are.'

'That's Sunny and Angela from the club. The others are her friends or family, I have no idea who they are. Where the hell did you get this?'

'I'll tell you when I'm ready.'

'What are you waiting for?'

'A letter.'

'From whom?'

She did not answer.

'By the way, you didn't tell me how you met Jade's son'

'That's right, I didn't.'

'A WHO WASIT'

She RECEIVED AN E-MAIL FROM Mike some weeks later. She clenched her jaw, frightened of the possible bad news and the devastation she knew it would bring to an enthusiastic young man looking for his father. Let alone the consequences which would resonate throughout her own family if Jimmy Lee was not Mike's father, leaving Jack the very possible silent partner in the affair.

Dear Mrs. Nielson,

I am thinking of you all so often and perhaps you are thinking of me and wondering how it has all turned out. The answer to that, it is a disaster.
It took me a few days to get an appointment with Jimmy Lee since he is semi-retired and only goes to his office occasionally. He asked me why I should believe I was his son. I told him what my mother had told me. He looked as though he was sorry for me. Well, I was sorry for me too. It was not what I had

hoped for. He was very kind and told me how he had an affair with my mother and, in fact, he had loved her very much. She wanted him to divorce his wife but that was impossible and he had no time to help her because he had become ill and had to go abroad for immediate treatment.

He knew my mother had gone away to stay with family. He said he had never heard from her again.
I asked him whether it was possible my mother was carrying his child when he left. He said that it was not. He said it with such certainty, I had to believe him.
Then he suggested we both have a DNA test to prove he was telling the truth.

I am so shocked, I don't know what to do or think.
I was sure my mother was telling the truth. I asked him if he had any idea who my father could be. He shrugged his shoulders and then he remembered she was in a group at the Yacht Club and his relatives had told him she had held wild parties before she left. He seemed genuinely upset and wished me luck and hoped I would one day find my father and that we would stay in touch.

I am leaving next week, I would so like to see you all. May I telephone you when I get back?

Love Mike.

P.S. The test proved he was not my father.

Jack, she decided, was going to have a DNA test. He owed that to both of them, to Mike and to her. And she was not going to take 'No' for an answer.

*

She thought Mike looked both sad and angry when she eventually met him at the beach house.

'Why didn't she tell Monty and me that Jimmy was not my father?' His voice broke as he spoke.

'Perhaps she didn't know for sure,' she suggested. 'Perhaps it was easier to stick to her story which once told would be difficult to change.'

She gazed down to the beach imagining how Jade had loved Jimmy so desperately that she had thrown herself into the 'why not' syndrome when he left her, accepting love from whoever offered it. She felt only pity for this young woman who had worked herself into a hopeless situation.

She sat talking to him for what seemed hours trying to convince him that, no doubt, his mother had her reasons for what she had done, what she had told him. He would probably never know the truth unless he found those who knew her at that time and, perhaps, might even be willing to have a DNA test if they had slept with her and were honest enough to admit doing so. Though she doubted many men would agree to that. Mike had looked at her in astonishment.

'I don't know of anyone who could be my father.'

'Perhaps one of those in that old photograph.'

'I don't know who those people are,' he replied, sounding apathetic.

'Well, I think we are looking for a European.'

'I have European blood in me, my great grandfather was French,' he snapped, angrily.

'Sorry, I didn't know that. But we can still start with Jack,' she suggested, hopefully. 'It doesn't change anything.'

'Jack,' he replied, in amazement. 'What the hell did he have to do with my mother?'

'Nothing that I know of,' she lied. 'Except he was at her party and Helen recently made a suggestive remark which, of course, says nothing. Anyway, we have to begin somewhere.'

'I don't believe that's possible, Jack my father. That would be a turn up for the book,' he muttered, obviously stunned. 'If not for you then for me,' he grinned, warming to the idea.

'Anyway,' she continued, 'don't throw away Monty's hair brush or tooth brush, or anything which could hold his DNA.'

She did not know why she threw Monty's name into the hat since he was still married to Fleur when Jimmy left Jade. But, then, she considered men were easily influenced by a beautiful woman. Perhaps, Fleur had turned cold after her miscarriage.

*

Getting Jack to have a DNA test was no small thing but eventually, under duress, he admitted his one night stand could have been longer though he was unsure how long. As far as he knew Jimmy had only been gone a couple of weeks before Jade's party.

He also admitted he did not really know whether she had other lovers, though he thought there was another man after he had left. As far as he was concerned, it had been just a bit of good fun. He had gone on to say that he thought it better, easier, to keep a low profile and that he would probably go off again.

'Have you seen Helen again?'

'Yes, a couple of times,' he admitted.

'You said you were finished with her.'

'I didn't say that. I can't just drop her. We're just good friends. She brings some stability into my life and, whether you believe it or not, there is nothing to finish. My God, I've known her for over thirty odd years.'

'You've been seeing her all the time.'

'Not true.'

'Liar.'

'I've told you the truth. She's lonely and it's somewhere to go with all this going on. I'll say it again, we are just good friends.'

'Just friends are the most dangerous. Just friends don't exist and you know it. You are so naive, she winds you round her little finger. I hope you'll find your stability. God only knows you need it.'

He had walked into the garden and climbed onto his motor bike.

'Don't assume things you don't know. I've not had an affair with Helen but now I'm thinking about it,' he added, angrily. 'Let me know when the results are in.'

'We shared a dream, nobody does that.'

He sighed. 'You don't get it, do you? I'm sick of all that psychic rubbish. Why can't you just be normal, there is nothing else. We live, we die, that's it.' He shrugged his shoulders. 'Just give me a bit more space and time,' he added, more mildly. He revved up his motor bike. 'Listen, we'll talk about it when I get back. Okay?'

'Don't bother,' she yelled as she slammed the back door and then cried over the kitchen sink, smearing her makeup on the drying up cloth.

She had poured herself a glass of wine and flopped down in a chair to consider Helen and how she had decided not to sell her cottage in spite of the recent tragedies. She had wanted to warn Jack of Helen's nonchalant acceptance of death and remind him how the lake intermittently claimed those who were careless, but her anger had overcome all else. Now, she felt, he could look after himself and to hell with him and his 'bonhomie' charm.

A shiver ran through her as she recalled how Helen had recently asked her to go alone to the cottage, which she now connected with Rob's death, and her unlikely story of how Belle had wandered out into the night without her knowing.

'Oh, God,' she murmured. 'I don't trust you,' and once again felt concerned for Jack and his almost childish outlook on life, on Helen.

*

She breathed a sigh of relief when the DNA results finally arrived. Jack was not Mike's father. Mike looked a little sad for she thought he would have liked to be one of the family.

'What now?' Mike asked.

'Well, we'll try Monty. Do you have anything which could hold his DNA?'

'I have kept his silver-backed hair and coat brushes and an expensive razor and shaving brush set. I even found an old toothbrush of his which I had thrown in a garbage bag in the garage.'

'That's fantastic. I believe this kind of test will take longer and cost more but it's worth a try. I'm sure it's not him,' she added. 'He was still married to Fleur, he wouldn't have done that.'

She set her uncomfortable thoughts aside as she studied him sitting, silently, staring out to sea. His dark hair was parted so that a lock fell across his face and she was unable to see whether he was depressed, or even crying. She felt full of maternal love as she put her arms around him. It was then she noticed numerous small grey hairs between the dark. Perhaps he would become prematurely grey as Monty had done.

'I think you should go for it', she continued, trying to sound enthusiastic. 'You never know, you might get a nice surprise,' she said, hopefully.

'I've had enough surprises to last me a life time,' he answered, bitterly.

'Come on, we have to do something,' she murmured, feeling puzzled how she had developed such deep feelings, how she had become so involved with a young man she hardly knew.

He looked up at her. 'You know, if my mother knew for sure Jimmy was my father then she would have looked him up at some point.'

'Listen,' she said, trying again to sound hopeful. 'If it's not Monty then I'll ask Helen if she has anything of Rob's which can be tested.'

She omitted to tell him that the chance of Helen having kept any of Rob's personal possessions was minimal.

'Okay,' he agreed. 'But I know it will be a waste of time and money.'

'Good, we won't give up so easily.'

'Why didn't she get an abortion?' he asked suddenly.

She paused for a moment to try to figure that out and to give him a logical answer.

'Well, perhaps because she loved Jimmy so much she hoped the baby was his. Maybe she had religious principles.'

'That's possible,' he replied, thoughtfully.

'Well, she was a good mother. That must count for something.'

He nodded in agreement.

'Enough to forgive any human failings, don't you think?'

'Nothing could change my love for her.' He paused. 'What a pity Monty died when he did. Just too soon. He probably knew much more.'

'Yes, I'm really sorry. I wish it could have been different,' she murmured.

*

It seemed a long time before they received the results which they closely studied over her kitchen table.

'You see, you were right. Unbelievable, Monty was my father. No wonder he was so kind to me.'

'It really is the most obvious, when you think about it,' she laughed, nervously, as she thought of all that had happened during the last months.

'I find that really strange. My mother has an affair with Jimmy Lee, he leaves her and she goes on to have an affair with Monty and perhaps even one with Jack,' he added, cynically. 'She must have known one of them was my father. I don't understand why Monty didn't take a DNA test. I can't understand why he didn't do that.'

'Well, perhaps, he found it good as it was. Anyway, he left everything to you, I think that says something. He probably guessed it.' She paused. 'You know, I've been thinking about your Christian names, James, Michael and John. Well, James is Jimmy, Michael is Monty's name and John is the real name for Jack.'

'My God, I've never thought of that', he said sounding shocked. 'It's like she left a trail of clues. Now I understand why I have so many names.' He stopped. 'Take your pick,' he added, angrily.

'Anyway,' she continued, quickly, to ease the tension, 'my home is always open to you. You can come and go as you please. Whatever else, you have a family here with us.'

'How is it between you and Jack?' he asked, as though he was finished with it all.

'Okay. As you know, he is a man of few words though he did manage to say he had enjoyed his freedom.' She laughed, bitterly. 'We've agreed to stay together and he can come and go at his leisure. Nothing has to change. He's got a good deal, at least I think so.'

'Emy, have I caused this?' Mike asked, sounding concerned.

'Naa, his mother was a gypsy.'

'Really?'

'No, but she could have been. Come on, let's drink to your good news. The girls are on their way down and we're going to celebrate.'

She held the papers down as a small breeze lifted them gently off the table and, just for a second, she thought she heard the wind bells on Mrs. Chung's veranda.

'Jade,' she whispered. 'Of course, Monty didn't want a DNA test, everyone knew about you and Jack.

Sometimes, it is better not to know the truth, sometimes it is better to leave well alone.'

THE STORM

It WAS EARLY FEBRUARY when Mike telephoned to say that the estate agent, who was selling Monty's house, had told him of an unusually high sea and storms which had battered the beach house and damaged some of the roof.

He thought she might like to go down to check on her possessions and that he had already arranged for John Marlow to board it up, if it was possible to do so, and he would go down there the following weekend. She said she would go immediately and take home what she could salvage. She put the phone down irritated that Jack was away on one of his shorter 'get-away' modes.

She decided to 'phone the girls to say where she was going, threw a change of clothes and toiletries into a small overnight bag and left, hoping the traffic was not too bad and the weather had quietened down.

*

The house was better than she had expected. John Marlow was already on the roof when she arrived with a nail between his teeth while he hammered another into a board to cover an exposed rafter.

'Could 'ave been worse. The shed caught the most of it, you can pull that down, that's for sure. I's found a box of books on a shelf, I's brought them inside to dry out.'

'Thanks,' she shouted to him as she entered the house. 'I'll make a coffee, you must be cold up there.'

'You could say that,' he agreed.

It did not take long for her to throw her few household articles into the car along with the box from the shed which she had already opened and glanced, briefly, at what she thought were old schoolbooks. She smiled to herself as she realised Jade had kept, as any loving mother, exercise books belonging to her most valuable possession, her child.

John Marlow appeared at the patio door.

'I's got to go into the village. I needs more of those boards,' he said, pointing to the roof. 'Won't be more than an 'our. If ye moves ye car then I can back out.'

She climbed into her now full car and wound down the window. 'I'm nearly finished, I might be gone when you get back. I guess Mike will be down this weekend, I might also come.'

'Maybe I'll be finished, maybe not. 'Ave to see about that.'

'Okay, we'll see,' she answered, amused at his casual slant on life.

She was on the point of going home when a gust of wind banged the sunroom door against the outside wall just as it had done once before. She glanced down the beach, a figure was standing by the shoreline. She watched, mesmerised, as a woman looked up at the beach house then faded into the spray which formed a fine mist.

Surprised and shocked, she ran across the dunes and down to the beach, uncertain of what she had seen, shouting to the woman to come back. Then, throwing off her shoes and coat, she splashed clumsily into the outgoing tide, plunging forward towards what she thought was an outstretched arm but, when she pulled it towards her, it was only a long sliver of dark green seaweed, its bulging leaves formed like fingers.

She turned in panic as the current dragged at her saturated clothes while the stinging sand rushed outwards across her feet until she fell back into the icy water. She struggled to stand up and gain her balance, aware she was losing the fight against the pulling tide until, suddenly, a small rock in the sand became exposed. In the moment between failure or success, she thrust herself towards it, screaming to God for help as she did so. Then, clinging onto the rock she waited until the sea receded and she was able to crawl up the hard wet beach.

She laid breathless, stiff from the bitter cold, aware that if she didn't get up she might even die of exposure. She clenched her jaw to control her shaking body and, focusing on the house, stumbled bent double, against the wind with Daisy jumping at her as though angry at her ill judgement.

The door to the sun room was still banging when she staggered towards her car, pulled out her overnight bag and ran upstairs to the bathroom.

'Oh God, why did I do that when I didn't really know if she existed,' she sobbed, as the hot water beat down on her. Aware, as she stood with her hands against the white tiled wall, that she must not tell anyone what she had done for no one would be able, or even willing, to understand her.

Mike 'phoned after she had returned home. He sounded so normal in her abnormal world. She wanted to tell him what had happened but, instead, she told him how Marlow could probably batten down the roof enough to keep out the rain and how the shed was a total loss.

'Actually,' she said, 'I'm not insured and I really don't care if I lose it all.'

He ignored her remark and laughed and said he was happy the house was still standing and that he had already contacted the insurance company, everything was under control. They agreed to meet the following Saturday when they could discuss the details. He sent her his love and she felt once again incredibly close to him, a closeness near to love. She felt tears welling in her eyes and realised she was becoming sentimental, something she had never tolerated in others.

It was the middle of the following morning before she began to store her pots and pans in the garage and bring the bed linen and the plastic bag full of wet clothes into the house.

She laid Mike's box on the hall floor near the radiator and forgot about it for another day. It was only when Daisy took an interest in it did she lift it onto the kitchen table and opened the first book, which was the most recently written. It took only a few seconds for her to realise the handwriting was adult and that she was reading a diary. She opened more exercise books, all were in chronological order and neatly written. She felt guilty for here, she felt, was something private, not to be read by others. She wanted above all to close the box and give it to Mike but, on the other hand, she was unsure whether he aware of its existence. She decided that probably he did not know, otherwise he would have taken it with him and not left it at the beach house. Supposing, she thought, that by being honest she was paving his path to unhappiness, opening a Pandora's Box.

With that in mind, she fell back into a deep chair and began to read the books in chronological order. Aware her curiosity had won over her sense of decency. After all, whatever else, the books did not belonged to her.

*

Jade was over three months pregnant when she left home to live with her aunt some distance from the city. She wrote of how she had immediately found work and how her aunt had taken all the money which Jimmy had given to her before he left. She had felt misused since she also had to work as a child minder for her aunt's extended family, giving her little time to rest especially as she became more pregnant.

She had kept in contact with Monty until she had read in the newspaper how Fleur had been found dead outside her house. She had felt full of guilt and remorse and broke her contact with Monty by changing her job and address.

Luckily, she had found work in a private house where she had a room in the servants' quarters. Here, she could be with her baby and pay a young girl from a village to look after him while she was working.

Jade had not written in her diary everyday but only when there was a particular event. After some years, when Michael was around six years old, she had tried to find her old friends but the Europeans had mostly moved back to their own countries and her friends had married and did not want her around them, which she could understand.

She had visited her old house and stood crying at the iron gates, begging Fleur to forgive her affair with Monty.

An old lady who was tending orchids in the garden opposite recognised her and invited her to come in and rest for a while, since she had walked a long way from the main road. She had offered her tea together with some romantic story about Jimmy Lee. Jade wrote that she did not disillusion the old lady but listened attentively, nodding in the right places and sympathising where necessary.

She had thanked Mrs. Chung and wished her a long and healthy life. The old lady had laughed lightly, reminding her how old she was.

The rest of the exercise books were about Michael growing up, her working and saving until she had eventually found Monty.

She wrote of how she and Monty had married and how generous he had been to both of them and how he had bought the beach house where Michael could take his friends. She wrote how she had learnt to sail though sometimes she preferred to be alone and walk down the beach, read and write her diary.

Then, she wrote about having cancer, her treatment, and how kind Monty had been but how she saw little of her son since he worked in London.

The diaries carried on noting family birthdays and other significant events until she eventually came to the last entry. It was written on a Saturday.

'I don't know what to do anymore. Michael has decided to look for Jimmy, he thinks he can find him. He wants to come here but I have asked him not to drive down if the weather is bad. I don't want to talk to him about the past.

I went to the hospital this week. They told me my cancer has returned. It is now hopeless. Perhaps I will tell Michael if he comes tomorrow. I have not told Monty yet.

She closed the exercise book and wondered what happened on that Sunday afternoon, if Mike had decided to visit his mother. Daisy jumped up onto her lap and looked up with her melting eyes.

'Mrs. Chung, your story was almost true,' she whispered, as she stroked the dog's curly hair. 'Jimmy was ill, he did go away and Jade did leave later. I am sure Jimmy named his yacht 'The Gull' to please her. Actually, Mrs. Chung, your story held a lot of truths only it was just a little too flowery. An innocent cup of tea with you, so many years ago, opened up a can of worms for me now. I wish I had stayed home that day.'

She put the exercise books back into the box and decided the best thing to do was to give them to Mike and pretend she had not read them. She thought it inconsequential who knew what when. 'It doesn't changed anything. 'It is as it is,' she sighed.

*

The following Saturday was a beautiful day, cold but sunny. She and Mike had inspected the little house and surveyed the damaged shed which gave her the opportunity of telling him how Marlow had found a box of schoolbooks and, because the box was damp, she had taken it home to dry out.

He had looked surprised. 'That's interesting but I can't remember my mother keeping anything.' He opened the first book, smiling shyly. 'These are not mine, this is my mother's handwriting. Where did Marlow find them?' he asked, sounding puzzled.

'In the shed under some old tarpaulins.'

'They must have there for years. Why did she put them there?'

'I don't know.'

There was a tense silence as he began to read and she guessed he had chosen the first book which was the most recently written.

'I'll put the mats outside to dry,' she suggested, wanting to give him some privacy. 'Maybe we should go for a walk later.'

She sat on the patio wall staring out to sea until, eventually, Mike appeared in the doorway.

'I'll get my coat,' he muttered.

The wind had dropped but the sea was still choppy when they strolled along the desolate beach.

'Dangerous sea, here,' she remarked. He did not react to her obvious statement so she continued. 'Something incredibly strange happened when I was down here this week. Marlow had gone into town and I was just about to leave when I was overcome by a feeling that something tragic had happened, here along the shoreline. I had a feeling that a woman drowned and that she had something to do with the beach house. I don't know when it happened, it could have been a long time ago.'

'I've never heard of anything happening down here', he replied. 'Maybe it was before Monty bought the house.'

'Who knows. Did you come down that Sunday afternoon?' she asked, curiously.

He turned, sharply. 'You've read her diaries?' he asked, accusingly.

She blushed, profusely. 'Just the last page where she wrote you might come. It was the day before she went missing.'

He turned to her, the sides of his jacket flapped in the wind showing his dark blue jumper which fitted tightly against his slim body.

'Yes, I came down. I waited a long time but she didn't turn up. I 'phoned Monty to ask where she was but he didn't know either, he thought she was with me. You know, there's just one thing which could explain what she did. I told you how they found her cancer had returned when they did the autopsy. The hospital confirmed it was terminal. According to the last entry in her diary, it seems she did know. Perhaps she was tempting providence when she took 'The Gull' out. I'll survive, or not.'

'You'll never know.'

'I'll never know,' he repeated.

They returned to the beach house and she brought a mug of coffee to Mike who was sitting on the floor, his head lowered as though depressed. She sat on a chair behind him and cradled him in her arms, his head pressed against her breasts. She felt the most extraordinary sensation, that of a mother wanting to comfort her child.

He smiled as she stroked his hair, she was so motherly, so kind. He wished he could tell her the truth of what happened that fatal Sunday afternoon.

He had met his mother at the Beach House, excited he would soon be going to Hong Kong to find his father.

She had looked away. 'Please don't do that, you will not be the happier for knowing.'

'Why not, why shouldn't I meet him?'

'Because,' she said softly, 'he is not your father.'

'What are you talking about?' he shouted.

She had not answered him, refused to discuss the matter further, just as when he was a child. He had been angry, terribly angry, and she had walked in the dunes to get away from him.

'I love you,' she shouted. 'What does it matter who your father is as long as I love you?'

'You're little better than an easy lay. Little better than a pickup.'

'I was in love,' she screamed, desperately.

'But your lover was not my father, explain that. I have the right to know who my father is.'

He had followed her through the blustering wind and rain, shouting and calling her names as she ran down to the water's edge. He had grabbed her coat and thrown her towards the icy sea, pushing her again and again until, finally, she fell back into the crashing waves. She had stood up, her tears indiscernible in the driving rain, her mouth open as though to scream in fear and desperation.

Then, suddenly, she became silent and gazed at him calmly. He stopped, aware of her change, aware she had retreated further into the sea. He thought she smiled, he thought she became the young woman he knew in his youth. She looked once more up at the beach house before turning to him.

'I love you. I'm sorry, I'm sorry', she mouthed, as she threw herself forward into the gully, the flowing river behind the shallow water.

He had knelt on the cold hard sand screaming

for her to come back, begging God to bring her back, begging God to forgive him.

He had walked slowly back to the house aware he had to tell Monty what his mother had done. He would have to explain why she was on the beach in such weather. He could have driven home and waited for the news she was missing had he been sure Monty was unaware of their meeting. He had decided to take a chance, he would cover up the truth.

He found the keys to 'The Gull' on his mother's key ring so he put on his thick jacket and pulled the hood over his wool hat and drove her car down to the harbour. There was no one is sight though he could hear loud talking and laughing from the Bar of a Pub. He waited for a moment before opening the cabin then, quickly, hung his mother's bag on a hook, as she always did; took off his clothes and piled them neatly on the mooring along with a towel. He shivered from the ice cold wind as he untied the ropes, pulled up the anchor and pushed off. The tide was still on the ebb and he managed to manoeuvre 'The Gull' until it was at the harbour entrance. Then, praying to God for help, he jumped into the sea, as near as possible to the slimy green harbour wall, and swam, hopefully, unnoticed, to the mooring. When he looked back 'The Gull' was drifting out to sea.

Eventually, he pulled himself up onto the mooring where 'The Gull' had been anchored, dressed quickly and made his way back to the Beach House, crossing small isolated coves and climbing over rocks which would later be covered by the incoming tide.

Once back, he dried his hair, made a hot cup of chocolate and tried to unwind as he hoped, against hope, he had not been seen. Then he 'phoned Monty on his mobile.

'Hey, Monty, I've been waiting a couple of hours for Mum. She said she would meet me here, at the Beach House, is she with you?'

'The Gull' had been found quickly and his mother several days later. It was assumed she had taken the yacht out and the police had seen it as a tragic accident.

He returned to the present. Emy was still stroking his hair, he lifted his head upwards while he slowly moved over her body until their lips touched. He felt she was ready to be loved and he ran his hand down her body, she shivered and for a moment he thought she would surrender to her desires. Instead, she drew back, unwillingly, and pushed him gently away.

'We have to get going. Marlow's obviously not coming,' she said, standing up.

'We can wait a bit longer,' he suggested, looking at his watch.

'No, we can't. It's a long drive home.'

'I want to stay here with you forever,' he continued, persuasively.

She purposely did not answer for she was old and wise enough to draw a line. She could not use any more regretted emotions.

'No one is going to miss me,' he whispered, insinuating she might still stay. 'And you?'

'It's already late. I'm going home,' she said quickly. 'Tell you what, if you have nothing better to do next weekend then come and have some lunch with me. Maybe the girls will come.'

'I would love to and I haven't yet seen where you live.'

'Well, here's your chance.'

She never really knew why she had asked him for lunch, after what had just happened, but he seemed hurt and lonely, as she was, and dangerously attractive. He had inherited Jade's good looks and Monty's mannerisms, quietly spoken, extraordinarily polite and perhaps gallant.

She sighed deeply as she remembered the past. She had been so in love with Jack and life had seemed so simple. Now it was as though everyone had secrets, told half truths, including herself.

It was then she decided Jack's 'freedom' days were numbered. It was decision time, crunch time. He would have to play by the rules and, if not, he would be out on his neck. And Helen? Well, she really did not know what they had between them. After all, what good would it do to know the truth.

'What I don't know, I don't have to worry about,' she muttered, suddenly feeling confident. 'It will all turn out right in the end.

* * *

Helen 'phoned a few weeks later and asked if Jack was home. She had been trying to reach him for days, it seemed he had turned his mobile off.

She had handed the telephone to Jack and smiled knowingly as he shifted from one foot to the other. Eventually, he plucked up enough courage to say that he would be staying home for a while and would get in touch later.

She heard Helen's telephone click as she hung up. Jack turned to her.

'I think I heard the whistle blow.'

'I would say the score was even?'

'Want some extra time?'

'Only if you play by the rules.'

'Rules are made to be broken.'

'Only if I say so.'

He grabbed her wrist and she knew she had him back again. She closed her eyes and leaned her head against his chest so that she could feel the warmth of his body through his shirt.

Everything would return to normal, Jack would make the coffee and she would take Daisy for a walk. And, if that did not happen, then she would tighten the reigns, pull harder on the bit, keep the runaway beast under control. She would be the driving force in their marriage, not her husband who chased his youth.

'I just need a bit more time'. She thought she sounded like Jack.

A CARELESS VISIT

It WAS IN THE MIDDLE of a heat wave when Helen telephoned. Her first reaction was to hang up for she had little reason to listen to anything she might have to say.

'Don't hang up, Emy. I just want to ask you something.'

'What?'

'I'm clearing out the cottage and there are so many things of yours here. I thought you might want to have them.'

'Chuck it all away. I don't want anything.'

'Okay, but Jack lent Rob some of his tools when he was doing up this place. I'm sure he will want them back. They are expensive to replace.'

'Why didn't he pick them up on one of his freedom calls?'

'I guess he forgot, as I did.'

'Like hell,' she muttered. 'Right, okay, I'll tell him. Perhaps you can bring them if you are coming this way.'

'If he wants them he has to come and get them. I'm not his run around. I'm contemplating selling the cottage that's why I want to tidy it up.'

'I thought you had decided to keep it. What changed your mind?'

'Don't really know. Just thought I should get away from here.'

'Perhaps you need a new start, get away from the past,' she replied, sarcastically.

'Yes, that's just what I need,' Helen chuckled, as though amused.

She sighed, she did not want Jack to go alone neither did she did want to go with him.

'Tell you what, I'll pick them up. I'll be with you as soon as I can. Jack's gone to his mother. I'll leave him a note.'

'Okay, see you soon.'

'I'll just pop in and out, can't stay.'

'Fine, whatever you want.'

Helen was sitting on the porch when she arrived. 'Glad you could make it,' she said, sweetly. 'I've missed our weekends together.'

'Really,' she answered coldly, as she turned towards a box of tools in the corner of the room. 'I'll put them in the car.'

'No, later, there's no hurry. Come on, you've driven a long way. Let's sit outside and dabble our feet in the water one last time. I'll make some ice tea. For old times' sake. How about it?'

She hesitated, after all she did not really know if there was anything between she and Jack and she did not want to look like the jealous, suspicious, wife.

'Yes, why not. One last dabble in your haunted lake.'

'You go on down,' suggested Helen. 'I'll make the drinks, I won't be a minute.'

She slipped off her sandals and dangled her feet in the cold green water. It was a lovely day and just once in a while a small fish jumped and Daisy was in her element, sniffing and digging in the soft mud by the edge of the lake.

She turned to see Helen coming towards her with a tray of glasses and plates.

'I've got to finish the apple tart off,' she said, nodding her head towards the plates.

'Lovely, I'm feeling quite hungry.'

She actually didn't know what happened except that she was immersed in the cold lake. She spluttered and thrashed with her arms, gasping for air as she surfaced while, at the same time, aware Helen was tugging at her blouse. She was also aware of Daisy barking excitedly on the mooring followed by a splash.

When she came round, Jack was pushing down on her chest and Helen was patting her face and calling her. She knew she had been saved but was unable to say anything as sickly water slowly dribbled out of her mouth and down the side of her face.

Then, after what seemed a long time, they supported her between them as she stumbled to the house.

'What happened?' she asked, coughing as she spoke.

'You lost your balance,' Helen replied, quickly.

She turned to Jack. 'How did you get here?'

'You left me a note, don't you remember?'

'Oh, yes. Thank God I did.'

'Come on, I'll get you home,' Jack was saying.

'No, let her stay here. She can lie down for a while. We'll get her upstairs.'

She was aware of Helen and Jack discussing what to do until Helen won the argument and helped her upstairs and onto the bed in the spare room. A bed which she and Jack had shared so many times in the past. They were both incredibly concerned as Jack dried her with towels and Helen put on one of her T-shirts with 'Sweet Dreams' printed on it.

'Jack,' she said, after they had wrapped her loosely in cotton sheets. 'I don't feel right, I can hardly breathe.'

'I'll call the doctor if you don't feel better. Just wait until we get our wet clothes off.'

'I have a pain in my chest.'

'The local doctor is on holiday,' Helen informed her. 'If you don't feel better soon then we will have to take you to hospital. See how you feel later.'

'Jack,' she called, as they left the room but her voice did not seem to hold any volume and she knew she needed to get home.

She tried to get out of bed, to stand up, but she felt incredibly tired, unable to find the energy to call out or go downstairs to look for help.

And Daisy, where was Daisy? She tried to call her but once again her voice was faint, just as she was, faint.

Everything seemed to be against her even though she knew she was lucky to be alive, to be lying safely in bed, albeit a bed in Helen's cottage.

She passively watched the dust floating in the sunbeams like she did at home. Home, she thought, I don't think I'll ever see home again. She could feel herself slipping away as the pain in her chest worsened. She became conscious of everything becoming misty, lulling her into a sleep.

When she opened her eyes Jack was standing next to her bed again.

'It's okay darling, try to relax. You'll be alright.'

'No, I'm dying,' she whispered.

'Of course you're not. We saved you.' He turned around as he walked towards the door. 'Emy,' he whispered, softly, 'I've always known what happened. A push or a helping hand, who knows, I don't. I only know you were screaming mad and swiped out at me. I can remember a gull, but whatever happened, I deserved it.'

'Jack, I swear I didn't push you, a gull swooped and I went to grab your shirt but you stepped aside and slid. I thought you were dead. When I got back to the cottage, George and Pat were in the hall. I wasn't out of breath from running, I wasn't shouting for help, how could I calmly tell them you had just fallen down a cliff. So I made up a story which I couldn't take back anymore,' she coughed violently as she spoke, only managing a word one at a time.

'I know, don't worry. Don't talk anymore. Try to sleep, we are just going to have a coffee. I'll be back in a few minutes. It's okay. I believe you, that's why I've never mentioned it before. It will be alright. I'm home now. I'm sorry I put you through all of this. I'll be back in a minute, then we'll go home.'

The mist was clearing when Daisy ran up to her wagging her tail and barking excitedly. She ruffled her curly black hair.

'Come on, sweet girl. Let's go for a walk. Let's sit on the bench and wait for Will.'

THE INQUEST

The CORONER HEARD all the evidence, how Mrs. Nielson had been sitting on a small mooring with her feet in the water. How her friend, Mrs. Bennett had gone to fetch drinks and how Mrs. Nielson had stood up to help her with the tray and, at the same time, Mrs. Bennett tripped over Mrs. Nielson's dog. The tray flew out of Mrs. Bennett's hands and hit Mrs. Nielson on the head causing her to lose her balance and fall into the lake.

Mrs. Bennett had jumped in to help her but Mrs. Nielson had struggled wildly making it more difficult to rescue her.

Mr. Nielson had arrived just in time and together they brought his wife to the side of the lake. Both Mr. Nielson and Mrs. Bennett thought she seemed well enough to rest in Mrs. Bennett's cottage before returning home later.

Mr. Nielson had left his wife in bed sleeping. She was dead when he returned to check up on her.

A verdict was brought in of Accidental Death by Post Immersion Syndrome or Secondary Drowning.

The Coroner sympathised deeply with Mr. Nielson, who was devastated by his lack of medical knowledge, and praised Mrs. Bennett for rescuing her best friend.

A detective in the police force followed the case with interest. Perhaps it was his years of experience which made him feel something was not as it seemed.

Helen Bennett had obvious feelings for Nielson but he was unable to detect whether they were returned. She was a wealthy widow and, after some investigation, he found Nielson seemed to have had some kind of a mid-life crisis.

The Nielson's marriage had been shaky for some time and his daughters said their mother disliked Bennett intensely.

The story of a heavy tray knocking Emily Nielson into the lake seemed farfetched though there was a cut on her head which matched the side of the tray.

Nielson said he had been at his mother's Care Home some fifteen minutes drive from the family home. He had only stayed a few minutes since his mother was having a difficult day, she suffered from Alzheimer's, and the staff could confirm Nielson's short visit.

Nielson said he had returned home and found a note written by his wife on the kitchen table, telling him she had gone to Bennett's cottage to pick up tools which he had lent to Bennett's deceased husband.

The timing of his arrival at the cottage was more than fortuitous. In fact, one might say a miracle since he was just in time to help Bennett save his wife from drowning.

Nielson had told the Court how Helen Bennett had insisted his wife would fully recover and it would be a good idea if she were to rest for a while before driving home. He had taken her advice and had a sandwich with Bennett before checking on his wife again. She was dead when he found her. It appeared, according to Forensics, that the 'quick' sandwich was probably a little longer than was said. However, the cause of death was as found since there were no other extenuating circumstances.

The detective wondered why Nielson had not called a doctor or even gone to a hospital directly after the near drowning. It all seemed so unlikely that he had not done so.

He thought, perhaps, Nielson was a bit of a dreamer, unable to see the consequences of his actions. He knew there were people like that. He had come across them before. People who were unable to acknowledge a dangerous situation or even to act logically when faced with one.

He had to admit Nielson seemed broken by his wife's death and blamed himself for not taking her immediately to a doctor or hospital.

Daisy, the poodle was found drowned under the mooring. Bennett said the dog had jumped into the lake to be with Mrs. Nielson but she was too old to swim for long and eventually disappeared. She did not know the animal was dead until later.

It occurred to the detective that Emily Nielson's death was caused by careless neglect, perhaps even wilful neglect bordering on a criminal act. Perhaps an unexpected opportunity arose which they misused. He thought Bennett was capable of that though but he was unsure about the husband, unless he was under Bennett's influence.

He noted Bennett's husband and mother-in-law had recently died in and by the lake though it seemed Bennett had nothing whatsoever to do with their deaths. He wondered how she could bear to stay alone in the cottage after two members of her family and a close friend had died there within a very short period of time. Surely, he thought, that must say something about her.

One way or another, he felt that the case should not be closed. Somewhere, there was a loose end only he did not know where to look for it and he had no manpower and no budget to keep the case open. He threw the file down on a pile of 'Closed Cases'.

PART TWO

Leaves in the Tea

AN ANGRY YOUNG MAN

Michael MONTAGUE-LEE, for that was what he called himself, sat in a small nondescript car as he watched the people drift sadly out of the Coroner's Court, amongst them Sophie, Jillie and, of course, Jack.

He studied the three of them as they stood huddled together on the windy pavement. Helen joined them, nonchalantly nodding to both girls, while she stood closely against Jack and kissed him fully on the mouth. Then, she smoothed her now auburn hair, straightened her jacket and walked arrogantly towards a small Jaguar, clicked the key, and stepped elegantly into the car and drove away.

A feeling of excitement ran through him as he followed her through the heavy traffic. He felt alive, he was a man with a Cause.

He glanced at a paper bag on the seat next to him recalling how he had found a well-worn trunk in Monty's attic. He had sat back on his heels, almost gutted by surprise, as he pulled out an old police uniform, letters of recommendation, a police badge, an identity card and the jewel in the crown, a gun and a box of bullets; obviously the possessions of Monty's father who had been in the Hong Kong police force.

He had carefully picked up the gun, checked it was unloaded, and placed it in his pocket along with the box of bullets. After all, he could not look a gift horse in the mouth and it could even help him to settle two scores, both with Helen Bennett. The first being the humiliation of his mother years ago and the second Emy's unnecessary death. The first reason for revenge was debatable, but not the second.

His mother had not wanted to visit the Bennett's just after she and Monty had married but Monty had convinced her that she would enjoy meeting up with old acquaintances and, anyway, he was proud of her. He wanted to show them how happy he was with his new wife, his mother.

The visit had been disastrous for the 'Helen woman' had talked not only about the past but had even mentioned Jimmy Lee. He had seen tears in his mother's eyes and Monty had tried to cover up Helen's insinuations.

Eventually, he had borrowed a pair of swimming shorts from Rob Bennett and dived into the green water hoping it would help lessen his frustration. He had swum further out than he had intended and had casually kicked away the waterweed when it touched his legs, but each time its swaying tentacles returned as though determined to entrap him, pull him down into the dark water below.

He had panicked while those on the mooring ignored him, thinking he was having fun. In the end he had shouted for help. Monty and Rob had jumped into the boat and pulled him, ignominiously, out of the water. They had left soon afterwards and his mother had cried in the car going home. Monty had told her not to care, the Bennett's were nobodies and had nothing better to do than gossip. They would never see them again.

He had left the visit for what it was until Emy died. He missed her, she did not deserve to die. She had treated him as a son and cried with him over his losses, his hurts. Gradually, he had found himself the centre of her universe and enjoyed her excessive interest in him. He had never been so important to a woman before, not even his mother had lavished so much attention on him.

He recalled the afternoon when Emy had told him how Helen was obsessed with Jack and how he had continued seeing her, even though she had asked him not to.

'I'm married and looking for love,' she had whispered, sadly. He had held her tightly in his arms but she had, unwillingly, pulled back.

He questioned Emy's death, had she died because of Jack and Helen's abject carelessness or had they taken advantage of an opportunity? Whichever one, he decided Helen needed to be taught a lesson and he would do his best to teach her one, no matter how dangerous the outcome.

He thought of Jack. Jack the Peter Pan who had raced around on his motorbike while Emy waited for him at home. Jack a poodle, a wimp under Helen's control. Jack who had, most probably, screwed his mother when she was young and vulnerable. Helen the viper, the snake in the grass, Jack's loyal lover. He would deal with Jack later.

He turned his attention back to the small Jaguar which had now turned off in the direction of a village. He stopped in a picnic area and lit a cigarette. He knew exactly where Helen was going, he no longer needed to follow her but only to carefully consider how far he was prepared to go.

It would take another ten minutes to reach the cottage. He thought it unlikely anyone would be around, it was a lonely place and, at this time of year, it would soon be dark.

*

Helen was sitting at the kitchen table with a cup in her hand and reading the newspaper when he entered the back door. She looked up startled, then amazed.

'What do you want?' she asked, sharply.

'To see this place again. I have memories.'

She laughed nervously. 'From so long ago?'

'Memories don't always fade.'

'No, not always, but they can be inaccurate,' she added.

'I have some old scores to settle.'

'What old scores?'

'Hurting my mother for one. You let her die for two.'

'I can't remember hurting your mother and I've just come away from the Inquest. It was an accident, as simple as that.'

'Nothing is simple,' he answered, taking the gun from out of the paper bag.

'Are you mad?' she shouted, hysterically.

'Perhaps.'

'You won't get away with it,' she gasped.

'What do you think I am going to do?'

'You tell me.'

'I will. We are going to take a row on your lake,' he answered, smiling slightly. 'You know, I haven't seen it for so many years.'

'Why do you want to do that?'

'I want you to have an experience.'

'What experience?'

'To feel fear. Now walk,' he said, pointing the gun at her forehead.

She looked down.

'You aren't listening. I'll give you a fighting chance, otherwise you will die now.' He grabbed her arm. 'I mean it.'

The closing autumn evening was fresh and slightly misty as she walked down to the lake. She stood on the mooring for a second in the hope that someone may be taking their dog for a walk but, of course, it was deserted. There was no one in sight.

'Get in and row.'

'Where to?'

'The middle, of course, where else.'

She felt her hands perspire and swell from the effort of pulling the oars through the water while she tried to plan how she might be able to dive into the lake before he could shoot her.

Eventually, after what seemed ages, he told her to stop rowing. She looked up, searching his eyes for pity, for some kind of mercy, but there was none.

'Jump in,' he commanded. 'It's full of weed but you might be lucky and make it to the side, or maybe not. It will be your fate.'

'It will be yours when you get caught,' she answered, angrily. 'I'm a strong swimmer. I'll easily make it.'

'I hope you will. I'm giving you a chance which you didn't give Emily Nielson.'

'I saved her,' she shouted.

He leaned forward. 'Like hell you did. Know one thing, if you succeed don't go to the police because I will stir up Emy's death so badly you and Jack won't know what hit you. And a gun, what gun? Your word against mine. Now jump or I'll shoot.'

The soft slimy waterweed stroked her skin, slipped between her legs and curled around her arms. She could see his opaque form as she swam underwater, pushing the swaying weed aside with a breaststroke, and heard the lapping water against the side of the boat when she was forced to surface.

'Helen,' he shouted, pulling the trigger several times. 'The gun's not loaded.'

*

Michael Lee drove back to London that evening, went to bed early, and contemplated the afternoon and whether Helen had managed to reach the side of the lake. It was not his intention to actually cause her death but rather to let her feel panic as Emy must have done. Sooner or later, he would hear whether she was dead, alive or missing. He was, suddenly, overcome by the consequences of her going missing and the possibility of his DNA being found in the boat. Now he wished he had scuttled it.

He shrugged his shoulders, he could do nothing about it, and let his thoughts return to his youth when he and his mother were living a poor existence in Hong Kong.

He had just finished his final school exams and was looking for a job, or a cheap IT course, when his mother pulled the newspaper down, peered over the top, and told him not to bother.

He had looked up, irritated she had interrupted his search.

'We're going on holiday.'

'On holiday, where on holiday?'

'England.'

'Where in England?'

'The south coast. To Monty. He has invited us to stay for a month.'

'How come?'

'He found us, we found each other.'

Monty had met them at the airport and driven straight down to Devon. His mother had acted coyly, flirtatiously, as though she was on a first date. Within a very short time, they announced they were to marry. He could hardly believe it. He could understand his mother would have a good life, would no longer have to work, but the idea of leaving a bustling city for the extreme quiet of a small village by the sea, in Devon, was not what he was looking for. Not at seventeen, without his peers.

He had not been happy at the prospect of living in the back of beyond, no matter what its beauty. Monty had understood his misgivings and offered to find a college in, or around, London.

'You'll see, you'll settle down. Just give it time.'

He hadn't been so sure about that, he wasn't going to make any promises though he had realised he was tied down, thousands of miles away from home and without any money. He had felt frustrated for he had been trying to find his father, Jimmy Lee, a missing parent who shared a common surname with his mother. She had told him many times when he was a small boy how his father had let her down. It was only when he grew older did he realise what she meant. The old story, girl loves man, man is married. Nothing new about that, he thought.

He had tried to question his mother but she had remained secretive.

'Not now,' she would snap, dismissively, gesturing with her hand whenever he broached the subject.

'It's not over yet, Mum. I'll find him with or

without your help,' he shouted, innocently, ignorant of the truth.

Amazingly, Monty turned out to be all his mother had said. He bought the beach house which he and his eventual friends could use weekends and holidays. Of course, it was a 'win-win' situation, he free while the romantic couple enjoyed their privacy.

Looking back, she had actually been a good mother and even a good wife, but there was always something between she and Monty. Something he could not place until he recently discovered Monty was his father. The paternal culprit, if one could call him that, with Jack as a possible runner-up.

It seemed his mother's New Year's party had freed her inhibitions and he questioned whether she was a loose woman, which he had accused her of being, or a sad looser manipulated by opportunists.

For the first time, he felt sympathetic towards her and wished he had given her a chance to explain her difficult youth on that fateful Sunday afternoon. He did not want to think about it, he considered it a part of life. A part which had encouraged him to abandon the idea of looking for his father so he could keep Monty company, whenever possible. Monty had even stayed at his flat visiting art galleries and museums while he was at work. It was only when Sophie went down to Devon did he realise Monty was not as lonely as he had thought. His cultural visits to London had a purpose.

He was on the point of renewing his plans when suddenly Monty died of a heart attack. He could not believe it. Monty had seemed so relaxed, he was even planning to remarry.

Sophie had come and tearfully packed her possessions into boxes. She had hung onto him crying and he had rubbed her back and made her tea and said all the right things. They had kissed and promised to keep in touch. A few weeks later he had invited she and her family to the beach house where he had met her mother. Somehow, they had clicked and he had offered her the use of the beach house.

He had spoken to Sophie before leaving the country, she had been on his wish list and he reckoned she would need comforting, something he was very prepared to do, an act of kindness. However, she had not reacted as he had hoped. It did not worry him, he would take his time, sympathise, and eventually win her over. He mostly got what he wanted.

Two days later he flew to Hong Kong to find the man who was not his father.

A dark shape moved across the room, he dismissed it as a shadow from the branch of a tree for there was full moon that night and, after all, the curtains were not entirely drawn. He turned over and fell into a troubled sleep.

*

Emily Nielson stood at the end of his bed. She felt his hurt, his loyalty, his anger at her death. He had fortunately not killed Helen but rather not helped her to live, comparable to Helen who had been forced to save her then left her to die. She decided Michael Lee needed a new life, one which did not include Sophie, for this was a troubled young man.

An elderly Chinese man flashed before her and she somehow knew he would be the solution. She just had to arrange it.

*

Michael Lee had signed documents at the solicitor's office, a few weeks after his return from Hong Kong, then dropped in at 'The Cutter'. It was a popular little inn used mostly by casual visitors rather than actual holiday makers and decorated with seafaring objects; large sea shells and unusual pieces of timber found on the beach.

He planned to drive straight back to London and bypass the beach house which now frightened him. After all, Emy must have seen something otherwise she would never have known there had been a tragedy.

He turned his thoughts back to the difficult weeks after Monty's death, sorting out his personal possessions and checking the house was ready to be viewed by prospective buyers. Monty's cleaning lady had helped with the beds while he had emptied out the clothes cupboards.

He stopped, as though his mind slammed on a brake, as he visualised one of the guest rooms: two windows on either side of the dressing table, built-in closets, a chest of drawers, two bedside tables and a bed. A queen-size bed with two duvets. Both duvets had been turned down, the bed had been slept in.

He stared at his empty coffee cup as it dawned on him that the spare bedrooms were seldom used, if ever. Someone had slept in that bed, perhaps not 'one someone' but 'two someone's'. It had to be Emy, she was the last to visit. He could imagine Monty might have drunk too much and she had stayed the night. Knowing Monty's appreciation of good wine, he thought that was more than likely.

Of course, it was possible Emy had automatically turned down both duvets. He could hardly bring himself to believe that she had shared the bed with Monty while he was planning to marry her daughter.

Now, he felt irritated that he had not asked either of them about the two days they spent together. He felt a sense of jealousy, rather like a child standing in the corner of the playground while the others played together.

'Bizarre,' he muttered, aware he had also thought of both Sophie and Emy as future trophies. He wondered if Monty had the same kinky thoughts. 'Like father, like son', he muttered, smiling broadly, as he stood up to pay the bill.

HELEN

She USED A BREASTSTROKE as she swam, pushing the weed to the side. It was not difficult, she would win this battle and then she would report Michael Lee to the police and have him put behind bars where he belonged. She hoped he would eventually be deported.

'Lee' was rowing in the direction of the cottage when she looked back, she gave a sigh of relief as she concentrated on getting to the side of the lake.

Pictures of Emy formed in her mind. Pictures of her struggling; thrashing the water; Daisy paddling hopelessly around and she pushing the animal under until it became too tired to swim; Jack arriving, unexpectedly, and helping to keep Emy's head above water; his stupidity at being persuaded to leave his wife upstairs while they had lunch; the second glass of wine; the cheese and biscuits; the extra helping of pie. It was all so intimate until he began to fidget, wanted to check up on Emy. It had taken a lot of persuasion to keep him with her but, inevitably, he had gone upstairs. He had found her dead and shouted, blaming her for distracting him. It was her fault.

By the time the ambulance arrived he was crying, pathetically sobbing, which embarrassed her. She thought he was too upset seeing how they had experienced some 'personal' times together. Surely, he could see the positive side of Emy's death, to experience freedom just as she had done when Rob died.

She was exhausted when she crawled up the muddy bank and made her way back to the cottage. There was no sign of 'Lee' or his car and for the first time she was afraid of the loneliness, the isolation, she had become so used to. He had warned her not to go to the police to report their differences and, if she did, he would tell them about she and Jack. She really did not know what Emy had told him. It seemed the two of them had some kind of special friendship but she was not sure how special; whether Emy had confided in Lee; whether he knew enough to make the police suspicious of her death. She thought it was not worth the risk. She would have to think of some way to pay him back for humiliating her, to wipe the supercilious grin off his face. She would have to give it some thought.

She closed her eyes as she stood under the shower and let the hot water beat down on her as she imagined Jack stood close behind her, caressing her body, kissing her neck. She would be patient, wait a while, he would return to her. He just needed a little time to come to terms with what had happened. She would wait.

She drove home that evening, too insecure to stay in the cottage alone. She thought of Rob, something she tried not to do too often, and how they had met.

Her father had been sent to work in Hong Kong and she, without a steady boyfriend or a particularly interesting career, had accompanied her parents and joined the club. The club of young women who were looking for husbands, successful young men who could offer them a good life both out east and at home, in Europe. Rob had ticked all the boxes, overseas manager of a company which imported luxury goods, earned a good salary with an excellent bonus every year, pension scheme and above average home leave.

It was her mother who had pointed out Rob's financial advantages which had not been the reason for her enthusiasm, but rather she had revelled in making her girlfriends jealous of having such a suave beau, a seemingly sophisticated man of the world.

They had married quite quickly, actually within six months, which had surprised her and her parents, who seemed uneasy at the speed of their courtship. Her mother had openly asked her if she was pregnant and her father even seemed to have some kind of aversion to Rob himself.

Looking back, she realised how quick, rushed,

their first time together had been, as though it was something to get out of the way. She had imagined it would be something special, a something which would carry her into a realm of yet unknown delights. Instead, it had not been a something she would want to remember or even do again though, of course, there was always the possibility of being overtaken by a storm of passion, thunder and lightning. Instead, their spasmodic lovemaking remained a soft drizzle.

It had not taken long for her to realise she had been trapped for Rob needed to cover up his sexual inadequacy to the world at large. Marriage would keep women at bay and even men who might find his fine features, fair shortcut hair and slight build attractive. She was young, inexperienced, caught in an almost sexless marriage with a man who showed no inclination to alter the situation.

She had resigned herself to a life of useless coffee parties and afternoons at the swimming pool with spoilt, grizzling, children who were too young, hot and sticky, to appreciate their mothers' lifestyle.

She had despaired for the choice was either to accept it, or not.

The only person who seemed to guess there was a problem was Rob's best friend, Jack, who she found excruciatingly handsome. She had tried to get him on her side, into her bed, but he had remained loyal to his best friend, which she had found disappointing since he was the 'not' she was desperately seeking.

Then Jack had an open affair with a beautiful Chinese girl, called Jade, who had just broken up with her boyfriend. Jade had held a party and Jack had stayed the night, in fact many nights. He admitted to Rob that he had been careless. Rob was sympathetic and she was scathing. Then, to her relief Jade dropped Jack for another lover, at least he thought there was someone else, though he did not know who it was. Anyway, he had been happy to be let off the proverbial 'hook' and so was she.

She had been heartbroken when Jack was called back to London and it was only when Rob retired did they meet up again.

The depth of her jealousy had not surprised her when she heard Jack had married Emy, a divorcee with a daughter called Sophie and, years later, had another daughter with Jack, Jillie. Most probably Jillian.

Later, she thought it would not be too much of a problem to usurp Jack's new love; conquer him by whatever means necessary. She thought that possible once the icing was off the matrimonial cake.

DINNER WITH SOPHIE

Sophie AGREED SHE WOULD MEET him Saturday evening, so long as Peter looked after Tom. He had recently become obsessed with the idea of taking care of her and her offspring, just as Monty had done with him and his mother.

But now it occurred to him that he was already seventeen when he arrived in England and Monty had not been obliged to raise a small child, suffer toys and rubbish, messy eating habits, spilt chocolate milk, scratches on his shiny furniture and all the rest of it.

He shuddered at the thought of his gleaming minimalistic apartment being less than that, his highly polished floor, his white transparent curtains, his perfect kitchen, his bathroom with towels hanging exactly in line with each other, all at the mercy of a small boy. His life was orderly and he did not think he was able, or wanted, to change it. He realised how Monty must have thought and that he had probably inherited his fear of sticky fingered and runny nosed children from him. He shuddered again. He wanted Sophie but not her baggage, not some child from another marriage, not the hassle of an irritated father who was only interested in laying his latest girlfriend and paying the minimum alimentation for his increasingly expensive offspring.

He did not want another man's child and all the complications which went with it. He might, eventually, want his own child who would not have to share love and possessions with another sibling from another marriage. Actually, he did not even know if Sophie wanted another child, maybe her career was paramount in her life.

He decided to follow a more traditional plan; a romantic dinner, followed by a nightcap at his apartment and the ensuing night of love. Then he would drop her. He thought that would probably be the best for him, for her and her child.

*

Sophie looked tired when he picked her up on Saturday evening. She said she had worked late all week and was now paying someone to look after Tom. She could leave him with Jack in the school holidays if she, or Peter, was unable to take time off, but he was reluctant to have him for more than a couple of days at a time. He said he was trying to get his life together and did not want to look after children for too long. She had felt hurt and wanted to shout that he would do it for Jillie, if and when the occasion arose, but not for her. She wasn't his child and Jillie was. That made the difference.

He felt stunned, Sophie was saying just what he had been thinking. It was as though she was confirming his thoughts.

He had sympathised; told her how he understood her feelings; poured another glass of wine and continued to commiserated. After all, he had also been a stepchild. He knew all about it.

'I never thought of it like that, Monty spoke so kindly of you. It never occurred to me he ever saw you as anything else but his son and, in the end, you were his child. What a pity he never knew it.'

'My mother, Monty and Jack were all connected. Can you imagine a scandal, from around thirty five years ago, coming back to haunt you?'

'What do you mean?'

'You don't know?'

'Know what?'

'Jack could have been my father. It was a tossup between him and Monty. It seems Monty was the alpha male.'

Sophie stared across the table in amazement.

'Who told you that?'

'Your mother, she said Helen told her.'

'You mean Jack had an affair with your mother, Jade, all those years ago and Helen told my mother about it. What was the point of doing that, unless it was to hurt her.'

'Yes, Helen was a bitch to tell her. Monty told me he knew your mother and father in Hong Kong. What's his name?', he added.

'Guy Gaywood. Yes, Monty and my father worked in the same office.'

'Did they socialise?'

'I don't think so. As far as I know, they disliked each other at that time.'

'But not anymore?'

'No, seems not. Monty heard Guy was looking for a job for me. He knew of an opening and told my father. That was how I met him.'

But how did Monty know that?'

'I don't know, good question. Perhaps my father bumped into him. I have no idea.'

'Did you tell your mother?'

'No, not until later.'

'She must have felt left out.'

'It wasn't a secret, I just didn't tell her. It all went so pear shaped. I can't begin to tell you how guilty I feel.'

'Why should you feel guilty? If anyone is guilty then it's Helen and Jack. It was their fault your mother died.'

'Bloody Jack', she murmured.

'Did Monty ask your mother to visit him so that he could tell her about the two of you getting married?' he continued.

'Yes.'

'And did he?'

'No, he got cold feet and left it to me. I went down to see him, he had 'The Gull' in the water and we went sailing. I dropped in to tell Mum on the way back on the Sunday evening. She was pretty angry about it all, she found him too old. She reacted really badly, I knew she would but, in the end, she seemed to accept it. Though, knowing my mother, that doesn't say anything. That's why I asked Monty to tell her about us when I wasn't around.'

'And did she confront Monty after you had told her.'

'I don't know. It was all so quick. I suppose she could have 'phoned him.'

'Monty died the following Thursday only a few days later.'

'Am I supposed to make some kind of a sum from that. Are you suggesting something?'

'No, but she could have gone down to see him, maybe they had a fight and he dropped dead.'

'Oh come on. I don't believe that and you don't know that.'

'No, I don't know that, just throwing a few scenario's around.'

'Well don't,' she snapped, sounding upset.

'It really doesn't matter. It doesn't change anything.'

'I am wondering if you're right,' she muttered, thoughtfully. 'Maybe she did upset him and he had a heart attack.'

'Try not to think about it,' he said, kindly. 'It doesn't help to chew on things you can't prove.'

He looked at her lovingly as he placed his hand over hers, wondering if he had made the right decision. Maybe he would take her out for a while.

'Shall we go to my place for a nightcap?' he suggested, filling her wine glass and then leaning intimately towards her.

'Why not,' replied Sophie, thinking of Mike's inheritance and the easy life it offered her. 'By the way, you can't guess who 'phoned me the other day.'

'Who?'

'The bitch, Helen.'

'Is she still alive,' he joked. 'What did she want?'

'I don't really know. She just asked how we all were. Oh, yes, she went on to ask me your address. I told her I couldn't give her that before asking you, but in the end I gave her your telephone number. I would have hung up if I had known she had hurt my mother.'

'It's okay. I don't mind speaking to her. Maybe she has something interesting to say,' he answered, amused that Helen wanted to contact him. He considered it to be either a sign of weakness or she was planning something devious to repay him for his dangerous teasing at the lake. 'Come on, let's go,' he said, standing up and taking her chair.

'You have such nice manners, just like Monty,' she remarked, partly because it was true and partly because she thought it might be time to take his interest in her seriously.

*

She had not planned to go to bed with Mike but the wine had made her feel sexual. She wanted to be loved and make love. By the time they arrived at his apartment she felt the beginning of a bad headache, probably from the wine, and decided to take a shower in the hope it might lessen.

She felt guilty as she locked the bathroom door behind her. She wanted to be alone, to consider what she really wanted, for she still felt some loyalty towards Monty though she had come to realise that their age gap had been too much.

She remembered the numerous times she had left Tom with his father when she went down to Devon. In fact, Monty hardly ever saw her offspring. He had hinted that he had looked after Jade's son and perhaps that was enough. Once he had even said, 'give him to Peter', as though he was a dispensable pet. She had wanted to say that Mike was hardly a child when he arrived in the U.K. but she said nothing since it would have driven a wedge between them.

She had begun to accept that, most probably, her mother had been right. Monty's life style had paved the path of love. She tried to clear her thoughts, her memories of Monty, and consider whether it was wise to get involved with Mike.

She stood with her hands against the white tiles and let the hot water beat down on her neck and shoulders. She felt strangely overwhelmed by a sensation that there was something she should know, something she had forgotten, something in the past which she should recall. She thought again of her mother and felt as though she was her, that her mother had stood under a shower as she did now but she could not recall when, or where, that could have been. She felt herself overcome by a feeling that she must leave, not after sex with Mike, but now. She felt a panic which she had never experienced before, an urgency to get dressed and get out before reaching the point of no return. Get away from the past, Monty and now Michael Lee.

She dressed quickly and 'phoned Peter on her mobile.

'Can you pick me up?' she half whispered.

There was a pause. 'Where are you?'

'At Mike Lee's place. I want to leave but I don't have my car and I don't want him to drive me home. You know where he lives?'

'Yes, you banged on about his flat until I asked where it was. Remember?'

'No, I don't remember. Anyway, there's a little Chinese restaurant opposite his flat. I'll be there in ten minutes,' she answered, ignoring his comment.

'Be careful,' he said, suddenly sounding concerned. 'I don't like you walking over streets late at night. Wait downstairs in the lobby. I'll pick you up there.'

'Okay, don't be too long.'

She unlocked the bathroom door to find Mike standing behind it, obviously aware something was wrong. He looked at the mobile in her hand.

'Who are you calling?'

'Peter, I've asked him to pick me up. I don't feel well and you have drunk too much to drive.'

He looked at her coldly. 'You could have stayed here.'

'It's okay. I've arranged it.'

'Please yourself,' he answered, coldly, as he walked into the colourless lounge and played a cd.

He hardly turned his head when she opened the front door.

'Sorry, Mike,' she murmured.

'I couldn't care less,' he said, bitterly, as he turned the music up higher. 'Oh, by the way,' he added. 'I believe your mother slept with Monty when she was down there those two days. She was probably the cause of his death.'

'And what do you base that lie on?' she shouted, her voice breaking up with anger and hurt.

'A double bed in a guest room which had obviously been slept in. And, seeing how your mother was the last to visit, it could only have been her.'

'Liar,' she screamed, hysterically.

'She couldn't get enough of it, if you ask me.'

'You pathetic liar, you disgusting nerd. I hope you drop dead. I hope,' she screamed, hardly able to catch her breath, 'I hope you smash your bloody sports car with you in it.'

'And don't use the beach house again. I'm having the lock changed.'

'Get lost. Do what you want. I hope I never see you again.'

He called her a name under his breath when he later found the bathroom untidy and decided there was nothing deader than dead love. He had not meant to hurt her but she had rebuffed him and no one did that twice. There were plenty of others who would enjoy a night with him. Sophie had overstepped the mark, she had not even given him a chance to entice her, excite her. 'Serves her right,' he muttered.

He fell back into his white armchair and thought of his mother, how she had worked long hours for various families while he sat in the kitchen doing his homework and, more often than not, helping to prepare vegetables or do other menial chores. He had seen how she had scrimped and saved for tickets to go to the U.K., at least up until Monty had sent her a big fat cheque, so to speak.

It seemed she was eternally grateful and showed it by pampering him and keeping his perfect house perfect and her willingness to please him sexually. At least, that was what he supposed since, once in a while, he listened outside their bedroom door. It was something he was not particularly proud of doing but he had a need to know, to understand why he spoilt her.

He thought of Mia, Jimmy's granddaughter who he had met on his mission for truth. She was beautiful, fine, charming, well mannered. In fact, she became even more attractive with every passing day. He thought the time was nearing to visit Jimmy again and see what he had to offer and whether he could charm Mia out of the trees. He thought he could and if not her then another.

SECOND TIME AROUND

It WAS THE FIRST TIME SOPHIE had driven alone with Peter for what seemed ages. She could remember how she had fallen in love with him at college and how they motored around in his old Fiat Panda which was, rather like its place of origin, temperamental.

They had shared a cramped flat for some years after leaving college. She had become pregnant and expected Peter to tell her to do something about it but, perhaps because of his upbringing, he insisted they should marry. She had been elated, to marry your first love was almost unthinkable. All had gone well for some years, in fact their actual marriage had lasted nearly seven years, in keeping with the 'seven year itch.'

'How is Salome?', she asked, before they got to his flat.

'I've told you her name is Sallyann.'

'I always get it wrong.'

'You get a lot wrong.'

'For example?'
He did not answer.

The flat was warm and cosy, Sallyann was in Peter's dressing gown stirring a cup of hot chocolate and did not hide her surprise when Sophie entered.

'I thought Sophie could share Tom's bed.'

Sallyann did not react to his statement.

'No, that's okay. I'll pick up Tom now, if you'll take us home. Leave you two in peace,' Sophie suggested, to break the atmosphere.

'No, it's too late,' replied Peter, firmly.

'If she stays, I'm going,' snapped Sallyann, angrily.

'Do what you want, it's up to you.'

'I can go, no problem,' Sophie suggested, forcefully, not wanting to be in the middle of a fight.

Peter did not answer.

'Fine, I'm off. Luckily, I have my own car, I don't have to rely on my ex-husband to look after me,' Sallyann announced, as she walked into the bedroom and slammed the door.

'I had no intention of causing a scene,' she said, guiltily.

'It's okay. Don't worry about it.'

'This is what you want, isn't it?'

'To be honest, yes.'

'Am I being used?' she asked, wearily.

'No. We have to talk.'

'What about?'

'Us.'

'Us,' she repeated.

Sallyann came out of the bedroom with a large bag hanging over her shoulder. She gave her now ex-boyfriend a hard look.

'Good luck with the bitch,' she shouted, banging out of the front door.

'Actually, you phoned just at the right time.'

'To save you from something, something called Salome?'

He laughed lightly. 'Yes, you could say that. Listen, I know this might sound a bit lame but I miss you. Tom keeps asking me when am I coming home. You see, I want to go home.'

'So why did you leave?'

'You kicked me out, remember?'

'Yes, I remember very well, something called Tessa came between us.'

'I didn't want a divorce.'

'You didn't leave me too many options.'

'I made a mistake. You couldn't forgive me.'

'Did you expect me to. Why is it men think they must prove themselves, their sexual prowess.'

'And women don't? It didn't take long before you were in bed with that old man.'

'He was not an old man. He had charm, more than you ever had.'

'Come on, he was more than old enough to be your father.'

'Why should you care, what's it to you who I see or don't see. I don't see you acting like a monk.'

The lounge door opened. Tom stood in his pyjamas dangling a large plastic dinosaur by its tail.

'Can I sleep with you in your bed?' he asked innocently.

'You know, Tom, I think that's a really good idea. You can sleep between mummy and me.'

She turned, prepared to be angry, to contradict him, to ask him if he was mad. Did he really think she would slip into the bed where Salome had just been. He looked back at her and she could see a sign of despair in his eyes, a longing she had not seen for so long. She closed her eyes for a moment and tried to remember her feelings for the father of her child; their passion, her love, which had turned to anger with a tinge of hate. The idea that he still loved her and the acceptance that she had never stopped loving him. Michael Lee had tried to smash her trust in those she loved, had loved. And here was Peter offering renewal of old love. She loved him, she had never not loved him.

'I agree with daddy. Let's all cuddle up together like we used to do but first I want to change the sheets.'

He took her in his arms and she remembered how they had loved, his tenderness, his warmth. She felt a tear rolling down her cheek. She had lost him to some cheap pickup who had drawled down the back of his neck until he gave way. She could understand how it had happened, she had wanted to say it did not matter, but it did. Her pride had been irreparably damaged, so she had thought. He stepped back a little and saw the tear.

'Oh, Sophie, I never stopped loving you.'

'I know. We'll take it a step at a time but for the moment, I'm going to crawl into your bed with a small buffer between us.'

He smiled. 'Come on, Tom, we've got some sleeping to do. Some catching up to do.'

It was somewhere in the early morning hours when she woke up with a start. Michael Lee's remarks had hung on her, depressing her, she even thought she had dreamt about her mother and Monty's house but the dream evaded her. She stared up at the ceiling, it was then, suddenly, she remembered the last time she went to Monty's house to collect her belongings. She had walked past the spare bedroom and noticed both duvets were turned back as though the bed had been slept in. She had noticed it but not registered it, not questioned why. But Michael Lee had done the same only he had guessed, not known, just guessed.

Now, as she lay in the dark room with Tom squashed between she and Peter, she gasped at the idea of Monty and her mother sharing a bed when she was visiting. Surely, she thought, her mother had only vaguely known Monty all those years ago. It was hardly likely she would jump into bed with him. It was not possible that either of them would do that. It was just Mike's lousy conjecture, intention to hurt her.

She toyed with the idea of checking up on the two days her mother spent with Monty but dismissed the thought. She had no desire to do so. That would be a step too far, though she realised how much of her mother was in her, fifty percent, and her curiosity was part of that fifty percent. She riled at the thought of inheriting her mother's genes. The genes which made her mother so irritating.

No, she did not want to be like her mother but she feared she was.

She glanced over to Peter.

'Can't you sleep?' he whispered.

'No, I'm thinking.'

'What about?'

'Nothing important.'

He reached across and stroked her auburn hair. 'You are so beautiful, Sophie. Please give me another chance. I am so sorry.'

She turned her head. 'You know what I like about you?'

'No, what?'

'Being able to say sorry. So few people can do that. They see it as weakness, I see it as strength.'

A MULTIPLE OF LOVE

Helen TELEPHONED MICHAEL LEE a few days later. He was amazed at her friendliness and asked her directly what was the name of her game. She had laughed and said she was sorry that he felt she had purposely let Emy die. How could she know anything about secondary drowning. She was alright when she and Jack left her in bed. It had been a terrible tragedy and she hoped he would see it that way. Perhaps they could meet and have a drink together. She would try to convince him that she had been lonely after Rob had died and had known Jack way back in Hong Kong when he and Rob were still bachelors. Perhaps, she could persuade him to see her in a different light. She could tell him about the old days when everyone knew his mother as a beautiful young woman, hardly more than a girl, and desperately in love with Jimmy.

He had, in turn, apologised for his behaviour at the lake. He said he had watched her swimming, he would never have let her drown.

She silently mouthed 'liar' as he talked on.

It seemed to him that she accepted his apology and they agreed to meet at a small Bistro near Hampstead Heath. She would book the table.

He snapped his mobile closed and laid back, enjoying the various scenario's which might take place. He liked the idea of an older woman, unprotected sex; no surprise pregnancies; her character formed; no need to grow towards each other; the give and take costing years only to realise that one of them always took more than the other. He thought mostly the woman wanted to change the man, first get married and then to work.

'The Changlings,' he muttered, to himself. No, he definitely did not fall into that category. If anyone had to change it would be the woman, she the weaker sex, subservient, would have to please him. He didn't think he needed to change the status quo by adapting to some woman's idea of Mr. Perfect.

Yes, he thought, he might string Helen along for a while. They might even find some common ground, above and beyond their intense dislike of each other.

*

She lit a cigarette and smiled broadly, amazed how easy it had been to arrange a date with Mike, which made her wonder whether she should be even more careful than she had planned to be. She decided they were similar, both capable of committing bad deeds, after all he had been willing to leave her to drown as she had Emy. It took one to know one.

In fact, it was almost funny, he clicking an unloaded gun while she swam to the side of the lake. It would certainly have been poetic justice had she drowned. Now she had to decide how to pay him back, financially would be too difficult though she would love to clean him out. Perhaps, she could seduce him and drop him just when he thought she was in love with him. She thought that sounded juvenile, rather like a teenager plotting a vendetta in her bedroom between her discarded soft toys and Barbie dolls. However, she could not think of anything better.

*

She met Mike as planned. He ordered oysters and she reminded him of how they were an aphrodisiac and purposely let the juice roll slightly down the side of her mouth. He had taken his napkin and gently dabbed the careless dribble and she had smiled, the kind of smile which spoke the unsaid word. He reacted magnificently and they spent the next two hours eating and drinking too much good wine until it was time to leave. They had taken a taxi to her apartment and fallen on the crisp white sheets and made love as though their hunger had not been satisfied.

'I did not mean this to happen,' she lied.

'I did,' he replied, smiling the smile she had hated. 'Is Jack out of the picture?' he asked, as she laid back smoking a cigarette, something he did not approve of but let it go as part of the evening's entertainment, enjoyment.

'Yes, I guess so.'

'Does that bother you?'

'Not anymore,' she laughed, softly, as she turned and kissed his firm young body.

'That's okay then,' he replied, kissing her breasts in return.

He smiled to himself as he pictured her as a sophisticated woman in the nineteen thirties, dressed in a slivery evening gown with an extremely deep cleavage and cut to the waistline at the back; a slender creature with a cigarette holder in one hand and a glass of champagne in the other.

He thought of the woman who had married a 'would-be' king, she must have had something about her. It was not her body, so what was it? He compared Helen to her as he passed his hand over her sparse breasts again.

'More than a handful is a waste', he thought, and he wondered if the Duke had thought the same about his Duchess.

*

Months later, she stood on the mooring staring across the still water. It was a place which held secrets, it had dominated her life, her emotions, her love for Jack. She sighed as she remembered her feelings when she watched divers search for Rob under the melting ice and how Rob's mother had been found between the frozen reeds. Of course, she should have protected her but she really could not see the point of saving an old lady who would grieve for the rest of her life. After all, you put an animal down if it is in constant pain.

She thought of Emy who had died in some wondrous way, not the way she had planned. The cost had been high, indecently high. It had brought only unhappiness and driven Jack away. She tried to convince herself that she was not responsible for anyone's death. She had not killed anyone, rather not helped to avoid their deaths, but not more than that.

She even wondered if the lake would be the death of her as she watched the green water slowly turn black as the sun set.

She sighed again, she seemed to sigh a great deal nowadays, what was the good of all this sentimentality. Jack had cheated on his wife and now he boo-hoo'ed. She thought he should face facts, Emy and Rob were dead and they were alive.

Luckily, Mike was in her life, which somewhat boosted her now low morale, lunching on a regular basis, a show in town or a film. She felt as though she was young again, being wooed for the first time though she was unsure whether she was enamoured because he made her feel special; attentive to her mood; the single red rose left on her pillow; the special handmade chocolates or the expensive perfume. She loved romance, in fact, she found it more important than the act itself for without romance sex was just another enjoyable pastime. Romance, she thought, took it a step further but she wondered how long she could keep him before he became tired of her, before some beautiful young girl crossed his path, though up until now he seemed quite happy with their arrangement. She could not understand how she could return his passion after she had secretly loved Jack so much, for so many years.

A love she would have died for, even killed for, and she wondered if she would feel the same about Mike. Would she die of love for him, she thought not.

*

It was when her cold would not clear up, when her cough seemed almost chronic, when her weight loss was becoming unattractive, when her tiredness was beyond normal, did she go to the doctor.

He had given her a full examination and, finally, suggested she should go to hospital for immediate blood tests. He had looked at her sympathetically, as though to prepare her for some dreadful result. She had known, instinctively known, that something was wrong and her thoughts jumped to every possible terminal illness.

'I'll phone you when I get the results. It might take a little longer than usual because I want to do a whole range of tests.'

She had agreed to wait for his call and meanwhile she was get a lot of rest and not to have any sexual contact until she had heard from him.

Her mind raced to cancer of the cervix or the womb. She could hardly believe what he was saying, surely he was only doing extra tests to be sure.

'Oh, God,' she murmured. 'I don't want to land

up middle aged and sick, I'm not ready for that, I'm not ready to be ill. I'm not ready to die. I'm not ready to die unloved.'

Mike phoned her a few days later, he had not contacted her earlier and she had not cared.

'Listen,' he said, sounding apologetic, 'I have to go to Hong Kong.'

'Again? You've only just got back.'

'Yes, I know, but I want to make a safe investment. Jimmy Lee has a couple of good leads. I'll phone when I get back.'

'Fine,' she replied, sounding as depressed as she felt.

It was over a week before she sat opposite this serious looking doctor who seemed to avoid eye contact as he studied the papers in front of him. Eventually, he glanced up at her and then back down again to the papers.

'I'm afraid you have HIV. Try not to worry,' he quickly added. 'There are new medicines, it's not like it was before. It's not life threatening anymore. You can lead a normal life. Have you any idea who may have passed it on to you?'

'No,' she gasped. 'Though it could have been my husband. He died recently. I always suspected something was not quite right but I was never sure.'

'Well, any partners you've had will have to be told and tested,' he added.

'Yes, of course,' she agreed, hardly listening to anything more he had to say.

She drove home in a daze, her mind racing as she tried to recall anything which might give her some clue as to who carried the illness, Rob, Jack or even Mike. There would be hell to pay, whoever it was.

She grimaced, if she sought to revenge Mike, then revenge she had. But Jack was now involved, that she felt would be the ultimate tragedy unless, of course, he was the one infected. And as for herself, well the joke was also on her.

*

She had never heard Jack so angry. He had shouted that Emy was bloody right, he should have listened to her. Everything which had happened was her fault, not his, and now this. He would like to wring her neck.

'I have to know if you are infected,' she added, quickly, aware their conversation was going to be short and sharp. He slammed down the telephone.

Well, she thought, that's the first, now Mike.

She knew she could reach him on his mobile but she had no desire to be screamed at again. She decided to send an email and hoped he regularly opened up his laptop. She sighed as she typed a small message.

'Mike, Something rather terrible has happened, please phone me immediately. It is very important you do so. Please take this mail seriously. Helen.

She waited for a minute before hitting the 'send' button, sat back and waited for the next round of insults. Strange that, she thought, why should I get the blame. One of them gave it to me. One of them should be shouting at the other, not at me.

Mike returned her email. He had no time to 'phone at the moment.

She mailed back to say the only reason why she contacted him was tell him he needed to be tested for HIV. His health was his problem. She had warned him and, as far as she was concerned, she need do no more.

He sounded hysterical when he 'phoned her.

'I want to know who you've been with.'

'And I want to know who you've been with,' she shouted back.

'I'm asking you, bitch.'

'You know who I've been with. You for one.'

There was a silence.

'Are you there?' she asked, angrily.

'Yes.'

'And?'

'How do you know this?'

'How do you think I know? A doctor told me, how else would I know.'

'Why did you go to one?'

'Why do you think? I felt unwell. You have to get tested quickly.

'I'll look into it.'

'Do that,' she screamed, slamming down the receiver.

*

The hurt and insults hit her hard, first Jack and now Mike. They both blamed her, she was the common denominator, she was to blame. Neither of them commiserated with her situation, neither of them thought passed themselves. She hated them, she hated men.

She stared at the row of bottles on the kitchen table, barely able to believe that this was to be her life. Pills and yet more pills, visits to doctors and blood tests.

*

She opened the front door to Jack a few days later. He brushed her aside, waving an envelope.

'I don't have it, it's not me,' he shouted. 'Thank God I've not been with you for months. So who is it, who the hell have you been sleeping with?'

'What I do is my business. Aren't you overlooking the obvious?'

'What obvious?'

'Rob.'

'Rob,' he repeated, as though amazed at such a plausible suggestion.

'Come on, Jack. You know as well as I do that Rob wasn't interested. I've always wondered if he was on two sides.'

'He wasn't homosexual.'

'How do you know that? Come in, I have to sit down. I'm worn out. I don't know what to do, we can just as well hate each other sitting down.'

'I know,' Jack almost spat out, as he followed her into the lounge, 'because he told me something he never told anyone else, that's why I understood him. He relied on me and I tried to be there for him.'

'What something?'

'I promised not to tell anyone,' he said, as he flopped down in Rob's chair.

'I'm not bloody anyone.'

'I need a whisky, with ice,' he stated, as though incapable of proceeding without one.

She grudgingly fetched his drink feeling like a servant to a man she suddenly disliked. She was surprised at her feelings, how could she ever dislike Jack. She adored him, he was her reason for living. She could and would not stop loving him, she would reject any hidden anger.

'And you were saying?'

Jack swirled the whisky and ice around in the glass before he took a mouthful. He let it linger for a few seconds, as if he was a connoisseur, before finally swallowing it.

'For God's sake, get on with it, don't be so childish. Say it as it is,' she shouted, bitterly.

'He was sent to a boarding school because his father thought he was becoming a mummy's boy and needed toughening up. Well, that's not what happened. He was raped on a regular basis by some senior bag of shit.'

'Oh, no,' she gasped.

'It broke him. His schooling became a disaster and, in desperation, he was brought home and sent to a local private school where Charles was teaching. I don't know if his father guessed what happened. His mother certainly didn't know. Anyway, he got through his education but the experience ruined his life. He never recovered.

'But why did he tell you?'

'I don't know, maybe he needed to confide in someone.'

'More likely he was giving you a hint.'

'Rubbish, he wanted a normal married life but he just couldn't get it together.'

'And me, what about me?' she screamed. 'Did he marry me in the hope he could learn to screw?'

She could feel herself gasping for breath and for a second she saw Emy on the bed doing the same. Gasping for air, for life.

She ran to the bathroom and threw up over the toilet.

She heard Jack behind her.

'I'm sorry,' he said. 'You wanted to know. I never wanted to tell you. I promised Rob I would never tell anyone. It was not Rob who gave you HIV, it's not me. So who the hell is it?'

'It's not your business,' she gulped, as she rinsed water through her mouth. 'You still can't be sure whether Rob found solace with another man.'

'I'm one hundred and one percent sure Rob never looked at another man. He leaned on me, he looked to me for support, he did nothing without telling me,' he half sobbed with emotion.

'And you found that normal. Poor Emy.'

'Poor Emy,' he shouted, angrily. 'What a pity you didn't think of that sooner.'

'Yes, what a pity,' she screamed back 'You were not Rob's friend, you were his crutch. You held him back. You helped him to ruin my life.'

She was aware of a stinging pain as he hit her across her face.

'I'm sorry, I'm sorry,' he stuttered, his voice choking back yet more emotion.

She knew she was out of control when she beat him with her fists, tore at his shirt and scratched his face. She also knew their relationship was irrecoverably broken. He would go, never love her again. She felt tears streaming down her face though she was not aware of crying and her body shook as she semi collapsed, hoping he would catch her, hoping he would comfort her.

She heard herself give a pitiful cry, like an animal that had lost its mate, an animal in pain, but still he made no movement towards her.

'Get out, get out,' she screamed. 'It was all for nothing, nothing.'

There was a dreadful silence as he slowly turned around. 'What do you mean by that, all for nothing?'

'I don't mean anything.'

He grasped her arm tightly. 'When I arrived Emy was nowhere near to the mooring. How could she have been so far away?'

'How should I know? She splashed around. How should I know?'

'She was where she was because you pushed her there. You weren't saving Emy, you were helping her to drown.'

He pinned her against the wall. 'What did you do, what the bloody hell did you do?'

'She fell into the water, I tried to help her.'

'You're lying. How could you, how could you. I loved her,' he choked, as he released his grip. He trembled as he leaned against the door frame. 'How could you,' he cried, as he sank down onto his knees.

'Please believe me. I would never have done that. I would never have hurt her.'

She watched him from her lounge window as he walked, stooped, across the road and out of sight.

'What about me?', she cried, unable to absorb the misery of a man who realised he had made love to a woman who was prepared to go to any lengths and the terrible consequences of her obsession.

She fell back into a chair and wept at the deceit of Rob and the naivety of Jack, aware of the thin line between love and hate, for now she hated Jack as she had hated no one else. 'If Rob had only told me, I could have loved him,' she whispered. 'He had only to tell me, we could have worked things out. All that for nothing. All the years of blaming myself and then despising him, for nothing. What a waste, what a waste of our lives.'

She sat down at Rob's desk that evening and gently swivelled the well worn leather office chair as she turned over Jack's account of Rob's childhood trauma. Rob had confided in Jack which did not surprise her for she had always viewed them as being secretive, only she could never have guessed why.

Her attention was pulled to a narrow drawer in the middle of the desk where Rob had kept his mobile. She had cast it aside since it was too large and out of date to match her now rather chic wardrobe. She plugged it into a socket in the kitchen while she reluctantly made something to eat.

She considered food a necessity, no more than that.

An advertisement on the television reminded her of the now charged mobile. She really did not expect to find anything very interesting when she searched through it. However, there was just one number she could not place in the address book. A number without a name. She pressed the call button. Sam Somerford answered.

'Who is calling?' he asked, sounding surprised and perhaps concerned.

She quickly closed the mobile, both amazed and curious. He was Rob's financial advisor and she had visited his office, just once, to sell Rob's shares.

She had never met him before then, only knew of him. He had turned out to be a rather thin, sallow, looking man, his mousey brown hair streaked with grey, his forehead deeply lined above his almost invisible eyebrows. He had kept his light brown eyes cast down as he fumbled through Rob's portfolio.

'Sell it all. Lock, stock and barrel,' she had instructed him, firmly shutting the door to any suggestions he might have to the contrary.

'If that's what you want,' he had replied, sounding indifferent.

She told him how she liked to see her assets printed on a bank statement, preferably with a row of noughts. Not bits of paper informing her of the price of some commodity, or product, which could vary almost by the minute and which could burst like a bubble at the push of a button on some investment banker's computer.

She had left his office feeling strangely dissatisfied. He had noted her instructions and then shown her the door as though he had ended a job interview. He had avoided direct eye contact; had not tried to persuade her to keep at least some of Rob's shares; had kept their conversation short; not offered her tea or coffee; not asked her how she was managing or written down her new address without commenting on how she lived in a nice area. In fact, she was out of his office almost before she had crossed her legs. She did not like him.

She had thought of Belle as she drove home in a taxi, a miserly old woman not like her husband, Charles, who was generous and rewarded her after their discreet holiday frolics. She was unsure whether Rob knew about his mother's hidden fortune, she thought not for he often slipped her small amounts of money.

'Buy yourself something nice,' he would say fondly.

'You scheming old bag,' she mumbled, remembering how Belle had let her house become dilapidated, refusing to have a home help or a gardener. Constantly complaining about being cold while she kept the thermostats on the radiators low. She was not sorry she had died and was happy she had been so 'careful' since it had gone towards an exclusive apartment near Hampstead Heath.

Now, she wondered if Somerford would return her call. She thought he might need some time to weigh up the pro's and con's, after all careful judgement was his business.

Fifteen minutes later the 'phone rang.

'I believe you've just called me, Mrs. Bennett, can I help you?'

'Yes, perhaps you can. I would like to see you. I was looking through Rob's papers again. I've been thinking, perhaps I should buy back some of the shares I sold after he died. That is, if they've dropped in price since then.'

There was a silence before he answered.

'Yes, would you like to come to the office next Wednesday? I believe that is a quiet day. Actually, perhaps we could have lunch together.'

A gut feeling ran through her as she hung up, he was far too friendly.

*

It was a cold miserable day when she met Somerford in a restaurant off Baker Street. He stood up as the waiter showed her to the table and gave her a firm handshake.

'So, have you any ideas on what you would like to invest in?' he asked, after ordering drinks.

'No, you're the expert. Actually, I am more interested in your friendship with my husband. Rob told me you went to school together,' she bluffed, since she could not really remember any details.

He sat back in his chair and turned a knife over several times before answering.

'I suppose this is the real reason for your visit. What do you want to know?' he asked, sounding resigned.

'I believe my husband had a medical problem. I would be grateful for your help. I'm not well.'

'I'm sorry to hear that,' he replied, looking at her directly. 'I thought he had told you.'

'When did he know?'

'After I found out I was infected.'

'And that was?'

'Over two years ago.'

'So long ago and he didn't tell me.'

'Yes, that was very remiss of him.'

'Remiss! I would say bloody criminal. How did it happen?'

'I went to South Africa some years before. I had an affair. I didn't know I was infected. I'm sorry.'

'And what did Rob say. That's alright, old chap, I understand. I just happen to be married and have probably passed it on to my unsuspecting wife.'

He put his hand over hers sympathetically.

'But why didn't my doctor tell me, why didn't he say anything?' she continued, trying to control her anger.

'Because he went to a Clinic. They told him to go to his doctor. I guess he didn't go. I guess he didn't feel ill and he hoped you hadn't been infected.'

'And if I had a friend?'

He smiled at her, whimsically. 'I don't think he considered that an option.'

Her anger rose at his subtlety, his insinuation that she was too old or unattractive to be loved by another. She controlled her emotions, not wanting to dignify his remark with a response.

He lowered his voice as he continued. 'We broke up when he found out I'd had an affair. I carried on with his finances but that was all.'

'I believe you were at boarding school together.'

'Yes, but we didn't meet again until Rob returned from the far east.'

'Why did he leave school?'

'He was expelled, we both were.'

'Why?'

'We experimented. Boys do that, sometimes, you know.'

'No, I don't know. Perhaps you would like to enlighten me.'

He sighed and grimaced at the same time as he straightened the cutlery on the bright red table cloth.

'We were born like that. It is not a choice. Rob married you truly hoping he could turn it around. I accepted how I was. You must have known. I always expected you to divorce, you must have loved him very much not to have done so.'

'I must have missed the telltale signs,' she snapped, bitterly, now appalled at the idea of Rob being attracted to this rather unappealing man.

She hated Rob now, more than she could ever have imagined. She felt she must have been aware that perhaps he had a dual sexuality but she had not wanted to know, not to have it definitely confirmed. Only once, when she was young, did she have him followed for a few weeks, but it had been an expensive business and she had given up. Perhaps the detective had followed him precisely the wrong weeks, perhaps he was not actively involved with other men at the time.

'Was it only you or were there others?' she continued, almost politely.

'As far as I know, only me.'

He put his hand over hers. 'Let's go to my place, it's not too far from here. I'll get a taxi, we need to talk privately.'

Her instinct was to walk away, to get up and go, but she wanted to hear more. She wanted to hear it all.

Sam Somerford lived in an expensive block of flats boasting a doorman and a thick carpeted elevator with mirrored walls.

The decor in his luxury apartment was carefully chosen with just a few ceramics and a couple of very modern pictures. It surprised her because to look at him one would think he was just an ordinary, nondescript, kind of man. A man with no particular aesthetic talent for design.

'How are you?' he asked, as though she had a simple cold or headache.

'How do you think I am. Frantic, desperate. Frantically desperate.'

He did not answer as he walked into a shiny white kitchen and opened a large refrigerator.

'Wine?'

'No,' she answered, shortly, for she did not think he deserved any unnecessary courtesy. He was the enemy who had infected Rob and perhaps, through her, Mike. 'I heard Rob was raped by some senior bum at school. I suppose that's also a lie.'

'Yes, it is.'

'But his father knew the truth?'

'Yes, both our fathers were called to a meeting with the headmaster. Rob's mother was not there, it seems his father thought it unnecessary and my mother was away on holiday.'

'Did his mother ever know the truth?'

'No, she would have been devastated. They simply told her he was unhappy at school. It was because of her he lived the lie. I am really sorry this has happened, that you have it.'

'You talk of 'it' why can't you just say the word out loud. Say it for what it is, HIV.'

'If that makes you feel better.'

'Do you have any idea of what you have done?'

'Of course, I would be a moron not to understand the consequences. What can I say to make it different, to help you. I've tried to be honest. I hope you will take that into consideration.'

'Yes, I'll give you that much.'

'How did you know about Rob and me?'

'I didn't, there was a telephone number without a name and you didn't come to his funeral. I bluffed. I knew he had known you at school and his friend, Jack Nielson, told me some story of how he was raped. I just put two and two together. I would not have known if you hadn't told me. Thanks for that, if nothing else.'

She got up to leave and turned as she opened the front door.

'I hope you feel guilty for the rest of your life.'

'Don't worry, I'm sure I will. What about the new investments,' he added, almost hopefully.

She gave a hard, pretentious, laugh. 'Over my dead body.'

He smiled, almost kindly. 'Over our dead bodies, darling.'

She emailed Jack when she got home. She thought it would do him good to know Rob, his confidant, his best friend, had lied to him for years. Had it never occurred to him that Rob's arm around his shoulder and his constant admiration were perhaps exaggerated. Perhaps there had been a touch of homosexuality about it. Had he really not noticed that. Had he been selectively blind to protect Rob's fine feelings, had that been more important than reality, her reality.

She went on to call him names and hoped he had a conscience. He had helped Rob to mislead everyone and, most importantly, her. As far as she was concerned, she would see them in hell.

*

She fell into bed that night aware there was something she had to line-up, something she must focus on.

Rob had homosexual tendencies at a young age and his father knew of it. Therefore, their marriage must have come as a surprise to Charles. Either Rob had passed through a difficult stage in his young life or he had used her as a cover-up. Charles would have known, he would have been able to recognise the signs. Why then did he have his 'holiday flings' with her. Was it 'kinky' to sleep with his son's wife; was he sympathetic to her needs; did he take what he could get whenever, wherever, he could get it?

She sat up and turned the light on as she remembered Charles had always taken precautions. Perhaps he could never be sure of Rob's preferences and she could be a carrier of goodness knows what illness.

She fell back on the pillow, hurt and disillusioned.

"Is nothing as it seems,' she sobbed.

*

It was some weeks before she heard from Mike. He emailed her saying he wanted to see her. He did not mention an HIV test and a sickening feeling overwhelmed her for his message was not friendly, not that she had expected it to be. She did not reply to his mail, she thought it purposeless to do so. It would not change anything.

'I could kill you, you stupid bitch.' His voice sounded cracked and sharp on her mobile. 'I want to see you.'

'Why, what good will it do? If you are positive then I am sorry. Believe you me I am sorry and I am also sorry for myself.'

'I don't have the final results yet. I have to be free of you for a bit longer. You've had a life, mine is just beginning. It's not worth anything if I'm infected.'

'That's not entirely true. You aren't the only one, there are tens of thousands of people in the same boat. You can still have a reasonably good life, meet someone, even if you're positive.'

'I did meet someone, that's the problem. Do you see what you've done. Ruined peoples' lives.'

'Are you coming here, or not?'

'Are you willing to take the risk that I might shoot you.'

'I'll take the risk, what have I to lose.'

She clenched her jaw as she closed her mobile, burdened with guilt. How could she help him when she could not help herself. She even thought Mike would do her a favour if he put her out of her misery. It was true, she had lived her life, lived it badly.

It seemed to her that everyone she had loved now hated her and Rob, who she had learnt not to love, had cheated on her. Not once, but her entire married life. She felt a despair which she had felt only once before. A heart breaking despair which she tried not to recall.

She opened the glass doors of a cabinet displaying her special pieces. She wondered why she had collected valued items, items which did not add to the value of life.

'Everyone knows you can't take them with you, so why bother in the first place. What do I need them for, I never use them. I'm alone,' she sobbed, pitifully, as she carefully lifted a fine porcelain teapot, cup and saucer from out of the cupboard. She decided, as she walked to the kitchen, that she would use everything she owned, enjoy everything she possessed, and when they became boring she would sell them. All of them. And if they became damaged, then so what. Possessions were no longer important and she almost felt a sense of relief, a sense of freedom.

She found a packet of loose tea in the kitchen cupboard, then boiled a kettle of water, warmed the teapot as her mother had instructed her, and spooned the tea carefully into the pot. She was so careful, so precise, she felt as though she was performing an ancient tea ritual. Eventually, she poured the honey coloured tea into the cup and stared at the leaves floating on the surface.

'Things always get in the way,' she murmured, as she carefully spooned them out and added the milk. 'That's love, it never stays clear for long. Something always comes along to make it murky.'

Mike arrived late as though staying the execution. There was no warm welcome only a bitter confrontation.

He pushed past her just as Jack had done, his face white with anger.

'Well,' he shouted. 'What have you to say for yourself. Who else did you sleep with apart from Jack?'

'My husband.'

'Other than him,' he shouted.

'Just Rob. What do you think of that. I am not the slut you would have me be. I found the culprit, Rob's old school buddy who had an affair in South Africa. It seems he was infected for years without knowing. Rob caught it. End of story.'

'Was Rob gay?' he asked, in disbelief.

'Seems so. I had my suspicions but I was never really sure. He covered it up well, I didn't realise he was on both sides. In the end I just thought his sex drive was limited, that maybe he was born like that. I thought he might have taken after his mother. His father told me she was cold.'

'I've been with Jimmy Lee's granddaughter, Mia.'

'Congratulations,' she snapped.

'Well, you must have known we would not go on forever. You're old enough to be my mother.'

'Thanks for that, Mike. I didn't notice you worrying about it.'

'I didn't say I worried about it, I am just stating a fact.'

'So, what about this new love in your life?'

He looked away.

'Did you take precautions?'

'No, she said she was on the pill.'

'Does she know?'

'I haven't told her yet.'

'You mean you left her, without saying anything?'

'I had to. I can't be around if she is positive.'

'Why not?'

'What do you think her family will do to me?'

She felt suddenly sorry for him. 'Try not to

worry, from what I've read the chances of picking it up are quite small. Not everybody gets it. There's more than a good chance neither of you are infected.'

She noticed how she called HIV 'it', just like Sam Somerford. She felt almost sorry for Sam, of course he felt bad just as she did now.

'So what's next?'

'Nothing, I have to be free of you for some time before I can be finally tested. I can't go back,' he added. 'Whether she has caught it or not, I can't go back. God help me if she has it.'

He walked to her refrigerator and poured himself a large glass of wine.

'I'll be in big trouble if her family find out. They will go ballistic, they will probably have me killed.'

They sat until late, drinking and talking until Mike lay along the sofa completely drunk. She kissed his forehead and he stirred a little as she covered him with a blanket.

'I still love you, Mike,' she whispered. 'I don't suppose you will ever forgive me.'

JIMMY LEE

Jimmy LEE WAS ALMOST AWAKE when he vaguely thought of Michael Lee, unfortunately not his son. His wife had given him four beautiful daughters, a son had seemed important years ago but now it seemed irrelevant.

The young man had turned up unexpectedly. He had liked him, he seemed so friendly, so open, so sincere, almost to a degree of naivety. He had even written to him suggesting he should return to Hong Kong, to his grass roots, which would bring him more happiness than slogging alone in another man's land. This brilliant, vibrant, successful city held huge potential. It was his homeland as it had been his mother's.

He was in his garden practising Tai Chi before beginning his day. He believed this form of art kept his mind and body healthy. He had told his beautiful daughters to practice Tai Chi every day and they were to teach their children, his grandchildren, to do the same.

He looked up to see one of his daughters walking towards him.

'Ah, my dear Linda. What brings you here so early?'

'This man, Michael Lee. What do you know about him?'

'Nothing, except that I knew his mother long ago.'

'You know Mia was seeing him.'

'Yes, my lovely granddaughter, Mia. Is there something wrong?'

'He has dropped her. No goodbye. Left the country without a word. She is heartbroken. He told her he would work for you and then ask Lex and me if they could marry.'

Jimmy pulled a towel from the back of a garden chair.

'I don't understand. He left without saying?'

'Yes, and I'm left with a daughter who won't stop crying. I think she has been to bed with him. I'm not sure but I think it very likely.'

'There has to be a reason.'

'Whatever it is, she won't tell me. I am worried there is more to all of this. Perhaps he is married.'

He put his arm around his daughter. 'Try not to worry. I will ask Chia to see what he can find out. Is she having a baby?'

'No, I am sure she is not, thank God.'

'Go home now and don't talk to anyone else about this.'

Linda kissed him lightly on the cheek. 'I will let

you know if I find out anything, maybe she will tell me more.' She bowed slightly as she left. 'Thank you, father.'

Jimmy Lee frowned as he walked slowly into his house. Why would a young man suddenly drop his beautiful granddaughter. A young woman who had everything to offer him. A chance to return to his own country and settle down with excellent prospects in his company. What would make him leave so quickly.

He picked up the 'phone. 'Chia, I want you to do something for me. I want to know everything you can find out about Michael Lee. You met him once, he was with my granddaughter. I want to know every 'phone call he made and received. I want to know who he saw and when he saw them while he was here in the country. I want to know where he is now and every move he makes. I don't care how long it takes or how much it costs. Do you understand?'

He hung up. Chia was a thorough investigator, if there was something to find then he would find it.

It was nearly a week later when Chia handed Jimmy Lee a list of telephone calls. Only one was to London. The others were to Mia except for one to a Clinic.

'What clinic?'

'A clinic for HIV, AIDS.'

Jimmy gasped, his face whitened and his lips formed a tight thin line.

'Do you know why he 'phoned them?' His voice trembled as he spoke.

'No, they won't give any information. They

won't even confirm he called. I've tried to bribe them, even threaten them, but I don't believe they will talk.'

'Do you know where he is living?'

'He has an apartment in London but seldom uses it. He seems to spend his time with a Helen Bennett. An older woman who also lives in London and owns a small cottage in the country.'

Jimmy Lee swivelled his chair around until he faced the windows. He stared out at the high rise buildings all reflecting the sun, all reflecting wealth.

'Find out more, see if he visits hospitals or doctors. Find out if he takes any medicines. Then, when we are ready, we will ask him a few questions. I want him watched day and night. Arrange it.'

He telephone Linda when Chia had left.

'Linda, see Mia does not have any new boyfriends.

'Why?'

'Because Michael Lee might be carrying HIV. Try not to worry, it could well be a false alarm. I am just being careful. Maybe there is nothing to worry about.'

He heard a gasp, almost a small scream.

'She will have to be tested now and again in a few months time, just to be safe,' he added, softly. 'Try not to worry.'

He heard his daughter cry and he hung up quickly. He could not cope with such unhappiness. First, he must find out if Michael Lee was infected and, if he was, did he know it when he took his granddaughter out. If he did, then it was tantamount to murder and he would be dealt with accordingly.

He closed his eyes and let himself return to a time when he had loved Jade. She was so beautiful, so incredibly beautiful. Her features chiselled, her movements elegant, her thoughts still pure but exciting. How could he not love her as she did him. He had promised to marry her, to leave his wife. He wanted to do that though he doubted it would happen for there were too many family ties, too much family money, to extricate himself without causing a turmoil. Then, unexpectedly, his world collapsed. It was as though some ancient family spirit came to his help, came to free him from the web he had spun, he became ill. He did not even know he was sick until he had a medical check-up for a new insurance policy.

He had tuberculosis. He could not believe it, he had nearly no symptoms, just a little tired. His father had panicked and immediately arranged for him to go to an expensive clinic for treatment. He had not argued and he was gone within two weeks. He had barely said goodbye to Jade. Just a telephone call to tell her his accountant would transfer money to her bank and that she must go to the doctor to be checked for tuberculosis. He was sorry, he was sorry. He had heard her crying and he had put down the receiver and wept. He never saw or heard from her again and he had not tried to find her.

Then, recently, her son had contacted him. He did not even know she had a son and concluded she had married and lived somewhere on the island.

However, it seemed the young man was living in England and was only on a short visit. He had agreed to meet him for he was keen to hear what had happened to his old love, his Jade.

He had liked Michael, he seemed well educated, polite and charming. However, he had been shocked to hear how Jade had said he was his father, of course he was not his father. A feeling of disappointment overwhelmed him to learn Jade had found another lover within a few weeks of his leaving for treatment. He thought she must have acted on the rebound and remembered how she had sobbed when he told her their affair was over.

He had offered to take a DNA test as proof and the unhappy young man had reluctantly agreed and, perhaps out of sympathy, he had introduced Michael to his family.

*

It was another two weeks before he heard from Chia. Indeed, Helen Bennett and Michael Lee had visited a hospital together. Chia's agent had managed to bribe a local chemist as to the pills they were taking. He had slipped him 'an envelope' and the chemist had discreetly written down names of pills, all were for a Mrs. H. Bennett. The medicines were antiviral.

'You mean they are used for AIDS,' Jimmy asked, his voice sounding low and almost guttural.

'Probably, HIV. The fact that only the woman is taking them suggests he is not infected or, of course, he has medication from another chemist which we don't yet know of. It's still inconclusive.'

'Keep watching him until I give you further instructions.'

He sighed deeply as he 'phoned his daughter after Chia had hung up.

'Linda, how is Mia?'

'Extremely depressed. Luckily, she has tested negative but they will test her again in a couple of months to be absolutely sure.

'He won't get away with this. I will make sure he regrets the day he set foot in my house. I will revenge her,' he hissed.

It was over two months before Linda 'phoned him. He swivelled his chair so that he could stare at the other skyscrapers and the ribbons of blue sky between them.

'Pa, she is totally clear. She hasn't got it, she hasn't got it,' she gasped with happiness. 'Lex says we are all to go on holiday. I can't tell you our relief. Poor Mia, she has so suffered but we tell her it is behind her and one day she will meet a man who is known within our circle.'

'We will celebrate,' he laughed, loudly. 'We will have a party before you go. It is good you take her away.'

They chatted on for a while and eventually his elated daughter said goodbye and thanked him for all the support he had given the family.

He redialled when she had hung up.

'Chia, get hold of the little bastard. I want to know if he is infected and, whether he is or not, I want you to make sure he never enters this country again. Give him a clear message that he is not welcome here, ever. No need for extremities but the message must be clear. Do you understand what I am saying?'

Chia replied that he understood very well what had to be done and would arrange for his wishes to be carried out. Coincidentally, there was a Chinese restaurant opposite his flat. It would be easy to arrange.

The aging man put his hand to his forehead and sadly shook his head. Michael Lee had shown himself to be treacherous. He could never forgive that, never.

TWO OF A KIND

Helen HELD MIKE IN HER ARMS when he received the results of his test. She wished she could think of something to say to help him but there was nothing. She felt empty and for the first time without a plan, any plan. Useless idioms and clichés rushed through her mind, fruitless remarks which would not add to his situation, their situation.

They curled around each other at night and she wished they could be found like that for her love had been fatal. She had wanted to shout to God, why had he done this to her, had she not suffered enough in a loveless marriage, a childless marriage. She recalled, as she so often did, her child born only to die minutes later. The tiny limp body of their baby boy had been taken away before she had a chance to hold him. It was like that in those days. Babies were not held by their parents with love until they slipped away. Such an infant death was something not to be spoken about after the first sympathetic words from family and friends.

Rob had seemed just as devastated as she was. He had held her in his arms and cried. She had never seen him cry before, she had not expected that.

She had sat for days in a rocking chair clutching a finely knitted baby shawl. It was weeks before she could bring herself to carefully pack the tiny clothes between tissue paper, dismantle the cot and return it with the pushchair to the baby shop, which guaranteed their return in case of such tragedies.

Later, Rob had taken her away for a month to Australia and she had managed to block the hurt and even enjoy herself for a while. They never spoke of the child again. It was as though their pain was buried with him, an unspoken subject, almost a taboo.

Rob's coolness had continued and she slowly learnt to accept her marriage for what it was though she hoped, someday, someone would charge into her barren life. However, no serious suitor arrived and she spent her time sewing patchwork quilts and sketching the colourful world around her, breaking the monotony with the odd short affair or 'one night stand.'

She turned slightly and studied Mike who had fallen asleep. A lock of his thick dark hair fell across his forehead, his skin smooth but pale, his long lashes outlining the shape of his eyes, he was beautiful, so beautiful.

*   *   *

It was a cold miserable evening when Michael Lee left his apartment to go shopping. He often stayed with Helen but he was slowly trying to pick up his life and had returned to his own apartment. Sometimes, he ate in a small Chinese restaurant opposite but tonight he would go shopping to fill his almost empty cupboards and refrigerator.

He was thinking of Mia and whether he should contact her and tell her about the trouble she might be in. He thought he should do that, in fact he knew he must, but he was overwhelmed by fear of her family and certainly her grandfather. He decided he would email her that evening, it was the only decent thing to do.

He was walking down the almost deserted street towards the supermarket when he became aware of someone behind him, he turned to see two men closing in on him. His heart was beating fast as he hastened his step and began to run but the men quickly caught up with him. He felt a man's arm around his neck and his left arm pulled behind his back while the other man hit him violently in the stomach. He gasped in pain and tried to bend over but the first man still held him tightly.

'Talk,' the second man said.

'What about?'

'Your illness. Somebody wants to know when you knew you had it.'

'What illness?'

'Don't mess around if you want to live.'

'After I arrived in Hong Kong,' he gasped.

The second man punched him between his legs and he groaned in agony as they semi dragged him along the road and down an alley. He knew where he was. It was a side entrance to the Chinese restaurant.

'When did you know you were infected?'

'I told you, after I arrived in Hong Kong. I got an email from someone who had just found out she had it. I 'phoned her and she told me I could have HIV. I mailed back to say I was leaving and that I would get tested at home. I left. I went home.'

'Can you prove that?'

'The mails are on my computer.'

'We will go to your flat. We will see if you are lying and if you are, you're as good as dead.'

'I swear to you I'm not lying.'

They pulled him across the road and he hoped there would be someone in the lobby and that they would run off, but there was no one in sight as they took the lift to his apartment. They hit him on the jaw as they flung him down in his lounge.

'Find it,' the first man shouted as he crawled to his laptop.

'There,' he gasped, pointing at the screen. 'I'm not lying.'

One of the men took out a mobile and dialled as he walked away, speaking softly so that he could not hear what he said. When he returned he pulled him up by the collar of his coat.

'Be warned,' he spat, his spittle wetting his face. 'If you return to Hong Kong, that will be the last thing you ever do. Understand?'

He nodded then received one more blow in his ribs and another to his jaw.

'You are being watched, do you understand? Every move, every telephone call, everyone you meet. Everything you do. We have our agents everywhere. If you put one foot in Hong Kong, you are dead. Understand?'

'Yes,' he groaned.

He remained bent double for some time as an excruciating pain throbbed throughout his body.

He ran his tongue along his bleeding gums to check none of his teeth were loose or broken, then he slowly reached for the telephone. He wanted Helen, she was the only one who could help him. His mother and Monty were dead. He had no brothers or sisters. No close friends he could confide in. He had no one apart from her, the woman he had intended to destroy had destroyed him. Ironically, she was now his only friend.

Helen found him sitting on his blood stained sofa after he had 'phoned her for help. He looked up at her, rather like a puppy which had been hurt.

'What happened, for God's sake,' she cried, as she ran to him and put her arm around his shoulder.

'I think I got a visit from Jimmy Lee's friends. They warned me not to return to Hong Kong. I guess my leaving suddenly made them suspicious. They have probably been checking up on me.'

'And what is there to check?'

'Not much, only that I 'phoned a Clinic but I didn't go. I decided to come home to get checked. I've no doubt they know I did that. They wanted to know when I knew I had HIV and I told them it was after you mailed me. They dragged me here and I had to show them your emails. Thank God I could prove I was telling the truth. I don't know what would have happened if you had 'phoned me instead. Then one of the men made a call and afterwards they beat me up a bit more and warned me never to return to Hong Kong. I think Mia must be in the clear. That's all that matters. I think I would already be dead if she had caught it,' he cried, slightly, as he spoke.

'You're not staying here. Come on, we're going home.'

*

They were at the cottage, months later, when he told her he was not only unable to return to Hong Kong but was also in the U.K. on a work permit, for however long it might last.

'I have nowhere to go, I have no family, I have no country.'

'Did your mother take her citizenship here?'

'Yes, Monty thought it wise to do so.'

'But you didn't.'

'No, I wasn't sure what to do, so I did nothing.'

'Well, I suggest you apply for it.'

'It will take years,' he whined, miserably.

She sighed at the new problem facing him and felt even more responsible for his situation. She stared across the lake, it was a beautiful day, small fish came to the surface causing circles on the almost still water and, once in a while, a dragonfly darted through the reeds.

'There is a possible solution, don't be shocked, it's only an idea.'

'What?'

'We could marry. Should anyone ask, we can say we have known each other since you arrived here and I knew your mother from years ago. My husband died. I was alone, you were alone. Our need for each other turned to love. As simple as that.'

He looked staggered, staring at her as though he had not heard her correctly. She waited for him to react, perhaps sneer at such an unlikely suggestion. Instead, he grinned broadly.

'Brilliant, truly ingenious. Why didn't I think of that. Would you really do that for me?'

'Yes, of course. Why not? Listen, I don't know the law, it could be that getting married does not necessarily mean you are entitled to become British, but I think you would have the right to stay here. Not forgetting, your mother had a British passport, you studied here, worked here, lived here for a long time, married a British citizen. You have a very healthy bank account. That must say something, that must help.'

'And don't forget Monty was my father.'

She frowned. 'Of course,' she replied, thoughtfully. 'Only how can you prove the DNA is from him. It could be from some other man. I mean he's not here to prove it.'

'Yes, I can see that's a problem. It might not work. We'll stick to our plan, we can always try later if we have to.'

'You don't have to marry me if you don't want to,' her voice broke with emotion as she spoke.

He took her hand. 'I can't think of anyone I would rather be with. You are so kind, so caring.'

She looked away as tears ran down her cheeks.

'No one has ever said that to me. I am so afraid you don't mean it.'

'I mean it, Helen. Maybe I don't need you to get a U.K. passport, I don't have the answer to that. But I do know we are two of a kind, we need each other, for better or worse,' he laughed.

She dabbed her eyes with a tissue. 'You know we have enough money to do nice things, go to nice places, live it up a bit,' she said, softly. 'That is, if you want to stay with me for a while.'

'I can't think of anywhere else, or anyone else, I would rather be with. You are beautiful, Helen. We can make something of it, of life. Thank you for being so kind to me. Strange Monty helped my mother, now you are helping me.'

She laughed as she began to cry again.

'You know, we could have an extended honeymoon. Get away from here. I think I will keep Hampstead Heath and sell this place. Too many unhappy memories here.'

'I'll put the beach house up for sale, same reason. Too many unhappy memories,' he agreed.

'You know what, we could go away every winter to somewhere warm.'

'A lot of people go to Thailand,' he said, thoughtfully.

'Can you imagine months on a beach.'

'Yes, I can. And the food is to die for,' he grinned.

'We would have to take a supply of pills,' she laughed through her tears.

'Yes, I guess so. We could also get married on the beach,' he suggested, teasingly.

She looked up surprised. 'What a lovely idea. We could ask a couple of passersby to be witnesses.'

'Another problem solved. I really wouldn't know who to ask.'

'Yes, that's what we'll do. Marry on the beach on Christmas Day. And if the paperwork is too difficult, then we'll marry here and still have Christmas somewhere on a beach in Thailand.'

He pulled the weekend newspaper off the garden table and thumbed through the pages. 'Here we are. Thailand. Let's see. There's a beautiful island called Koh Phi Phi near Phuket.'

'Then, of course, there's Jamaica.'

'We'll toss for it.'

'Jamaica, Thailand, here we come.'

'And when we get back I will look for a job and get my life together.'

'Let's drink to that.'

He raised his glass. 'To our new life,' he toasted.

She sat next to him, her head resting on his shoulder. 'Did you really hope I would drown when you forced me to jump into the lake?'

'Did you guess Emy might die because you didn't take her to hospital?'

She paused for a moment, a little shocked at his direct question.

'I think there was a madness in me. I was desperate to be loved. I didn't think further than myself. Jack was a sort of 'have to have'. I turned to him just after I married, when I realised that Rob was all about nothing.'

She drank some wine to give her support.

'But, true to form,' she continued, 'Jack was loyal to his best friend. I thought of him just about every day of my life and when we eventually met up again, he was married. He became a challenge. It would have been alright if Jack hadn't have gone back to Emy.'

'So what are you saying, you left her to die?'

'No, how could I know she would die. I just didn't want to admit to myself that she needed Jack's attention. I suppose it was a sort of power struggle. That's what love does, makes you a bit mad.'

'Well, we all do stupid things, who am I to judge. I nearly fucked up Mia's life and almost left you to drown. I don't suppose I am much better,' he replied, not adding that he was also partly responsible for his mother's suicide.

'I hope not. I hope you are as bad as me. If not, then we will probably start playing the 'better than thou' game.'

'I'm not very good at playing games. I like to win.'

'Do you feel you have won now?'

'Sort of. I have you, haven't I?'

'Forever and ever.'

He looked across the still lake and imagined Emy sitting on the mooring, dabbling her feet in the green water.

'You know', he said, softly. 'Perhaps we should wait a little while before selling this place or the beach house. Prices are still rising. We can always do that later.'

'Whatever you think best,' she whispered.

She kissed him and for the first time it was a kiss of affection, as a mother kisses her child.

A kiss for her baby who had not lived long enough to know love, a kiss for her baby who had escaped the pain of life. A kiss which broke her heart.

PART THREE

Champagne for Tea

WILL AND ROSIE

Will WINDSOR SAT ON THE BENCH at the 'Crossing' remembering his inevitable desire for Emily Neilson. How could he not have fallen for her and hoped she had been, at the very least, impressed by his wit and humour. He thought shared humour led to a special kind of friendship, possibly a special kind of love.

It seemed impossible that he would never see her again walking towards him with her small poodle jumping through the heather; never discuss life and love and whatever else came to mind. She had been so alive, so present. Now she was gone. Gone, just like that.

He remembered how Emy had told him Jack was home and that one of her girlfriends, Helen, was chasing after him. He had listened, sympathetically, but there was nothing he could say to help so he had changed the subject and told her how Rosie wanted to marry in the old chapel.

He stared across the heath as he envisaged the small outbuilding attached to the house, a sombre place offering Calvinistic austerity, stone altar, a crude Cross, two candlesticks, stone floor, pews straight and unforgiving to the back and two coloured glass windows. A heavy wooden door led to a gravel path in the garden which Rosie's mother had insisted was to be left open every day so that those looking for spiritual comfort, or even just a rest, could sit there for a while. It had been blessed, over a century ago, by a religious splinter group and had flourished for a while until the congregation dwindled to a couple of old people and then to none. It had stayed a chapel though no one knew when the last Service had been held or even by whom.

He had suggested marrying in a registry office but Rosie was adamant and, after a heated discussion, he agreed to the chapel and Rosie vaguely agreed to putting the house up for sale when they returned from their short honeymoon. He could only assume the place held some kind of sentimental value for he could not think of any other reason why Rosie would want to marry there. After all, he knew her well, she had been in his life since he was a small boy, she was his soul mate and lover, had welcomed him home at the end of a field trip, welcomed him into her kitchen and bed. As Rosie always said, they were comparable to an old pair of comfortable slippers.

He always smiled when he thought of her.

*   *   *

He and Rosie had married as she had wanted, the chapel was decorated with summer flowers and garlands of red and white roses fell across the altar. The choice of colours puzzled him for, as far as he knew, red and white flowers stood for blood and even death. He wondered if Rosie knew that or maybe the superstition was outdated.

The local priest had blessed their rather old union and he had kissed the bride as expected. They were about to walk back down the aisle when, suddenly, Rosie pulled herself up onto the altar and waved her bouquet while she did a small dance. He had laughed and clapped with the guests, while the priest played down any feelings he might have harboured in his spiritual breast. He had, lovingly, lifted Rosie off the stone slab and led her back down the aisle while the guests continued to clap and cheer. He thought everyone had seen it as Rosie's day of glory for which she had waited far too long.

They had an offer for their house far quicker than expected. A retired couple had fallen in love with what they called the 'original features'. Rosie had cried and told him she could never leave her family home and he had spent weeks trying to persuade her why they had to, how he could no longer afford the heating bills and the upkeep. In fact, he had never been able to afford them and their burden would disappear with the stroke of a pen.

She had refused to be reasonable and he had firmly held her arm and pointed to the high ceilings, the stone floor which led from the vestibule through the hall to the kitchen and scullery. Ice cold areas which were not to heat in the winter. Not to mention the sash windows which were constantly jammed, the creaking staircase, the huge hot water boiler in the bathroom, the temperamental central heating boiler and the damp basement All these things pressed down on him, depressed him, made him want to run away whereas they could be solved.

He had walked angrily out of the house and onto the heath and sat now for the first time, in what seemed ages, on the bench at the 'Crossing'. He closed his eyes, imagining Emy might suddenly appear in the distance, hastening her step when she saw him waiting for her. He could not believe she would never come again, laugh at his jokes which blended with her own dry humour, deep discussions over religion, politics and the world at large, including love. 'To love', she had said, 'was to suffer'. Now he suffered a pain, the pain mourners suffer.

He turned his thoughts back to his youth and the first time he had come to 'Tower Lodge', a rambling house with an equally rambling garden stretching over two acres.

His father, who was called Reginald, had already divorced his mother who he remembered as a bright, jingling, jangling, woman. Their marriage had lasted ten years and then, he supposed in a hopeless well of desperation, his mother left him and his father for a car salesman. He had to admit he sold sports cars. He could sympathise with his mother as he grew older though he never really forgave her for

abandoning him. Everyone said that opposites got on well together but he thought that was a 'load of codswallop' for Reginald had been a precise man, his hair perfectly parted and sleekly combed. He was tall, well built, immaculately dressed, polished his black shoes every night before going to bed and wore a pair of gold rimmed glasses. He was an accountant, a man of his time.

His very strict and rather bullying father had told him that Stella, the owner of 'Tower Lodge', was the nicest woman he had ever met and she was going to be his new mother, since his real one had other interests, and he would have a sister called Rosie.

Later, he had learnt how his father and Stella had met over a sandwich lunch, in a rather mediocre café, and that Stella worked part time in a library not far from his office. Her husband, who had been much older than she was, had died leaving her a large house, rambling garden, a meagre pension and a small child.

Reginald had comforted the widow, Stella, and before long had moved in with her which was a solution to her financial difficulties and, perhaps, a good investment for him in the future, if he could lay his hands on her house, if he could persuade her to marry him. After all, he insisted, living together was living in sin. Unfortunately, for him, Stella was a broadminded woman, not of her day, and refused to get bogged down in the ensuing paperwork. A Marriage Certificate.

However, Reginald moving in with Stella was his saving. Her daughter, Rosie, was two years younger than he was and Stella was a warm and *loving woman. He had been lucky to have arrived in this family and forgot his mother rather quickly.*

Two years later, he was sent to boarding school which he surprisingly enjoyed. Rosie stayed home and, because she was shy and insecure, it was decided to leave her in the local school. In any case, Stella wanted her child near to her, she loved her, she was all she had and was not about to hand her over to some institute. He liked Stella immensely, certainly more than his father who he disliked just as immensely.

He had been in his second year studying archaeology when Stella telephoned him to say Reginald had disappeared for some considerable time, in fact three months. He had, of course, asked her whether she had reported him missing to which she replied that she had been forced to do so, seeing how his office insisted on it. His father had been suspended from work until he returned, hopefully with a satisfactory reason though she could not think of one herself.

He had been astounded for his father was not an impulsive man, rather the opposite.

'I can't believe it.'

'I know, I can't either, but he has. He's taken all his clothes except for his dark suits and briefcase. It looks as though he wants to start a new life.'

'Who with?'

'No idea.'

'I'll come down tomorrow.'

'No need,' Stella replied, firmly. 'You can't do anything, wait until the end of term.'

Stella had seemed only slightly depressed when he arrived. Reginald had indeed packed a suitcase with his most informal clothes, which were rather limited, together with his passport, wallet, cheque book, gold watch, gold pen and a pair of spare glasses.

The police had done their best to trace him but they had only found his car, with the keys still in the ignition, parked somewhere outside Dover. It had been thoroughly examined for foul play but only his and Stella's fingerprints had been found and they had drawn a blank. They had concluded that Reginald had met someone, left the car, and driven away with whoever it was. They had no reason to think otherwise and Reggie became one of many thousands of missing people who might, or might not, resurface.

Stella thought he had probably taken off to the Continent though there was no trace that he had done so. Still, she reckoned he was a quiet man and no one really knew anyone.

His archaeological work had taken him away from home and he had felt a degree of sadness every time he left to go on some 'dig', for he not only loved Stella but also Rosie who had turned out to be incredibly beautiful. Her long hair was a mass of curls, her eyes bright blue, her skin almost translucent and she dressed in a sort of bohemian style. Whenever he saw a field of flowers, he thought of Rosie running through it, her slim body almost discernible under her thin cotton dress, her blonde hair flying in a light breeze. She was for him the personification of beauty.

He had, unwillingly, hidden his feelings for he could not imagine she would ever be interested in a stepbrother who had teased her when she could not keep up with him.

But Rosie, who had always giggled and flashed her eyes at him, had changed. She seemed to ignore him and he felt hurt because somehow he had always been close to her, shared silly secrets, climbed trees, cycled to a stream a little further from their house, fished for tiddlers and cooked potatoes in a fire; everything which made an idyllic childhood. He could not understand what had changed between them, he was the same, he had not changed, not that he knew.

He had expected to hear how Rosie had a steady boyfriend, was engaged, getting married. But every time he came home she was still drawing and painting and writing. Stella said there had been interested young men but Rosie had brushed them aside, though she was sure the right one would eventually come along. He had wanted to shout, 'I'm the right one,' but he held back in case he might be instantly rebuffed.

Then, suddenly, Stella died of a stroke which had left both he and Rosie devastated, though her death confirmed she and Reginald had never married. This, luckily, simplified her Will in which she had, generously, left the house to both of them. This seemed to please Rosie who said he could help with any future upkeep while it gave him a permanent pied à terre. He thought Stella had somehow tied them together even if it was only through property.

But, Rosie still remained distant and he had sadly given up and married an assistant to the college bursar and lesbian. After an inevitable divorce, he and Rosie settled back into their old routine in 'Tower Lodge' until the following Christmas when they had gone upstairs together. He had laid next to her and slowly, carefully, made love. He was surprised when he realised she was not a virgin and decided that her brief engagement to a Belgian schoolteacher had been more sexual than he had wanted to admit. Anyway, the Belgian had returned to the small country he called home and he was thankful he had done so. He still shuddered at his disastrous marriage and the idea of Rosie living alone, without him, on the Continent. Then, suddenly, it occurred to him that Rosie had broken her engagement at almost the same time as his divorce. He wondered if that had been coincidental or whether Rosie had been waiting for him, as he had for her.

He had intended marrying Rosie but she had put her finger over his lips and said it was alright as it was. She said that maybe marriage might spoil the magic of their love.

He had not been entirely happy but he had accepted her decision, after all he had one notch in his belt and he could not afford to make another mistake, though he thought Rosie could never be a mistake. He would ask her again, sometime later.

He turned his thoughts back to the present and decided to ignore Rosie for a while to see if she would change her mind, if she would get round to his way of thinking, to accept the generous offer for the house and be rid of it and its ability to swallow any money they might have.

A yellow butterfly fluttered around him as he stood up to leave. He thought of Emy.

Rosie seemed unperturbed by his coolness and finally, in a rage, he had shouted at her and called her selfish, something he had never done before. She sighed deeply and replied that he would be happier not to know the why's and wherefore's which made him shout even harder for her resilience was insufferable. He threatened to leave her, she could have the house for all he cared and she would never see him again.

Tears formed in Rosie's eyes and he wanted to hold her, comfort her, tell her he would never leave her, but instead he stamped upstairs and pulled a suitcase from out of a cupboard and began to pack.

When he looked up Rosie was standing in the doorway. It seemed to him that she grew lovelier as she grew older, her hair was still the mass of curls though a little thinner now and the lines around her eyes made her look even softer, tender, more loving.

He sat on the bed and she stood in front of him and held his head against her body.

'You are all I have, ever had. I loved you from the moment we met,' she whispered.

'Then why, Rosie. We could have a lovely life together. Why hang onto this old place. Why?'

Rosie sighed. 'Because of what happened.'

'What happened?'

'No one else can live here.'

'Why, why can't anyone else live here?'

'You can't guess?'

'No, what must I guess?'

Rosie sat on the bed next to him sobbing, hot tears rolled down her ruddy cheeks and her curls stuck against her face which she tried to wipe aside with her sleeve. She drew her breath in as she spoke.

'Your father. He never left, he's still here. He's in the chapel,' she managed to whisper, her voice breaking up between light wails.

'What are you talking about?' he eventually managed to gasp as a feeling of deep apprehension flowed through him, stifling him, so he could hardly answer her.

'He is in the chapel, behind the altar. I'm so sorry, I'm so sorry.'

He wished he could assimilate what she was saying, wished she had not said it, wished he had just accepted it all as it was.

Rosie bent over, her head in her hands, as she told him how his father had attacked her, raped her, in the chapel. How her mother was at the local hairdresser's and not expected to return for some time but when she arrived at the shop it was closed as the hairdresser's daughter had been taken ill.

Her mother had heard her screaming when she returned and, in horror, had picked up a brass candlestick and hit Reginald on the head with it. She spoke quickly, stuttering, as she tried to explain what happened.

How she had sat with her mother at the kitchen table and persuaded her that what she had done was understandable, a normal human reaction, and she did not see why Reginald should spoil their lives. Why tell anyone, why have the social services across the floor, police investigations, court hearings, all the dirt spread across the local and even the national newspapers and, not least, poor Will. The humiliation and pain he would suffer, perhaps he would leave and never return. Neither of them could bear that.

She had suggested hiding Reginald under the stones in the chapel where he would be nearer to God. Anyway, moving him would only leave a trail of evidence. Her mother thought the stones would be too heavy for them to lift so she suggested asking Uncle Henry, her mother's brother, to help because she did not believe he would let his sister be arrested for manslaughter, or even a more terrible crime.

They had discussed the matter at length, her mother being unsure whether Henry would be prepared to go to such lengths for her, but she assured her that it was the best solution to an insolvable problem.

Eventually, her mother had agreed that Henry would most probably help since he hated Reginald and would, most likely, be extremely sympathetic to his long suffering sister.

Henry had stayed a few days with them, telling his wife how he needed to help Stella since

Reginald had gone off, probably with some woman, and how Stella said that Reginald was sexually overactive and his disappearance did not particularly surprise her. She had expected something of the sort. They would just wait and see whether his fling was to be short lived and perhaps he would come home with his tail between his legs, so to speak. His wife promised not to tell anyone and hoped he could be of comfort to his sister and Rosie.

Henry had thought it better if they removed the stone paving behind the altar and dig deep enough to bury Reginald in a sitting position, since the less stones removed the better.

They had carefully shovelled the sandy earth into heavy plastic bags, making sure that no surrounding stones were chipped or damaged. In fact, the exercise was far more difficult than they had anticipated for the hole had to be made wider as it became deeper.

Eventually, Henry thought the hole was good enough to place Reginald in with his back leaning against one side and his feet against the other. Then they brushed his hair, placed his glasses on his nose, his spare ones in his pocket along with his gold pen, wallet, cheque book, bank pass and passport. They checked to see his gold watch was still on his wrist before they bent him over as far as possible, said a small prayer and threw the sandy earth back over him. They thought he had everything he needed in another world, only he was sitting around in this one probably feeling very bored.

Henry then replaced the stones, hammering them down gently, rather professionally, with a special hammer made for that purpose. The floor was brushed clean and, since there was no cement between the stones, he hoped the disturbed sand would quickly blend in with the rest.

'Don't tell anyone he's missing until you have to,' Henry had warned them. 'The stones have first to settle and please if you get caught keep me out of it. Just say the two of you did it alone. It is possible you could have done it. So please shut up and for God's sake stay in this house until after I've died. In fact, until you are both taken out between six planks.'

They had sworn before the simple wooden Cross that they would do that and never divulge their secret. Not to anyone.

Her mother had packed Reginald's casual clothes into a suitcase, removed all makers' names and a dry cleaning tag from his linen jacket and filled the case with stones.

When it was dark, she and her mother drove to a deep fast flowing river and threw the suitcase over the bridge. They had held hands as they watched bubbles form as it disappeared and sighed with relief as they walked away.

They reckoned if the suitcase or clothes were found then tracing them back to Reginald would be almost impossible.

Next day, Stella had driven Reginald's car to Dover, left it on a lonely picnic area, and driven back home with Henry who then drove home to his wife.

Will sat dumbfounded, shaking his head as the story unfolded. Eventually, he said he found Rosie and Stella very brave and Reginald had deserved what he had got. If he had been there he would probably have done the same. Though he was not entirely sure that was so.

He frowned. 'But why did you want to marry in the Chapel?'

'I suppose it was a sort of revenge, dance on his grave. He stole my best years, we lived in fear of being found out. I think it killed my mother. I finally decided to tie the knot when you and Emy were chasing behind each other. Now, I've had to tell you because you want to sell the house.'

He sympathised as he held Rosie in his arms.

'You should have told me. Now I understand why you didn't want to marry all those years ago and why you didn't want to have a family. You poor thing. But your Belgian fiancé?'

'Marcel? He was a nice man but I couldn't go through with it and I wanted to make you jealous.'

'You did that and you also dug yourselves into a hole. Reginald is the toad in the hole,' he laughed, nervously.

'Yes,' agreed Rosie. 'But there's just one small problem. Henry is in a Care Home. I went to see him a few months ago and to my horror, in front of a nurse, he asked if Reginald was still sitting in the chapel.

It seems he is a little fragile, mentally fragile. Sometimes he can remember things from long ago, sometimes he doesn't even know who I am. Luckily, the nurse ignored him but what if he tells them he buried Reginald behind the altar. What if the Care Home tells the police?'

'Yes, that could be a problem.' He considered the situation. 'There are two options, as I see it.

Either hope for the best or dig him up and bury him somewhere else. I think that's the best.'

'I agree. We will have to make sure we have all the bones, if we leave even one behind and the police find it, then we're in trouble.'

'Don't forget I'm an archaeologist.'

'Yes, of course, I forgot that.'

'And then we can sell the house?'

'The very next day,' Rosie agreed, elated that she had shared her secret and would be able to put Reginald to rest at last.

'Rosie,' he asked, softly. 'Is that why Stella left me half the house, she thought perhaps she owed me something?'

'I don't know. But I do know she loved you. She saw you as her own son, perhaps that was her way of keeping us together.'

He found he had to dig deeper than he had anticipated since the bones seemed to have sunk into the sandy earth and the hole became wider as he dug further. He had found the skull almost immediately and had held it up, rather like Hamlet did Yorick's, and studied it as though it was just another relic on some field expedition in some god forsaken place.

'Yes, he got quite a hit.'

'Sorry, he was your father,' Rosie murmured, standing on the edge of the hole with a container bag, grimacing as each bone fell upon the last, while he tried to convince himself that his father deserved his fate. 'After all,' she murmured, 'he could have landed up in prison and, at least, he was buried in a chapel which is as good as it gets.'

'Doesn't matter. I could never get on with him. I think he sent me to boarding school just to get me out of the way.'

'You're right about that.'

He stopped digging and looked up.

'He was around me for years. Passing too close to me, touching my breasts by so-called accident. I said I would tell my mother, but he told me I would be hurting her and she had a nice life and he would give me anything I wanted. I told him I didn't want anything from him.'

'What a creep. You poor thing.'

'It's a long time ago, I've put it behind me.'

'You've had a bad time, Rosie dear, carrying such a burden alone.' He climbed out of the hole and kissed her. 'I'll make it up to you,' he promised. 'Don't worry, we'll have this settled by tomorrow and then we'll put the house back on the market.'

'It will come right, won't it?'

'Of course it will,' he answered, bravely.

He was almost finished when someone banged on the locked door.

'Mrs. Windsor, Rosie, are you there?'

'Oh, my God, it's that Carter woman. What do we do?', Rosie whispered, almost hysterically.

'Get rid of her, don't let her in for God's sake.'

Rosie walked to the large chapel door and squeezed out onto the garden path, closing it behind her as she did so.

'Whatever are you doing?' asked the woman noticing Rosie's dirty hands.

She paused for a second. 'Oh, Will and I are going to replace the chapel floor.'

'Why do you want to do that?'

'Because,' she said, slowly, while her thoughts raced for a reason. 'Because we thought we would bring the chapel into the house to open up the hall.'

'What a good idea. Can my Ben help you?'

'No, thanks. Absolutely not, we'll give you a ring if we need any help. Nice of you to offer.'

'Well, you know where we are if you need us. What a good idea,' she repeated.

Will 'phoned a stone mason offering him a good quality flagstone floor together with three slabs of stones which were the altar. The mason was keen and said he would be around the next day to have a look. He explained that the stones had still to be lifted off the ground but they were not cemented in. He casually mentioned that he had begun the work himself but had found the stones too heavy for him to lift. The stone mason told him not to worry. It was all in a day's work.

Will looked down at where he had removed the stones, 'I'm going to have to lift more. I can hardly say I started by the altar. I'll begin in a corner and make it look as though I've made my way up to here,' he puffed through his lips at the thought of the work ahead and his backache which was worsening by the day. 'And then I have to fill the hole in.

'Can I help?'

'No, just make dinner, I'll either drop dead from stress or I would have worked up an appetite. I don't know which one it is yet. What a bloody mess this is.'

'Actually, there was very little blood,' Rosie, remarked, thoughtfully.

'Thank God for small mercies,' he muttered.

The mason seemed rather pleased with the floor and the price he had paid for it. Removing the stones had not been a problem and he really did not understand why anyone would want to replace them. For him, stones were the centre of the universe; they were his work, his hobby, his life. He saw them as other men saw a woman's body but, unlike a woman, they never changed their shape unless he wished it.

Rosie giggled and Will said he had never thought of stones in that way.

Later, Will pulled a sports bag full of Regie's bones from under his bed where he had hidden it after his 'dig'.

'Where's the best place to lay him out?' he asked, sounding worried.

Rosie thought for a moment. 'No one goes to the tower, not unless I take them there.'

'Good thinking, I'll start now,' he answered, as he made his way to his study to find his field bag.

He was busy brushing off the excess earth from Reginald's bones when Rosie arrived with a cup of coffee.

'He had a bit of arthritis. I reckon Stella saved him a lot of pain.'

'Well, that's something,' Rosie replied, trying to sound positive.

'I think we're missing a small bone from his right foot and a couple of teeth. You don't happen to know if he lost any teeth, do you?'

'No idea. Never looked in his mouth.'

'You can be happy for that,' he laughed, now beginning to find the exercise even more bizarre than he had anticipated. 'I'll have to dig again but, first, I want to visit my mother, I haven't seen her for ages, perhaps she can shed some light on his missing teeth. I think it's time to hear her out, she's just moved to a small flat down by the coast.'

'Now you can introduce me as your wife.'

He smiled, lovingly. 'Yes, I can do that now.'

'You should go more often.'

'I never know what to talk about,' he complained. 'What can I say to her after all these years. We have nothing in common.'

'She's your mother. She's old, be kind.'

'I'll see what I can do,' he mumbled, turning away so Rosie could not see him gripping his teeth at the thought of a long overdue visit.

*

Poppy, real name Petronella, was still as bubbly as he remembered her on the occasional visits he had made over the years. Her now thin blonde hair was frizzy from too much peroxide and too many 'perms'. Her lips were streaked with bright red lipstick which seemed unable to find the outline of her rather indefinable lips.

She welcomed her child with open arms, forgetting he was middle aged and not the ten year old she had forsaken. He placed his arms around her frail body and gently rubbed her back while she smudged his summer jacket with makeup and black tears from her mascara painted eye lashes.

She eventually pulled back. 'You never come,' she almost whispered. 'I am so lonely, I have no one, only you, and you don't want to know me.'

'That's not true, Mum,' he replied, looking uncomfortable as he lied. 'It's just that I have been so busy. I want to ask you a few things. I want to get it all sorted out before it's too late.'

'Before I die.'

'Yes, to be honest. There are so many loose ends, things you have never told me about Reginald.'

'Reggie?' she queried, suddenly sitting up and looking a lot stronger. 'What about him?'

'I want to know why you left him.'

'He was the meanest sod I have ever known. He was older than me, I was too young, too innocent, and too pregnant when I married him. He took my money and gave me so much per week and I had to write down exactly on what and where I had spent it. Meanwhile, he bought anything he wanted for himself.'

He sat upright as though to defend himself.

'And me then. You left me with him. Was your freedom worth more than me?'

'I had already introduced him to Stella,' she replied, guiltily. 'I made sure they met again just before I was divorced. I connived a bit, but it worked out in the end. I didn't leave before I was sure their friendship was definite. You see, I had to leave you behind. My late husband, Rodney, as sweet as he was, didn't want to get tied down with children. He was always off on some car rally or another. He wanted me but you weren't part of the bargain. So I had to make a choice. I thought that you would have less than ten years with the bastard whereas I might have a lifetime. I believe Rodney loved me and that does not come around very often.'

'Don't you think you were a bit selfish?'

'Perhaps, but I knew Stella was a good woman and I did keep an eye on you and when you went to boarding school I knew you would be alright, get a good education, get away from him.'

He wanted to shout that she had been a selfish tart and that he despised her and had only come to find out just a little more about Reggie's physical attributes.

He cleared his throat. 'I'm doing a study on inherited physical features. Do you happen to know if Reggie ever lost a couple of his molars?' he asked, in a cold controlled voice.

Poppy looked amazed, 'I don't think I can remember that. Well, let me see, he did have a couple of wisdom teeth taken out.'

'No, not wisdom teeth, other teeth.'

'Well, he once told me that his school dentist took a couple of teeth out to make room in his mouth for others to grown straight. The only reason

I remember that is because I took you to the dentist and he said he did not think you would ever need to lose any teeth since your mouth was wide enough.' She giggled. 'Big enough.'

'Right, fine, thanks Poppy,' he answered, not sharing her joke. 'I know enough.'

'Are you coming again soon?'

'Whenever I can.'

Poppy turned to Rosie. 'Your mother and I were such good friends.'

'Friends?' repeated Rosie, her voice rising a couple of octaves from surprise.

'Of course. If you want to get rid of your husband you must tell your girl friends how unhappily married you are.'

'Really,' replied Rosie, coldly.

'One of them will always take the bait, if she is single or unhappily married. Guaranteed success,' she giggled. 'It worked out well, your mother was looking for a new husband and I had one to spare.' She giggled again, closing her now weak eyes as she did so. 'Where is Reggie?' she added.

'We don't know. He disappeared long ago, we've never heard from him,' Rosie informed her.

'Well, I'm not surprised. Stella wouldn't marry him. She was going to but never did. Your mother saw through him, he was after her house or at least half of her house. He probably found someone else who was more obliging. Though I must say they stayed together for quite some time. Longer than I thought they would,' she added.

'We only found out they weren't married after Stella died,' Rosie informed her. 'Had she married

Reggie and had he owned half the house then there would have been a problem settling her estate, since he is missing. You know, Will and I never realised we were not stepbrother and sister until after my mother died', she added, as she stared across the room at a photograph of a young couple leaning against a sports car.

'Well, if everyone had known the truth they would only have thought you were having if off together. It would have been strange if you weren't,' Poppy added, sniggering a little.

Rosie sighed. 'My mother was not the kind of woman to live with a man. I guess she had too many financial problems.'

'Yes, lack of money can be the biggest reason why women tolerate men,' sighed Poppy, as though she had her own memories. 'Anyway, she saved herself the bother of a divorce. Perhaps he found another widow. Good riddance to him. Poor Stella,' she added.

'That's always a possibility,' agreed Rosie, smiling at her suggestion.

'Whatever, he's been gone for so long he is probably already dead,' Will suggested.

'Maybe he lived in some beautiful villa in South America and had a really good life,' added Rosie, enjoying the conversation.

'Sooner or later, he would need to renew his passport,' pondered Poppy, frowning as it occurred to her that it was more than likely he was still in the country. 'Passports can be a stumbling block,' she murmured.

'You can buy anything, if you have enough money,' Will replied. 'Do you like living down here?' he added, changing the subject.

They stayed longer than they had expected. In fact, Rosie found Poppy rather refreshing, honest. She had wanted to dislike her but somehow could not and she could see Will felt the same way. She thought it would be good for him to see his wayward mother, from time to time, and she was sure that deep down Poppy felt bad about leaving her child. She decided Will should make it up with his mother, offer the olive branch, before she died.

'Well, Poppy, enjoy the Kent coast,' Will said, kindly, giving his mother a warm kiss. 'We'll be along as soon as we can, we have just a few things to do.'

'You must come for a few days,' suggested Rosie. 'That's if you want to.'

Tears formed in Poppy's eyes. 'Do you really mean that, would you have me?'

Rosie felt a lump in her throat. 'Of course,' she replied, gently. 'Why not, then you can see my mother's house.'

'Oh, I saw it decades ago. Your mother and I were school friends.'

'I never knew that,' replied Rosie, rather stunned.

'Has it changed much?'

'Well, that's what we are doing now,' Will replied.

*

Mrs. Carter and her husband, Ben, were standing by the locked chapel door when they arrived home. Agnes stood with her handbag dangling over her stomach while Ben doffed his cap in respect.

'Ah, there you are,' she gushed. 'Ben and I think we, and the village, owe you so much. All those meetings, meditations and positive thinking, here in the old chapel. Ben says he wants to help you.'

'That's most kind of you,' replied Will, acknowledging Ben as he stepped forward, as though volunteering for some dangerous mission.

'I'm a bricklayer. My boss has a good name around these parts. I can recommend him and I can do a bit extra for you.'

'Right, I'm sure we can use both of you.'

'I've 'eard you want to pull a wall down.'

'Well, yes, but I don't think we can do that so easily. It's an outside wall.'

'Don't you worry about that. My boss can arrange all of that. Perhaps I can 'ave a look at it?'

'Come in,' Will invited, nervously.

'Can you come back at the end of the week,' suggested Rosie. 'We've been out all day and we want to eat something and have a rest.'

'That's fine Mrs. W. Let's say Friday evening after work. I expect my boss will come along.'

'Excellent,' Will sighed. 'Until Friday.'

'Come along Ben, let these poor people have a rest,' his wife said, assertively, pulling on his arm.

'I need a drink,' Will muttered.

*

He was on the point of climbing out of the newly dug hole, after digging for hours looking for his father's lost bone, when he looked up to see Ben's knees.

'I've just come to say that Mr. Willard will see you Monday afternoon, if that's alright with you. What's that 'ole for?', he added, innocently.

'This hole,' Will replied, clearing his throat to give himself time to fantasize, 'is for a pool, perhaps with a fountain.'

'Yea,' Ben drawled. 'That's nice, a door at each end, one to the 'all and the other to the garden. You would see the fountain from the 'all, that's real nice.'

'Yes, Rosie and I thought it would bring life into the old place. I thought I would dig out the shape of the fountain and at the same time see what the earth is like.'

'Everything is sand around here, I can tell you that now. Not going to be a round pool then?'

'As I've just said, we're experimenting. Rosie thought an oblong shaped pool would be more modern with perhaps some gold fish in it and water lillies, or whatever. She is leaning towards a more clean look. I prefer something more classical, goes better with the room, but I guess she will get her way in the end. That's why we are digging it out now. Just to see how it will look.'

Rosie appeared at the chapel door.

'I'm just telling Ben how we are going to put a small fountain in here and how you would like a more modern look, a sort of oriental look.'

He could see Rosie blush as she broadened the lie.

'Yes, it will make it seem peaceful, enable one to find tranquillity within oneself,' she cooed, as though she had suddenly become overwhelmed with oriental serenity.

'We once went to a Chinese restaurant,' recalled Ben. 'Nice but I prefers me roast beef and Yorkshire pudding. Can't wait to get that 'ere opened up,' he enthused, knocking on the thick wall between the chapel and the hall. 'That'll make the place seem bigger, lighter, and the 'all as well. Can't wait to do that.'

Will cleared his throat. 'Well, if your boss can arrange all the paper work.'

'He'll be right on it, don't you worry. We'll have this finished in no time. My wife will like this. She's been telling everyone in the village 'bout it.'

Rosie glanced over to Will who was visibly perspiring, large damp patches showed on his azure blue shirt and he wiped his forehead with a handkerchief already soiled from the sandy earth.

'Thanks, Ben, it's so nice having people like you around. A job shared is a job halved.'

'Don't you mean a trouble shared is a troubled halved,' Will corrected, sharply.

Rosie looked irritated. 'No, I don't mean that. We don't have any troubles, so if you don't mind, I'll leave it as a job shared.'

Ben laughed loudly, 'Well said, Mrs. W. It's going to be a pleasure digging out that fish pond though I think you've dug deeper than necessary. Don't you worry, we'll have it fixed in no time.'

He walked away still laughing as he left the chapel door open behind him.

'Well, we don't have to close the door anymore, the whole village knows what we're doing,' he grumbled.

'I see it as a blessing. We can get on with what we're doing and everyone will think it is what it isn't.'

'Fine, but we'll be left with a bloody great bill paying for opening up the wall, new floor, fish pond, fountain and God knows what else. We're going the wrong way, Rosie, we are supposed to be pulling the money in not giving it out.'

'Perhaps the price of the house will increase when it's finished,' she suggested, hopefully.

'I don't even know what we are planning to do, let alone finishing it.'

'We are going to make the most marvellous entrance hall to a beautiful house full of original features. The hall will open out into a pure white plastered room, white marble floor, which can be used as a chapel or, with a bit more imagination, into a dance floor or even a casino,' she giggled.

'What a good idea. Why didn't I think of that,' he answered, sarcastically. 'What shall we call it. 'Reggie's Hideaway'. Bar and Dancing facilities.'

Rosie grinned broadly. 'Something like that. I'll have to think about it.'

'Meanwhile,' he added. 'There's someone in the tower who still needs a permanent home.'

Rosie did not seem at all bothered with their predicament, in fact she was becoming more enthusiastic over the idea of a pool with a fountain, potted plants and an extra room. She was even at the stage of planning a wall of windows, glass doors to the garden and windows in the roof. The chapel would become a conservatory. Selling the house had been swept under the carpet while he was left arranging a mortgage with the Bank.

Plans were submitted and passed by the local Council and Will wondered, on a daily basis, how had it got this far. If Agnes Carter had not arrived when she did, if Rosie had not made up the story of replacing the old stone floor, if Ben Carter had not seen the huge trench he had dug out looking for a bone. All 'if's' he thought, as he pondered on Reggie who was now rolled up in a couple of towels in a sports bag in the tower.

*

It was a book on Feng Shui which finally tipped Rosie into the realms of fantasy. The word Bagua was flung around, a compass was found and a Bagua map drawn up. It seemed that the opening to the hall and the doors to the garden were exactly what were required for the energy to flow through or was it for the spirits. He really could not grasp it all.

She spent hours reading and making notes of the correct plants needed and even fish. It seemed to him that Rosie had found her niche in life. He knew she had always been inclined towards alternative thinking, even spirituality, and he had no inclination to contradict her at any stage of the operation. If she was quiet, he was happy.

An oblong pool was dug out and lined. Water dribbled over two large round smooth stones, spiky grasses and flowering plants were pressed into colourful pots filled with the right kind of soil, of course. Expensive fish were gently eased into the well balanced water and dim lights, tucked under the white marble tiles, lit the pool at night.

He had to agree it was all very charming and could only add to the value of the house. In fact, people had already asked if they could have a small peep at the wonders they had achieved and wished they had the space in their houses to do the same.

Rosie had collected a library of Feng Shui books and walked around their rather large, au natural, garden with her trusted friend, the compass. He knew it was a bad sign and had come to hate the round box with its ever swinging needle and realised it would not be long before Rosie would find a corner where Feng Shui, which he now visualised as an unwelcome entity, would feel most at home.

'We need a Feng Shui rockery,' Rosie casually informed him one afternoon. 'The position here is perfect and the energy can pass through the front door, down the hall, across the pool, through the conservatory, out of the glass doors and over the rockery. All this was meant to be,' she added.

'Rosie, it will cost thousands.'

'Yes, I know but you see it is the kindest thing we can do for poor Reginald. Can you imagine the spiritual peace he will have under the rockery.'

He flopped down in a chair in the now colourful conservatory and was overcome with the desire to splash his weary feet in the pool, clouding Shui's water, disturbing the fish and changing the direction of Feng's wind.

Actually, he thought, after he had stilled his worried soul, Reggie under the rockery was not such a bad idea. They would, of course, have to return him to the ground before the work on the rockery could begin and he felt a strange déjà vu feeling pass through him. Was not digging up Reggie the reason why Feng Shui had arrived in the first place.

Now Rosie was suggesting they should rebury Reggie so that he might rest forever in Feng Shui's energy field. He wondered whether there was something he was missing, something he did not quite understand. Eventually, he decided not to query Feng Shui let alone question a woman's logic.

Rosie found a Feng Shui expert through the local garden centre and called him in for advice on how to lay the rockery. He was a quiet man, slightly built as was to be expected, probably because of his healthy diet, who implicitly agreed with Rosie's choice of site and obviously admired this pretty middle aged lady in her flowing frocks and sandals.

Arnold Waters, also known as Arnie, seemed very keen on his Rosie and promised to supervise the work since it was really important how the stones were laid and, of course, the choice of plants. Rosie willingly agreed a price with Arnold Waters which staggered him and his bank manager who, nevertheless, seemed quite happy to offer him an even larger loan since their house was collateral.

Will winced, he had not forgotten the reason for this whole exercise and Reggie under the rockery would once again put a damper on selling. After all, a new owner might not like Fen Shui's rockery and dig it up only to find a bag of bones.

He sighed, Reggie's final abode was inevitable for he realised that throwing the silly old sod into a river was not really appropriate. After all, he should show some kind of respect even though he thought Reggie hardly deserved such a nice resting place.

*

'I was thinking,' said Arnold, pointing to a corner in the garden. 'You have so much unused land, whether you might consider putting down a green house. You could grow your own plants, even grow biological vegetables, seeing how you have so much space. There is nothing like home grown products.'

'We could sell them here and I could do teas in the conservatory,' enthused Rosie.

Will closed his eyes as he visualised a board outside the front garden advertising flowers, biological fruit and vegetables, morning coffee and afternoon teas. However, he had not seen Rosie like this for a long time, bubbling enthusiasm, keen, full of ideas. The Rosie from long ago. He felt he owed her for all the misery she had suffered over so many years. Arnold stood with his eyes open, he had found his soul mate, the woman he admired so much had spark, spontaneity, spirituality, adaptability; a jewel hidden in a stuffy old house. He would open up her life and slowly bring her into his culture, the one his mother had taught him. He felt fate had brought them together and he would be happy just to see her every day and perhaps innocently touch her hand. In fact, any small morsel from the table of admiration would satisfy him.

Will watched it all with an interest which bordered on connivance, as though he was encouraging a 'special' friendship. He knew he could turn Arnold away but then, maybe, Rosie might harbour a hidden resentment. He thought there was something odd about Arnold and he wondered if Mrs. Arnold had her own tale to tell. In any case, Rosie's friendship with him was platonic, not like Emy who was looking for love.

'Fine, Arnold, I think we can work something out,' he muttered, his thoughts turning back to Emy.

Arnold marked out the position of the rockery which was in line with the conservatory's glass doors. He said it was perfect for the flow of energy and could be appreciated from within the house when the weather was unfavourable.

Will had glanced over to Rosie who seemed to have forgotten about Reggie in the tower, and his lost bone, as she absorbed every word her guru offered.

'Rosie,' he said, softly, after Arnie had gone home, 'we still have to put you know who to rest.'

'I thought we had already decided on the rockery,' she replied, as though the deal was done.

'Yes, but I have to clear the ground, dig a hole. What will Arnie say to that? Won't he find it strange if I do that myself?'

'I know, we'll ask Ben to prepare the ground, so to speak. Then we can dig it out a bit deeper, put Reggie in and cover him up.'

'I don't know, I feel we're involving too many people.'

'Well, it's a bit like 'the bigger the lie, the more it's believed'. No one will think anything, what with Ben and Arnie around and then the gardeners. There's nothing to think about.'

'I hope you're right.'

'They're coming next Monday.'

'Who are?'

'The gardeners. Arnie has organised it for us.'

'Is Arnie going to pay for it?'

'Don't be silly.'

He turned away, seriously wondering whether he had made a mistake, perhaps running away with Emy would have been simpler after all. He felt he was digging himself into a deep hole alongside Reggie.

Arnie measured the area where the rockery would be placed in great detail. It appeared that the sun played a large part in Feng Shui's energy field and he assured them that the rock plants would grow better there than anywhere else in the garden and, along with the enhancement of the pool and conservatory, would bring a peace and fulfilment into their lives which they had not yet encountered. Will wondered how he could be privy to such information about their personal lives.

Ben was summoned to clear the area and, just in case it was necessary, to dig a little deeper so that the rocks would have a good foundation.

'You's got something about digging 'oles,' he laughed.

'Looks like it,' Rosie chirped in. 'You and Agnes must come soon, when the weather is a bit brighter and have tea with us. I was actually thinking about opening up the conservatory and having a little tea room. You know when people have walked with their dogs across the heath, they might just like to have a cup of tea or coffee along with scones and cakes,' she smiled, sweetly. 'Of course, people will have to know we are here. I don't see how I could advertise. Word of mouth is always the best. I suppose, if it were to become popular, I might even have to get a catering licence. Don't you think that's a nice idea, Ben?'

Ben grinned knowingly. 'I'll tell Agnes. She knows just about everybody.'

'That's what I was thinking. Come on in and have a beer.'

Ben cleared the patch rather well and dug a small foundation for the intended rocks. Will grudgingly took his spade and set to work when he had left, praying he would not return with Agnes as they had done when he was digging behind the altar. Luckily, only the neighbour's cat came to watch him and when it decided there was nothing to be gained walked slowly away, twitching its tail as though irritated that all this labour had not produced a field mouse or two. A robin was his next visitor but its attitude was quite different and seemed happy at every turn of his spade.

He wiped the sweat from his forehead as he drunk a glass of beer which Rosie had brought him.

'How deep do you want to go?' she asked, her voice sounding slightly tense.

'As far as I can before a pair of handcuffs are clicked on my wrists.'

'You worry too much.'

'So should you.'

'Let me know when you're finished.'

'Thanks for the support,' he muttered, wondering how it was possible he was hiding his father's bones while one of the perpetrators of his death calmly read books on growing biological vegetables.

The gardeners came and, under the supervision of Arnie, laid a rockery along with a small stream of water which gently trickled down the Purbeck stones. He shuddered at the rising costs but his priority was to find Reggie a permanent home, bury him for eternity, so they could get on with their lives. Rosie thought they would meet up with him again in some parallel world.

'Heaven forbid,' he had muttered, in horror, as he walked away quickly in case the discussion broadened.

He gave a sigh of relief when Arnie appeared and Rosie followed him around the rows of biological veggies. He smiled, Rosie was off his back and seemed to be extraordinarily happy. He could get on with his life which mostly consisted of patching up the house. Still, it could have been worse, he thought, so long as he could pay the bank every month then nothing was amiss.

*

It was the middle of Spring when Poppy came to visit. She was surprised not only at the conservatory and fountain but at the rockery and the extensive planting of flowers and vegetables.

'You have made a lot of changes,' she observed. 'I wonder what Stella would think, she liked gardening. Sometimes, when the sun shone.'

She watched her son that evening and thought she knew him well enough to recognise the signs of stress. She thought only a mother knew her child, even a prodigal mother. She guessed he had a financial problem so she thought it was time to step in and offer a solution which would not only benefit him but her as well.

'You do realise that I have some money put away. It's all yours,' she informed him, a couple of days later. 'You can have it now, if you like. I'm sure you can use it.'

Will smiled but it was an uncertain smile.

'Think about it,' she added, softly.

'Thanks Poppy, if I can just chew on it for a few days,' he answered, aware that everything had a price tag.

Poppy was reading in the Conservatory that evening when a young woman and her mother came to the door. It appeared she was going to marry in

August, a rather quick unexpected wedding, and had heard how beautiful their old chapel had become and how the garden was a sight to be seen.

Will raised his eyebrows as Rosie gushed enthusiasm and asked if she could help in any way.

'Well,' said the mother, who called herself Pat. 'We were wondering if we could use this beautiful room for the reception, perhaps even for the wedding seeing how it was once a chapel.'

Rosie stepped back in amazement. 'Well, yes, as far as I am concerned. But I don't have the facility to serve food. I mean I can't do the catering, not for a wedding.'

Pat assured her that would be taken care of by outside caterers who would only have to put their equipment in the kitchen and supply the tables and chairs.

'And the wedding, I don't know if you are allowed to marry here,' she added, now sounding a bit breathless.

'Oh, my husband, George, will arrange for the Registrar to come here. He is so good at organising.'

Rosie frowned, the names George and Pat rang a bell, someone had mentioned them. She would have to think about who it had been.

'Emy,' she said, out loud, as though the name had been put in her mouth.

'Emy,' repeated Pat, looking concerned.

'I believe you went on holiday with Emily and Jack Nielson.'

Pat shifted uncomfortably. 'We try to forget about it, strange couple,' she added, her tone indicating the subject closed.

'She told me what happened,' Rosie informed her, as though protecting Emy's good name.

'I heard she drowned recently in a lake,' Pat said, suddenly open to any gossipy news.

'Yes, her friend tripped and fell against her and, somehow, she fell into the lake. She was rescued, of course, but later she died of secondary drowning.'

'How tragic,' Pat remarked, without showing any emotion. 'She should have known better, she should have known to keep away from water after their holiday fiasco. Now let's get down to business.'

It seemed to Will that all was signed and sealed within the hour and he glanced over to Poppy who seemed completely fascinated by the turn of events.

'Do you know,' Poppy said, after they had left. 'I have been thinking these last few days that, indeed, this could be used as some kind of a centre for events. I must say weddings had not come into my mind. If you were to divide the garden into little areas with tables and chairs and old objects from past gardens, pottery, urns, old gardening tools, wicker baskets and what have you, it would be really charming, really charming.'

Will thought Rosie was about to explode with happiness.

'Marvellous idea,' she gasped. 'Arnie can make the plans and plant it out.'

*

It only took a couple of good summers for 'Tower Lodge' to become known for its teas. Poppy helped with the scones and cakes, a Chef was hired for parties, Agnes helped in the kitchen and Ben helped in the garden when Arnie suffered a feminine breakdown, mostly when the Feng Shui plants took on a life of their own or after the rabbits feasted on his biological lettuces.

Slowly their red bank account changed to black. Poppy sold her flat by the sea and invested in 'Tower Lodge' by converting three rooms for herself; one a bedroom with an 'en suite' and the other a sitting room with a corner for making coffee or tea.

Later, she stripped Rosie's old comfortable kitchen and installed a new one, which would be the envy of any restaurateur. Then she modernised the whole house beginning with the central heating which she found above and beyond all other necessary requirements.

'You know,' Poppy said one evening. 'I was sitting in the garden when I saw a toad in the rockery. He had his head poking out from a space between the stones.'

'It was probably a frog,' Will answered, too quickly, suddenly overcome by something not quite natural.

'No it was a toad. He walked, he didn't jump, and he was brown with lots of ugly markings on him. I would know a toad anywhere.'

'Well, so long as he feels at home,' muttered Rosie, avoiding Will's glance.

Poppy laughed a little too loudly. 'Do you know, I think I'll put a 'toad in the hole' on the menu for the children. They love sausages cooked in batter in the oven. Reggie was a toad,' Poppy laughed again. 'And most missing people are under the rockery,' she added, grinning knowingly.

'Who knows,' Will chuckled, trying to sound amused.

'Not me,' Poppy answered, dunking her biscuit into her cup of tea. 'And if I did know, then it would go with me to my grave.'

Rosie thought Will was about to have a fit for his face became slowly bright red and his hands trembled slightly as he placed his cup on the saucer.

Poppy put her hand in her pocket. 'Look what I found this morning on top of that heap of sand in the corner of the garden.'

'What?' asked Rosie.

'A bone. I think it's a phalange, a foot bone. I was a trainee nurse and we had to learn all the bones in the body. I've never forgotten, it was so stamped into us. I think your interest in archaeology came from me, Will.'

'Could be from a rabbit,' laughed Rosie a little stiffly. 'Would you like another cup of tea?'

'Would you like something in it?' Will asked, hoping that might silence his dried up old mother who had an equally dry humour.

'Not now,' answered Poppy, smiling. 'I think I'll make a 'Toad in the Hole', tomorrow. Then we'll drink to the other toad. God bless him, wherever he is.'

FIRST LOVE REVISITED

It WAS SOME TIME BEFORE Will Windsor saw Jack Nielson sitting on a bench by the 'Crossing' with a black Labrador dog sniffing around nearby.

'Jack, Jack Nielson,' he called. 'How are you doing?'

He had invited him for a coffee and could see how Jack reluctantly accepted. He was not surprised for he could imagine Jack might not want to be confronted with anyone who knew something about him and Emy and their past.

'What do you think of our new conservatory?' he asked, trying to lighten the tension between them. 'And, as you can see, we have renovated the kitchen,' he added, as the coffee machine spurted and hissed into life.

Jack made the obvious, polite, comments of admiration as he swilled the 'Expresso' down in three large gulps.

'And here she is,' he muttered, as Rosie came through the back door with a bunch of flowers.

'Oh, Jack,' she exclaimed. 'How nice to see you. Have you seen our new conservatory and garden?'

'Yes, Will showed me and I've just had a quick coffee. I have to be off because of Vici,' he added, trying to make a getaway.

'I'll come with you, I have to freshen up the flowers on the tables outside,' she stated, walking into the garden.

'Actually,' he said, having given up the idea of escaping from her, 'I've been meaning to 'phone you, I want to thank you for being such a good friend to Emy. She didn't know too many people, we probably shouldn't have moved down here.'

'So many people do that,' she replied, sounding irritated. 'Reach retirement and then move away from where they have lived for years. I don't know what they are thinking. The grass is seldom greener on the other side. It's difficult making a new life when you're older. Will wanted to move. I dug my heels in the local mud. Over my dead body, I told him,' she stopped for a moment remembering how it was over a dead body. Will's father's body.

She cleared her throat. 'Well, anyway, yes. We did build up a friendship.'

'I guess she told you about us.'

'A little, not as much as you might think. She loved you too much to say anything bad about you. You were a lucky man to have such a loving wife.'

Jack hung his head and studied the path.

'You're right, Rosie,' he said, bravely. 'I wasn't there for her. I didn't protect her,' he murmured.

'It wasn't your fault. These things happen. She believed in an afterlife. Perhaps she is with you, watching you.'

He wanted to say, 'God, I hope not' but instead he managed a small smile. 'You never know. I'll have to behave myself.'

Rosie gripped his arm. 'I shouldn't tell you this but I've seen her. By the bench at the 'Crossing'. She was sitting there, as large as life. Then she smiled and disappeared.'

Jack stared at her to see if she was taking some pleasure in shocking him, but he could not see anything in her expression to support that.

'That's a nice thought,' he replied, clearing his throat. 'Something special I should say. I hope she's at peace,' he added.

He wanted to tell Rosie that he had also felt a presence by the 'Crossing' and that Vici often wagged his tail for no apparent reason.

'It's a very special place,' she continued.

'Yes, I believe Emy told me it was a pagan worshipping site until a Christian monk pinched their land.'

Rosie stepped back slightly. 'Well, not exactly. But I guess something like that. Did she tell you about the lights there at night. I can see them from the tower in my house.'

'Yes, she mentioned it. Hope to see you again soon,' he murmured, quickly backing away.

'Emy is still around, remember that,' she called, as she left to go back into the house. 'You will probably see her one day. Probably at the 'Crossing' or when you're walking your dog across the heath.'

Rosie smiled as she entered her beautiful conservatory. She had done exactly what she intended. Jack would always look over his shoulder, he would never be sure if he was being watched. She would try to contact Emy tonight when Will was asleep. The shadow which passed at the end of her bed, it was either Emy or Reginald. She liked to think it was Emy.

Will watched Rosie talking to Jack who fidgeted until he eventually broke away and quickly strode over the small paths between the heather towards his house. He doubted he would see him again in the near future.

He went into the garden and asked his customers if they were satisfied. Poppy was tidying up the kitchen when he returned. He had forgiven his wayward mother who was not only in her element but, diplomatically, kept out of their way in the evenings by retiring to her rooms and watching every sitcom imaginable.

It seemed to Will that they had all settled down to a rather nice life style, without debts and the weight of an old house pushing down on his shoulders, all thanks to his mother. All in all, he felt content, except for the fact his father was under the rockery and poor Emy. He thought she did not deserve to die when she did, she was far too young, far too bright and active. He thought life was cruel.

*　　*　　*

Jack hurried back over the heath trying, unsuccessfully, to forget the past and even considering whether he should move away from the area. He knew he needed someone, something, to fill his life and Vici did not do that. It was a nice dog, a friendly dog, but he slobbered leaving wet streaky lines on his trousers and had a rather demanding character. He thought he did not really have the patience for an animal and felt guilty thinking as he did. However, he had given the dog a good home and Vici was lucky not to have been put down after a too long stay in the kennel.

He could see a black form sitting astride a motorbike as he approached his house. He frowned, he could not think who it could be. The form took off its black helmet and medium length blonde hair straggled down a woman's face. A woman with a motorbike was not in his address book, not that he knew.

'Jack Nielson?'

'Can I help you?'

'Don't you recognise me?'

'Have we met?'

'I think you could say that.'

He recognised the voice. 'Charlene?'

She smiled as he recognised her. 'Yes, me.'

He felt stunned and slightly worried, something between happiness and dread. He had left to go abroad. He really had no option, anyway they were far too young. He could not possibly get tied down at the age of twenty one, even though they had been going out for some years. He had realised that she expected to get engaged and all that followed. His new job had arrived exactly on time, the opportunity to work overseas and to break with Charlene. After all, he told her, he had to consider his career and how could their friendship go further without him first building his future. She had cried, he had expected that, but he had firmly kissed her goodbye and promised to write. Well, he did write a few times.

He invited her into the house for a coffee and talked briefly of the past. Then she kissed him. He could recall the warmth of her body against him, recall the feel of her, their secret lovemaking. He remembered how she had sat behind him on his motorbike, hanging on to his jacket while he showed off as he took the corners too sharply or swerved between the traffic. They had biked around the countryside until they came across some nice little dale, a clearing in a corpse, a trickling stream. It had been romantic but he never forgot to be careful, he was very aware of that. His father had just once broken the ranks of his stuffy, stiff, fellow peers who were almost unable to say the word 'sex', though he reckoned most of them would grab an opportunity if offered by some willing female, assuming they would not be caught, so long as they could get away with it.

His father had handed him a book on reproduction and, at the last minute, confided in him. It was probably the biggest secret the man held and he had divulged it in a moment of confidence.

'Your mother and I had to get married.'

He could hardly believe his ears.

'It was not the best way to start a marriage. Be careful,' he had warned.

It had been the first time his father had shown any signs of being less than perfect. He wanted to shout 'Hurray. Good for you', but he kept quiet to help his father retain his dignity.

'I'll be very careful,' he promised, sincerely.

And he was, except for his affair with Jade when, for some reason or another, he loved with abandonment until he managed to get his brains in a row. He cooled off and she dropped him. He could not blame her, he had not been very diplomatic.

He was more careful after that though Emy had become pregnant. Strange that, he thought. She was on the pill, she swore she had taken it, she said it must have been an upset stomach though, in truth, he could not remember her having had one.

Luckily Charlene, who now called herself 'Charlie', was too old for that which was a plus point since young women were unpredictable, if they thought they were about to lose their lover. He had fleetingly considered rejecting Charlie but, on the spur of the moment, he had suggested they went down to the beach house and stay the night and, perhaps, the next day they could walk along the beach. After all, he thought, nothing need happen, it was just a case of renewing an old friendship. Charlie had jumped at the idea.

He had taken her upstairs to find some underclothes which the girls always left behind. She had pulled two pairs of panties from out of a drawer together with the top Emy had died in. He had kept it, he could not bear to throw it away and he had been startled when she held it up

'Sweet Dreams,' she read. 'How cute.'

In fact, it had been Helen's T-shirt and he remembered how she had worn it on the weekends when he and Emy had stayed at the cottage. How she had come down the stairs into the lounge showing the tops of her legs, almost to the point of exposure. Emy had ignored it because she considered Helen rather plain and certainly not sexually dangerous. It was only later did it dawn on her that the so-called quiet ones, even the so-called plain ones, were just as dangerous.

'I'm sorry, I would rather you didn't take that one, there must be another.'

She looked at him a little surprised and guessed it had some kind of sentimental value.

She held up a plain unadorned shirt. 'What about this one?'

'Yes, that's fine. Listen, I have to drop Vici with the neighbours. They don't mind having him for a day or two. I'll be back in a couple of minutes. Help yourself to another coffee,' he added, as he ran quickly down the stairs.

*

The ride down to Devon had been stressful. He had swerved between the traffic and dangerously overtook whenever he could, while Charlene hung onto his jacket as she did years before, probably closing her eyes in fear and probably wishing she had not agreed to his racy invitation.

He had already regretted asking her to go with him by the time they both wearily climbed off the bike and straightened their stiff backs.

'It's lovely here,' she said, watching the sand as it blew across the beach and gulls swooping overhead. 'Is it yours?'

'No, it belongs to a friend of my daughter,' he answered, as he inserted the key in the kitchen door.

He tried to turn it, took it out and tried again but there was no movement in the lock.

'Strange,' he remarked, as he walked around to the patio and held his hand against the window so he could see in. The room looked empty, no trainers untidily thrown on the floor, no beach towels drying on the backs of chairs. There was nothing except for a couple of armchairs and a coffee table. By this time Charlene was standing on the dunes staring down the beach.

'I'm just going to 'phone my daughter,' he shouted to her, sounding worried.

He walked to where the dunes sheltered him from the wind.

'Sophie, I can't get into the beach house.'

'No, Michael Lee has changed his mind,' she answered, bitterly. 'We can't use it anymore.'

'I think he's changed the lock.'

'Yes, he said he would.'

'Why, what happened?'

'I have to go. I'll 'phone you back. What are you doing there? You didn't say you were going.'

'I know,' Jack replied, shortly. 'I'll speak to you tomorrow evening.'

He hung up quickly. He did not want to go into details.

'Sorry. Charlene, change of plans,' he shouted, as he walked towards her. 'The owner has decided to sell the house. I didn't know, seems he told Sophie. We'll try 'The Cutter'. Nice little pub in the village. I've been there with Emy.'

He purposefully dropped Emy's name to give Charlene a hint of the night ahead, but she did not react.

The Bar was full of local people and holiday makers when they arrived.

'You'll have to wait,' the barman told them when they asked for a table. 'We're real busy tonight.'

Jack's enthusiasm waned yet more as Charlene signed the hotel register, grinning as though she had won the lottery.

'I didn't ask you your surname,' he remarked, reading 'C. Redman' in the hotel register.

'We haven't actually discussed anything about each other. You could be a serial killer for all I know,' she laughed, perhaps nervously.

'You never know,' he replied, as they pushed their way through to the noisy bar and ordered drinks. He watched the congenial barkeeper while Charlene brought him up to date with her life.

He listened, vaguely, while he thought of the weekend he and Emy had spent together at the beach house. He knew he could have been kinder, warmer. He wished he had apologised for all the misery he had caused, made it up properly, loved her as she wanted to be loved. He realised how tolerant she had been to accept him on his terms, his selfish need to be free.

He did not want to remember the past, his last meeting with Helen, he did not want to know what her intentions had been. He did not want to remember Helen, at all. Now he was drowning in guilt. Floundering in hopelessness. He was already in hell and he did not believe it would ever be different.

He thought of Rob, someone he also did not want to think about. He would, normally, have felt sorry for Helen but that was now impossible. He thought they deserved each other. Any sympathy he might have felt for either one of them had now turned to contempt.

He turned his attention back to Charlene who was already planning the next day. They would have a walk down the beach, then stroll through the village and then take a light lunch. Then they would go home to his place and, maybe, she would stay the night with him. Of course, she would eventually take him home to meet her children.

His aversion to Charlene increased by the minute and he was happy the beach house was locked up. He even hoped it would pour with rain next day so he could avoid walking along the beach which he felt would contaminate his memories. He shuddered at the thought of going to their room after dinner.

*

The bedroom and bathroom were decorated pink and white and Charlene giggled as she flopped down on the pink candlewick bedspread. He knew she expected him to lie next to her but instead he walked over to the window and looked down at the almost silent street below.

He puffed softly through his lips, closed his eyes and wished he was home.

Charlene was in the pink bathroom when he turned around.

'Oh, what a cute bathroom,' she cooed.

He wished she would stop using the word, 'cute'. He wanted to tell her to act her age, she was not seventeen. He knew the night was going to be a disaster and it would be his fault.

When he looked again, Charlene was fluffing up bubbles in the bath. He knew she expected him to wash her back, work his way down her body, around her breasts and between her legs. Instead he stayed in the bedroom watching the late night news as though that was more important than satisfying his possibly nymphomaniac ex-girl friend.

She returned to the bedroom drying her hair and wearing the uninteresting T-shirt.

'I'm finished if you want the bathroom,' she informed him, sounding worried and disappointed.

'Thanks,' he replied, sounding unenthusiastic.

'Listen,' she said. 'It's all a little too quick, for me, for both of us. Shall we take things slowly.'

Jack looked down at the pink carpet. 'Sorry, it's my fault. Emy's death is too new. I thought I could sweep it away, get over it, but I can't, not yet. Perhaps in a little while.'

'That's alright,' she answered, sympathetically. 'I understand. I'm tired. I think I'll call it a day.'

'Yes, so will I. The traffic was heavy.'

He felt mean, in fact he felt very guilty as though he had encouraged her when he knew full well it was not really what he wanted.

He removed a bedside table and pushed the twin beds together to soften the tension. Charlene smiled, as though her damaged ego had been slightly repaired, when he got into bed and turned on his side to face her. She smiled gently and he kissed her cheek and she returned mouthy kisses.

He suddenly stopped. 'I can't, I don't have a condom.'

'We don't need one of those, nothing can go wrong at my age,' she laughed, lightly.

'Yes, it can,' he answered. 'I always wear one.'

He knew he sounded as though he slept around on a regular basis and that such a remark was suggesting one, or both, of them was possibly carrying a social disease.

Charlene sat up, horrified. 'You know what, Jack Nielson, I don't know you and I have a feeling I don't want to. Perhaps you have too much baggage, too much past. How do I know where you've been and who with.'

'I'm just careful.'

'No, you're just insulting.'

She got up and pushed her bed away from his as he walked across to the window to breathe in the fresh night air and look at the stars glittering in the dark blue sky. A yellow butterfly resting on the windowsill flew up and fluttered around his head before disappearing. He did not know why but he thought of Emy.

'I love you, Emy. I will never forget you,' he murmured, as he returned to his bed.

Charlene laid on her side with her back to him and he thought that was what he wanted. He had no need, at this moment, to relive his youth with her again. He wanted only to concentrate on the years he had with Emy. He would return home and talk to Rosie. Maybe she could help to make him feel better.

He woke with a start as a black shadow moved across the room.

'Emy?'

He looked up to see the butterfly resting on the pink lampshade above his bed.

'Don't leave,' he whispered. 'I need you.'

LOVE IN THE MIST

It WAS LATE SPRING WHEN POPPY panicked. Arnold Waters, landscaper and almost permanent gardener, had not turned up for the fourth day in a row. She tut-tutted as she 'phoned Jack Nielson to remind him that he had once promised to help out whenever necessary and Jack, the gentleman that he was, kept his promise.

He had been weeding flower beds for some time before Poppy asked if he would like a beer and a sandwich. He had happily taken up her offer and she walked away mumbling about people who let other people down.

He sat down, wearily, on a garden chair remembering how Poppy had buttonholed him at Emy's funeral. He could think of better things to do with his time, not least something more recreational such as replacing his motorbike with a small yacht. He had brushed aside Emy's suggestion of joining the local sailing club but now it all seemed such a bother to go too far afield.

He would seriously think about it as life had ground to a standstill and Charlene was long gone. He was sorry about that but he felt nothing for her, she no longer appealed to him and he wondered what he had ever seen in her. Well, he probably did know, youth with an overdose of testosterone

Poppy reappeared with the beer followed by Rosie, a slightly built man and a young woman.

'Arnold's turned up', Poppy said, obviously embarrassed. 'There was a misunderstanding, he pulled his back', she added, sounding flustered as she quickly disappeared back into the house.

'Jack Nielson, whatever are you doing,' Rosie asked, glancing at his boots and dirty hands.

'Just helping out. Poppy was a bit desperate.'

'I'm Arnold Waters,' said the man, holding out his hand. 'I'm sorry Poppy roped you in. Sorry about that. This is Alison, my daughter.'

He shook her hand. It was a noticeably firm handshake.

'I've thinned them out,' he informed her, looking down at a bed of sad looking flowers. '

'Oh, you shouldn't have done that. They're Nigella, 'Love in the Mist', They always look a bit straggly.'

'Appropriate name,' he chuckled. 'That just about sums it up. Love I mean.'

He looked away embarrassed at his comment.

Alison laughed. 'I know all about it. I walked around in a haze for some time. When it cleared, I found myself at sea.'

'Very good. That says it all. I'm still battling the storm,' he chuckled at their repartee.

'Well, I have to get to work. My father pulled his back but he won't lie down.'

'Have no time to do nothing, Alison.'

Rosie pulled him away. 'Come with me, Arnie. I'll make you a drink, you look tired.'

'Gardening is about the only thing I do these days,' Jack informed her.

'It's my work,' she grinned. 'This is how I earn my bread and butter.'

'I can think of worse ways. Do you live around here?'

'Yes, in the village with Dad. He and my mother divorced. She went up to Yorkshire to visit her sister and never came back. Everyone's happy.'

'What about you?'

'Nobody has ever asked me that. Good question, I'll have to think about that one.'

She took out a cigarette. 'Dad needs me. He can't run the business alone. I'm just happy I'm here to help him. He really likes working by Rosie, he's designed her entire garden. They have a lot in common,' she added. 'They're both a bit spiritual. People find him strange which rather isolates him. Some people even think he is 'on the other side' but he isn't. He's just not macho.'

'He doesn't have to be, everyone is different.'

'He thinks he sees spirits, actually I think he does. He was just saying the other day how he once in a while sees a woman sitting on the bench by the 'Crossing'. She has a dog with her.'

Jack looked stunned. 'What kind of dog?'

'I don't know, I'll ask him. Does that say anything to you?'

'No, of course not. I'm just interested. That's all. Where do you work?' he asked, wanting to change the subject.

'As I said, I help Dad. He owns the Garden Centre. At the moment, he's tied up with Feng Shui and Bonsai so I do most of it now.'

'He's done this nicely,' Jack observed, looking around the garden. He stood up. 'Well, I guess I had better be off.'

'I think I've seen you at the Garden Centre though not recently,' she rushed her remark, as though trying to keep the conversation going a little longer.

'Yes, I used to go frequently. Not so much anymore, since I lost my wife.'

'Yes, Rosie told me about it. I'm sorry.'

He turned as he heard a sound on the stones between the flower beds.

'Still here?' asked Rosie, slightly out of breath.

'Yes, I've been talking to Alison.'

'Alison is my surrogate daughter, aren't you dear?'

'If you say so,' she replied, sounding reticent.

'I don't have any children and she seldom sees her mother. What more can I ask for?'

'I've a couple of daughters you can adopt, Rosie. I can see you've made a good choice.'

Alison lowered her head. 'Thanks for that. All compliments kindly received and accepted. Shall we form a mutual admiration society?'

'Good idea, but you'll have a job finding something to admire,' he replied, sounding sad.

'Would the two of you like to come to

supper?' Rosie asked, quickly, sensing Jack's unhappiness. 'Poppy is making a 'Toad in the Hole'.

'I would love to,' answered Alison.

'Thanks, fine. I'll just go home to let the dog out. He's been alone for some time,' replied Jack, sounding happier.'

'I'll walk with you, I'll get Megan. She's in the house, probably being spoilt by Poppy.'

'Megan?'

'My dog, she comes everywhere with me.'

Jack stood almost frozen with disbelief as they entered the conservatory. Megan was sitting on Poppy's lap being pampered. She was a small black poodle.

Alison picked her up and ruffled the soft curly hair on her head.

'She's beautiful. I wasn't planning to take a poodle but I couldn't resist her. I got her from the local dog's home.'

'That's where I got Vici. I hope he behaves himself, he could make mincemeat of her,' he said, sounding worried.

'Don't you worry about Megan. She's a girl who can hold her own and, if not, then I'll carry her. It's such a lovely afternoon to walk across the heath. We can sit on the bench when we get back and see if we can call up dad's lady friend, the spirit and her dog.'

He winced but Alison did not notice. Why should she.

ALISON WATERS

The AFTERNOON WAS BRIGHT but still slightly cool when she and Jack made a turn around the heath with their dogs. They had strolled behind each other in semi silence, since the paths were narrow, arriving back at the old bench by the 'Crossing'.

She had expected him to carry on home but, to her surprise, he sat down and stared across the heath while he told her how he had taken an early retirement and moved with his wife, Emy, to where he lived now. He doubted whether the move had been wise, though his wife's death would have happened wherever they had lived. He sounded both sad and wistful.

In return, she had told him something of her past, giving him the impression that she was recovering from some recent love affair. She had lied. If she was recovering from anyone it was a seventeen year old schoolboy, called Philip Price, Phil. A schoolboy who had left behind not only a beautiful daughter but a deep scar within her psyche. She painfully recalled the one careless afternoon, over twenty years ago, and wished she had chosen another name for her daughter. Any name other than Philippa, so obviously his name.

Jack Nielson seemed to enjoy their discussion and had continued to confide in her about where he had been and what he had done. She wondered whether his memories were perhaps just a shade too colourful and concentrated not only on what he said but how he said it.

Perhaps he had become conscious of his openness, and her thoughtfulness, for suddenly he became reserved. She felt strangely hurt at his sudden change of mood and covered her feelings by being flippant and teasing him by pretending to call up the spirit of 'the woman with the dog'. The one her father had claimed to have 'seen' sitting on the bench where they sat now. Jack had looked uncomfortable so she changed the subject yet again and asked him if he had any future plans, discreetly referring to the loss of his wife. He had answered her rather shortly as though his personal affairs were, after all, not her business. She decided he was controlling and was unsure whether she admired that or not.

By the end of the afternoon, she considered Jack Neilson to be a pretty cool customer, she also considered him to be just the man she needed. She thought he must have been very handsome when he was young, he still was. He was a man she could admire; be seen with; be connected to; belong to. She considered their age difference irrelevant so long as it did not physically interfere with her objective, her goal.

'Why don't you come to the Garden Centre and chose some plants?'

'I don't know what I need. I just rake the beds over, pull out the weeds, mow the grass. I seem to have ground to a standstill.'

'Oh, you mustn't say that. Come on, you're still young. Don't sit and wait for God.'

He looked surprised. 'Well, I'm not exactly that far. But you're right. I have to do something,' he agreed, laughing lightly.

'Sorry, I didn't mean to be rude.'

'You weren't. You know, I'm thinking of buying a small sailboat. Do you sail?' he added, as an afterthought.

'No, I don't but I would like to.'

'Well, I'll let you know,' he replied, quickly, conscious he was backing off.

'I would love that. I hope you can find something.'

'Oh, there's plenty for sale. I have only to put my mind to it.'

'Can I help in the search?'

He gave a positive grunt, now aware he was on dangerous ground. He was cautious after the disaster with Charlene. He really did not want to go down that road again, not have a woman shout at him, telling him what he was, and was not, before finally slamming the door in his face. Let alone the catastrophe with Helen. He shivered at the thought of the last years, a DNA paternity test followed by an HIV test. He considered that abnormal. He did not know anyone who had been subjected to both of those, let alone one of them.

He realised he had too many secrets, too much baggage, he really could not see how he could begin again, certainly not with a young woman the same age as his eldest daughter. He dreaded any family upsets, Sophie and Jillie would never accept her. He decided it unwise to take Alison on board, be it a boat or his life, even if he would like to do so. He would stand firm, resolute, and suppress any awakening desires.

'I have to go,' she said standing up and walking back towards her van. 'See you later,' she called.

'I'm going home to clean up.'

'We could always have a cup of tea together. Nothing too dangerous,' she laughed.

'A cup of tea in Rosie's garden. Yes, we must do that.'

She drove away uncertain whether he would take the bait. She thought probably not, he was far too experienced to fall for her invitation although he was alone and lonely; an excellent combination.

The leafy lanes, once ancient tracks, twisted and turned between high hedgerows, the sun flickered through the branches and leaves, mesmerizing her, calming her, enabling her to return to the painful past and him. One fateful afternoon with him, Philip Price.

❧

It was a beautiful day, the first Friday in September, a day she would never forget. A day when she allowed Philip Price to touch her as he had done numerous times before. She had felt almost faint from the now familiar warm feeling which throbbed throughout the secret parts of her body. A thrill she had up until then managed to control; to subdue.

She felt strangely faint as she allowed him to ease her onto the settee, vaguely pushing his hand away as he touched her; giving little screams of excitement; until suddenly she stopped aware of a searing pain within her body. She tried to push him off but he leaned too heavily on her and held her wrists down as he continued his jarring movements. Eventually, he gave a strange groan, screwed his face as though in pain, and abruptly stopped, silent. She lay motionless until he sat up, took a half dirty handkerchief from out of his pocket, wiped himself and zipped up his trousers.

'Good, eh?', he said, grinning, as she carefully stood up and ran sobbing to the bathroom.

Blood was smeared between her legs together with a slimy substance. She was aware of feeling sick, sick from fear and humiliation, sick in case he should tell his friends about her and what he had done. She had imagined her first time would be a tender, loving, experience but he had not once thought of her, had not uttered a kind word, a word of concern; nothing.

He was sitting on the settee watching television when she eventually returned. He looked up and smiled.

'Good, eh?', he repeated.

She wanted to say it was not good, she had not wanted that to happen, she was frightened her mother would find out; she was frightened she would become pregnant. She had heard stories of that happening to other girls. He pulled her towards him again but she broke loose.

'You have to go, quickly. My mother will be home any minute.'

He gave her another mouthy kiss.

'See you tomorrow. Only two more weeks and then I'm gone.'

'Gone?'

'To Australia.'

'For a holiday?'

'Don't think so, they've got permission to emigrate. They waited for my exam results,' he explained, almost incoherently. 'I've told them I don't want to go but they won't even discuss it. I can't tell you what I feel, losing you and all my friends.'

She had stood frozen, her mouth dry.

'But just now,' she whispered. 'What you did just now.'

'You love me, don't you?'

He pulled her to him and snuggled his head against her neck. 'You enjoyed it, didn't you? I will always remember this afternoon. It's my first time, our first time. That must be special.' He kissed her again. 'I do love you.'

She had continued seeing him but she had pushed him away when he wanted more than just a kiss and a fumble.

'You're going away, leaving me. What is the point of doing that anymore?'

'But we'll keep in touch. I promise to write. I will never forget you. No matter how far away we are from each other. Perhaps, one day, you will come to Australia and then we'll get married. I love you, I always will.'

She had not let him love her again.

He had left, just as he said he would, and she had waited for a letter, a card, but none came. The pain was deeper than she could have imagined but it was only the beginning of a constant ache. One which would never to go away.

She had done everything she could think of, taken medicine which gave her stomach ache, jogged countless miles, skipped, jumped from small heights and rolled down grassy slopes. Nothing happened, nothing moved within her body. She was pregnant.

It was just after New Year when her mother became aware of her condition. She owned up and all hell broke loose. When her father returned home that evening he was bombarded by what his only daughter, his only child, had done.

She tried to explain she had only done it once. He, Philip Price, had left the country with his parents two weeks later. She had not meant it to happen, he had overwhelmed her. She had cried as accusations of who was to blame, apart from her, were thrown around. She watched her parents fighting; they fought over everything and anything. Her mother was the one who complained the most and she had felt sorry for her father, a small rather insignificant man, who was told his failings on a daily basis. The words 'always' and 'never' were bantered around, words mostly used by her mother. She felt those two words should be banned, deleted from the English langue, any language, since they were inaccurate. Nothing was always and nothing was never. She hated those words and swore she would never use them. She also felt her father should not have married since he was too kind and considerate to stand up for himself against a dominant, strong minded, woman such as her mother, although he had tried to protect her by shouting back at his wife.

'Leave her alone, Connie. She's just a child, she didn't realise what she was doing. Done is done, making good decisions is what's important now. Your shouting doesn't help anyone. She needs to be loved, not yelled at.'

'I'm not yelling at her. I'm yelling at that little bastard. I know his mother, she's my hairdresser. She's been talking for years about emigrating to Australia. How could she have let this happen, what kind of a mother is she?'

Her mother had sobbed as she spoke and she had sobbed with her.

'Well, I'm sure she didn't know anything about it. You can't blame her,' her father replied, sympathetically, as he put his arm on her shoulder which made her cry even more.

In fact, she had cried on and off all evening and most of the night and at regular intervals during the next months.

Her mother had sat on her bed early next morning and stroked her hair. She had brought her a cup of tea, something she had never done before, unless she was sick.

'We have to find a solution. Who knows about this?' she asked, kindly.

'No one.'

'Does this boy know?'

'He was gone before I knew it. I've never heard from him. One of his friends said he was living outside Sidney. That's all I know.'

'Your father and I have been talking. We have decided that it would be better if you and me go to Aunt Flossy in Yorkshire. You will have the baby up there. No one down here has to know.'

'And the baby?'

'We'll see when the time comes.'

'I'm not having it adopted.'

'We'll see.'

'No, we won't see. I'm not giving it away.'

Her mother's sister, Florence, known as Flossy, lived alone in a farmhouse on the edge of a small town in Yorkshire. The two sisters had inherited the property, which included a large amount of land, after their father died. Her mother had agreed to Flossy staying in the farmhouse and, in time, Alison being the only offspring between them would inherit everything.

Flossy, who had remained single, had no inclination to carry the burden of the smallholding as her father had done. Her sister had sympathised and together they agreed to sell the land to the neighbouring farmer except for an adjoining field. Flossy had then taken over a local florist shop with her half of the proceeds, which seemed to be financially successful, and had admitted to being *happy for the first time in her life, while her mother admitted she was jealous of her sister's freedom.*

Aunt Flossy was a kind woman, looked with tenderness at her swelling abdomen, and began to knit baby clothes in the evenings. Eventually, her mother had joined in, at first reluctantly but later it seemed as though both women were excited at the idea of a newcomer in their midst.

Her mother had tried to explain to her what was ahead, the pain was natural, it was only for one day and then she would have a beautiful little girl, a fact established by a scan at the hospital.

A trainee midwife, a young woman who seemed not to have too much experience, or diplomacy, looked down on her patient. 'Hadn't she heard of the Pill, hadn't he heard of a condom?' Her mother had pulled the girl into the hall and protected her against the sharp judgemental tongue of the young woman. She had felt loved, for the first time her mother had actually demonstrated love, something she had never done before, not to her or to her father.

She had been happy at the display of affection but it had not change how she felt, had not made her feel less imprisoned, caught between two women who had total control over every aspect of her life. She thought that would never change, she would grow old as they grew even older. She would become one of them. Sometimes her father visited, tense occasions which he kept as short as possible.

Once she had walked with him to the gate, tightly holding his rough hand.

'I want to come home. Please, wait for me daddy, please let me come home.'

He had held her in his arms and whispered, for her to be brave, it would be alright, she could come home whenever she wanted, he would wait for her.

The frightening day arrived. She thought it was rather like waiting for death, something so unavoidable as that. She suffered, as she had been warned, and grasped held her mother's hand, along with Aunt Flossy's, while any pride disappeared as she became overwhelmed with pain.

It was a nice baby, she realised that, and had held onto her in case some strange woman came and thrust a pen in her hand and said, 'sign here or you'll be sorry'. Instead, Aunt Flossy had begged she and her mother to give her the baby, she would look after it and Alison could visit her whenever she wanted. She could get her life together and when she was settled she could take her child back home. She would understand, she would give the baby back without a scene, without a tear.

'Yes, fine. Whatever,' she had answered, trying to ignore the small pink thing with a demanding, screechy, voice. 'Anyway, I'm not giving her to some stranger.'

'Well, actually,' her mother had said rather softly. 'I've decided not to go home. Your father and I don't get on that well together. We won't divorce immediately, just live apart for a while. We've discussed it already. He doesn't seem to mind. In fact, he doesn't mind at all. He's already agreed.'

'Oh, Connie, would you stay here with me and the baby? Would you do that?' Flossy had gasped, sounding completely overwhelmed.

'Yes, I don't have a problem with that. It's all for the best, the two of us looking after the baby. What do you think, Alison?'

Flossy turned to her. 'What do you think, dear?' she asked, excitedly.

'I don't know. I guess it's okay. Whatever.'

'Listen,' her mother said, sounding too controlled. 'You can't look after a baby, you know you can't. Daddy and I have been living apart for a long time. I'm happy here with Flossy, in our old family house. Philippa would have a good home. We'll be honest and tell her you are her mother and I'm her grandmother and Flossy is her great-aunt. What do you think?'

'When do I get to go home?'

'When everything has quietened done. After a year or so, if you want to.'

'You can come with me to the shop. I'll teach you all about flowers, their names and how to make bouquets. You will like that. Then, maybe, you can go home and help your dad in the Garden Centre. If you still want to,' offered Flossy, breathlessly.

'And what will she call me?'

'Mama or mummy. You will always be her mother. Mama, Nana and Auntie Flossy. Perfect.'

*   *   *

Philippa, called Pippa, was nearly three years old when it became obvious she saw her Nana as her mother. Nana became Nama.

She did not blame her mother for her muddled child, after all she was with her all day and came out of bed at night to comfort and soothe her. She could never compete with that and, in truth, she had not wanted to.

She had taken Pippa back home with her a couple of times and tried to settle her down alongside she and her father, but the child had only cried to go back to Nama and Aunt Flossy and the little Shetland pony, called 'Jogalong,' who lived in the field behind the farmhouse. She realised she had lost the momentum of being a mother and also realised that pulling her away from the two women would be selfish. She had slowly given up any claim to motherhood and returned to her father to help him in the Garden Centre. Her training in Aunt Flossy's flower shop had worked out well and they had settled down to some kind of a routine and, once in a while, she went up to Yorkshire to visit her blossoming child.

She had tried to bridge the gap as Pippa became a teenager by sharing an interest in pop music, clothes and makeup. Their true relationship was swept under the carpet, discussed by no one and certainly not by Pippa who was not only aware she was her birth mother but her young father lived somewhere in Australia.

Now, twenty years later, she thought Pippa looked like her father, a pretty girl, tall and slim, blue eyes and dark curly hair, unmistakably Philip Price's daughter. Once in a while, she held an old school photo under a magnifying glass so that she could remember how he looked, how he had been good at sports, involved in school activities and even a Prefect. She thought he would have appealed to any girl, she had just happened to be there when he was ready to explore, exploit, his manhood. She wondered how innocent she really was, she must have known that bringing him home nearly every afternoon to an empty house would end in trouble. And, of course, it did.

She had tried a few relationships over the years simply because her mother and aunt thought she should get her life together, but they had not worked out. However, she had recently met David Coleman who sold biological compost to the Garden Centre and who had been in the same class as Philip Price.

Neither of them mentioned him, Philip Price, and it seemed the world at large believed her younger sister, Pippa, who lived with her divorced mother in the north, was an 'afterthought'. A product of her parents who may, or may not, have been a factor in their separation.

All in all, she thought the truth had been well hidden and that, most probably, Philip had not shared his fun afternoons with his friends. Maybe he waited until he got to Australia before he boasted about his conquest. He would be safe there, without her hysterical mother banging on his parents' front door.

She turned her thoughts back to David Coleman who had picked up a beer mat on their last visit to a Pub and read the handwriting on the back.

'Listen to this,' he had said, laughing rather loudly. "Sex is not the answer. Sex is the question. Yes, is the answer". What do you think of that?' he questioned, looking at her squarely in the face.

'Depends on what you want.'

'Everyone wants sex, don't they?'

'I guess so.'

'Well, then. What about it?'

She had paused for a moment to consider what she wanted. Pippa had 'phoned to say that she had just got engaged and would be bringing the love of her life, Mark, down to see her. He was mad for horses just as she was. She said she had never been so happy.

'I thought you were planning to come and live down here,' she had asked, a little hopefully.

'Naa,' Pippa had answered, too quickly. 'My life is up here. Why don't you come up here to live?' she replied, insincerely.

'Because like you, my life is somewhere else.'

'We'll talk about it.'

'Nothing to talk about.'

She had hung up quickly, suddenly aware of being alone. No mother around the corner, no siblings, no child. In fact, no one except her father.

'Well,' David asked, impatiently. 'Your place or mine?'

'Yours. My father's at home.'

They had driven to his house in silence. It was a simple place, not somewhere she would want to spend the rest of her life. His bedroom was untidy and the sheets looked as though they needed changing. She avoided looking at him as they undressed each other. It was all so planned.

She had wished she could feel sexual but she remained tense as he pulled her down onto the bed.

'I'm on the pill,' she whispered.

'Great.'

She hoped she might enjoy his touch, she even thought, for a moment, she felt sexual. But then, just as so many times before, she controlled any natural desires. She bit her lip, determined to overcome her feelings and act the part of the easy lay, she would let him think she enjoyed it. She gave little screeches at the right time, his sweat moistened her breasts along with his slimy kisses. She groaned, he roared, she screamed.

'Good, eh!' she stated, as he rolled on his back and offered her a cigarette.

'Fantastic.'

'Can't get enough of it.'

'That's easy to fix.'

'Then that's what we'll do. Fix it until we've had enough of each other.'

He looked surprised. 'Have you any idea how long that will take?'

'No idea. Probably when the mutual interest enters a black hole.'

'That doesn't sound very optimistic.'

'Why not? An pessimist is only an optimist with more information.'

'Or experience,' he laughed. 'Perhaps you would like to share one or the other with me. On the other hand, I'd rather you didn't. Funny, I never saw you as someone who lived in the 'fast lane'. I guess you've been around.'

'I heard you married,' she asked, changing the subject.

'Yep, that was a real disaster, followed by a long standing partner who was last seen riding into the sunset.'

'Perhaps she was long suffering,' she muttered.

'Could be, she said she was. But I don't think so. She flew out the window when my money flew out the door.'

'Don't you mean her horse jumped out of the window, with her on it?'

'Probably.'

'I think it must be easy to love a man with money.'

He laughed, loudly. 'You're betting on the wrong horse. 'It ain't me babe It ain't me you're looking for, babe'. Did you ever marry?' he added, after he had finished his musical fiasco.

'Why should I want to do that?'

'I thought all women wanted to.'

'Not me. I like it as it is. No strings attached. Not too many emotions, keep it simple.'

'That makes life easy. Feel like it again?'

'As often as you want.'

'Great,' he moaned, as he began again to satisfy his needs while she bit her lip again, aware that any physical pain or mental anguish were worth enduring for the greater scheme of things, her greater scheme.

They drove back in silence until they reached her house. The light was on, her father always waited up for her. She loved him because he cared for her though he pretended not to be concerned if she was late home.

She stepped out of the car. 'Thanks for an interesting evening.'

'Are you doing anything tomorrow night?'

'I'll give you a call,' she answered, almost certain she would not be fertile for at least another week.

*

She was surprised when Jack Nielson turned up next day at 'Rosie's Tea House.' A petite blond girl was with him who he introduced as his daughter, Jillie.

'Come for a cup of tea?' she asked, smiling broadly, hoping he had come to see her.

'I'm looking for Rosie. What are you doing here?' he replied, sounding surprised.

'My father's back is still bad, not that he will admit it. He can't even stand up. The doctor came this morning, I don't think he will be doing much for a while. Probably sciatica.'

'That's painful. Do you know where Rosie is?' he added.

'She's gone into town. Poppy is in the kitchen, she'll make you something,' she informed him, trying not to sound disappointed at his lack of interest in her. 'Shall I get her or are you going in?'

'Would you like to have a drink with us? That's if you can spare the time,' he smiled, the smile which made him so attractive.

'I'm my own boss. I can do what I want, when I want,' she replied, proudly.

'What a luxury, hang on to that.'

They chatted about things in general, mostly about his daughter who was enthusiastic about history and seemed quite politically minded, leaning heavily towards the left. She found youth so pure, so full of good intentions and rightly critical of the establishment.

Jillie looked around obviously embarrassed.

'If you don't mind, I'll take a look at the Conservatory, haven't seen it yet,' she said, standing up rather too quickly, obviously beating a retreat.

Jack smiled proudly as he watched her walk in the direction of the house.

'Now, what about that drink?' he asked.

'You won't find anything alcoholic here. I'll settle for a tonic water.'

She watched him saunter off to find Jillie and Poppy. She thought he looked very Scandinavian, lightly tanned, his fair hair now mixed with grey and his surname, 'Nielson', was not typically English.

'I wonder what neck of the woods his forefathers came from,' she murmured.

When she looked up a little later, Jack and daughter were returning from the main house. Jillie held a tray with glass dishes filled with ice cream and fresh fruit and Jack two cokes and a tonic water.

'That looks good. They should be from the garden,' she said, pointing her spoon towards the fruit. 'There's some raspberry bushes at the back.'

'I've never seen all of the garden,' Jack said, curiously.

'Okay, eat up and we'll go for a stroll. I'll show you our tea roses. They're really beautiful.'

'Do you mind if I go home. I have some books to catch up on,' Jillie butted in, unable to share their enthusiasm in flower beds and potted plants.

She frowned, her mother had said exactly what she was now thinking. She felt more like her every day. In any case, she was not planning to hang around while her father sized up this 'Alison woman', who, in return, showed an obvious interest in him. She was sick of men, they were all the same.

'No, go ahead. I won't be long,' Jack replied, smiling broadly, which added to her annoyance.

'That's okay, Don't hurry,' Jillie replied, as though it was of no importance. 'Raspberries are my favourite fruit,' she added, scraping her dish while glancing sideways at Alison who she thought found herself rather interesting.

'I'll get a bowl and pick you some,' she offered, only too happy to please.

'Thanks, but you don't have to do that.'

'No, I don't have to but I'd like to.'

She watched Jillie leave the tea garden, satisfied that she was on the right track by appeasing the critical daughter.

She stretched her bare legs, laid back and closed her eyes, conscious of Jack next to her, probably summing her up. She knew she looked good and smiled confidently.

Sometimes, in the summer, she would wipe her arm across her face and absorbed the sweet smell of her moist skin, a mix of sun and flowers. She loved summer; she thought she could love Jack Nielson. His presence confirmed her maternal instincts, she wanted a baby. She was already thirty six and very much aware she was running out of time. She had given birth to Pippa but that was all. She had never been hers but rather a gift, a present, to be shared between her mother and aunt.

She opened her eyes and caught Jack studying her and smiling his beautiful smile. She desired him, for the first time since Philip Price she felt sexually attracted.

She thought of the night she had been with David Coleman. A feeling of horror ran through her as she thought of her decision in the pub. She had decided that a child with him was about as good as she could get, she would allow herself to become pregnant and then, if she did conceive, she would visit her mother for a couple of weeks, have an imaginary affair with some non-existent guy, come back home to her father and surprise, surprise, she was pregnant. A child conceived, by chance, with some unknown man who she had met in a pub and screwed in an alleyway. No memory of how he looked or where she had been. Simple.

Now, she was faced with the fact that she did not want David's child nor did she want a child from frozen sperm stored in some hospital. She wanted Jack Nielson's child. She would buy the 'morning-after' pill first thing tomorrow, in the unlikely event she had conceived during her unromantic night with David Coleman.

Then, she would follow her original plan if she got what she wanted from Jack Nielson, though she was pretty sure he would carefully consider his actions. It was not going to be a walk over.

*

Jack Nielson looked rather embarrassed as they sauntered between the flower beds discussing various types and reading the names on the hanging labels. Finally, they came to the kitchen garden where she, unnecessarily, pointed out the raspberries climbing between canes, red and black current bushes, a few gooseberries bushes and straggling blackberries climbing mostly out of reach within a bordering hedgerow.

'We try to use our own fruit whenever possible,' she informed him.

He noticed how she used the word 'we' as though she was part of Rosie's family. Perhaps she read his thoughts.

'Rosie told you, she sees me as her surrogate daughter. Sweet. I've never understood why she and Will married so late. Both of them alone for so long, they could have had a family.'

'Yes,' he agreed. 'But I expect they had their reasons. There's usually more to it.'

She stepped back, with the intention of returning to the house, when her foot slipped off the path and down the side of a vegetable bed. She gave a sharp scream of pain.

'Oh, my ankle,' she cried.

Jack lifted her up and she put her arm around his shoulder for support.

'Can you hop back?'

'If you don't mind me leaning on you.'

'Lean on me when you're not strong,' he sung, continuing to vaguely hum an unrecognisable tune.

'A singing knight in shining armour,' she laughed. 'What more could a damsel in distress ask for?'

He blushed, obviously embarrassed. 'Come on, let's get you back.'

She wondered how she had managed to get it together as she limped painfully back to the house; it was as though someone, something, had arranged for her to fall almost into his arms. She realised that this was her chance of making him more aware of her, while unaware of her need for him.

Rosie was obviously a little hysterical when she phoned next day. She could hear Poppy in the background shouting, 'ask Alison to ask him.'

'Ask what?'

'Poppy wants you to ask Jack Nielson if he could help out for a few days. I've got one temporary help but he's away on holiday. You and your father can't come and I have no one else to ask, unless you know of somebody.'

Of course, she knew numerous, untrained, young men who would like to earn an extra buck.

'No, Rosie, I don't think I know of anyone except, of course, Jack Nielson. I'll give him a ring. See what he says.'

'We don't like to ask him. Not after Poppy roped him in for nothing.'

Jack Nielson did not seem surprised when she contacted him.

'Of course, I'll help out. Just say when.'

'Oh, thank you so much. What would we do without you?' she gushed.

'What's the order of the day?'

'Well, my foot is still swollen and I'm not supposed to put any weight on it. It could still take a while before I'm back to normal. I thought perhaps you could pick me up so I can show you what to do. Would you do me a favour,' she added. 'Could you first give me a lift to the chemist?'

'No problem, I'll be right over. By the way, what about the Garden Centre, who's going to run that?'

'We have an old hand and a couple of trainee boys, my father isn't going to lie in bed longer than he has to and I'll pop in and out. It will have to run itself for a while.'

'Where do you live?'

'First star right of Venus.'

He laughed. 'Of course, where else.'

'We live on the premises.'

He hung up a little puzzled. Alison was able to hobble around in Rosie's garden when she should be at the Garden Centre. He brushed aside the idea that, perhaps, he was being used and that, most likely, he would land up driving both she and her father around. He did not care if that was so. He felt happy for the first time in what seemed ages, he felt needed. He even wondered if there was a life after Emy.

JILLIE

Jack WAS SWEEPING LEAVES in the front garden when Jillie arrived in her old second hand car. He strolled towards her, happy to see her, for her visits were too short and too seldom.

She greeted him with a warm kiss as she made her way to the front door. Jack followed her, recognising how much she took after her mother, her movements; the way she held her head; the small side glance; the grin. Everyone said she took after him but he could not see it. Still, he had to admit she had inherited his blond hair and love for sailing.

'Good you could make it. It's been too long since your last visit.'

'I've been studying like mad. I have to make a decision about next year, whether to go on or not. I mean, what can I do with history.

'There must be something.'

'I'm thinking about genealogy.'

'That sounds interesting. Is there any work to be found in it?'

'Probably not, but I'm going to look into it.'

'Well, you can start with my side of the family. I mean the name Nielson must say something. Traces of an invading Viking who ravished some wild peasant girl.'

'Possibly,' she laughed. 'Maybe, he was known as 'Wilfred the Winner'. That's if he had a name.'

'More likely 'Jacque the Loser'. I think I'll change my name to Jacques de l'Oser-Nielson.'

She laughed again and threw her arms around his neck. 'That's French. Anyway, you're not a loser, never have been and never will be.'

'I lost your mother. You can blame me for that.'

He turned away, aware that he had never spoken like that before. He had actually spoken words he hardly dared to admit.

'Don't talk like that. It's not true. She had bad luck, really rotten bad luck. Anyway, talking of Mum I have something to tell you.'

He suddenly felt nervous. 'What?'

'I think I've met her.'

He felt a jolt pass through him, a basic human fear of the unknown.

'Impossible.'

'Yes, I know it is. But something happened, something I can't account for.'

'What?'

'Do you remember the last time I was here. I went home while you stayed in Rosie's garden talking to that girl, Alison. Well, I sat for a while on the bench where the paths cross. A woman walked towards me, there was something about her which seemed familiar. Anyway, she sat next to me and, of course, I got up to leave but she began talking to me so I had to be polite and stay. I wasn't really listening to her until she said she had lived in Hong Kong.

Then, everything she said seemed to be familiar, as though it fitted our lives, Mum's life. And, then, she said something about our meeting being inevitable, that it had to happen. She got up to go and, of course, I also stood up. She took my arm and kissed me on the cheek, exactly as Mum used to do, and said, 'you will never forget me, you will never forget today'. And then she left. I watched her for a while then I looked down at my book for just a moment, when I looked up, she was gone.'

Jack made a humming sound as he turned over the facts.

'Do you know what I think?'

'No, tell me.'

'Well, to begin with, most people kiss on the cheek and to say you will never forget her, well yes, that was clever of her. Of course, you will always remember her, she planted an idea in your head and it will stay there, forever. That's what I think.'

'I am sure you're right, Pa, only is it not a coincidence that she lived in Hong Kong?'

'Thousands of Brits lived in Hong Kong. That's not so special.'

'That photo, the one you took of Helen's lake.'

'Yes, what about it?'

'Well, this woman talked about it. I mean, she

couldn't have known there was one, not in a thousand years.'

She walked across to an enlarged photograph taken at Rob and Helen's cottage years ago.

Her mother had told her how it was taken on a beautiful day, the willows were mirrored in the water and the sun had formed a beam which faded onto a nearby clearing. It was an unusual photograph.

She remembered how her mother had mixed emotions about going down to the cottage and Helen, though she never said why.

'It all sounds too romantic. If you ask me, it's all coincidence. No more than that. Did she look like your mother?' he asked.

'No, I don't think so.'

'Well, then, she wasn't. There's a good film on the telly tonight. Something historical, I believe.'

'Fine, I'll clear up then we'll put our feet up and have a glass of wine. In vino veritas.'

'In wine there is truth,' he sighed.

'Perhaps I'll find the truth in a glass of plonk.'

'I've tried that. It doesn't work. Next day, the truth is just a bloody headache.'

She curled up in bed that night turning over the story she had told her father. He had scoffed at it, she had expected him to do so. It was no surprise. But still, as her father said, the woman had planted something in her mind, something she could not shake off. She felt it was not only what the woman had said but rather how she had said it. Her tone, the inclination of her voice, was familiar.

She got up and crept downstairs to the lounge and pulled a book from out of the bookcase, one she hardly ever read because she thought it would make her feel guilty if she did, so she did not.

Vici looked up and then went back to sleep. At least, he pretended he was asleep but, most probably, he was just laying with his eyes closed listening to her every movement. She was glad her father had taken him, he was company. She stroked his soft silky head before going back to bed.

She knew where to look for the information, it was not difficult to find. It was the gospel of St. Luke, Chapter 24, the story of how the dead were not only able to contact the living through thought, or even as an apparition, but through the flesh. It was not that she thought her mother was nearer to God, so to speak, but rather the fact that if it had been done once, perhaps it could be done again. Perhaps it was an everyday occurrence which no one knew about or recognised when it happened. Perhaps, she thought, the world was full of unrecognised people who were spirits incarnate, who appeared to give the living a message; to comfort the grieving; a memory of past love; to tease those who were too self assured. She even thought death could have a fun ending, there were so many people she would like to haunt, she hoped in a good way, if she liked the one to be haunted.

She held the Bible tightly as she tried to sleep.

*

'I've been thinking,' she said, after breakfast. 'I want to do an Open University Course. I can live with you. That will cut costs. Maybe I can get a bit of work around here.'

He laughed. 'You can help Rosie in the garden or in her tea house.'

'Only if I have to.'

'Just do what you want. I'm not going anywhere and I can use the company.'

'What about Alison?'

"What about her?"

'Just thought you got on rather well together.'

'Well, I wouldn't say it's more than that.' He laughed again, slightly too loudly. 'Women cost a lot of energy.'

'Yes,' she agreed. 'Women cost both energy and money. Especially young ones,' she muttered.

'Your mother didn't really ask for much, just love.' He tried to laugh at his remark, again surprised at his openness.

He thought maybe he needed to talk about Emy and who better than his girls. He would ask Sophie and Tom down for the next bank holiday weekend. Perhaps they could all do something together.

'Can you come down for the Bank Holiday,' he asked, hopefully, changing the subject. 'I'm going to ask Sophie if she can make it. I thought we could have a sort of family weekend.'

'Super, it's time we got together. You know what we were talking about last night, well I want to go back to the bench once in a while. Maybe, the woman will return, then I can find out more about her.'

'Don't waste too much time. It's what I said, if you say enough vague things some will fit. That's what she did. She probably goes around talking to people on park benches. Every now and again she hits the jackpot.'

'You're probably right. Still, I can just as well read a book on a park bench than indoors, if the weather is right.'

'Of course,' he agreed, picking up the Sunday newspaper.

'Do you want to talk about Mum?'

He laid the newspaper on his lap.

'What is it you want to hear?'

'About the two of you, how you were together. What happened.'

'I was faithful to your mother all my married life until.'

'Until?'

'Until I got that stupid motorbike and had the feeling of wanting to relive my youth. Now it sounds so pathetic. A man my age rushing around the countryside trying to be twenty.'

'I can understand that. I can understand life being dull, suffocating. I'm sure Mum understood. She said she did.'

'Everyone who loves another cares. I'm sure your mother cared. She hid it well, I must say.'

'Perhaps she also enjoyed her freedom, ever thought about that?'

'Yes, of course, I realise that. But she didn't rush off on her bicycle, did she.'

Jillie giggled. 'She would have to do a hell of a lot of peddling to get very far. Though she did get to Devon.'

Jack looked up. 'When did she go to Devon?'

Jillie blushed. 'Oh, it was nothing. That man Sophie was running around with, he asked Mum down to talk about he and Sophie getting hitched. She went but he didn't tell her, I guess he got cold feet. It's not important anymore.'

'Who was he again?'

'Some man called Montague.'

'Oh, yes, now I remember. I didn't know she went down to see him,' he muttered, sounding puzzled. 'I wonder why she didn't tell me.'

'See, we all have our secrets. I guess you whizzing off made her feel she didn't have to tell you everything. I can understand that. Anyway, how did 'Helen the Horrid' fit in,' she added, not trying to hide her dislike of the woman.

'She had been chasing me since kingdom come. I had a weak moment and I succumbed to kingdom come,' he smiled at his rhyming.

'Did that cost Mum her life?'

'Why do you say that?'

'Because if Helen hadn't been around, she would be alive today.'

'We can't control everything,' he muttered.

'You could have seen the consequences, if you had chosen to,' she shouted.

Jack turned away.

'I'm sorry, I didn't mean that. It's just that there is so much unsaid, what really happened. Why you left her upstairs alone. She might still be alive if you hadn't done that', she sobbed, as she ran upstairs, trying to hold back her tears.

'And I don't give a damn what you think. It was Mum I spoke to. I know it was her because she told me her dog had died recently in an accident. And for your information, I am going to wait for her on the bench by Rosie. I will never stop looking for her. I will find her and then.' She slammed the bedroom door behind her.

Jack gave a deep sigh. It was true, he had never given a full account of that day. He could not and, so long as he need not, he would not. Nor would he ever reveal his last meeting with Helen or that he had an HIV test. He had crawled through the eye of the needle and now he wanted to be quiet, to live simply, to mourn Emy. To accept he had been undeserving of her love. He had hoped he could love Charlene, as he did in his youth, to lessen the pain. But it had been a disaster, it was not to be and now the idea of another love was out of the question, at least for the moment.

He made two cups of coffee and took them upstairs. Jillie was sitting on her bed watching television with a tissue in her hand.

'I have to take Vici for a walk. I was thinking of going to the 'Crossing'. I thought you might like to come with me. I have also something to tell you. You're not the only one who has seen your mother, you're not the only one who has seen her by the 'Crossing'.'

*   *   *

A week later, Alison Waters invited Jack home after work. Her father stood up, painfully, and gave him a warm handshake. He was happy to see his daughter so animated since he felt a burden or, at least, he was becoming one. He was also conscious she had sacrificed a great deal to work alongside him and keep him company.

He frowned as he remembered how he and Connie had fought fiercely over their only child, over their daughter's teenage pregnancy, discussing at length what should be done, what was the best solution. He knew she would win, she always did, that was until a letter arrived addressed to Alison just before she left for Yorkshire. Connie had snatched it from him and made him promise not to tell either Alison or Flossy about it. They had quarrelled, hissing at each other since Alison was upstairs sleeping.

'You are not to tell her.'

'Why not?'

'Because I say so.'

'It's for Alison.'

'Listen to me, what do you think will happen if I were to give her every pointless letter he sends. He's seventeen years old and lives on the other side of the world. All she will do is sit around moping and hoping he returns. And the truth is, he won't. He'll meet another girl, probably already has, and she gets even more hurt. Leave it as it is. She will eventually get her life together and settle down. I'm asking you not to say anything, it can only make things worse.'

'How many letters has he written?'

'Too many. Luckily, I start work after the post has been. You are not to tell her. And you are to give me any more letters he sends. Understand?'

He had not given up, as she had expected, and the fight had escalated into name calling. He could not remember the exact details except that he had pushed her a couple of times, slightly too hard, called her a deceitful bitch, and that what she was doing would come back to haunt her. Connie had stood silent as though her anger had subsided, as though she was happy he had shouted at her, as though she was relieved he had crossed a line. She had suddenly become relaxed and they had calmly discussed the details of their future together, or rather their separation. Later, he had felt a sense of relief as though a weight had been lifted off his shoulders, off both their shoulders. Their marriage was irrecoverably over, 'finito', finished.

Alison had joined him at the Garden Centre three years later. He had felt both happy and sad for she had all but lost Pippa and knew nothing about the letters from Australia. He had kept his wife's secret just to keep the peace between them all and, perhaps, Connie was right. He no longer knew at the time what was best for Alison and her child, though he was sure Connie and Flossy did what they thought best. Still, he considered it cruel to keep back letters from the father of her child. Flossy would never have agreed to that had she had known.

He thought of Flossie with fondness, they had a great deal in common, not least flowers, and he knew she was aware of how he felt. Sometimes they spoke when she 'phoned Alison about Pippa. Their conversations were always warm and loving, there was an unspoken word between them. He loved her and they both knew time was running out but there was nothing be done about it.

It was when he stepped back after shaking hands with Jack Nielson did he realise a spirit was present. Rosie had already told him she had seen Jack Nielson's deceased wife so it was no surprise that she was with him now. He would confide in Rosie as soon as he could. He smiled, such a lovely name for a lovely woman. She was a rose, a beautiful rose and he had designed a beautiful garden where she could blossom between all the varieties of roses he had planted.

He turned his attention to Jack Nielson.

'Alison tells me you want to talk to me,' he said, happy to begin a conversation about his favourite subject, the paranormal.

'Actually, it's my youngest daughter, Jillie, who would like to talk to you.'

'About seeing her mother.'

'Yes. I guess Alison told you that.'

'She did,' he said, honestly. 'Your wife was just here, I've seen her several times. She seems to be taking care of you all, if she's able,' he added, quietly. 'Tell your daughter to come and see me next time she's here. It seems she has decided to change her study.'

'How do you know that?' he asked, amazed, since he had not told anyone.

He did not answer but smiled kindly. 'Don't worry it will all come right in the end. Give it time.'

'Yes, thanks,' Jack muttered, as he left the small house as quickly as possible.

He drove home, a puzzled and somewhat troubled man.

*

She had gone home with Jack a few days later and sat at the kitchen table while he poured drinks; whisky for him and wine for her. She watched him as he swirled ice around in the glass before he took a mouthful. She knew he probably had an alcohol problem but somehow it seemed to be a part of who he was. The whisky glass suited his image and she wondered if he was aware of that.

'Shall we sit out here?' he suggested, walking towards a rather beautiful conservatory.

She looked around, critically. 'It's lovely but it's lacking something. Something green,' she joked. 'I could arrange for some plants. Would you like me to do that?'

'Anything to make you happy, Alison.'

'Well then, that's what I'll do. I like to be made happy.'

'You're already a happy person.'

'Am I?' she replied, wanting to contradict him.

'Well, you seem to be.'

'Looks can be deceiving. How about you?'

'Same thing. I've almost forgotten what it feels like to be happy, no problems.'

'And what are your problems?'

He stopped for a moment as though weighing up the correct answer.

'Too many hours in a day. I think that sums it up.'

'You can get a lot done,' she teased. 'Some people might find that a luxury problem.'

'Of course you're right. I'm grateful for what there is. It's what there's not.'

'And that is?'

He stood up. 'Want another?'

'Let's throw caution to the wind.'

'Why not, who cares anyway,' he muttered, as he walked away.

She felt overwhelmed by sympathy and tenderness, aware such feelings were not in her agenda. But, then again, she was prepared to take a chance, so long as the lover played by the rules.

Jack appeared with the drinks, this time he shared the chaise longue with her. She could tell that he had probably swilled down a second drink in the kitchen and this was, at least, his third. It suddenly seemed irrelevant whether she became pregnant, she wanted him regardless of her hormone level and whether she could be fertile. He leaned towards her and she waited to be kissed. She was almost breathless, intoxicated by her feelings, languishing in anticipation. She wanted him.

He suddenly pulled back.

'I'm sorry,' he said, quickly. 'I forgot I have to go out tonight. My neighbour has a birthday and I promised to go for a drink. I'm sorry.'

She sat back as though unaware of any intentions either of them might have had.

'It's getting late,' she stated, glancing at her watch. 'I had no idea of the time.'

She stood up and walked, still slightly limping, to the front door.

'I'll pick you up tomorrow.'

'No need, thank you. I've too much to do at the Garden Centre. Maybe Monday but with a bit of luck I might be driving by then.'

'Let me know,' he replied, feeling guilty and aware he had enticed her, then dropped her.

'I'll do that,' she replied, coldly.

He felt depressed as he drove her home, conscious he had backed off twice when love was offered, first Charlene and now Alison. He doubted he would ever be able to have a relationship again and the thrill of love would become a vague memory. It would have been so different if he had just made one 'phone call. If he had called for an ambulance, Emy would be alive today.

FROM AUSTRALIA WITH LOVE

Alison WAS ONCE AGAIN HELPING in the tea garden, something she had little time for. Rosie calling her a surrogate daughter was just, perhaps, a little devious since she was forced to act as one or, at least, make some show of doing so. Rosie's landscape agreement, if there had ever been one, was with her father who had planted it out, with love and care, and kept it under control at an extraordinarily reasonable price; one she felt bordered on being unfair. However, she could see that he was enamoured by this charming lady and, since he had little in his life, she left it for what it was. A labour of love.

In fact, she felt she could no longer cope and realised that, sooner or later, she would have to employ an experienced help but that would cost money which they could ill afford. Her father's crush on Rosie was actually an expensive hobby and she was not entirely happy with the situation. She would have to speak to him when, or even if, Rosie's hold on him lessened.

The tea house was rather busy and she, Poppy and a local woman, Agnes, were working hard to keep the visitors happy. She had just brought cold drinks to a crowd of rather rowdy men and vaguely listened to their conversation. It was not until one of them said 'fair dinkum', did she realise he was from Australia while, at the same time, she noticed David Coleman coming through the garden gate. She turned and hurried back to the house.

'I'm not feeling too well. I think the heat got to me,' she complained, as she entered the kitchen.

Poppy looked up surprised. 'Sit down a minute, dear,' she advised, kindly. 'I'll get you a cold drink, how about some elderberry juice. Would you like that?'

'Thanks, Poppy, if I stay here maybe you and Agnes can do the tables. I don't mind clearing up and making the food.'

'Whatever you like, dear. Agnes and me are old hands. Aren't we Agnes?'

Agnes nodded enthusiastically. 'I love serving on tables, better than in here.'

Poppy turned around. 'Can I help you?' she asked, suddenly aware of two men standing at the kitchen door.

She could feel herself weaken, it was David with a dark haired man, tall and handsome.

'Hey, Alison, remember me?' the stranger said, grinning. The grin she remembered so well, the grin from over twenty years ago.

'How could I not?' she replied, reeling with happiness which was instantly overtaken by fear. Fear of hearing how happy he was, how he had a family who were the centre of his universe. She did not want to remember what happened between them, how he had broken his promise to write to her. It was as though her body wept with hurt, throbbed with pain. She wished she was allowed to cry streams of hot tears, push him aside as she ran passed him while, at the same time, pleading with him to stay. Instead she smiled.

'Thought we could have a drink together.'

'Can't, I'm working.'

'Okay, after work then.'

'I'm busy tonight.'

He took her arm. 'No you're not.'

David turned away. 'See you outside,' he called, diplomatically, as he returned to the group in the garden.

'Did you come alone?' she asked, expecting him to say he had a wife and children tagging behind him.

'No, my mother's with me. My father died a couple of years ago. She wanted to see her old friends and I thought it would do her good to get away for a while. My sister, my twin, couldn't come, she's too tied up with her work.'

'I'd forgotten you had a twin. What does she do?'

'She's the brainy one, she's into all things which sliver, crawl or have four legs, sometimes two, a Vet,' he told her, proudly.

'Clever girl,' she replied. 'You like it out there?' she added.

'I did.'

'Why the past tense?'

'Just divorced.'

'Who isn't,' she answered, dryly.

'Thought I'd get away, visit the old country. See everyone again. Relive a few old memories.'

She dug a little deeper, relieved he was free and not about to tell her how happy he was. 'Do you have children?'

'Nope, she didn't want any. She was a nature freak, said the wild needed her and there were enough children in the world without her adding any more.'

'You weren't suited.'

'You can say that again. What about you?'

'Well, that's a long story. I'll save it for another time.'

'When are you off?'

'About six-thirty.'

'Okay, I'll pick you up here.'

'I'll have a pot of tea waiting.'

'I thought of something a bit stronger than that. Tea isn't my scene. I've heard they've opened a restaurant by the Ford. It's a bit of a drive but I want to see the countryside again. I've almost forgotten how beautiful it is over here, so green.'

He touched her arm as she turned to fill the dish washer but she ignored him, aware the past had finally caught up with the present, 'the moment of truth was nigh'. She had dreamt of this moment, the satisfaction of showing him how she had survived.

Now, she was unsure whether the truth was better left untold. She almost wished he had not come for his visit was about to disturb her routine, bring more uncertainty into her already emotional life. For the first time in over twenty years she wished him away. She would give it some thought, deep thought, before jumping into the turmoil of confession and soul baring, before she told him he had a daughter, a beautiful daughter.

She thought of Jack Nielson who now seemed totally irrelevant and suddenly too old.

She studied him as they drove down the country lanes. He was broad shouldered, his skin slightly tanned, his dark hair fell across his forehead and he wore a pair of well fitting denims and a white open necked shirt. He was gorgeous. Her heart ached for all the lost years, years of secrecy, of a daughter he had without knowing. She knew she would have to tell him, but when.

He smiled at her and said very little and she also did not want to make some stupid, useless, comment or ask some mundane question. She was speechless as though unable to form intelligent thoughts, let alone a conversation.

They eventually entered the newly opened restaurant where tables and chairs were arranged around an old watermill. The sun shone through a window onto the shiny glasses which, in turn, formed a prism of colour on the freshly painted ceiling.

'That's pretty,' she whispered.

'Now you can tell me the story of your life. You promised me that,' he said, as he studied the wine menu.

'Did I? Well, perhaps it's not appropriate for a first time out.'

'Well, that's food for thought. Talking of food, take a look at the menu.'

He spent the next five minutes discussing wine with the waiter and ordered, loyal to his country, an Australian wine from one of the well known valleys.

'So, tell me all. Tell me all you've been doing, recently?' He emphasized the word 'recently'.

She looked at him across the table aware that, most probably, David had been talking about his night of passion with her.

'Not everything. I must keep a few secrets otherwise you won't have a reason to ask me out again.'

'Have you something going with David?' he asked, directly.

'I had a one night stand. I don't know if you would count that as something going.'

'Not if it's over.'

'As I said, it was just the once.'

'I would like to ask you something.'

'Yes,' she answered, her heart pounding which made her hands damp as though she was fifteen years old again.

'Why didn't you answer my letters? I wrote so many, you didn't answer one. Not even a Christmas card.'

'What letters? I never got any.'

He frowned. 'They can't all have gone astray. I wrote to you, regularly, until the end of January. You must have received a couple of them.'

'Perhaps they were purloined. Perhaps there was someone who intercepted them.'

'Your parents?'

'Let's say my mother. She would do that.'

'But why, why would she do that? I mean, I couldn't do any harm thousands of miles away. It's not like you were about to jump on a plane the next day.'

'I'll have to ask her,' she replied, almost choking on her words.

'Please do. I would like her to tell me why she did that, if she did do that,' he added, sounding emotional.

There was a pause before he spoke again.

'Took me a long time to settle down,' he said, softly.

'I expect you missed your school friends,' she said, hoping he would say he missed her.

He did not answer but drew an old school photo from out of his wallet. 'Remember this?'

She took it in her now trembling hands.

'I also have this one. Sometimes, I even look at it.'

'Really! You know, I want to apologise for what happened between us. I shouldn't have done it. I knew we were going away, it was unforgivable of me. I thought about it so often. That's one of the many reasons I wanted to see you again.'

'And the other reasons?'

'You are just as pretty as the last time I saw

you, more so,' he replied quickly, not answering her question.

'I didn't want anyone, not after you.'

'Oh, come on. That was twenty one years ago. You must have had a lot of admirers. I'm amazed you're not married.' He frowned. 'How come?'

'Long story, I'll tell you one day, perhaps.'

'Don't take too long. I'm only here for a month before I return to the mess waiting for me at home.'

'What mess?'

'My 'ex' got half my money. I have to sell everything to pay her off.'

'Life's a bitch. We all have our crosses.'

'And what is yours?'

'Not now. Tell me about the outback.'

She hardly listened to what he said, only felt her jaw tighten and her lips form a thin line as she realised her mother knew what he had written and she did not. The idea of such an intrusion fired her to a degree of hate she had never known before. She realised how lucky she was not to live near her mother, not to be able to storm over to her house and shout and scream until her mother begged her to stop. So was her anger and, most of all, her hurt. The only good thing was that Phil did not know of the result of their afternoon together and, therefore, could not have written about it. She could only hope he had written three words, the words every girl wants to hear. Or any boy for that matter.

Three passé cliché words. 'I love you.'

*   *   *

'I'm coming up to see you. Pippa 'phoned to tell me she is engaged. I have a little present for her and I want to meet Mark again.'

'That's nice, dear. When are you planning to come?' Flossy asked, excitedly.

'I'll leave here Saturday morning, stay the night, and leave Sunday afternoon.'

'I'll tell your mother and Pippa She's not so well, you know.'

'Who's not well?'

'Your mother. I keep telling her to go to the doctor but she won't. She's so stubborn. Maybe you can persuade her.'

'I'll try but I can't guarantee any success. Anyway, I'll see you Saturday afternoon. I'd like roast beef and Yorkshire pudding with all the trimmings.'

'I'll have it all ready when you get here.'

'See you Saturday then,' she hung up, feeling depressed.

She liked Flossy so much more than her mother, she was softer, gentler and probably more honest. She dreaded the confrontation ahead of her and hoped not to drag Flossy into it, though she thought it impossible for her not to hear the inevitable fight.

Her father seemed surprised and a little hurt when she told him she was going up north to see her mother over the weekend. His back was slightly better but she doubted whether he would ever be able to do heavy work again. She really had to seriously consider getting help. Good strong help, not the youngsters who worked so they could go out Saturday night and showed no real interest in what they were supposed to be learning. She would look around after the weekend but first she had to talk to her mother, more likely shout at her mother, and then there was Pippa She had to be told, she dreaded that more than anything else.

'God, this is going to be a f. awful weekend,' she muttered.

Flossy met her at the door full of hugs and kisses. She was so unlike her mother who gave her a peck on the cheek as she walked away.

'Where's Mum?' she asked, after taking off her coat and dumping her bag in the hall.

'Upstairs, sleeping.'

'Is she okay?'

'I don't really know. Your father 'phoned her a couple of times. I don't know what that's all about.'

'Strange. He seldom does that.'

'I know and since then she seems to have only headaches. I've told her to go to the doctor but she won't. Mumbled something about the past and no one can put it right.'

'I have a small idea what that is. Got a cup of tea?'

'Of course, dear. Pippa is coming over this evening with Mark. Such a nice young man. They have all these plans but I'm afraid it's going to cost too much money. That's youth, first do and then think about the consequences later.'

'Try not to worry. It will all come right in the end,' she murmured, trying to sound convincing as she heard her mother coming down the stairs.

Creaking stairs and bumps in the night belonged to the old farmhouse, no one thought anything about it. She didn't like the place and it had always surprised her that it had never bothered Pippa

'How are you, Mum?' she greeted her mother who now looked suddenly a lot older and pale. 'You don't look well.'

'I seem to have migraines. Never had them before.'

'Go to a doctor.'

'Doctors can't help.'

'Why not?'

She did not answer as Flossy set a cup of tea in front of her.

'Flossy says dad has recently been in touch.'

'Yes, a couple of times already.'

'Any particular reason?'

'I think you know why.'

'Do I? Why don't you tell me.'

'Because he's returned. Your Philip Price is back. Everyone knows. Your father seems to think you have already met him. He's come back to make trouble.'

'Who says that, who says he is going to make trouble. It was always more than likely he would return one day. Most people do, see the old country just once more.'

'What did he have to say?'

'About what?' she answered, trying to wind her mother up.

'Have you told him?'

'About Pippa, not yet.'

'Do you have to?'

'Of course I have to. That's one of the reasons I'm here. To tell Pippa her father's resurfaced.'

'You'll only upset her.'

'Well, whether I do or not she has the right to know and so does he. Do you know what Phil told me?'

'No, what?'

'That he wrote to me from the end of September until the end of January. He wrote to me.'

She could hear her voice crack with emotion, feel tears burning her eyes, feel the familiar lump in her throat, the pain which seemed to run throughout her body.

'So where are they, where are my letters?' she could hear her voice raised in anger.

'I didn't throw them away. I don't know why but I kept them.'

'Where?' she shouted. 'Where are they? Get them, do you hear me, get them before I kill you,' she screamed, as her body shook in uncontrolled rage.

Flossy fell back into a chair, sobbing. 'Please, please, Alison, keep calm. I am sure Connie didn't realise what she was doing. I'm sure she did everything for the best,' she whispered, as the tears rolled down her cheeks.

'I didn't see the purpose of giving them to you. He was thousands of miles away, seventeen years old. What was the point of upsetting you. He wasn't going to come back. You would only have yearned for something you couldn't have, ruined any chance with another young man. It was the best for you, the best for Pippa,' her mother shouted back in defence.

'It was not for you to decide what was best for me, for us. I would have done it differently. I would have taken Pippa home and looked after her. I would have sent photographs and letters. It would have been our decision what we did next. Not yours,' she wailed.

'Pippa had the best. We never kept anything from her. She knew you were her mother, she knew her father was in Australia. She had everything any child could ask for. She had love from both me and Flossy. And I didn't see you rushing up here every other weekend.'

'I didn't have the money to rush up and down every other weekend. And', she added, fiercely. 'how come you could love Pippa so much and not me?'

'Don't talk such rubbish, I've always loved you. You're a hypocrite, Alison. He turns up and suddenly we've done it all wrong. Ask Pippa if she was unhappy. Ask her whether she would have been happier with you than with us. Ask her,' she screamed, hysterically.

'You're missing the point. I dreamt of him coming back. He might have come back for me, taken me away, married me,' she sobbed. 'I couldn't make it with anyone else just in case he came back. I waited for him,' she cried.

'Well, you waited a long time,' her mother replied, bitterly.

'He didn't know I had his baby.'

'I did what I thought best.'

'Exactly, what you thought best. You know the trouble with you, Mum, everything is about you. Do you know what I think. I think that after the initial shock you and Flossy liked the idea of having a baby.'

'You're talking a load of rubbish,' her mother, snapped.

'You were just over forty and your marriage was zilch. I think you used the situation, you found a good reason to have a fight with dad so that you could leave him and Flossy was conveniently waiting to supply you with a home. No rent to pay, no need to go to work with Flossy helping out financially. You had it made, the timing was perfect. You used Pippa for your own ends.'

'Hang on there,' yelled her mother, angrily. 'This house is as much mine as Flossy's. It was left to both of us and I ran it when Flossy went to work and, what's more, I put my measly alimentation into the housekeeping pot.'

Tears ran down Flossy's cheeks. 'Please stop, Alison. Please stop. You helped to keep Pippa as well.'

'Come on, I didn't earn anything for years. It was dad who helped to support Pippa, not me.' She turned to her mother. 'There was a business to run, what do you think was left over after dad paid for you and helped towards Pippa while he kept me? I had pocket money, a pittance.'

'If I'm not mistaken all of this is because of you.'

'Yes, I got pregnant and what you did after that was your choice.'

The living room door opened, Pippa stood in the doorway.

'What choice?'

There was a deadly silence between them all.

'Pippa,' said Alison, almost out of breath. 'Something has happened.'

'Obviously.'

'Your father is over here on holiday. I haven't told him about you yet. I wanted to tell you first. Ask you what you think about meeting him?'

'Well, I should think that's obvious. Of course, I want to meet him. That saves Mark and me a lot of trouble.'

'How come?'

'We were saving to go to Australia for our honeymoon to look for him. Now we won't have to do that. When do I get to meet him?'

'You aren't upset?' she asked, stunned.

'Why should I be upset? I've had a good life, I had everything I wanted and more. I was spoilt to death by my lovely Nana and Flossy. You could never have given me what they gave me.'

Pippa walked over to the two sobbing women and put her arms around both of them.

'Don't fight, you all did your best, I know that. So don't worry. I have Mark now and you have each other. Be as happy as I am. We have such marvellous plans for the stables and Mark has found me a new horse. We're going to pick him up next week. If you want to make me happy, then you be happy. That's the best present you can give me.'

Mark turned up a little later and they sat around the dining room table discussing Philip Price. How he would react to his new family, catch up on his life and he theirs. It was exciting, no bad feelings, no one could help what happened. It was only sad for her, Alison, she had suffered the most and they, Pippa and Mark, were going to make it up to her. Perhaps, take her on a holiday with them.

Only she remained silent, wondering whether their enthusiasm was not, perhaps, a little premature. Would Phil forgive her mother for all the lost years. She could hardly forgive her let alone forget what she had done. But, for the time being, she was willing to let it go for the sake of Pippa and the rest of the family.

Her mother pressed a bundle of letters into her hand as she was about to leave.

'Here they are, all of them. I'm sorry. You are right. I should not have taken them. Please forgive me, please forgive me.'

She put her arms around her mother and rubbed her back.

'You did your best, you brought up Pippa so much better than I could ever have done. I've never said thank you. I am also to blame. Don't worry, it will all work out in the end.'

*

She had left her mother at the end of the path dabbing her eyes with a small handkerchief, though she doubted she was really crying.

'Love you,' she called, half heartedly, as she waved her hand through the open car window.

'Love you too,' her mother managed to say with a small degree of hesitance.

Flossy joined her mother and placed her arm around her shoulder as she waved goodbye. They both seemed so sad, so lost, so insignificant, as though they had completed a task and were now irrelevant, expendable.

She gently stroked the bundle of letters and cards on the seat beside her, wondering whether she dared to read them. She prayed he had not only written about the beaches, surfing, his new friends, where they lived.

'Oh, please not, Phil. Please write about us.'

*

'I'd like to see you again,' she said, her voice trembling a little.

'Great, when and where?' he answered, in his charming Australian accent.

'Rosie's tea garden. I feel secure there.'

'Why do you need to feel secure with a big bloke like me to protect you?' he laughed.

'Perhaps it's you that makes me feel insecure.'

He laughed again. 'You like puzzles. Well, then, puzzle me tomorrow after work.'

'Fine, see you at Rosie's around six thirty.'

She hung up almost sick from fear, nauseated, rather like taking an exam at school knowing you had not studied for it. In fact, she had not finished school, she had been just old enough to slip through the 'education net' and work in Flossy's flower shop.

It had been a relief escaping to the sweet smelling room filled to the brim with various house plants and flowers. There was a small kitchen at the back of the shop where they made tea or coffee after she had bought Danish pastries or doughnuts from the baker next door. She had treasured those years, loved by a warm hearted woman who did not seem to see her faults as her mother did.

Eventually, she had decided to leave the Yorkshire countryside and make a new start without Pippa. Her decision had been eagerly accepted by her mother who tactfully added it was better for Pippa to have a stable life and the odd visit from her was enough, nothing too emotional.

The new start was with her father who had taken over the Garden Centre from the last owner. It had been a coincidence that both he and Flossy found joy in plants and flowers. She felt that he had married the wrong sister. Flossy would have been a far better choice. She wished Flossy had stepped in when her mother stepped out.

She would have pushed them together had she had been old enough to understand the complexity of relationships.

*

She met Phil in a small lean-to in Rosie's garden which smelt of impregnated wood, with perhaps a whiff of oil, and decorated with hanging baskets, an urn and dried flowers.

This romantic shelter was one of many scattered around the garden and surrounded by shrubs and hedges which afforded privacy to the guests. They were popular beyond words, perhaps because it recalled the past, elysian days, simple times which had all but vanished. Whichever one, they were always occupied and sometimes even reserved for special occasions. Rosie's tea garden had caught on in a big way and she was proud of her father who had designed it.

'So,' he grinned, when they met. 'What's the puzzle?'

'There is no puzzle, just facts which I would rather not have to tell you.'

He looked worried. 'Are you about to tell me something bad? Do I have to know?'

'It's not bad, just a little more than surprising. I am the one who feels bad.'

She could see him eyeing the gate as though he would run away, if he could, if he had to.

'Okay, let's have it. What's wrong?'

'Nothing is wrong, just not right.'

'For God's sake say it. What?'

'I have a daughter, Philippa, Pippa.'

He gazed at her, silently, as though stupefied.

'What are you saying?' he asked, his voice lowered.

'I was pregnant when you left.'

'Oh, my God. I never knew. Why didn't you tell me. I wrote, you had my address.'

'I told you, my mother took your letters. I never received them. I went up to see her last weekend. She gave them to me. She had actually kept them. I've read them. They are lovely.'

'So, what happened to my daughter?'

'I had her by my aunt, up in Yorkshire. My mother came with me and never returned home. I stayed there with Pippa for nearly three years then I came back here to live with my father. My mother and aunt looked after Pippa. No one knew I had a baby, for all intents and purposes she was my sister. I've always told Pippa the truth, it seems she was planning to find you.'

'I hardly know what to say.'

'I can imagine.'

'I have a daughter, I have a child. I always wanted a family but my 'ex' wouldn't even discuss it. I have to thank my sister for introducing me to her. But all the time I had a daughter. I can't believe it. Does she know I'm here?'

'Yes, I told her on the weekend.'

'And?'

'She was terribly excited. She wants to meet you as soon as possible. She's just got engaged to Mark. Mark Bourne. Nice boy, you will like him. He's about seven or eight years older than she is. They have a lot in common, mad for horses. The joke is, when I called her Philippa, I didn't know it meant 'lover of horses'. Anyway, as I understand it, she and Mark want to eventually take over a riding school, or something like that.'

He held his head in his hands. 'I can't believe it's true,' he gasped. 'You know I can remember David once writing that you were no longer on school and that he thought you had gone with your mother up north. I thought you were angry at me for what I did and then leaving you. I can't believe what I did.'

'Well, it's true and you did.'

'You must have had a bad time of it.'

'Yep. But I survived. Couldn't get it together with anyone else. I sort of hoped one day you would come along and I told myself that if you were married with a family then I would do my best to settle down with someone else. Only thing is, you took so long coming back. I'm thirty six and I have no one.'

He held her in his arms and she cried, tears which she had held back since Pippa was born.

'I'm so sorry. I'm so sorry,' he murmured, as he stroked her hair. 'I had no idea. You must have been so hurt.'

He kissed her hot face and wiped the tears from her cheeks.

'I'll make it up to you. I promise I will. I have thought of you so often, especially when my marriage failed. You know it was not what we did, it was our friendship. You were my best friend. Somehow, I never managed to replace you, you were so special.'

'I thought you had used me. A bit of fun before you left. No harm done.'

'Never, that was never my intention. I didn't think as an adult. I wanted you and thought I would make you remember me, forever.'

'You succeeded. How could I have forgotten you.'

'Alison Waters, we will start all over again and, if you can bring yourself to love me, we'll get married.'

'Just like that?'

'Yep, just like that.'

'It all sounds so romantic and I'm not that anymore. I'm realistic, I have my father, he has a business to run, I can't leave him. He could never cope without me.'

'Then I'll stay.'

'What, just like that?' she repeated.

'Yep, just like that. My mother is here, she is happy. I've never seen her so happy and she said, only yesterday, if it wasn't for me she would stay. If she could.'

'And your sister?'

'She married a New Zealander, they live north of Wellington. They don't seem to need my mother, let alone me.'

'It sounds too easy. I don't believe anything goes that easily.'

'Well, now it does.'

'You don't know me.'

'And you don't know me but, from what I remember, we saw each other every day for years, played together on primary school and did our homework together later. And a bit more,' he grinned. 'Unless you have a split personality you are still who you were then. People don't change. I haven't changed and I bet you haven't either.'

'No, I haven't changed. Still the same, warts and all.'

'I can't see any, perhaps I should take a closer look,' he chuckled.

'Listen, Phil, I'll be honest. I want another baby. How do you feel about that?'

'I feel complimented. After all these years, all the hurt I have given you, you want another baby with me.'

'Yes.'

'Alison,' he said, firmly. 'We are going away. rather like a rehearsal for our honeymoon. We're going to drive around France, Italy, wherever you want to go and, as I've just said, if you like me enough, love me, we are going to marry the moment we get back.'

She laid her head against him and felt a tear run down her cheek.

'No tears, Alison. We're going to spend the rest of our lives laughing.'

'We could marry here, in Rosie's garden. People do that all the time. They walk through arches of flowers to the arbour and if the weather is bad they marry in the conservatory. Did you know it was once a chapel?'

'You can marry wherever you want,' he replied, kissing her lips lightly. 'Can you get help for your father if we go away?' he asked, sounding concerned.

She thought for a moment. 'I know a man, Jack Nielson. I think he will help out. He lost his wife and doesn't seem to know what to do.'

'Okay, if you can get that together. But first I want to meet my daughter. Does she look like you?'

'No, she's the splitting image of you.'

'That's a disadvantage if ever there was one,' he laughed. 'When am I going to meet her?'

'Next weekend, if that's alright with you.'

'I'd best get brushed up.'

'Don't, they seldom get out of their riding clothes. You know,' she said, thoughtfully. 'We are thinking about taking on someone to help run the Garden Centre. If you should need work then,' she did not finish the sentence as he kissed her long and lovingly.

'Alison, I am going to love you to death,' he murmured.

She closed her eyes and smiled, remembering their last kiss. He was right, perhaps people don't change. And their kisses, well perhaps they do, just a little, perhaps a lot.

AN INDEPENDENT PARTY

Sophie STARED AT HER LAPTOP with apathy, devoid of ideas or even the will to search for any. She had been instructed by her editor, Jonathon Jenkins, known as JJ, to produce an unbiased report on the increase of train fares and that seemed impossible. How could she be unbiased when she suffered the ignominy of being transported, twice a day, in what she considered little more than a cattle truck. Repeated high cost journeys pressed against people who sent sms messages or, worse still, held imbecilic conversations on their mobiles. How could she be unbiased?

She decided that if she were to write an article then it would be short, sharp and scathingly critical. In fact, she thought her job as a badly paid junior reporter, for a rather mediocre rightwing newspaper, almost untenable though she was very much aware she was lucky to have a job at all in the newspaper world. She also decided that if she had a political party then she would take her son's paint box and swirl a wet brush in the blue, red and yellow squares. The resulting colour would represent her party which would probably be a mixture of lounge socialists and idealists. The thought amused her, she would like to have her own political party. She could see herself standing on an orange box or, if successful, on a town hall balcony with stirred crowds below cheering her on to improve their position in society and, most importantly, the money in their pay packets.

She typed a heading for the proposed article, aware her friends considered her job to be interesting. She was careful not to disillusion them, to keep the bubble floating so they could envy her. Joke, she thought.

She pursed her lips as she thought of Peter, her 'ex' husband, now her legal partner. She thought that had a ring of equality to it, though she was unsure whether she would ever be truly equal even though he helped around the house, was a good father to Tom and a good friend and lover to her.

However, there was just one small problem, if it could be called a problem, he wanted another child. He said that Tom would not have anyone if anything happened to them. He knew how it felt to be an only child, he knew how it was to be alone. He wanted Tom to have a brother or sister. She had not answered him directly, only pointed out that by the time she had another baby, if she could have one, there would be too many years between the siblings. Peter had immediately answered that an age gap was insignificant as they became older. She had not argued the point because she did not know herself what she wanted; a successful job, another baby, or both. She thought the answer to that was obvious.

Anyway, why should anything happen to either of them, she dismissed Peter's reasoning as being rather dramatic. She frowned as she thought of her mother's two day visit to Monty, in Devon, when he was supposed to tell her about their affair and how they intended to marry. Monty, had backed off, got cold feet, and said it was better she should break the news to her family, not he.

Her mother had reacted hysterically when she told her, shouting how Monty was old enough to be her father, how she had known him years ago when she was young, how he had too much baggage and so forth. She had realised her mother would not appreciate their age difference but her reaction had been exaggerated, excessive, which made her query why that should be so. After all, she would not be the first woman to marry an older man.

Three days later, Monty died of a heart attack and a few months later her mother also died, an unnecessary, pointless death. Then Michael Lee had insinuated her mother and Monty had shared a bed while she was visiting him. Her first reaction was hate for Michael Lee, followed by the need to prove whether there was any truth in his assumption but, in the end, she had let it go. She had no desire to check up on her mother.

'Love hurts', she muttered. 'And so does the truth', she added, still staring at her laptop, blank except for the heading

'Is it FAIR to increase FARES, Are the Fat Cats Clawing at our Cash. Do the Public get a 'FARE' shakedown? Privatisation or Nationalisation.

She smiled as she wrote the article which her editor was never going to agree with. Right wingers do not support nationalisation. Still, Jonathon Jenkins was more modern than the last editor who had retired after a heart attack. No surprise to those who knew him.

She logged off, looked at her watch, too early to leave, pulled her coat from the back of her chair and waved goodbye to those still intent on finding eloquent words to keep their jobs. She walked, nonchalantly, into the fresh, but polluted, London air determined that she was done with it all. Let someone else who enjoyed writing insincere articles take over. She could not and would not comply to the views of her editor, any editor. She felt free. She would go home, pick Tom up from school and later tell Peter her plans for their future.

The telephone rang at five o'clock. It was JJ.

'I'm reading your article,' he said, sounding not too unfriendly.

'I know, I should have written it differently.'

'It's not what you'd call unbiased.'

'No it's not. It's just the truth.'

He laughed. 'Fat Cats don't share their cream, that's why they're fat.'

'True, but what we have to pay to stand on a cattle train is absurd. I can't write about something I don't believe in.'

'Also true, tell you what. We'll run it. I'm looking for a bit of a fight with a certain government department. See what happens.'

'Really!'

'Okay, don't be late tomorrow morning. See you left early this afternoon, any particular reason?'

'Just a bit frustrated.'

'Have you got any other confrontational articles up your sleeve?'

'Hundreds.'

'Well, let's see them.'

'If that's what you want.'

She hung up amazed and shocked since she had expected to lose her job, to be fired on the spot. She had pictured herself filling a cardboard box with her few worthless possessions and slinking off like the brokers and bankers who were caught with their fingers in the till. She would never be seen in the reporting world again.

She heard the front door open, it was Peter.

'Have a nice day?' he asked, as he always did.

'Yes, actually, I think I did. I have to work tonight, I have a few ideas to throw around.'

She sat back and typed the headline of an idea which floated around in her mind. It was, of course, just an outline and she needed facts and as much financial data as possible. She knew the chance of getting her article further than JJ was minimum. He would not find it feasible and she was aware he was probably right. Still, it was worth a try.

REWARD 'STAY AT HOME' PARENTS OR GUARDIANS

Modern society now views non-working mothers as being either rich or idle. I have heard it said that it is good for children to see their mothers go to work. Really! Is a child with a key around its neck better off, happier, than one who comes home to someone waiting for them? Are women happier with a duster in their hands? No, probably not. But the choice should be theirs to make.

I am suggesting that caring for children should be seen as a job, like any other job. I am suggesting the parent, or guardian, should receive a 'StayAtHome benefit' (SAH).

There are many positive sides to this contemporary idea, not least time to bring up families in a more nurtured environment; the return of family values and freeing jobs for those desperately seeking work. Unemployment benefits could be transferred to SAH benefits.

So, let's think out of the box. After all, the children of today and tomorrow are the wealth of the nation and their behaviour formed by their childhood experiences and memories. YOU are the mentors of the future generation. YOU are the bearers and carers of the country's future wealth.

*

JJ leaned back on his chair, smiling as he read her article.

'Well, yes, I can see where you are coming from but it doesn't stand a chance. It's not new, never got off the ground. No one's interested.'

'It's only an outline. I've done a bit of homework,' she pleaded.

'I'm sure you have but it's a non-starter. Forget it.'

'I think it could be discussed again. Couldn't you give it some space, just as a try out?'

'No.'

'Isn't there another government department you would like to irritate, just a bit.'

'Many.'

'If you give working mothers a choice to take up the offer then you are also freeing the workplace and, in that way, helping employers to take on new staff. It probably won't appeal to career women, though you never know. It's meant more for those on the homely side who haven't got too much to lose and certainly for those who are stressed out by their children.

I think it deserves a discussion. Don't you think?'

'It's more likely for women who want an easy ride.'

'Or men. Whichever, makes no difference. It's all about family values and freeing jobs.'

'All you will get are swarms of unwanted kids because parents want to stay at home and get a handout.'

'Agreed, but there could be really watertight conditions.'

'Not discussable, there's no interest and no budget for this kind of idea.' He closed a file as though ending the discussion.

She felt depleted, perhaps it was her image which touched a hardened heart.

'Okay, write something. In your own time. I'll ask someone to hide it in the women's section,' he added. 'But I'm not making any promises.' He looked up at her wryly. 'Are you getting maternal, is that what this is all about?'

'Why should you think that?'

'Experience, I can see it a mile off. Women are not a good investment.' He laughed. 'Though a pretty woman in the office is a joy forever.'

'A thing of beauty is a joy forever, if I'm not mistaken.'

'I prefer my version. Go on, get to work,' he added, trying to hide his affection for her.

'Thanks, you won't regret it.'

'I don't intend to,' he replied, picking up the 'phone. 'Finch, get down here. I want to talk about that useless piece of reporting you did yesterday.'

She lay in bed that night aware she had awakened strong but, until now, dormant opinions. She was excited to have written a small article which gave a voice to those who were unable to cope with both a family and work. Probably those with little to lose.

However, she could also relate to those with money because that was good for the economy and, anyway, she also liked buying nice clothes and luxuries. She thought she made her life difficult by sitting astride the fence.

She considered her career. It had not been particularly impressive, she had not yet found her niche, but now she suddenly felt compelled to concentrate on socially orientated subjects. Perhaps, she could throw a lifeline not only to stressed, hardworking, parents but, perhaps, she could even make a small ripple in an ocean of smug, placid, politicians. She accepted she was an idealistic dreamer though, at the same time, not entirely unrealistic. She still thought she could have been a politician.

Peter lay against her back that night with his hand softly caressing her breast. She turned to face him and slid into the thrill of loving, forgetting her new objectives.

He was in a deep sleep when she awoke at three in the morning. She threw her dressing gown over her shoulders and quietly opened her laptop. She had another article to write. An issue which, as usual, lined the pockets of the fat cats.

She dressed rather carefully next morning, choosing her dark grey suit. She did not want to be seen as pretty but rather to be noticed for her reporting. Unfortunately, JJ was an editor who was not easily swayed by either man nor beast and, somehow, she had to convince him that her new article contained merit. She thought there must be someone, somewhere, who would agree with her.

*

JJ's secretary was too busy to do more than acknowledge her revised article on 'Stay-At-Home' parents and assured her that she would place her new article in his 'In Tray' and would draw his attention to it today, if she could.

She had left the room disheartened, realising she had worked up an unrealistic enthusiasm which had wasted her time and energy at three in the morning. She could just as well have turned over and gone back to sleep.

She frowned as she remembered how Peter had distracted her when they had gone to bed. Now she was unsure whether she had been careless. She popped a tablet from out of its packing, aware she had not done so for the last two days. She thought it would probably be alright. After all, a tablet here or there was unlikely to make a difference. Surely, her body was so full of hormones one more or less would not matter. She decided it was probably irrelevant whether she had been careless, or not. Peter did not give up easily on any issue, if he wanted another child then that was what he would get.

She was packing up to go home when JJ appeared.

'I've got a friend who wants a debate. He says he can use your 'SAH' article to open up a discussion. He'll find an unobtrusive place for it in one of his 'lefty' magazines. I've still to study your very socialistic views on property ownership. You're not a bloody Communist, are you?'

She laughed. 'I've first to buy the red flag.'

'Do 'Commies' wear short skirts and bright red lipstick?'

'I don't see why not. Perhaps I can convert you.'

But he did not answer as he walked away.

*

The 'someone' JJ knew appeared to be a rather unimportant member of parliament who believed the uncontrollable youth in his area was due to a lack of parental care.

It seemed he totally supported the idea of a benefit scheme to encourage parents, legal guardians, to stay home so they were able to tend to the needs of their children. Not least, cooking a proper breakfast which, dieticians said, improved children's learning ability and, hopefully, their bad behaviour problems.

There would, of course, be strict conditions which would have to be thrashed out. Perhaps a parent might still be allowed to work one day a week. The duration of the benefit and the income of any other partner would have to be carefully considered.

Such a scheme was not to be seen as an easy touch for all and sundry. It was not for those whose aim was to misuse a benefit system.

She deliberated on whether she would be prepared to give up her job to bring up a family, knowing she would probably never get it back again. She thought probably not, not unless she could do some freelance work.

A middle aged man was sitting opposite JJ when he called her into his office.

'This', said JJ, 'is Tony Stockwell. He wants to meet you.'

Tony stood up and shook her hand. She noticed his brown suede shoes, she always noticed men's shoes though she did not know the reason why. She also noticed his light coloured trousers, his navy blue polo jumper, dark jacket and a rather large gold wristwatch. She thought him rather attractively dressed and his looks were not to be totally disregarded.

'Nice to meet you,' he said, sounding sincere but, nevertheless, jovial. He reminded her of someone who might place a bet on a horse or be found drinking with the locals in a Pub. 'Thanks for your article.'

'Not at all,' she replied, wondering where all this was going.

'I'll get to the point,' he continued, ignoring JJ. 'As you may know, I'm a member of the 'Opposition'. I'm considering standing at the next election as an 'Independent'. I have too many views which do not seem to fit in with any particular party. JJ told me that you have a similar outlook on life, rather opposing the establishment. If I'm correct.'

'Yes, you could say that,' she replied, thoughtfully.

'Are you interested in helping me?'

'How could I do that?'

'Perhaps by writing a few articles.'

'I could write something in my spare time. At home,' she added, quickly.

'Perhaps if it all kicks off you would like to work for me.'

She looked over to JJ who looked amused at the openness of his friend.

'I like my job, I like working here and I like working for JJ,' she replied, trying to hide her fear that her boss might want to get rid of her and this was a good opportunity to do so.

'See, Tony, I told you. She's a loyal subject, you can't have her', JJ laughed. 'At least not on a fulltime basis. I'm not giving her away with a pound of tea. Still I appreciate your frankness, I must say you're direct, I like that in a politician.' He laughed loudly, something she had not heard him do before.

'Well, it was worth a try, you shouldn't have been so enthusiastic about her.'

'She's the rose between the thorns,' JJ said, smiling kindly at her.

Tony turned to her. 'I would appreciate you writing a couple of thought-provoking articles for me, good remuneration, of course. It was worthwhile seeing JJ's face just now.' He chuckled, deeply. 'We go back a long way.'

'I think being an 'Independent' will suit you. It would be a pleasure to write a few considered words for a good cause.'

He smiled broadly. 'I'll be in touch, you'll read about me in the newspapers in a few weeks time. I'm getting a manifesto together, perhaps you might like to skim through it. You might have a few ideas of your own.'

'Yes, I believe I might have a few,' she grinned.

They chatted for a while before she returned to her desk, feeling extremely happy that JJ had supported her and wanted to keep her.

She considered Tony Stockwell to be a kind man with a great sense of humour, she could use that. Laughs were hard to come by and he rolled off jokes as though he was a stand-up comedian. She liked him but admired JJ too much to ever consider leaving her job, unless she had to and she hoped that day was years away.

Still, she had now to juggle three men, Peter, JJ and Tony Stockwell. 'Challenging', she thought.

She was disappointed at Peter's reaction when she told him of her meeting with JJ and Tony Stockwell. He vaguely answered that she had been lucky to have been pulled out of the pile of mediocre reporters, or words to that effect. She thought he not only lacked enthusiasm but was condescending.

'It's not luck. I work hard.'

She stopped aware she had held this, almost exact, conversation with her mother who had also said that any success would be due to luck and being in the right place at the right time. Sometimes, she thought her mother stood behind her, nudging her memory so she could recall past conversations and feelings.

'I didn't mean it like that,' Peter continued, sounding a little repentant.

'You should be happy for me, it's a chance, a breakthrough. Maybe, I can even get a raise.'

'It doesn't matter whether you get a raise or not. I earn enough to keep us.'

'That's not the point. It's about me, my career. Not about your income.'

'It's about Tom having a mother at home, it's about giving him a brother or a sister,' he snapped, as he walked into the kitchen and poured himself a large glass of wine.

'Is that more important than my job?'

'Yes, of course it is. It should also be your priority, not pouncing around some lateral thinking failed M.P. who only wants to use you.'

'So you know him, do you?' He did not answer her. 'You are such a twit,' she added.

'If that's what you think.'

'No, that's not what I think. I just thought you would be proud of me, support me.'

'I do support you.'

'No you don't. You just want me to walk around with a duster in my hand.'

'And you have just written a load of shit about stay at home parents. Your hypocrisy astounds me.'

'And your selfishness astounds me,' she shouted, slamming the lounge door as she left the room.

He politely knocked on the bedroom door before he entered.

'I'm sorry. It's just that Tom needs you to be home. He's getting teased at school.'

'He didn't tell me that.'

'No, I met his teacher at the school gate. He was crying and I asked why.'

'Why?' she asked.

'Something to do with not being good at sports or P.T. I've already told you he needs to join a couple of clubs, football, judo, whatever. No one has the bloody time to take him.'

'Meaning me.'

'No, us.'

'So you want me to give up my job.'

'Probably, maybe, yes.'

'Our son's happiness depends on my staying home,' she stated.

'He's also lonely. It's not all about you. Not everything is about you.'

She sat on the bed and remembered why they had split up, even though she still loved him. Of course, it was not over the flamboyant, irresistible, Tessa who had so easily seduced him. It was over them, their silly fights, their inability to agree with each other. Now it was her career which, as far as she knew, had never been an issue and a sibling for Tom. It was not as though she disagreed, it was more the way it was demanded.

'I think I might have made a mistake with the pill. If so, your troubles are over. All I need now is a new broom to sweep the house clean. Along with our lives,' she added.

'Are you serious, do you mean that?' he asked, excitedly.

'Oh, yes. Very serious.'

He took her in his arms. 'We'll remarry,' he promised, vehemently. 'You know how I feel about having children out of marriage.'

She was amazed at his exaggerated reaction. Amazed he was so passionate. She felt she had lost ground, at least for the time being. She needed a Plan B, one which would satisfy everyone. She thought she might just be able to handle it, if she played her cards right, if she could work at home and freelance for JJ and Tony Stockwell. She knew the day after her maternity leave would be her first day without a real job.

'It's just that time is running out,' he murmured.

'You mean my biological clock.'

'Well, yes.'

She pulled away from him. 'For god's sake. I'm still in my thirties.'

'You know what I mean.'

'Oh yes, I know what you mean. And if I don't produce, what then. Another younger Tessa.'

'Now you're being silly.'

'I believe being silly is a structural fault in my character. I'll have to do something about it. I'm going to take a bath and go to bed.'

'Going to sulk in the bath, again.'

'Probably yes, it's a part of being silly. Silly people do silly things. Desperate situations call for desperate measures,' she muttered, as she closed and locked the bathroom door.

She laid up to her neck in soapy water wondering how it was possible to write an article on 'stay-at-home' mothers while, at the same time, getting herself 'banged-up'.

She sighed. Peter was right, she had written an article which made her look self-serving and he was not entirely wrong about Tony Stockwell. He did think laterally, but then so did she.

She climbed out of the bath and opened the door. 'Peter,' she called. 'Would you like to wash my back?'

*

Tony Stockwell 'phoned while Peter hovered around obviously unhappy and unsupportive of any extra work she might do at home. Still, she had a few new topics and she was not going to be restricted by any man.

Once, she had heard some idiot say that a woman's place was not at the kitchen sink but in the bedroom. She had attacked him verbally but Peter had shushed her up and even held onto her arm in case she swiped the half drunk with her shoulder bag. She still felt that some women had a long way to go to find the elusive equality but, on the other hand, she considered God helped those who helped themselves. However, she reckoned life was probably simpler for women who, when read the riot act, lay on their backs and accepted their fate, as they had done since the beginning of time.

The idea of moonlighting for Tony Stockwell was becoming more attractive by the day. If he didn't lose his deposit, then she was very willing to help him.

*

'How is my Sophie?' Tony was asking on her mobile. 'Have you dug up any skulduggery?' He laughed, obviously finding himself amusing.

'Yes, I am pretty worked up about the percentage of land owned by overseas investors. Have you any idea how much of our country is owned by foreigners?'

'Oh yes. That's one of my favourite topics.'

'I don't understand why it's allowed. I believe land and resources belong to the people. Not to overseas investors. Gas, electric, oil, coal, water, communication, whatever, belongs to the country.'

'And free trade?'

'I don't know enough about that. But it certainly doesn't make any sense importing a bottle of wine from the other side of the world, let alone a bottle of water.'

'That's called globalisation. Have you read the statistics?'

'Some of them.'

'Well, do so. They are very enlightening and very frightening.'

'I don't believe people understand what's happening,' she said, almost sadly.

'Ah, there's the rub. The man on the street doesn't really care just so long as he has a reasonable pay packet, his football and beer. After all, he can do little about it, even if he did know. Listen, write an article. I don't have the time. I'll try to use it.'

She hung up, unsure whether Tony Stockwell was misusing her since she had not yet seen a single penny, neither cash nor on her bank account.

She thought it was time to give Jillie a ring and arrange to have lunch together. Surprisingly, they both held the same opinions. It occurred to her that their similar views were the only thing they had in common. She thought of her mother whose rather radical ideas had irritated Jack.

*   *   *

'Sorry it's taken so long to meet up, I got bogged down earning some hard needed funds. I can't ask Pa for every cent I need. What are you having?' Jillie asked, looking at the menu.

'Can't make my mind up, I'm actually not very hungry.'

'Well, there's no hurry. We'll start with a coffee.'

'No, not a coffee, I'll have a mint tea,' she told the waitress who was standing with a pencil and notepad.

'Are you okay, you look a bit white?'

'I'm fine, just fine.'

'I've something to tell you. You can't guess. I'm going to take an Open University course in Politics. I'll live at home, keep the costs down and I'll try to find a job locally, probably land up helping in Rosie's kitchen or garden. Something I really don't want to do.'

Sophie stared with amazement. 'I can't believe what you're saying.'

'Why not, is that so strange?'

'Well, yes, it is. I met a chap through JJ. He's an opposition M.P. and wants to stand as an 'Independent' at the next election.'

'Interesting. I wouldn't mind meeting him.'

'He wants me to help him.'

'How?'

'By writing articles. Actually, I don't take it too seriously, it's more than likely he'll lose his deposit after the votes are counted.'

'That is a coincidence.'

'I don't know if I'm up to it,' she murmured.

'Just give a shout if you need any help.'

'I might do that.'

'You should take a Course with me, we could help each other.'

'Dream on,' she sighed. 'I've got something to tell you. Only Peter knows.'

The Italian looking waitress arrived and took out her notepad again.

'Would you like to order?' she asked, with a tinge of irritation in her voice.

'Okay,' said Jillie, looking across to Sophie. 'I'll take the Tagliatella, what about you?'

'Just a tomato salad,' Sophie replied.

'So?' Jillie asked.

'I'm pregnant. Peter wants a sibling for Tom.'

'Congratulations. Is that what you want?' she added, sensing it was not in Sophie's agenda.

'What can I say. He's right, of course, Tom is lonely. I need to be around more and, anyway, I'm earning a lousy salary.'

'And?'

'He wants me to give up my job.'

'Oh, come on. He can't ask you to do that if you don't want to.'

'I might be able to work from home, go freelance for JJ, if I am lucky, and something for Tony Stockwell if he succeeds.'

'Tony Stockwell?'

'The hopeful Independent. Peter wants to rush me off to a Registry Office,' she sighed, again.

'He's very honourable.'

'Yes, he is, a little too,' she added, softly. 'It would be nice to have a say in it.'

'You don't want to marry?'

'Yes, of course I do. It's just that I had hoped to get a career going.'

Jillie laughed. 'Does one exclude the other?'

'Peter wants a wife to take care of him and his creature comforts.'

'Do you regret getting back together?'

'I didn't say I regretted being back with him, it's just that.'

'You aren't suited,' Jillie finished the sentence for her.

'It's just that I feel a bit cornered. Is that so bad? You know, I've just written an article about mothers staying home to look after their brats. Look at me now. He always wins. You know, I forgot why we broke up,' she added, sounding miserable.

'The affair?'

'Yes, but I don't really believe that's ever the entire cause for splitting up. We were already bickering before that Tessa woman came on the scene. I think marriages are chipped away. Peter is terribly sweet but just a little bit dogmatic, assertive is another word. He wants his way. It's not that he's wrong, just irritatingly right, sometimes.'

'I can understand how you feel. You've got the nappies out of the way then nearly ten years later you begin all over again. I guess Mum had the same.

I've never thought of it before. But I guess that's what she wanted, Jack's baby.'

'She once told me she didn't take the pill on purpose. She never told Jack that,' she laughed at the thought of her mother conning her stepfather.

Jillie sighed. 'Just accept it, enjoy it, make Peter happy, he's a good guy. They don't come around very often. See how it goes. A day at a time.'

'You're right. Nothing ever stays the same.'

'I have something else to tell you.'

'What then?'

'You know I told you about the woman I saw by the 'Crossing', the one I thought was Mum. Well, it seems two other people have also seen her. Or think they have.'

'Who?'

'Rosie, from the tea house, and Arnold Waters from the Garden Centre. Both Rosie and Arnold have seen her on the bench at the 'Crossing'. You know, the one not far from Rosie's garden. I've spoken to both of them. They seem sincere. I don't believe they are making it up. That's a minor reason why I'm going to study at home. Arnold Waters runs a spiritual group.'

'You mean they call up the dead, Ouija boards and all of that.'

'I don't think they do that, it's more meditation and all that stuff. Anyway, I want to join, who knows what can happen.'

'That sounds interesting, I'd like to come with you. A day at a time,' she sighed. 'I'm dreading it. I love Peter but to begin again. God help me.'

'Don't worry, I'll drop in and do the dishes and

iron his shirts,' she laughed. 'He is a bit of an old fuddy-duddy. You really are so different.'

*

Jack was in the garden when Jillie answered the telephone.

'I'm in a mess. I can't cope. I will never be able to cope,' Sophie shouted, hysterically.

'Quieten down. What happened?'

'Twins, I'm going to have twins.'

'Oh, God. What does Peter say?'

'What do you think, he's over the moon.'

'You can forget your career, sweetie. That's not going to happen.'

'Don't I know it. I can't look after two babies.'

'Of course you can. Just the first three years will be a bit of a drag.'

'I'll be over forty by then.'

'So! Come on it's not the end of the world. You can manage, just plan your days. Peter will be only too happy to get out of bed at night,' she laughed.

'You think!'

'No, not really. But he has to.'

'By the way, I thought of getting married in Rosie's garden. It's more friendly that the inside of a Town Hall.'

'What a good idea. Seems Rosie organises the whole shebang, catering, everything. You have only to turn up looking lovely.'

'Sticking out half a meter.'

Jillie laughed. 'Five of you will be present. You, Peter, Tom and two babies. Do you know what they are yet?'

'Yep, a boy and a girl. Two different eggs. When I do something, I do it 'big time'.'

'Any names yet?'

'Emily and Jonathan.'

'After JJ?'

'Yes, but also after Jack. He is actually a 'John'. It's a nice name and I want to mend a few fences with him. And JJ is really kind, he says I can work from home. I'm just scared to death that I can't cope.'

'Of course you can. Keep calm. It will be okay.'

Jillie walked slowly into the conservatory and stared across the garden at the oak tree. She felt depressed, worried, conscious that it was not going to be alright.

Crows were flying in and out of the branches and a squirrel leapt from one branch to another.

She thought of her mother who could stare for ages at the bright little creatures.

*

'That's a coincident,' Rosie said, warmly. 'There's another wedding planned for the same day. Alison Waters is going to marry an old friend, Philip Price. Such a nice young man, came here on holiday from Australia with his mother. It seems he and Alison knew each other from school, before his family emigrated. A real whirlwind romance.'

'That's nice,' replied Sophie, not really that interested in the local love life.

'They went on holiday together and want to get married quickly. Perhaps she'll go back to Australia with him,' Rosie continued, sounding sad. 'Though I've heard he's helping Alison and her father at the Garden Center.'

'Well, what then?' Sophie asked, trying to move things along.

'It occurred to me,' Rosie said, thoughtfully. 'Seeing how your father and Jillie know Alison and her father, Arnold, rather well. And I was a good friend of your mother and Jack, of course. And everyone knows Philip's mother, Hilly, she owned the hairdresser's shop before she emigrated.'

She stopped for a moment to give Sophie time to absorb the tight structure of village life.

Sophie blinked and closed her eyes as she tried to work out who knew who and why this trivial information would affect her wedding plans.

'Interesting,' she replied.

'Well, what I am trying to say is that perhaps you and Alison might want to discuss a double wedding. I know Alison is going to keep it down to a handful of people. Are you planning a big wedding?'

'Absolutely not. Just a couple of friends and close family.'

'Well, think about it. I'll give you Alison's 'phone number. You can decide if you want to do something together. Otherwise, I'm afraid that afternoon is already booked. It would be fun having all these people meet up again,' she hinted, wistfully. 'It's such a small community.'

'I'll have to think about it. It is an idea.'

'Well, let me know, quickly, if you decide to have a double wedding.'

'It would be difficult. I don't know Alison.'

'Your father and Jillie do. They will probably be asked to Alison's wedding, anyway. You can ask them what they think.'

'Thanks, I'll do that. I'll let you know.'

It was several days later when Sophie called Alison Waters.

'I'm Sophie, Jack Nielson' eldest daughter,' she said, introducing herself.

'I've heard about you. Jack told me you were remarrying.'

'Yes, that's what I am 'phoning about. It seems we both want the first Friday in September. We're going on holiday the following Sunday.'

'What a coincidence.'

'Rosie thought it might be a good idea to have a double wedding, seeing how most of the guests know each other, at least the ones living around here.'

'Yes, Rosie told me.'

'What do you think about it? It seems a bit silly having two weddings within a short space of time, inviting almost all the same people.'

'I'll ask Phil, though knowing him he won't give a damn, he's so laid back. Probably because he lived out back,' she laughed.

'I heard he's from Australia and you were at school together.'

'Yes, that's right. Tell you what, a double wedding is okay. But, if you don't mind, I would like to marry first, seeing how it's my first time and, actually, that's a special date for us,' she laughed again, sounding embarrassed at her frankness.

'Fine, we'll meet up. I have still to tell Jack, he doesn't know I am marrying from his house.'

'I'm looking forward to all these people getting together. Do you know anyone from around here?' Alison asked.

'No, not really. I left home long before my parents moved down here.'

'We'll have separate cakes, if that's alright with you,' she added.

'Alison, everything is fine by me. I just don't want to get married in a Registry Office and this is something a bit in between, simple but special. We'll both be happy if a glass of champagne replaces a cup of tea.'

Alison laughed. 'Phil will go along with that. Champagne for Tea. What more can you ask for?'

'We'll drink to that on our wedding day.'

*　　*　　*

She threw her overnight bag down in the hall, greeted her irritable mother and loving Aunt Flossy and had a quick cup of tea with a piece of fruit cake.

Where's Pippa?' she eventually asked.

'At the stables, where else,' her mother answered, coolly.

'I thought we should discuss where everyone is going to stay. You and Flossy will stay with dad and me, of course, and maybe Pippa could stay with Sophie and Jillie.'

'Who are they?'

'Jack Nielson's daughters. I thought you should know that Phil and me are marrying on the same afternoon as Sophie. She's remarrying her 'ex', Peter. Don't be surprised when you see her stomach sticking out. She's expecting twins. It's going to be a double wedding.'

'Why?'

'Because we have mutual friends, local people. You must know some of them and it will take some of the spotlight off Phil and me,' she grinned as her mother looked uncomfortable at the idea.

*

She found Pippa mucking out the stall of her new horse, a large black animal with a white blaze. They made the usual motion of giving each other a light kiss, a floating kiss which might or might not land on the intended cheek. Their coolness disturbed her for it had never been her intention to have a similar relationship with her daughter as she did with her mother. She wondered if she was to blame but, then again, Aunt Flossy and she did not have a problem. Kisses and cuddles were abundant. She decided Pippa had inherited a 'cool' gene from her grandmother.

'You're a sweet boy, aren't you,' Pippa asked the animal who was impatiently scraping his hoof through the straw.

'What's his name?'

'Black Jack. It's a mixture of names. He's almost a purebred.'

She looked up grinning at her mother who had stepped back into the courtyard.

'Don't be frightened, he won't trample you to death. Not unless I tell him to,' she muttered.

There was a difficult silence until Pippa suddenly blurted out. 'And what about me?'

She raised her eyebrows in surprise. 'What about you?'

'I'm also getting married.'

'Yes, but not yet.'

She had not thought about Pippa getting married. Getting engaged was one thing but getting married was something else.

'Who says. Don't you think it would be nice for us to share a wedding. You and Phil, me and Mark. What about that?' she asked, sounding emotional as she bridled her horse.

'Why would you want to do that?'

'Why would I not?'

'It's a bit unusual to say the least. Mother and father marrying, incidentally for the first time, at the same time as their daughter. Not that anyone knows I'm your mother. Let alone Phil's your father.'

'Why not?'

'Why not what?'

'Tell anyone.'

'Because it doesn't serve a purpose. At least, not yet.'

'And what does Phil say to that?'

'He's told his mother and she has agreed not to tell anyone until we feel it's the right time. Can you imagine the whispering behind our backs when we are getting married. I really can't face that. There's a time and place for everything and it's not just before I get married.'

'Is there ever a good time?'

'No, probably not.'

'You didn't even ask me.'

'I told you we were marrying, I thought you would be happy for me.'

'I am happy for you, it's just that I would like to be included in something. Just for once. You are willing to have a double wedding with a woman you hardly know but it hasn't occurred to you that you could do that with me.'

'It's not a real double wedding. We marry first and have a drink, then she marries. We just share the reception because a lot of people know each other. Nothing more than that. Anyway, how do you know about it?'

'Grandpa told me. He wanted to speak to Flossy but she wasn't home so we had a cosy chat. He said you were going to marry at the same time as some female whose father, or step father, hangs around Rosie's garden.'

'He doesn't hang around. He was asked to help when your grandpa hurt his back. I don't think your grandpa likes someone else doing his work. He's possessive when it comes to Rosie's garden, that's why he's bit put out.'

There was a silence as Pippa flung a saddle over the back of her horse and ducked beneath to reach for the girth.

'You never think of what I want,' Pippa muttered, while vigorously pulling the girth tight.

'What do you want?'

'A normal family.'

'Well, you can blame your precious grandma for that. If she hadn't hidden your father's letters then he would have known about you. He would have put his name on your birth certificate, he would have come for me, for us. It would all have been different,' she held back her tears. 'And since when did you want to live with me.'

'Never, I never wanted to live with you.'

'Well, there you go.'

There was another sullen silence as Pippa adjusted the bit in her horse's mouth.

'I want us to have a double wedding. Then Mark and me will come back here and have a church blessing followed by a full-blown party. What do you think of that?'

'I didn't know you wanted a church service.'

'There is so much you don't know. We do it for his parents.'

'So, why the rush to get married?' she asked, suspecting there was more to it all. More than just being in love with the magnificent Mark.

'The rushed wedding is because there is a house here, on the grounds,' she replied, pointing in the distance. 'It's just become empty and if we don't take it someone else will. His parents accept we sleep together but they don't want us to openly live together. It's against their principles. Then you come along with all your neat little plans. Mark and me have talked about it. We marry down south and, to keep his family happy, we will have a church blessing up here. Okay?'

'But why do you want to marry down south?'

'Because I want a light hearted affair, between the flowers, in a field, on a mountain, on a beach. I don't know. This is the only chance I'll get to do that. Otherwise, his mother will meddle in it and push Mark into doing what she wants. This way, it's all arranged, she can't interfere, and we all get what we want.'

'My God, How controlling do you want to be. I've never heard of anything so ridiculous. Do his parents know I'm a single mother?'

'We haven't told them yet,' she replied, as she mounted her horse.

'Well, I hope you love each other enough to stand their wrath.'

'That sounds bitchy, Alison.'

'Yes, it does, but you have one strike against you. Me. Two more and you're out.'

'So says you,' she replied, as she mounted her horse in the yard.

'Yep, so say I.'

'Okay, enough of the sermon, yes or no.'

'If that's what you want, then so be it.'

'Fine,' Pippa answered as her horse impatiently turned in small circles, his hoofs clattering on the stones as he did so. 'By the way, all of this', she said, pointing with her riding crop across the stables and countryside is theirs plus a lot more. That's why we have plans to extend the stables and riding school. It will be ours one day. Could you help me?' she added, sounding impatient, as she bent over towards the gate.

She lifted the latch. 'Are you sure you want to do this?' she asked, pulling the heavy gate open. 'Are you sure Mark is right for you or is it just because you have your eye on this.' She waved her arm vaguely. 'What makes you think you won't be controlled by Mark as well. He's one of them. Are you sure you're in love with him or is it the land and a herd of horses?'

'Oh don't be stupid, Alison. Of course, I love Mark. He will arrange the Bans,' she called.

'Have a nice ride on Black Ass Jack.'

*   *   *

Jack Nielson put the telephone down slowly. He was used to surprises, he thought there was no end to them.

Jillie had recently informed him of her plans to study at home, perhaps an Open University course in politics, or something of that nature. He was happy, someone in the house, someone to care for and to talk to when he got up in the morning. He could hardly believe his luck, even if Jillie's kindness was most probably financially based.

But now Sophie had just 'phoned to say she was marrying in Rosie's garden and she and Tom would be staying with him the day before. That also pleased him, it was as though life was beginning to straighten out, things were falling into place, the summer months would end happily. Jillie would be living at home and Sophie settled again with Peter, though he had reservations since both were dominant types.

He had gasped when Sophie informed him she was pregnant with twins. He had wanted to feel happy for her, for them, but she had hardly been able to cope with Tom as a baby, let alone a couple of new ones. He thought it was a recipe for disaster but he did not have a solution. Some things were out of his control and this was truly one of them.

He startled as the telephone rang again. It was Rosie who sounded almost breathless as she asked him if he knew about the three weddings, all to be held on the same day; the first Friday in September. He listened patiently as she ranted on about the wedding of Alison to Philip Price together with her younger sister, Pippa, to a Mark someone or another. Then, afterwards, Sophie would re-tie the knot with Peter. And, what's more, most of the guests were from the village and everyone knew each other. It was all so unbelievably exciting. Nothing like that had ever happened before. Not that she knew.

Jack had laughed and joked with Rosie until she hung up, even more breathless. He sat back and stared at the photograph he had taken of Helen's lake. The one Jillie had talked about. He thought it was time to take it down and store it somewhere at the back of the loft. Had things been different he would have given it to Helen but the idea of seeing her was out of the question.

He was startled as the telephone rang yet again and amazed it was Helen ringing at the same time as he had been thinking of her. He thought there must be some kind of telepathy.

'How are you?' he asked, kindly.

'Fine, very well. I thought perhaps we could have a drink together, for old time's sake.'

'I don't think that's wise.'

'I don't believe you've stopped loving me.'

'Believe it. You had better believe it.'

'You're totally unable of taking responsibility for what happened,' she choked as she spoke. 'If I remember rightly, you were also there. And not just the once, remember?'

'I take full responsibility for what happened.'

'So, then, why can't we meet?'

'Because it's over. It should never have started. I can't believe I acted as I did, you can have no idea how I regret the whole thing.'

You know, Jack Neilson, there are a couple of words missing from your vocabulary and emotional development', she shouted.

'Interesting, and they are?'

'To love and to need. Be loved and be needed.'

'Since when have you developed social skills?'

'Since I met Michael Lee. We love each other and we are going to marry over Christmas, on a beach in Jamaica or Thailand.'

'Michael Lee. Isn't he a bit young for you?'

'Does that matter!'

'Not to me. Have you told him about your problem?'

'That's between us.'

'Well, then. I'm happy for you both and wish you a long and healthy life together.'

'I'm not finished with you yet, Jack Nielson. We go back a long way and I intend to be around a lot longer,' she shouted, slamming down the 'phone.

'Standard,' he murmured. 'She just couldn't resist telling me. God help Michael Lee.'

He frowned as he tried to work out why a young man would want to marry a woman old enough to be his mother and infected with HIV. He would have to think about it but, for the moment, it was above and beyond his understanding.

He set his thoughts aside, he had other things to think about, not least Sophie carrying twins.

He wished Emy was around. She would enjoy feeding them and patting their backs. He sighed as he wished there was something he could do to help.

A BAG OF BONES

Will STOOD STARING AT THE blocked toilet. It was not a pretty sight, not something he needed in his life, and Rosie was getting neurotic, not that he could blame her. Not when visitors asked to use their facilities. She was very fussy about them, toilets that is. They were to be found clean and left clean, hands were to be washed well with disinfectant soap and handtowels were to be changed at least once a day. Clean toilets were to be taken seriously and now this. A blocked lavatory totally unusable for visitors and staff, including he and Rosie. He had been plunging the offensive waste for days already and, once in a while, he thought he had won the battle. But, today, the rather large problem refused to disappear where it was supposed to disappear and plunging had not help.

'It's no good, Rosie,' he called to where she was standing some way down the hall, out of sight and out of any obnoxious odour which might float in her direction. 'We're going to have to get a plumber.

I can't fix it.'

'Do whatever you have to do, so long as it's done immediately,' she answered, walking into the conservatory away from the disaster area.

The plumber arrived very quickly, considering they were judged to be next to God alongside the vicar. He pushed a long wire brush down the offending pipe and twirled it around several times which made Will wince since he was sure he was scratching their brand new toilet bowl. He was not happy though the Plumber seemed to be.

'I don't think I can do much. If you ask me, you might well have a broken pipe somewhere under the house or in the garden. I take it you have a septic tank.'

'Yes, by the front gate.'

The plumber who was dressed in a blue overall followed him as though on a mission.

'When was it last emptied?'

'Have no idea.'

'Well, let's hope that's the problem. I'll arrange for it to be cleaned out. I wouldn't use your toilet again.'

'I have no intention of doing so,' remarked Will, irritated at the obvious advice.

'If it's not the tank then we have a problem. How old is the house?'

'I should think around a hundred and fifty years, maybe more, maybe less.'

The plumber grunted and smiled at the same time.

'Well, I'll contact you. Maybe it is nothing special, just a full tank.'

'You can see how urgent this is, what with visitors coming and going and a couple of weddings in a few weeks time.'

'Well, as I've just said, it could be a small thing like the septic tank but if it's a broken pipe it could take a couple of days to sort out. That's the trouble with these old houses. Sooner or later you have to replace everything. I think it's the turn of your sewerage pipe,' he laughed again, perhaps hearing a cash register ringing in his ears. 'I'll be back.'

'Please be as quick as you can. We have clients you know,' he reminded the man.

'See what I can do,' the plumber answered, still smiling broadly

'Thanks,' mumbled Will, aware this was going to cost him.

Sometimes, he thought he had inherited his father's love of numbers, money numbers. He tried to discard his guilty, uncomfortable, thoughts which jumped out at him whenever he passed the rockery, almost as though his father threw a stone at him to remind him where he was. He was not a happy man, not regarding his father and how he died.

Rosie was waiting for him at the front door.

'Well?' she asked.

'Well, nothing. With a bit of luck the septic tank is full and with bad luck the pipe is broken somewhere along the way. That's what you get from living in old houses. We aren't even connected to the sewerage system.'

'You worry too much.'

'You said that once before.'

'And I was right. Your father is nicely settled, we found Reggie a good home, didn't we?'

'Yes, under the rockery,' Will said, sounding concerned.

'Just relax. Come and have a cup of tea.'

'I have a bad feeling this is going wrong.'

'Why, why should anything go wrong?'

'Sod's Law, Murphy's Law, whatever. Take your pick.'

'Rubbish.'

'Rosie, if anything can go wrong, it will. I just have the feeling that my father will have the last word.'

'I can assure you he won't. He's gone, forever.'

'No, he hasn't. He's still here,' he whispered, trying to keep his voice down.

'Just wait. When is the man returning?'

'He didn't say. Knowing plumbers it will be next week or even later.'

'I'll give him a call tonight. See if I can persuade him to hurry it up.'

'How?'

'By using my feminine wiles, of course.'

'What else,' he grumbled.

The plumber came at the same time as the sewerage collector who drained the septic tank of its contents.

'That should help, let's try the toilet,' the plumber suggested as they all trooped into the house and waited while he pushed the shiny plate on the wall which hid the modern water tank. The water in the bowl did not move an inch.

The plumber leaned with his dirty overalls against the wall while he considered the options.

'Well, I think we will have to consider the pipe. Could be broken. Have you a basement?'

'You can look but there's no sewerage pipe down there, not that I've seen,' said Will, who had been deserted by Rosie.

They climbed down the narrow staircase to the damp basement. The plumber looked around and shook his head.

'No, nothing down here. Do you have any plans of the house?'

'Shouldn't think so. Not from over a hundred and fifty years ago.'

The plumber made a humming sound. 'I'll pop into the council office, maybe the planning department can point me in the right direction. They were probably laid recently, in the nineteen twenties.'

'You call that recently?'

'Well more recent than a hundred and fifty years ago, or more,' he laughed, loudly.

Will sighed, more time and money and nothing achieved. He was sure he was right, something was going wrong. It was an intuition, one he could not shake off.

*

The plumber returned next day with a sheet of paper in his hand.

'It seems your conservatory was a barn.'

'That's right,' agreed Will.

'And it seems it was built later, sometime after the house was built.'

'I didn't know that,' murmured Rosie.

'Now', he continued, 'here is the septic tank and here is the natural line which the pipe would follow to the house. Unfortunately, it seems to run under the barn.'

They both stood motionless, trying to absorb the consequences.

'How could they do that. How could they build over sewerage pipes,' cried Rosie.

'I think it's the other way round,' corrected the plumber. 'They dug up the earth floor and then laid the pipes.'

'That's why the old tiles were not cemented in. And then, we come along and lay a marble floor,' Will puffed through his lips in frustration.

'Now it may not be as bad as you think. A broken pipe doesn't have to be under your new floor. It can be anywhere up to the house. It could even be under the rockery. We'll start here, by the septic tank and run a line of rods with a camera at the end, it won't take long to find it. Fingers crossed it's by the septic tank or in the garden. You could still be lucky.'

'I knew it,' muttered Will, as he walked despondently away. 'I told you so.'

*

'Well it's good news and bad news, which would you like to hear first,' the plumber asked, with the same grin he had before.

'Good news,' Will replied, optimistically.

'Well the damage is not under the house.'

'And the bad news?'

'Actually, it's not that bad, it's under the rockery. You probably dug too close to the pipe and didn't compact the soil, this could have caused the pipe to shear. We'll have to dismantle the rockery, I'll take it apart very carefully so that it can be easily rebuilt. I'll be back tomorrow.'

'I'll ask Arnold to come along,' said Rosie, quietly. 'He can supervise it.'

'Why bother,' murmured Will, as he walked away.

Rosie followed him into the house.

'We're in big trouble,' he murmured, sounding worried and very depressed.

'I've something to tell you.'

'What?'

'It's not as bad as you might think.'

'I think it's as bad as it can get.'

'I haven't been entirely honest,' continued Rosie.

'Really,' he snapped. 'If I'm correct it's not the first time. What are you about to spring on me now?'

'You know I said your father was gone forever. Well, I meant what I said. After you buried the holdall, before the rockery was actually built, I dug it up.'

'Dug what up?'

'The holdall. Reggie's bones.'

'What. Why?'

'I thought that so long as you thought he was under the rockery we wouldn't move from here. You know how I felt about that, this is my family home. I can't move, I don't want to move. But I also did not want Reggie under the rockery still dominating our lives and, most importantly, if something happened to me you wouldn't feel free to move away from here, if you wanted. So I took the holdall and got rid of it. Reggie is not under the rockery. They can dig as deep as they want, there is nothing to find.'

'Where is he then?' he gasped.

'Where do you think?'

'I have no idea.'

'Where we put his clothes.'

'In the river?'

'Yes, in the river. I filled the holdall with stones, drove to the bridge and threw it in just as my mother and I did before. I was very careful, I removed all his teeth so that if ever his skull or jaw bone were found it would be difficult to trace him though, of course, there could still be DNA in his bones. I forgot about that,' she added, thoughtfully.

He stood totally stunned while at the same time relieved, he was free of the house if he wished. They would dig up the rockery and find nothing. It was on the surface excellent only he felt Rosie could do the most outrageous things, secretly, without his knowing, though he considered her to be his best friend. He wondered what other ghastly secrets she held. He thought he was even a little bit frightened of her, frightened of his sweet Rosie.

She stared at him. 'You are happy, aren't you?' she asked, hopefully.

'Yes and no. What did you do with his teeth?' he suddenly asked.

'Do you really want to know.'

'I think so,' he replied, hesitantly.

'Well,' she said, clearing her throat. 'I wrapped them up tightly in toilet paper and threw them down the toilet. They're probably in the bottom of the septic tank.

He gasped, shocked at what she had said.

'You know,' she added, aggressively, 'rape is a violation, both physical and mental. I was eighteen. If I had gone to the police they would most probably have insinuated that I had been flirtatious, led him on and I couldn't face police doctors and being cross examined, let alone see my mother arrested. And then there was you. You were in your second year at university, what do you think you would have done if it came out. You would probably have left, ruined your career, and disappeared into the back of beyond. We couldn't do that to you.'

'Don't you feel guilty? After all, your mother did kill him.'

'You still haven't got it, have you?' she shouted, angrily. 'I didn't dare to marry because of him. I got engaged to the Belgian because I was jealous of you getting married and I wanted to hurt you. But, of course, I couldn't go through with it because of all of this. And, we could have married years ago when we were young and had a family. I lost out on that. And my mother, can you begin to imagine how she feared every knock on the door, every police car seen in the village? She never ever got over it. He ruined our lives. No one can get over carrying such a secret. It killed her, in the end it killed her. I loved her,' she sobbed. 'We never had a quiet life because of him, he was always between us. Always there, under the stones in a chapel of all places. He didn't deserve to be buried in a chapel,' she covered her face as the tears rolled down her cheeks.

Will looked away unable to see her unhappiness.

'I wrote a letter, it's between my papers. You would have found it if I died first.' She sobbed as she walked across to a small desk in the corner of the room. 'Here you can read it,' she said, after searching for it between other papers.

He took it from her and carefully tore the envelope open.

'You don't have to read the first page,' Rosie said, still sounding angry and disappointed. 'It's only about how much I loved you. Past tense you will notice.'

He quickly glanced through it and turned to the second page.

'I wrote it so no one else would understand what it was about,' she explained.

"Will, I know I have asked you not to sell the house but, the truth is, you are totally free to do whatever you wish. There is absolutely no reason for you to stay here. I arranged everything a long time ago while we were still landscaping the garden.

Sorry for all the trouble I gave you, I have always loved you. Your Rosie."

'You see,' she said. 'I sorted it out so you could do what you wanted if I died first.'

'Why didn't you tell me?'

'Because you thought we had found a nice resting place for your father. How could I tell you his bones are in a holdall at the bottom of the river. That wouldn't have made you any happier, would it?'

'I don't know Rosie, you and your mother should have confided in me.'

'No, it was between us, be happy we left you out of it. Everything would have stayed the same if you hadn't chased around Emily Nielson. We would never have married and you wouldn't have thought about selling the house. You would never have known. It's also your fault. You wouldn't have known anything about it if you had just carried on as before.'

'Is there any more I should know? Some small incident, perhaps a body under the floorboards in the tower. A small poisoning, perhaps arsenic in the cakes, digitalis tea, egg sandwiches peppered with rat poison, sponge cake with e.coli in the cream?' he ranted, sarcastically. 'Actually, you've involved me in a murder, an accomplice to hiding a body.'

'He wasn't murdered. It was an accident. If we had gone to the police it would have been, at the best, manslaughter. My mother would have gone to prison. How would you feel if that had happened?'

'I'm sorry. It's just that you have a habit of keeping secrets.'

'Do you think I enjoy all this cloak and dagger stuff,' she cried, as she fell back into a chair still sobbing.

'Of course, I don't. It's just an enormous shock. I have to absorb it all. I mean I've walked a hundred times passed that rockery, every time remembering he was there. His bones in a bag. I mean he was my father. Even though I didn't like him very much.'

Her hair stuck to her cheeks wet from tears just as when she had told him how his father had died, how her mother had hit him with a candlestick when he was attacking her. He had loved her then, he loved her now. It was true, he had not really considered what rape meant to the one who had suffered the pain, humiliation and fear.

He frowned. 'But how could you have lived here all alone when Stella died and I was away on field trips?'

'I had no options. What could I do? I couldn't sell the house and, of course, I was afraid. That's why I always had a couple of dogs. Remember, you didn't like me having them in my bedroom? Now you know why I wanted them near to me. Then, eventually, you stopped work.'

'Oh, Rosie, I'm so sorry. You've been incredibly stoic. I don't think I could have done that.'

He kissed her wet cheek. He could forgive her for everything and anything. He held her close to him as he had done before.

'I'm sorry, I didn't mean to hurt you. I love you, Rosie. I will always love you.'

'Oh, Will,' she whispered. 'I am so sorry.'

'It's alright. When all this is over, when the toilet is fixed and the season is over, we'll go away together. We'll close this down for a few weeks or let Poppy and Agnes run it. Maybe Alison will come in once in a while. We will forget the past and get on with the future. No one else matters, just us.'

'And the rockery, what do we do about that after it's been pulled apart?'

'Everything can be put back as it was before.'

'Even broken hearts.'

'Yes, even broken hearts can be mended.'

He kissed her tenderly, just as he did the Christmas night when they first made love. It seemed so long ago.

THREE GOLD RINGS

Alison OPENED HER BEDROOM curtains, sighed with relief at the sight of the early morning sun, then fell back on her bed. She stared up at the ceiling and traced the crack which began at the light fitting and zig zagged towards a corner, while she absorbed the importance of the day. This would be her last morning in this bed, in this room, and she wondered if she should not feel sad, but that emotion escaped her. Tomorrow, she would wake up with Phil next to her, married to the man she had longed to be with for so many years.

She smiled as she remembered their first week together. The cool Spring evenings had remained half light until late while they made love in one of Rosie's garden shelters. Phil had hidden a camping mattress in the back of a tool shed which had, miraculously, gone unnoticed and she had brought fresh smelling cushions to make a bed of love. She breathed deeply. Today they would be together for as long as they lived.

She could hear her mother and Flossy pottering around downstairs and her father in the bathroom preparing for the day ahead. They had agreed she would use the bathroom last. She could take her time, there was no hurry, the wedding was not until the afternoon. She liked that, an afternoon with wedding cake and ice cold champagne. An ideal cocktail for a hot summer's day.

She and Pippa would marry first, as agreed. In fact, Sophie agreed to anything she had suggested and she wondered how enthusiastic she really was at her 'second time around' occasion.

Jack had recently cornered her in Rosie's garden and told her how Sophie was already five months pregnant and carrying twins. He was obviously worried and, perhaps, even hoped she would have some words of wisdom which might smooth his furrowed brow. She had told him not to worry, everything would come right in the end. She did not add that the 'end' could take a long time coming.

She felt a mutual sympathy for Sophie who seemed distraught as though she had somehow lost her way, as though unable to comprehend her future. Still, she could not worry about someone she barely knew, she had her own good news and she had pondered on whether to tell Phil before they married or save it for later. She thought she would wait just a little longer to be sure.

She turned her thoughts back to the day before and the difficult sleeping arrangements which she and Phil had solved, without treading on too many toes. Finally, it was agreed that her mother and aunt would stay with she and her father. Pippa, along with her Maid of Honour, would stay in Jack's house with Sophie and Jillie so they could bond before the wedding.

Phil was already staying with his mother in his aunt's house and had offered to have Peter and Mark stay with them. Another 'getting to know you', opportunity. And, finally, Mark's parents would stay in the local hotel; their grudging presence based on compromise. An immediate church blessing to take place the following Sunday.

They had insisted that vows taken in someone's garden did not constitute a marriage. A marriage was to be held and blessed in a church. Couples must swear before God that they would love each other, be faithful and respect each other. Only she wondered why so many did not keep their promises; even before God they broke their promises. She suddenly felt incredibly sad and tried to turn her thoughts to the day's arrangements.

In just a few hours she and her father would drive the short distance in an 'old timer', which Phil had borrowed from one of David Coleman's friends.

Then, at the same time, Pippa would leave with her girlfriend in a pony and trap decorated with sheaths of corn and flowers.

Later, Sophie and Peter would marry for the second time.

The bedroom door opened. Her mother stood holding a tray with three cups of tea while Flossy held a plate of uninteresting biscuits.

'We thought we would have a last cup of tea together.'

'I can remember you bringing me a cup of tea more than twenty one years ago, remember?'

'However could I forget,' her mother answered, sounding a little whimsical.

'All's well that ends well,' Flossy chipped in, still nervous her sister's deceit might not have been entirely forgiven by Alison, let alone by Philip Price and his mother. She turned to Alison. 'I can't believe you and Pippa are both marrying on the same day.'

'Neither can I,' she replied, quizzically.

'I don't much like Mark's mother,' Flossie stated, dunking a biscuit in her tea. 'I met her once at a village fête. I told her who I was and she turned away and started to talk to someone else as though I wasn't there. Probably saw me as one of the hoi polloi. As if she is something special.'

'Actually,' Connie whispered, as though she was frightened of being overheard. 'I did a bit of research the other day. It seems they own just about all the land around where we live and there is a title somewhere in the family.'

'Really,' gasped Flossy.

'I've been on the internet. Their land has been in the family for centuries.'

'Probably some crawling friend of a king was rewarded for slaughtering his enemies. You didn't get a title and land in those days without doing the king a favour,' Flossy informed them.

'Well, whatever. Mark's side of the family didn't get a title but they did get an awful lot of land, which they have managed to hang on to.'

'Pippa mentioned it,' she said, thoughtfully.

'Well,' her mother continued. 'It seems they're filthy rich.'

'Good for Pippa. That makes Mark even more attractive than he already is,' she said, brightly.

'That shouldn't be a consideration,' muttered Flossy.

'Of course it is. You can love a rich guy just as easily as a poor one. There's nothing wrong in having money. So long as you use it properly,' she added, trying to soften her opinion.

'I wish her all the luck in the world, she deserves it,' Flossy added, softly.

'Why does Pippa deserve it. Because of me?' she asked, sounding hurt.

There was a silence.

'No, not because of you,' her mother replied, obviously irritated.

'Well, then, perhaps because of you,' she snapped at her mother.

'What do you mean by that?' her mother asked, soundly equally angry.

'Well, for beginners, her father's name could have been on her birth certificate. That's because of you and, I have to tell you, Phil and me have already arranged for that to be changed.'

'Excellent,' said Flossy.

She watched her mother balancing the tray as she tried to open the bedroom door, obviously beating a retreat from any further confrontation.

'It would be nice if you could help me.'

She climbed off the bed and opened the door.

'Be careful going down the stairs.'

She closed her eyes and breathed deeply. It was her wedding day and she wanted to look and feel serene. Someone had once told her to throw her bad thoughts away. She thought she would open the container by the back door and mentally throw her mother in it.

She was just out of the bathroom when Pippa arrived. They gave each other the usual perfunctory kiss and immediately turned their attention to Pippa's wedding dress, though she had her doubts it could be called that; a cream coloured cocktail dress, short, strapless, made of stretch lace which fitted tightly and was decidedly sensuous. They looked at each other and giggled.

'Whatever is your future mother-in-law going to think. She won't like this Pippa.'

'Sunday's dress will go down better. It's the same colour with a high collar, long sleeves and pathetically boring. It makes me feel like 'goody two shoes'. It's so not me. I think Mark will explode when he sees me coming down the aisle. But,' she added, flashing her bright eyes, 'this dress is underneath. I just pull the skirt off and unzip the top. And hey presto, I'm ready to swing the night away.'

'I wouldn't count on taking over the stables just yet. You may have won the battle but you might still lose the war,' she muttered.'

A MAGICAL DAY

It ALL WENT ACCORDING TO PLAN. Nothing untoward happened, no faux pas or innuendoes were slipped between the champagne and the tea. It was all very relaxed, even Mark's parents seemed to enjoy themselves. Only the meeting between Hilary Price and her mother was openly hostile. Rosie, who saw all, stepped in thrusting a glass of champagne into their hands and leading her mother away to meet Will, while she introduced Phil's mother to Jack Nielson who turned his charm on like a tap.

Phil suddenly stood behind her. He kissed her neck and held his hands across her stomach. She wondered for a moment if he had an intuition that within her was a growing embryo.

'Penny for your thoughts,' he asked, softly.

'You don't have to pay for them. I'll tell you later.'

'Thoughts for the night!'

'You could say that.'

'I'll be waiting with bated breath,' he whispered, as he took her hand and led her to the small dance floor. She leaned her head against his shoulder as they played soft romantic music while she gazed across at the guests. Sophie was dancing with Peter who could no longer stand close to her and Pippa and Mark clung dramatically onto each other as though he was about to go to war.

She smiled at Jillie who seemed to be talking seriously to some man standing with his back to her. She thought that typical of Jillie who was most probably shredding historical events, misdeeds of kings and queens and parliamentary affairs.

When she looked around her father was walking towards the gate which led to the heath as though there was something he must do.

'I'll be back in a jiff,' she told Phil. 'I just want to talk to dad.'

Phil looked surprised. 'What about?'

She did not answer as she carefully followed her father until he stopped by the bench where she and Jack Nielson had sat, the day she found him to be an almost perfect candidate for making a baby.

She gasped at the sight of a woman sitting there. Her thoughts ran to the spirit which her father had mentioned but, to her relief, the woman stood up and turned around. It was Flossy. It was her Aunt Flossy who lowered her head as her father took her hand and kissed it. They were as a young couple, unsure, nervous of what they felt and whether the other would respond to their feelings. Then, he held her in his arms and kissed her.

She quietly returned to the party, stunned but happy. They had taken around forty years to find each other and she hoped they would have the strength to declare their true feelings to the world at large and to her mother, in particular. She tried to imagine Flossy coming down to live in her father's little house, helping him in the Garden Centre and lovingly looking after each other. She wondered how long they had known of each other's love.

'How good can it get,' she murmured, as she walked back to Phil.

'What was that about?' he asked, as they walked back to the dance floor.

'Tell you later.'

'At this rate, we'll be talking all night.'

'You think!' she replied, stroking the soft hair on the nape of his neck.

She glanced over to Jack Nielson who was in a seriously deep conversation with Hilly. She frowned as she realised they had both lost their partners around the same time. There seemed to be an apathy between them, an understanding, a sentiment. It occurred to her how little she had in common with Jack, actually nothing other than she was looking for a mate. Hilly, however, seemed sedately enchanted by him. 'Why not', she thought. 'Weddings are notorious for new love.' She warmed to the idea of Jack with someone he could relate to; he and Hilly forming a friendly bond.

It was only when she realised that both Jack and Hilly had stopped talking and were staring at she and Phil, then at Pippa, and back again to her, was she aware that their deep conversation was, most probably, not about their own lives, their past unhappiness, but over she and Pippa. Phil had told his mother their secret and she had promised to say nothing until the time was right.

She was overcome, convinced, that Hilly had told Jack Nielson that Pippa was her daughter from a teenage pregnancy and her son was the father. How poor Philip only found out when he came here on holiday. Her intuition overcame her. If the world was to know, then she would tell them. She would not be the latest gossip murmured in the local supermarket or hairdresser's shop.

She pulled away from Phil.

'What's wrong now?' he asked.

'I want to say something, I hope you won't mind,' she said, walking to the side of the arbour and picking up an old microphone.

'Hello everyone, I would like to say a few words.'

Someone softened the music.

'First, I would like to thank you all for coming to this very special day. It's not only the joining of three couples but much more. Today, a family has been united, Phil, me and our daughter, Pippa.'

There was a hushed silence, a deep silence.

'Phil and I knew each other from both Primary and Secondary school. We were best friends for all those years. We did our homework together because I was lousy at maths. Of course, what happened was inevitable. Once, just once, we loved each other before Phil and his family emigrated. I didn't know the consequences of that five minutes until weeks later and I kept it a secret for months. My parents thought it best for me to go to my Aunt Flossy up in Yorkshire to have my baby.'

She looked across to Flossy, who had returned from the 'Crossing', and then to her mother who looked shattered. She raised her glass.

'Well, the rest is history. Pippa and my mother stayed in Yorkshire and I eventually came back home to help my father, my very dear dad.

So the circle is complete. Phil and I have tied the knot and Pippa has a flesh and blood father, not the name of someone living thousands of miles away.'

Phil stepped forward, pulled her to him, and kissed her, lovingly. He raised his glass.

'To the mother of my daughter and to Pippa. May she and Mark be as happy as we are. I offer you a toast to Pippa and Mark, to Sophie and Peter, to Connie, Flossy and Arnold who played such a large part in our family happiness.

To my mother who came here on a holiday and found herself a grandmother. Is there anyone else?'

'Only me.'

Everyone turned around. Jillie was standing with the unknown middle aged man who turned out to be Tony Stockwell.

'Oh, Tony, when did you arrive?' asked Sophie stepping forward in amazement.

Tony took her arm and kissed her on both cheeks. 'Jillie asked me to come, to give you a surprise', he said, handing her a present which looked suspiciously like a book.

'What sweet of you, thanks. I thought you

were in Scotland.'

"I was but I wanted to celebrate your becoming an honest woman.'

'For the second time', she laughed, as she introduced him to Peter.

'You know Jillie's been helping me a bit', Tony said, putting his arm around Jillie's waist.

'Yes, she told me, that's nice. Very convenient, she can keep my laptop warm while I'm unavailable', she patted her stomach as she spoke.

'We've got it all under control', he replied, looking too admiringly at Jillie.

A feeling of jealousy, perhaps disappointment, rushed through her. 'Well, you don't need me then.'

'Of course, we do,' Jillie said, quickly. 'Once the babies are here and the worst is over, we will need you and your brains.'

Sophie turned to face the guests. 'To those of you who don't know, Tony Stockwell has won the Independent seat for Greater Wolton and Jillie and me will be helping him a little.'

Jack stood up and held his hand out. 'I don't think we've met. Nice to meet you,' he said, sounding jovial. 'What an afternoon, what an afternoon.'

Sophie pulled Jillie to one side while Tony Stockwell talked to Jack and JJ who had also been invited.

'Keep him at arm's length. He's old enough to be your father', Sophie whispered, seriously.

'I quite like him.'

'Well don't. He's only using you'.

'Oh come on, you're not my keeper'.

'I've been there, Jillie. Look for someone your own age. I happen to know he's got a lot of baggage.'

'Thanks for the advice.'

It occurred to Sophie that she had just repeated a conversation she had with her mother. 'Nothing ever changes,' she muttered. 'Everything is repeated history. Jillie, of all people, should know that.'

Jack Nielson and Hilary Price, who had sat huddled together all afternoon, were now dancing closely. In fact, they seemed to be on affectionate terms with each other.

'Lovely party, Alison,' he called.

She felt happy for him. He had found someone he could relax with, relate to. 'Good for him', she thought. 'At least Hilly is his own age.'

She could see Sophie was worried, perhaps even angry, as Jillie and Tony Stockwell danced until late into the evening, he holding her too closely and she acting as though she had just found the love of her life.

Sophie came and stood next to her and sighed, 'My poor mother,' she murmured. 'I gave her such a rough ride. I'm so sorry.'

*

The champagne was no longer cold and the icing on the leftover wedding cakes was soft but she did not care. The humid afternoon had now turned to cool evening and she and Phil danced closely, their bodies only slightly moving to the romantic music which drifted up into the motionless trees, it was as a stillness before a summer storm, an anticipation. She thought of romantic pre-Raphaelite paintings of lovers in forest clearings, by lakes or rivers. Camelot beauties in flowing gowns and handsome young men declaring their undying love.

'I've something to tell you,' she whispered.

'And that is?'

She whispered again, her lips touching his ear as she did so.

He stepped back. 'Really,' he grinned. 'This time I'll be around. Big time around. Forever around. Clever girl.'

Rosie placed her head on Will's shoulder and closed her eyes. 'Everyone wastes so much time and love,' she whispered.

He kissed her forehead. 'We didn't waste time, we just used it differently. We may not have married but we have always loved each other. Perhaps better than most.'

'I've never heard you talk like that before.'

'No, you haven't. But, I really believe true love can never be lessened by outside forces.'

'That is so beautiful. I'll hold you to it, William Windsor.'

POPPY's SPIRIT

Poppy SAT IN THE CONSERVATORY drinking a cup of tea. She had no need for music and dancing and silly behaviour. She was focused on the disappearance of her first husband, Reggie. She did not believe a word of Will and Rosie's story, not after she found a small bone on a pile of sand in the garden. It did not matter, she was not about to dig into the why's and wherefore's but she did think he was bumped off, probably by Stella, and she had a pretty good idea why.

Young girls were Reggie's weakness. He had called his dalliances 'careless mistakes'. He said they looked eighteen, or even older, and he had not thought to ask them their ages, why should he? The petty young things had been very willing and, in fact, he believed they enjoyed his advances and the goodies they could buy with his money afterwards. It was only when one of their mothers had complained did she find out the truth about the precise accountant she had married. He had paid off the mother with a substantial sum of money and appeared to be penitent.

She had met Kenneth, the sports car enthusiast, a little later. She was charmed by him and his various sport cars but he had not wanted her child. She was forced to chose between Will and him. She had chosen him but not before she had found a good mother for Will.

She had introduced Reggie to Stella, who she knew had a financial problem, brushing aside the fact that she had a little girl, far too young for Reggie to be 'careless' with. In any case, Stella was around as was Will. Rosie would be well chaperoned and Reggie had promised to keep his hands to himself.

It was when Will and Rosie showed her photo's of their simple wedding did she become aware of something strange on one of them. A photo of someone drifting in the smoke of a candle while Rosie danced on the dreary stone altar.

She frowned as she tried to organise her thoughts. Reggie was killed, his body hidden, so why did she find a human bone on a pile of sand in the garden? Unless, of course, it resurfaced when the chapel was renovated.

'So,' she whispered, 'he was buried in the chapel and they had to rebury him, but why and where? Not in the rockery, that was recently dismantled. Anywhere,' she answered, rhetorically.

*

Emily Nielson watched the old lady as she pondered on Reggie's whereabouts. She thought it possible to help Reggie's spirit to move on, to find peace. And she? Well yes, but not yet. She still had too much to do what with Sophie's twins on the way, Jillie with the wrong man and Jack, of course.

She looked up at the golden clouds. Of course, she had a solution for Sophie and her babies. She would enter Jack's early morning dream and he would react, enthusiastically. Happy to help his step-daughter, happy to make amends for her mother's death.

'Here's your chance to put things right, Jack. Send in the Clown', she laughed.